AND
BY
FIRE

Also available by Evie Hawtrey

Written as Sophie Perinot

Ribbons of Scarlet
Médicis Daughter
A Day of Fire
The Sister Queens

AND
BY
FIRE
A NOVEL

Evie Hawtrey

CROOKED
LANE

NEW YORK

Copyright © 2022 by Evie Hawtrey

Published in the United States by Crooked Lane Books, an imprint of The Quick Brown Fox & Company LLC.

Crooked Lane Books and its logo are trademarks of The Quick Brown Fox & Company LLC.

Library of Congress Catalog-in-Publication data available upon request.

ISBN (hardcover): 978-1-64385-993-4
ISBN (ebook): 978-1-64385-994-1

Cover design by Kara Klontz

Printed in the United States.

www.crookedlanebooks.com

Crooked Lane Books
34 West 27th St., 10th Floor
New York, NY 10001

First Edition: May 2022

10 9 8 7 6 5 4 3 2 1

CHAPTER 1

Present-day London

Sunday

"Doesn't it bother you that they got the spot wrong?"

"What?" O'Leary's comment snapped Detective Inspector Nigella Parker's focus back to the road. She slammed on the brakes, and they screeched to a stop at a red light.

"The point of ignition for the Great Fire of London." O'Leary wiped away the coffee splashed onto the lid of his Caffè Nero takeaway cup by the sudden stop, took a slug, and then grimaced. "Ever since 1666, when it burned the city end to end, historians insisted the Fire started in Pudding Lane, and then some aging House of Common's Clerk discovers it's all wrong."

"Not *all* wrong. The Fire started two hundred and two feet from Wren's monument, exactly as years of history said—just sixty feet east of where everyone thought." Nigella tapped the wheel impatiently. It was ridiculously early on a Sunday morning, the City was dead, but she was stuck at the light despite the lack of cross traffic. This was what came from using her own car: no siren, no free pass to blow through lights. Although honestly, this one didn't justify flashing lights.

A nuisance arson: Why had the detective chief inspector called her out for that? True everybody called her "the moth" because she had a special affinity for fire cases, but she wasn't on the early worm. She was an off-duty DI in the Crime Investigation Directorate of the City of London Police, summoned abruptly from an early breakfast, although no one would have guessed that given her crisp oxblood blazer and the perfect twist of dark hair pinned up neatly at the back of her head. Nigella thought longingly of the boiled egg she'd abandoned, with its yolk just the right amount of runny, and hot buttered soldiers of toast waiting to be dipped in it. *It'll be fit for nothing but the bin when I get home.*

"Sixty feet off is wrong enough," O'Leary said.

She glanced at him sideways: red–gold stubble on his jaw, unmanageable hair sticking up over his forehead. Nigella had texted her counterpart with London's Metropolitan Police because she owed him one after the Postman's Park murder case, and she knew he'd been assigned the Haringey fire. Her message had clearly found him in bed.

"Why should that bother me?"

"Because, Ni, you have to straighten your toothbrush if it isn't precisely parallel to the edge of the basin."

The light changed at last, and Nigella made a sharper-than-strictly-necessary turn onto Fish Street Hill, catching O'Leary off guard and jolting a bit of steaming coffee into his lap. He winced, then gave her the look—the one that said, *"You just hate it when I'm right, Parker."*

Yeah, well, fuck him. No, she'd done that for a while, which might be part of the problem.

Ahead, odd portions of Christopher Wren's monument to the Great Fire of London appeared—a sliver of the base, the top of its massive Doric column sitting like a hat on a commercial building obstructing her view. Rolling up to the curve where traffic from Fish Street Hill bent left onto Monument Street, Nigella slowed. The department had erected a lean-to against the west face of the monument. The wide end of a soot "V" protruded above the upper edge of the tarp.

That's the spot.

The right-hand section of Monument Street, generally off limits to traffic, was cordoned off and full of police cars. *Lots of cops for a nuisance arson.* A sergeant peered through her windscreen, then moved aside a cone and waved them in.

Parking, Nigella grabbed her bag out of the back. She'd only taken a few steps when DCI Evans swung in beside her. "What's with the Yard?" He tilted his head in O'Leary's direction.

"The Yard," O'Leary responded, "thought this might be related to the arson last week that disrupted the East Coast Main Line."

"Not." Evans shook his head.

Nigella wondered how he could be so sure. Then they reached the tent, and he lifted the flap. Scorch marks defaced the stone, and at their base, on the pavement, a figure lay curled in a fetal position and entirely blackened.

"Holy Mary," O'Leary breathed.

So, not a nuisance. Self-immolation . . . or murder. Nigella's breath caught and her pulse raced. It felt as if her heart was rising upward to meet the air trapped in her lungs. And in her head she heard a voice from her childhood whisper, *"You're it, Jelly."*

"It's not what you think." A crouching man in a jumpsuit looked up from beside the blackened form. *Wilkinson—good. He's as precise as I am.*

"What do you mean?" She stared at the form, unable to determine if it was male or female. The nose was nearly gone. Not a scrap of clothing remained, just a naked, desiccated form so consumed by flames that it resembled charcoal riven with fissures.

"It's wood." Wilkinson rose. "Someone ought to tell the poor, terrified old woman who discovered it smoldering."

"I'm sorry to have called you out on your day off, Parker." DCI Evans cast Wilkinson an accusatory look, as if the forensic officer was responsible for the misunderstanding, though doubtless Nigella had been phoned before he arrived on scene.

"It's fine, sir—I can always make a fresh pot of tea." In the rush of relief that the body was *not* a body, Nigella worked to sound nonchalant. She felt anything but. Whenever she stepped onto a crime scene involving death by fire, Nigella was washed over by fear—the terror of the victim—fresh, urgent, and hot—conjured by a vivid imagination, followed by her own throat-tightening fear, always murmuring the same thing: *I can't die like this—any way but this.*

"Tea sounds good," DCI Evans replied. "I'm heading back to Wood Street. You lads have this, right?"

It wasn't really a question, but one of the younger police constables piped up, "Sir, shouldn't someone interview the witness?" He jerked his head in the direction of a blue and yellow striped police vehicle. Nigella could see a white-haired head through the nearest window.

"I'll do it," she offered. The uniform looked disappointed; clearly he'd thought by asking he'd be assigned the task, and there really wasn't any reason not to give it to him—nobody dead. But there was something about the humanity of the form, and the crazy boldness of bringing something that large to the center of the City and lighting it on fire at a monument to fire . . . Nigella's police senses tingled. All cops, or at least the best ones, had them—the result of a subconscious loaded with years of prior case experiences. Every copper's intuition was different, but each knew you ignored that "something is off" feeling at your peril.

"Right then, that's settled." Evans nodded, satisfied. None of the niggling uneasiness she was feeling, Nigella thought, looking into her guv'nor's composed face.

"What am I supposed to do? Take a taxi?" O'Leary asked.

"You"—Evans pointed to the PC who'd spoken up—"run the Yard wherever he needs to go." He looked at O'Leary. "Professional courtesy."

And punishment, Nigella thought. Not for O'Leary—for the uniform. Evans didn't like overeager. Never had. Overeager was getting the PC removed from the scene.

Evans didn't wait for a response, just strode off. O'Leary hesitated. "Thanks for the callout. Suppose now I owe you."

"You owe me nothing because you got nothing," she replied. *Just a coffee stain on your trousers and a ride home with a pissed-off junior officer.* She felt vaguely guilty over that coffee spot.

Turning her back on O'Leary, Nigella headed for the van and swung the door open. Nodding at the officer sitting opposite an elderly woman in a tracksuit, who clutched her hand, Nigella said, "I'll take it from here. Mrs.—"

"*Miss* Payne," the uniform said, filling in the blank as she was meant to as she slid out to make way for the DI.

As the van door shut, Nigella observed the witness's posture. Nothing defensive in it—nothing to suggest Miss Payne was anything other than a trim woman above seventy and a complete wreck. Nigella thought about taking the hand the uniform had dropped, but hand-holding just wasn't her thing.

"Miss Payne, I am Detective Inspector Parker. Let me start by telling you that the figure you found, however disturbing, was not human—it was made of wood."

The witness's eyes opened wide, full not so much of comprehension as a lack of it, and then she burst into tears. "What a cruel, cruel thing," she sobbed.

"Yes. This is someone with a twisted sense of humor, pulling an offensive prank. And we want to find them." Nigella picked up the tissue box from the seat and held it out, waiting while the witness wiped her eyes and blew her nose. "Can you tell me how you found the object?"

"I was on my morning stroll." The woman paused for two deep breaths. "I smelled something odd—smoke. I started down Fish Street Hill, and there it was, smoldering against the Monument." Miss Payne's hand contracted around the used tissues until they entirely disappeared. "From a distance I thought it was rubbish. I pulled out my phone to report the disgraceful thing, and then, as I got closer . . ." She stopped and put a hand over her mouth, reliving the moment she'd recognized what she'd thought was a human form. "I dropped my mobile, then picked it up and called."

"Did you scream?"

"I did." She colored slightly.

"Completely understandable." Nigella held out the tissues again, but the witness shook her head. "Did anyone come running or react in any way?"

"There was no one—no one but me. I thought perhaps there would be a policeman, a courier—anyone. Then I remembered it was half six on a Sunday, and the fact that things are deserted is precisely why I walk early."

Nigella couldn't help feeling disappointed. Fire this odd, this purposefully odd—she'd hoped the firestarter had stayed to witness audience reaction. Lots of arsonists couldn't resist that moment. *And this one wants an audience. I'm bloody sure of that.*

"Did you see anything unusual other than what you believed was a burnt body?"

The elderly woman's gaze bored into Nigella. "When you think you see a burnt body it's rather difficult to focus on anything else. As soon as I had the police on the line, I went round the corner where I couldn't see it. The dispatcher stayed on with me until an officer arrived."

First officer on scene—I'll need that name.

"Thank you, Miss Payne. I assume someone has taken your contact information." The woman nodded. "I'll have an officer run you home. Or perhaps you'd rather go to a friend's?"

Nigella gave appropriate instructions to the uniform outside the van. There were far fewer cops milling about, and fewer police vehicles. But the tent was still in place. She lifted the flap. Wilkinson stood, arms crossed, while a half dozen others strained to shift the burned figure onto a tarp. He stepped forward at the same moment Nigella did, and both peered at the newly revealed pavement.

"No spalling," Nigella said. "So maybe no accelerant."

"Maybe." He gave a half shrug, considering but not conceding the point. "The monument would have acted like a natural chimney, but still."

"Send me a copy of your longitudinal section study. I want to know if this thing blazed or smoldered." Nigella said.

Every fire had its own language, and watching the team Struggle out with their grisly wooden burden, Nigella wanted to understand the fire that had made it as it was—she *needed* to understand. *"Jelly, Jelly, ready or not, here we come!"* The voices in her head were faint but chilling, like a sudden cold wind, and

Nigella shuddered. A lifetime fear of fire and a desperate need to understand it in every particular hung upon those distant voices.

"You don't think we've seen the last of this fellow, do you?" Wilkinson asked.

That was why she had to know.

"'Fraid not." *And my instincts say, while this starts with a piece of wood that looks human, it's not stopping there.*

♦

Present-day London

Wednesday

Nigella slid a folder from beneath the paperwork for the case they'd just wrapped, paperwork she'd stayed late to clear off her desk. It contained Wilkinson's report on the monument fire. *Pinus sylvestris*—Scots pine, the commonest bloody pine in the UK. Why couldn't the suspect have picked something exotic? Scots pine wasn't going to be an easy trace point for this guy if she had to find him. She didn't have to find him, she reminded herself. *Not yet. But he is not done, and you know it.*

Nobody else seemed intrigued or concerned with the nuisance arson. In the three workdays since the incident, no one had even reviewed CCTV footage to determine how the wooden man had been delivered. The first officer to arrive on scene had been gobsmacked when Nigella tracked him down. "Evans put *you* on this case?" he'd asked, incredulously.

"Call it a hobby," she'd replied. The uniform shook his head but answered her questions because she was his senior.

Nigella slipped the site pictures out. The charred form lay in a classic pugilistic attitude—curled into a fetal position, hands raised to head—just as if the large muscles in real human limbs had contracted under high heat. The first time Nigella had seen a burned body she'd come all over in a cold sweat and thrown up her lunch. She would never forget that moment.

Did the form of the ghastly carving mean the suspect knew what fire did to a living, breathing thing? Or had the pose been chosen for some other purpose? Nigella looked idly around, but there was no answer in the semidarkness ringing her. Damn, what time was it? It had been hours since her fellow DIs in the Crime Investigation Directorate had gone home. And at that precise moment, her phone rang—not her mobile, the phone on her desk. Nigella started like a rabbit and was glad there was no one to witness it. Never let the lads see you jump; she'd learned that early on.

"DI Parker." Her voice was strong and much steadier than her pulse.

"Ni, still working, eh? Good thing you gave the cat to your mum."

"O'Leary, you lonely? Or just looking to be annoying?"

"Neither. I'm on call and I have one. You're going to want to get to St. James's Piccadilly." And then he was gone.

🔥

The taxi scooted down Duke of York Street, turned left, and dropped Nigella near an unmarked car with flashing lights. St. James's Piccadilly, all red-brick and Portland stone, stood bathed in a combination of streetlight and moonlight. But the acrid smell of smoke, not the church's impressive profile, grabbed Nigella's attention. Other than police vehicles, Jermyn Street was empty. Little wonder. She'd checked her phone as she'd swung into the taxi, and it was past two AM. A pair of uniforms stood at a cordoned-off alleyway. Approaching, ID in hand, Nigella stopped in her tracks. The narrow lane dividing the rear of the church from a commercial building pulsed, illuminated by a pillar of fire inside the narrow churchyard. At the conflagration's center, the figure of a man stood in profile, one arm stretched high, flames lapping at him and leaping into the air above his head. Another man stood, silhouetted, between her and the flaming object. Nigella waved her ID, lifted the tape and ducked under. She was two steps from O'Leary when he turned.

"Detective Inspector Parker, knew this would interest you."

His use of her full title made Nigella aware of the half dozen other figures, including a police photographer, camera clicking away, and several firemen holding a hose run down from Piccadilly.

"Got here a tick before the fire boys," O'Leary said. "Asked them to wait. Wanted to document this before they put it out, and I knew you'd want a look."

Peering through the yellow flames at the wooden carving, Nigella stepped forward until the fire's brutal heat stopped her. *Another human form. Please let it be carved from something other than Scots pine.* "Is he pointing at the church?"

"Sure looks like it. All right boys." O'Leary, took hold of Nigella's elbow, pulling her back as the firemen's hose blasted to life. The jet of water hit the burning man and the church behind him with such force that spray rebounded, causing the detectives to jump back and shake like wet dogs. In just a few minutes the flames went out.

A spotlight came on, illuminating the drenched and smoking form. Nigella looked at the outstretched arm, then at her fellow DI.

"He's giving the church the finger," O'Leary said, confirming her thoughts. "There's something really wrong with this boy."

"Who phoned it in?" Nigella asked as they walked along the fence toward the churchyard gate.

"Vicar. She was alerted by one of the homeless. The parish lets them sleep on the pews. Liberal parish. Anyway, the fellow smelled smoke, took a peek, and roused everyone. I asked the vicar to keep an eye on him so he doesn't wander off, but told her I'd interview them both tomorrow."

Passing through the gate, they approached the burned figure from the side. Nigella noticed it wasn't, strictly speaking, life-sized. Probably about sixty percent. "He's well endowed."

"Parker, I'm disappointed, I'd always hoped you knew better than to judge a man by size. But, um, yeah. Suspect asserting his masculinity, or doubting it?"

"Who knows, but it's a little gem to file away." Nigella pulled on a pair of gloves. "You have a torch?" O'Leary pulled a flashlight from his coat pocket and handed it over. She walked wide of the carbonized figure, panning the beam across the ground. "No visible footprints." Then she turned and ran the light along the fence. Beginning about two feet from where the figure stood, a dozen or more fence spires wore little light-colored splinters of wood, as if they were hats. She widened her field of vision. Further along, a large piece of heavy plywood lay on the ground.

"Could be how he got it over." She illuminated the board.

O'Leary moved past her. "And this"—he squatted beside an orange crate with a looped length of rope hanging out of the top—"might be how the suspect did."

Nigella nodded. "Clever. Sick but clever."

"Right," O'Leary said, "let's flip the board." Sure enough, there was a line of deep gouges on the back, just the right distance apart to have been left by the pointed fence. He stood the plywood on one long side and ran a gloved hand along the upper edge. "There's something else. Give me a little light."

Nigella directed the torch. There was an indent on the plywood's edge, just beside O'Leary's hand—as if the wood had been compressed. She moved the beam further along, revealing several additional marks, each about three fingers wide. O'Leary flipped the board round, standing it on the edge they'd just examined. "Identical depressions on this side." He paused and bent to have a closer look. "Movers bands to cinch our wooden fellow to the board before levering him over?" O'Leary speculated.

"I want the board and the crate," he called out to a member of the evidence crew. They were swarming into the churchyard now in their suits and slip-over shoe covers. O'Leary moved back to the figure and held out his hand for the torch. The moment the light hit the stone directly beside the base Nigella saw them—striated lines on the surface and chips of stone flaking away.

"Spalling," Nigella said as she and O'Leary squatted side by side for a closer look. "Question is, did he use an accelerant, or did that blast of cold water hitting the hot stone do this? Because at my fire"—she realized as she said it, she was taking ownership of the incident at the Great Fire Monument—"there was evidence of boiled linseed oil in the cross section, but no sign of accelerant splashed about."

"Interesting. We'll have to wait for the report." O'Leary rose. "But the lab can't tell us what interests me most: Why is this fellow sticking it to St. James's? Abusive clergyman father? Fondled by a vicar? Angry at God? Personal grudge against someone attached to the parish?"

"Maybe all or none of the above," Nigella replied. "I'll start a chart for lines of inquiry tonight because you'll be tied up here for hours." *Order out of chaos—best part of this job.* "Then tomorrow I'll find the CCTV footage for the Monument fire, send you a copy of Wilkinson's report, and—"

"Ni, don't start *anything* tonight. I mean this is intriguing as hell, but not urgent."

"Not yet, O'Leary, but come on—remember the Camberwell cannibal? You know as well as I do the weird ones have a habit of getting weirder in the worst ways."

"Yeah, they do. But that's still no reason to pull an all-nighter. Besides, there *is* no tonight. It is already tomorrow, and you won't be getting much kip before you're back at your desk as is."

"O'Leary, if you were my mum, I'd have given you the cat."

"I liked the cat." He tried to smile, but Nigella saw something else in his eyes, something that bothered her. *Damn, when is he going to get over it?*

"Can you delay notifying Evans til midday? I'm not on call, but if I can get the Monument incident, then—"

"Sure Ni, *if* you promise to go home and get in bed without your laptop."

"Yeah, Mum, fine." She almost asked him if there was anything or anyone else she shouldn't take to bed. She thought of the MFA graduate from the Slade she'd met at that exhibit for promising new artists, the one she was now hooking up with. A thought quickly followed by a more uncomfortable one— O'Leary might be older, but he was better.

"Let me get a uniform to run you home."

"Don't divert your manpower; that's why god created Uber." Nigella opened the app before O'Leary could argue. She'd had enough of his caregiver mode.

On the way to her flat in Bankside, Nigella said, "Hey Siri, make a new note," and started a "lines of inquiry" list on her phone. She wasn't about to switch off her brain just because O'Leary told her to. All her fellow DI's clergy-related ideas were on the list, but by the time she turned the key in her flat door, something about them was already bothering her. She stripped, hanging or folding her clothing neatly as she did. Slipping on a nightshirt she padded to the bathroom. *What seems off about the idea of someone angry at the Church of England or one of its vicars?* Maybe it would come to her while she slept. Turning down the bed, she arranged her four pillows, slid in, and flicked off the light. As she drifted out of consciousness, Nigella's last thought was not of the fiery man with his finger fiercely raised, but of the toothbrush she'd just used. Damn O'Leary for being right, it *did* have to be precisely parallel to the sink edge.

Thursday

"Sir, here's the paperwork on Fore Street." Nigella set the folder on the corner of Evan's desk. It was nine AM. He acknowledged her with a nod, then looked back down at what he was doing. She didn't move.

"Something else, Parker?"

"Yes, sir. I'd like you to give me the Monument fire. DI O'Leary had an incident last night that looks related. I think we have a serial arsonist on our hands. We both know that's right up my alley."

Evans leaned back in his chair and looked at her. "Didn't see anything in the papers."

Nigella had looked first thing; there had been nothing. "O'Leary must have kept it out. Likely figured this Chummy is looking for attention, so the last thing we ought to do is give it to him."

Evans nodded. And stared at her some more. Giving her a moment to retreat, which she wasn't going to do.

"You've got a full caseload already, Parker. And we both know if anyone from HR took a look at how long you're in the office, there'd be a lot of administrative blustering nobody wants to deal with."

"With all due respect, when was the last time anyone from HR was in early or late enough to clock my hours? They're strictly nine-to-fivers. But if it'll make you feel better, I'll set up a mini-command center for the nuisance at my flat."

Evans smiled. He was old style. Like her, he didn't *do* the job, he *lived* it—as his string of failed marriages attested. "What did O'Leary have, and how'd the scene look? And don't try to tell me you didn't go."

"Five-foot-tall figure of a man, burning out of control down along St. James's Piccadilly while flipping the church off. I'm expecting the Yard's report."

"And we both know you have Wilkinson's squirreled away already. So I'll transfer the nuisance, just don't spend a lot of time on it—department time—until it warrants it."

Nigella turned to go.

"To be clear, Parker, "warrants it" means we have serious property damage or a body."

"Yes, sir."

Now to find that CCTV footage.

When she'd watched it for the third time, Nigella downloaded the interesting bit—unorthodox, but there was nothing really confidential in it—then dialed O'Leary.

"Lunch?"

"We both eat at our desks. Or is this a date?"

"I don't date."

"True enough."

"I've got CCTV footage. I'll show you mine if you show me yours."

"I like the sound of that. Bugger it, we get an hour, let's take an hour. My ground or yours?"

"Halfway." It was meant to sound like a compromise, but the last thing Nigella wanted was to be in a pub booth with O'Leary when someone from her CID wandered past. Their past involvement had come dangerously close to being an item of discussion. And there was no gossip like police gossip.

"Right, then. Meet me at The Three Crows in thirty."

She was there first, of course. Better to wait than be waited upon. Bit of a Parker family motto that. O'Leary slid his messenger bag into the booth between them. He might have done it subconsciously, but Nigella saw it with a detective's eye for what it was—assured clear distance.

He waited until they'd ordered, then said, "Ladies first."

"White van—office cleaning company." She slid her tablet out of her bag and pulled up the image. "'Spiffy'—not the most original name. I plan to get on to them, but my luck and law of averages says they have a whole fleet. Plates neatly covered. Yet another reason, on top of the fact the City is nearly dead, to choose a weekend night."

O'Leary nodded. "No congestion charge, so no automatic number-plate recognition cameras operating to alarm over the masked plates."

"Rolls right up to the curb. Then nothing for a bit." Nigella lifted the tablet slightly higher to let the waitress put down their plates.

"Maybe because of that fellow?" O'Leary pointed a stick of celery from his ploughman's lunch at a male figure with some sort of terrier on a retractable lead.

Nigella fast-forwarded until the dog and man disappeared. "Here he comes." A figure in a light-colored jumpsuit climbed out of the van.

"Disposable shower cap–style head covering and a handy little industrial half mask. This guy may be crazed, but he's also cautious." O'Leary's tone was grudgingly respectful.

The suspect looked around before opening the rear van doors and sliding out the vehicle's ramp. He went up the incline, and a moment later a mover's dolly came into view with something swaddled in blankets strapped to it. Its descent was painfully slow to watch, and must, Nigella thought, have felt like an eternity to the suspect because he was exposed. She froze the feed for a minute. "He has to have practiced. Look at him ride that brake. And even, so his weight is thrown fully back to keep it from running away."

"Yeah, well, I don't have a lab report yet," O'Leary said, "but I asked them to weigh the St. James's figure—it's over five hundred pounds."

Nigella gave a low whistle. "So the bastard's clearly in great shape."

"Something to remember when it's time to nick him," O'Leary replied.

Once the suspect was down the ramp, he began to move quickly: unstrapping the blanketed mass, putting the straps and dolly back on the van, removing blankets. Nigella paused the video and used her fingers to zoom in.

"A perfect pine man," O'Leary said. "Look at those." Most of the figure was smooth, but there were noticeable rough patches, very rough. "Those don't look just unsanded; they look deliberate."

"That's what I thought. And notice where most of them are: the front torso, where they'll be sheltered by the curled form. He's built a little chimney. Now watch." She put the image in motion. The arsonist took a bag out of his pocket, opened it, and pulled out a wad of something. Crouching, he put one finger in his mouth, held it up, and then resituated himself. It was no longer possible to see the chest portion of the wooden man. When the suspect stood up, his hands were empty and the central curl of the figure burned.

"Time to get gone mate," O'Leary said to the image.

Nigella smiled—clearly he was about to be as gobsmacked as she'd been. Instead of making quickly for the van, the perp took a few steps back and looked up at the Monument. Then he lifted his right arm, middle finger raised.

"He looks just like the flipping figure from St. James's."

Nigella smiled. "Your turn. What did the CCTV show?"

O'Leary shifted in his seat. "Don't forget to eat." He pointed to the wheatberry, apple, and cranberry salad she'd barely touched.

"You didn't get the footage yet! You bastard! You lured me here under false pretenses."

"It's worse—there is no footage."

"What? You're trying to tell me Church Place is the one spot in London where a person can pick their nose without it being filmed?"

"Yeah, and get this—it's because of St. James's. The vicar told me they petitioned to have the cameras removed. No use opening the church and grounds to rough sleepers if they're scared off by fear of being watched by coppers and government types. Homeless are a paranoid population."

"Wouldn't you be? What else did our vicar say?"

"Awakened from deep sleep. Ran down to see what was burning." He took a bite of buttered bread, chewed, and swallowed. "Smart enough to know it wasn't human. Dialed 999, then ran into the church to calm the fellow who reported the fire and to make sure none of the other kerb jockeys spending the night were head banging over the incident."

"Not quite the model of compassion and political correctness, are you?"

"Gate to the churchyard was unlocked—just as we found it. In light of that, vicar fixated on why the suspect bothered to heave the carving over the fence."

"That's a civilian response if ever there was one."

"I pointed out—politely— that he might not have wanted the attention he'd have attracted if he'd parked on a major street and rolled that thing along on a dolly."

"And let me guess: no solid ideas of anyone with a grudge against the parish or its clergy."

"Nope." He gave an exasperated sigh.

"That's because I'm not sure this has anything to do with the parish. In fact, I doubt it has anything to do with the good old C of E or vicars past either."

"Come on, Ni, you're good, but not psychic. That's a premature conclusion."

"Is it?" She put down her fork and picked up the tablet again. A quick swipe revealed the frozen image of the suspect, middle finger in the air. "Before he said fuck you to St. James's, he said fuck you to a monument that isn't even remotely religious, except that it used to have anti-papist screed on it that has since been removed."

"We prefer to be called Catholics."

"I'm sure you do, O'Leary. And the homeless prefer not to be called kerb jockeys. My point is, unless our suspect is random—and watching the carefully choreographed way he executed my fire, we know he isn't—the locations likely share a connection."

"Hmm. Maybe he's sending a message." He drummed his fingers on the table. "The first location is an announcement that he's all about fire—a fire at the monument dedicated to *the* most significant fire in London's history is a good way to throw down a calling card. And the finger in the air could be a 'Hey, you haven't seen anything yet 'cause I'm more of a firestarter than that French bloke you hung for burning all London.'"

"Hanged O'Leary. Pictures, not people, are hung." She gave him a withering look. "History clearly not a passion for you . . . at this point everybody knows the Great Fire of London was an accident, not arson."

"Everybody including the criminally insane, Ni? You know arsonists even better than I do, with all their deep-seated pathology. I mean fire setting is associated with animal cruelty, being a victim of sexual abuse, and schizophrenia. So I'm not sure we can be certain what this guy thinks, let alone how that relates to truth." He took another bite of lunch. "Maybe the monument represents civic London. And then St. James's represents the Church . . ."

"There are dozens of spots more representative of the power of the state scattered throughout this city."

O'Leary paused, rubbing the lobe of his left ear between his thumb and first finger—a personal tick Nigella had originally found charming and ended up finding annoying. "Yeah, but what are the chances of lighting something on fire in front of the Houses of Parliament?"

"You're not convincing me," she said.

"I'm not trying to. Just brainstorming and simultaneously pointing out the connection may not be easy to find. Hell, if it weren't for the fact that both fires involved carved wooden men, we wouldn't even conclude they were related this early in the game."

Nigella closed the video display and opened her lines of inquiry document. "Humor me, O'Leary. What do we know about the fire locations?"

"Monument to the 1666 Great Fire. In the City proper—thus your ground. Most of it a big column—"

"A two-hundred-and-two-foot Doric column."

"I'll take your word for it, Ni. Topped by a viewing platform and a golden flaming urn. Built sometime after the Fire—"

"Don't be cute, O'Leary. Late seventeenth century, but let's find the date." Nigella opened her search engine.

"I remember when people were embarrassed to rely on Wikipedia."

"We are not relying on it. We're beginning with it. Approved by the city in 1671. Took six years to finish. Cost thirteen thousand four hundred and fifty pounds and odd shillings—that's a pretty penny if you're standing in ruined seventeenth-century London." She shook her head.

"It's a pretty penny if you're seated in The Three Crows right now and employed by the Metropolitan Police." He picked up their check and flipped it over.

Nigella's eyes moved down the screen. "All very Royal Society. Robert Hooke and Christopher Wren designed it, and their fellow Society member, Thomas Gale, did all those Latin inscriptions that ninety-nine percent of the population couldn't read then and still can't."

"So much for a Protestant education. At least we Catholics know our Latin."

"Good, next time we have a Latin clue, you can translate for me." She rolled her eyes. "But for now, let's move on to St. James's Piccadilly." She opened a new search window. "Corner stone laid 1676—so while the Monument was under construction. Design by Wren, but steeple later by one 'Mr. Willcox.' Seven thousand pounds from the piggy bank of the Earl of St. Albans. Here's something! St. James's was nearly totally destroyed during the Blitz. Look." Nigella enlarged a black and white picture of the church entirely engulfed in flame and handed the tablet to O'Leary.

"Kind of makes what our boy did look pathetic," he said, passing it back. "So it turns out both locations are related to major fires past. Both are seventeenth century—"

"And both share an architect, the revered Sir Christopher Wren."

"So you add all that to your chart, and what do we have? An overwhelming list for two nuisance arsons neither of our guv'nors wants us to spend time on. Speaking of which—"

He looked at his wristwatch, and Nigella flashed back to the first time she'd noticed it—a big, old-fashioned thing—and how charming she'd found the fact that anyone told time in a manner that didn't involve pulling out their mobile.

"We'd better get back to our desks, I'll wait for forensics. You follow up on that van. But most of all, we wait for what's next."

What's next is going to be an escalation. I can feel that in my bones and you can too, or we wouldn't be putting off-the-clock time in on this, Nigella thought.

"We have numerous points of intersection between the fires, but most of them are probably rubbish. You know what they say: twice is a coincidence, three times is a pattern. Let's wait for a pattern to emerge."

Nigella was about to argue. She wasn't good at wait-and-seeing, but her mobile pinged, announcing a text from James. Reflexively she looked: "Gallery do tonight, Spitalfields Odd-Art-Out? After party your place?" She stuffed the phone in her pocket, uncomfortably aware of O'Leary's proximity. Was he close enough to have seen the text? And why the hell did that matter?

"We done here?" She dropped a twenty on top of the check.

"Yep." He slid out. "Oh and Ni, on the train back you might consider changing the alert for that bloke—I seem to remember it used to be mine when I was the flavor of the month."

"If it makes you uncomfortable." Nigella shrugged, but it was she who was uncomfortable, very.

◊

James rolled off Nigella and lay naked on the floor in front of the sofa, unfocused eyes turned to the ceiling. The flat wasn't large and the bedroom wasn't far away, but when it was dark and North London glittered across the river . . . *Well who wouldn't rather do the deed with that for atmosphere?* Nigella thought.

"Damn, I'm winded. Takes a lot to get me winded." He rolled toward her and bit her shoulder. "You're something else."

And you're good to look at naked, but don't try to stay the night or say stupid things like "I love you Ni."

"Bottle of water?" She rose, slipped into the robe that hung over the end of the sofa, and headed to the fridge without waiting for an answer. She brought back two bottles and handed one down to him.

"You should have met me at Odd-Art-Out," he said. "The photographer's contributions were rubbish, but some of the painting was good, and there was a sculpture . . ." He took a slug of water. "Let's just say there is a reason I came here all riled up."

"What was the theme again?"

"Beauty Is *the Beast."*

Nigella wasn't probing that any further. "Speaking of sculpture, or rather of sculptors"—she sank onto the sofa—"do you all sort of know each other? I mean I'd recognize all the DIs and DCIs in the City Police. And while the Metropolitan Police is much larger, I've met or at least heard of most detectives there as well."

James scooted to sit with his back against the sofa, head not far from her left knee. "Can't know everyone. I mean there are doubtless hundreds of people who fancy themselves serious artists—including sculptors—working on masterpieces in their cellars or garden sheds that I've never heard of and nobody ever will. My great aunt in Surrey built this monstrosity out of rakes and it's included in the local 'arts walk.' But if you're talking about London artists showing in galleries who went to legit art schools—that's not a huge circle. Why?"

"I've got a case." Nigella hesitated. She wasn't particularly interested in James becoming intertwined with the nonphysical part of her life. He was a diversion—like the art shows she went to or the glasses of wine she had afterwards over a nice dinner. Mixing work with pleasure had only happened once, and she'd vowed it wouldn't happen again. But she needed an expert in sculpture, and there was one leaning against her sofa. She gazed out at the illuminated dome of St. Paul's—Christopher Wren's biggest post–Great Fire commission. In her mind's eye she saw the curled, burnt wooden man at the base of Wren's Monument to that fire and took a swallow of her water. "I've got a case involving sculpture. Is anyone doing figural stuff these days?"

"Well, it's not exactly 'of the moment.' But there are always people trying to set trends, not follow them." He paused, looking thoughtful. "I'd like to think I fall in that category. And there are certainly examples of recognized works that are figural. The piece of public sculpture in Spitalfields for example—the one about the refugees."

"Haven't seen it."

"I'll take you."

"Is it wood?"

"Steel. Really evocative. Not like some of the sculpture du jour we saw at *Ten British Artists to Keep an Eye On*. A number of those artists were brilliant, make no mistake. I was at school with Jeremy Owen, and people will be talking about him fifty years from now. But if you ask me, all the palaver over Ethan Fox is unwarranted. I mean what exactly is he doing that is so earth shaking? And he's certainly a pretentious twat."

"Which one was Fox?" Nigella asked. She and James had met at the show's opening, and the artists had been present, posing for photos, chatting—mostly with those from the press or those who looked like they could afford to collect art.

"The ginger standing next to what looked to be a purple metal clothespin with some oversized toothpicks leaning on it. Based on buzz, you'd be forgiven for thinking you needed to snatch that monstrosity up for your manor house, but I don't believe his work will hold its value once the press puffing is over. Then again, predicting who'll break out—who'll really be something—if that were as easy as those yearly 'look who's hot' shows make it seem, then a lot of art investors would be rolling in money. And lots of artists could afford places like this one."

Nigella knew he envied how she lived. A situation made worse when she'd mentioned that she'd inherited the money to buy the flat.

"There's a reason I advise friends to buy what they like. Most of the time enjoyment is all you'll get out of your investment."

"That," she said, reaching out to run her fingers through his hair, "is the part of you that works in the City talking."

"Maybe. And that's the bitter part. I mean obviously I'd like to be able to survive on my art. Have more time for sculpting."

Nigella became conscious of the fact that she had never seen his work. A stunning realization, almost as stunning as the fact she'd not noticed before. Well, she told herself, she'd only known him a couple of weeks, and maybe they were two of a kind—maybe he liked to keep sex and work separate. Work, after all, where it was a true passion, was personal. The acknowledgment that he was frustrated by the limits on his creative self was a serious admission on his part. She supposed she ought to say something reassuring, like "Don't worry, some day you will have more time, more fame," but how the fuck did she know if that was true? And did she really want to go down angst road? Presumably, James had an artistic temperament, so that was a long road and not a smooth one.

She wasn't ready to hand-hold James; didn't want to become invested in his hopes and dreams.

"So," she said, scooting over until her knee touched his shoulder, "tell me more about that sculpture at *Beauty* Is *the Beast*. I'm in the mood to have you riled up again." She ran a hand down over his chest, and he dropped his head back onto the sofa. The eyes looking up at her no longer contained thoughtfulness, only lust. And that was how Nigella wanted things.

It wasn't until she was in the shower, after James left, that Nigella realized she'd never asked him if he knew any artists doing male figures in wood.

CHAPTER 2

Whitehall Palace, London

February 1666
Seven months before the Great Fire of London

O glorious fiery beauty!

The thought quivered in the cold air like the lingering tails left by the rockets exploding over the Thames. In the dim before the next volley, Margaret Dove, Maid of Honour to Queen Catherine Braganza, pressed a hand to her bodice, trying to slow her breathing, which had become so rapid that flashes of light and color not explained by the royal fireworks interrupted her vision.

"No unnecessary excitement!" The voice in her head was her mother's. But excitement was *not* unnecessary. Without it, life was merely a marking of time—a thought that filled Margaret with an uneasy, restless despair. And to live dully . . . wasn't that rendered more tragic by the fact that her family and a constant stream of well-meaning physicians seemed determined to convince her that her life would not be a long one?

If they are right, I ought to live as brightly as the royal fireworks burn. But I do not believe they are, for pestilence and accident have taken so many thought healthier than I. Last year alone, the plague killed one hundred thousand souls in London—yet here I stand.

Still, Margaret knew she would get a lecture full of references to her delicate constitution from Lady Saunderson,

Mother of the Maids, should she be caught in the winter air. For this reason Margaret had waited until the rest of the court was assembled on the leads before creeping there. And now she clung to the shadows at the back edge of the viewing area while other courtiers pressed close to King Charles II and his brother, the Duke of York, as if there was power in mere proximity.

Well, there is, isn't there?

⌡ Or at least there was a possibility of favor and influence: two things everyone at court desired desperately, with good reason. The monarchy might have been restored for nearly six years, but the estates fallen to shambles and the fortunes depleted during the rebellion were not. The Royalist families of England, like the great city of London, had been grievously damaged by the Roundheads and would take more time to repair: time and money. So while some like the Duke of Buckingham lived in true affluence, for far more families, noble titles and lavish court attire were masks obscuring relative penury.

"You are twenty, daughter. I myself was four years married at your age. The expense of keeping you in Her Majesty's household is considerable, and that investment was meant to yield a wealthy husband. Yet, after nearly three years with the court, you have none." The lines were from a letter, received that morning. Margaret sighed. It was not that she was obstinate or declined proposals of marriage; she simply did not attract that sort of notice at court.

Little wonder. She'd been brought up far from the fashionable and famous, on account of her health, and rendered serious by an endless string of medical treatments for what physicians called a weak and whispering heart. Standing in the darkness, Margaret recalled the thirty days of waters she'd endured yearly: submerged in smelly sulfurous pools at sunrise, surrounded by other invalids, most of them older, and enveloped in a voluminous canvas bathing gown that swelled around her until she imagined herself a child's ball, not a person. And that treatment had merely been annoying and humorous. The things she'd been made to swallow to evacuate her bowels, the leeches so thick that she could no longer see her own arm—all the various treatments she tried to forget; chose not to dwell on—had been far more onerous. Books had been her refuge. Her father, a man of scholarly bent, indulged her similar inclinations, allowing Margaret to pass more time with her tutor than her dancing master and spend more money on her books than her wardrobe. But as her mind expanded, her world had not—remaining maddeningly bounded by the walls and fences of the family estate, and by admonitions not to overexert herself.

Sent to court, an excited Margaret had hoped for freedom but quickly discovered herself constrained in a different manner. Women in the Queen's household were limited by conventions that had little afflicted her in isolation. Set against courtly customs and feminine ideals, Margaret admitted to herself—if not to her mother—that her behaviors made gentlemen wary. She never seemed to laugh at the right time or be interested in the right things.

I've doubtless damaged my marital chances by asking the finance minister about the state of the Treasury and listening at the elbows of powerful men discussing war, rather than polishing my witticisms and arch looks.

Well, Mother, when an unseemly curiosity, blue lips, and a serious demeanor become valued traits at the court of merry King Charles, I will be its center, my hand sought by every duke.

The next volley of fireworks celebrating the court's return to Whitehall began, and Margaret forgot about her mother's letter, her own shortcomings, and her shortness of breath. Springing from the shadows, eyes fixed on the sky, she collided with a man crossing before her.

"Excusez-moi!" He swept off his hat, bowing as if the collision was his fault. "Etienne Belland, your servant. Forgive me for startling you."

By the light of the artificially illuminated sky, Margaret saw that he was tall, handsome, and not a courtier. His dove-gray, close-kneed suit, while of good quality, exhibited none of the decorative exuberance common among noblemen. And instead of a fashionable wig, natural, long, dark hair fell to his shoulders. His eyes too were dark and lively in a way that held

Margaret's attention fully. She wondered who he could be to warrant a place on the leads alongside royalty—or had he come here as surreptitiously as she?

"Mister Belland, it is nothing, I believe it was I who startled you."

"You did rather." He smiled. It was warm, wide, and not at all contrived. "Plain Belland is sufficient, My Lady." He bowed again. Apparently he had been taking in her appearance—the rich velvet of her mantle, the luxurious deep blue color, voluminous sleeves, and fine lace trim of the dress beneath—while she'd been examining his. "I am a fireworks maker to His Majesty, not a gentleman." There was a definite French accent, even though, now that he was no longer caught off guard, Belland spoke perfect English.

Not a man then, a magician! Responsible for putting the fire she so admired in the air. Margaret was undeniably intrigued. So instead of merely nodding politely and turning from him, she smiled back. "And Mistress is sufficient for me. "I am no duchess or dame. I am Margaret Dove, one of Her Majesty's Maids of Honour."

A chorus of "oohs" and "aahs" drew her attention to the sky. A single trail forked like the branches of a heavenly tree, each branch giving birth to a half-dozen glittering lines looping upward, mimicking the well-curled strands of a wig. As the brilliant gold ringlets sparkled, then faded, they made a sound like a farm boy trying to whistle between his teeth and failing. Margaret clapped her hands in delight.

"It worked!" Belland exclaimed. "I told my father it would." His cheeks colored. "How I wish I could see his expression at this moment. He is on the barge supervising the firing." He pointed toward a spot on the Thames where small fires seemed to flicker on the surface of the water. "Meanwhile, I lurk here among my betters, gauging the effect of our rockets so we may refine them." He rubbed his hands together in a manner suggesting satisfaction rather than chill. "Do you know, Mistress Dove, we just this week began to design a rocket that will climb higher than the tower of St. Paul's." His pride was evident.

The tower of St. Paul's Cathedral was visible throughout London, rising square and massive above all else. "I would like to see that," Margaret exclaimed. "Would like to learn how such a thing is made. Your fireworks appear magical, but I assume they are the result of science, not sorcery."

He looked at her more closely. "Are you a woman of science?"

"There is no such thing—rather sadly, I think. But I read the publications of the Royal Society. And before we were driven from London by plague last summer, I attended the demonstration of a telescope with a convex lens design."

Margaret recalled the initial shock of seeing the stars so close—how she had jerked back from the device's eyepiece, then greedily pressed forward again. Wonder had been followed by an overwhelming sense of God's divine love in giving man both the objects in the heavens and the wit to discover how to see them better. She had left the event, eyes dimmed with tears. But now, as Belland's eyes widened in astonishment, she was embarrassed. What must he think of her for showing an eager interest in such things! *This is why you are still unmarried.* Margaret lowered her gaze to the toes of Belland's boots; then, recalling he was at best the middle sort, so what he thought did not matter, she raised her eyes again, daring him to criticize her.

Instead he said, "You have seen a convex lens telescope? They are said to be a marvelous improvement! You must describe—" A great number of popping noises interrupted his thought. "The finale!" he exclaimed, moving to stand so close to Margaret that she swore she could feel the heat of him through the February cold. A great fountain of fire roared to life on a platform in the river, as the rockets they'd heard launch broke open in the sky, sending a shower of colored stars downward.

The sight was spectacular, but Belland shook his head, "Too many on the right and not enough on the left."

The fountain on the river changed colors unexpectedly as a second burst of artificial stars tumbled earthwards to the appreciative gasps of the crowd. Margaret dared not wait for the light to fade and the torches on the leads to flare. She needed to be waiting in the Queen's apartments, book in hand as if she'd never left. She turned to slip away, but a hand on her arm stopped her.

"Mistress Dove, if you would really like to see a rocket made, I would be happy to show you. May I send a note to make arrangements?"

She knew that she ought to say no. But given the number of women who slipped away from court to do more scandalous things, surely meeting a man to view an assemblage of paste-board and gunpowder was not so serious a matter. So she nod-ded before running for the stairs.

◊

Whitehall Palace

August

"Margaret, the Earl of Tyrconnell looks at you again. And what a look! He undresses you with his eyes." Winifred Wells, one of the Queen's Chamberers, and mother of a bastard by the King, smirked. "He is the youngest of sixteen you know. So, little Dove, should he manage to lift those leaden skirts of yours, you will spend the next twenty years on your back—in one manner or another."

Margaret could feel herself coloring, which was doubtless what Winifred wanted. She was always needling those in the Queen's service she felt were too fastidious about their reputa-tions. Margaret was saved from responding by the arrival of a gentleman asking Winifred to dance.

"Ignore her." Simona Carey took Margaret's hand, pressing it as they drew back from the edge of the dance floor until they could no longer see Tyrconnell. "In any case, why should you be ashamed if the Earl admires you? He has made it clear he seeks a bride, not a whore, and he is well established in York's household. You could do worse."

"I wish he admired you," Margaret replied, fervently. The horrible irony of at last having a suitor when she most defi-nitely did not want one had hovered oppressively over Margaret for weeks. At first she had studiously ignored Tyrconnell's little flatteries. But the Earl had made his intentions unavoidably clear only days earlier when they were of the same party at lawn bowling. If he wrote to her father, that would be the end of things for her . . . the end of her hopes with Etienne.

What hopes? You have none.

"I would be glad if he looked at me," her best friend replied. "But he won't. After all, you have that touch of red in your hair, and he is an Irishman." Simona leaned in until her lips nearly touched Margaret's ear. "And perhaps he has heard that, like his patron, you have a weakness for papists."

Margaret jerked her head back, tears pricking her eyes. Simona must have seen them and known she'd gone too far. "My dear Dove," she said softly, "tears change nothing. The world is the world. You must have a nobleman for a husband. I begin to wonder if I do right in aiding your trysts."

For the last half year, since Etienne Belland had first shown Margaret how a firework was constructed, Simona had helped her devise increasingly frequent clandestine meetings with the handsome fireworks maker.

"Do not say that Simona. Are you in such a hurry to break my heart?"

Simona narrowed her eyes, "Perhaps sooner is better than later."

Although they were now at the fringes of the gathering, Margaret took the precaution of opening her fan so that her mouth was hidden from all but her companion. "Fine, don't help me," she whispered fiercely, "even though you know my meetings are innocent, and we only talk." *And kiss.* The thought must have brought some color to her cheeks, for Simona's eye filled with incredulity. "I will go tomorrow, nonetheless. What will you do then? Run and tell tales to Her Majesty?"

Queen Catherine sat not far away, lips fixed in a slight smile, but eyes, as ever, haunted by sadness as they rested on her husband talking with the Countess of Castlemaine. The Queen's deep pink gown gave her cheeks a lovely hue. Not that King Charles noticed. Resplendent in pale blue petticoat breeches, matching silk stockings, and one of the waistcoats he was making popular, His

Majesty's eyes were on Castlemaine's bosom, rising above a neck-line many inches lower than the modest cut favored by his queen.

Simona sighed. "You know I would never do that. Only promise me, again, that you will not do anything foolish, like run off with your Frenchman."

"Must you *always* mention where he comes from?" Margaret bristled, for while those at court accepted foreigners with equa-nimity, the trading class and the great unwashed of London did not. And as the Dutch fleet drew close to the coast, Etienne had been called a Hogen-Mogen and been spat upon in the street. Never mind that he was not Dutch.

"I am sorry. But what will I tell Lady Saunderson if tomor-row evening comes and you do not appear at Her Majesty's card table? If, instead of merely losing yourself in the streets of London, you slip beyond the monsieur's workshop and are lost forever?"

Tell her I am not lost, but found, or that at very least, I have found the courage to make myself happy.

Not courage—selfishness, Margaret corrected herself firmly. Such an action would not only disgrace her family but ruin Etienne's career and subject him to a lifetime of being hunted, for her family would surely insist she had been abducted. A shortened lifetime, too, if they were caught, as her father would want Etienne prosecuted, the same as if any of his other valu-able property had been stolen. Margaret might be willing to subject herself to disgrace, to being beaten within an inch of her life, and to a future locked away on her family's estate, but she would never destroy Etienne—her bright spark of glorious, exciting fire.

🔥

The monthly great wash was well underway, although the sun had just risen. The open spaces of sprawling Whitehall, from the Great Court to Wood Yard, bustled with women and were crowded with caldrons. A smell of castile soap wafted on a strong breeze as Margaret ducked beneath lines strung tight and covered with dripping linens, then passed between an army of screw presses. She wore the simple garb of a tradeswoman, albeit a prosperous one, and just before slipping out a gate used by those supplying the palace's myriad kitchens, she slid a mask into place. When Margaret traveled with the court, she wore a stylish loo mask. But merely covering the area about her eyes was insufficient on a morning such as this. When she met Etienne, she was less interested in fashion than in safeguarding her identity, so only a full vizard would do.

He caught her up with an arm around her waist the moment she was in the street.

"Goodness, you scared me," she said as he released her, offering an arm.

"No I didn't. You knew I'd be here, and I have yet to discover anything that actually scares you. Your name should be 'Hawk,' not 'Dove'—for you are fierce."

"That is not a very flattering thing to say to a lady."

"It *ought* to be. You ought to be the feminine ideal. You are mine." He laid his hand over hers at the crook of his elbow.

"And that is enough." There was nothing fashionably witty about her answer, but it earned her one of Etienne's charming, broad smiles.

"The coach is in Craven Street."

As the vehicle's door closed, Margaret leaned back and lifted her mask. "You said you had a surprise for me."

Etienne rubbed his hands together, pleased at the idea of pleasing her. "Thomas secured that issue of the Royal Society's *Philosophical Transactions* containing Monsieur Auzout's piece."

"The one discussing the changes likely to be discovered on the moon by its inhabitants?" Margaret's voice rose excitedly.

"The very one. And he has found a book setting out how a telescope may be built by amateurs with scientific interests."

"To have a telescope!"

"Perhaps I ought not to have told you about the book." Etienne took her hand, where it lay on the seat between them, and raised it to his lips. "I cannot have you spend all your time looking at the celestial bodies; some of it must be reserved for me."

"I will only look at the stars as often as you look at your fireworks," she teased.

"I cannot be sure if you chastise me or make a fair promise. But either way, I think we must build a telescope."

Outside the coach, the Strand became Fleet Street, and they slowed as traffic backed up. Jetties protruded haphazardly from buildings on either side of the road until they nearly touched, keeping the sun from the carriage. But nothing could prevent the noxious odors from creeping in now that they were stationary. Wood and coal smoke mixed with the stench of dung and piss from the road—where animals and men alike relieved themselves—and from cesspools beneath the nearby houses. People pressed past on either side of stalled equipages, twisting, turning, and squeezing to be about their way. A gentleman beside Margaret's window jumped as a large rat darted between his feet. His eyes met Margaret's, and while she did not know him, she jerked back from the window, startled.

"Are you all right?" Etienne's eyes examined her for any sign of her condition: a bluing of her skin, shortness of breath, swaying that might presage a swoon. After so much time in each other's company, he knew them all. And he worried with a possessive caring that touched Margaret deeply.

"I am fine, Etienne." This time it was she who raised his hand and kissed it. "Only eager to be at Bradish and Son. How charming that Thomas added "and son" when little Raphe is not yet walking." Bradish was Etienne's favorite bookseller, and as she loved books nearly as much as she loved Etienne, over the past months Margaret had come to know the Bradish family well.

"I fear we must stop on our way if His Majesty's grand fireworks display, intended to distract from pleasures missed because of the cancelation of the Bartholomew Fair, is to go forward."

The fair, with its labyrinth of stalls and various entertainments, drew Londoners highborn and low to West Smithfield the last two weeks in August, providing a diversion from the late summer doldrums, dust, and heat. But this year's fair had been cancelled by the Council to "prevent contagion." There had been much disappointment and grumbling at Whitehall, with more than one courtier pointing out that if plague continued to be of any real consequence, the court would not have remained in the city.

"The miscreant's establishment is in Warwick Lane," Etienne continued. "I promise to keep my lecture short."

The shop was closed. Etienne knocked, attempted to peer between the shutters, mumbling to himself in French, then knocked again. Nothing. As he turned away, a man of middle height and broad build crossed from a butcher's shop opposite, wiping his hands on his blood-streaked apron.

"Can I help, sir? My friend opens late today, for he has a new grandson. But you can leave word for him with me if you like."

"I would. My name is Etienne Belland. Your friend will know it well, as he's had money from my purse for more than twenty gross of pasteboard these last months. But now, having been promised four gross more by the twentieth of August, I have nothing." Etienne drew a deep and aggrieved breath. "Well, not precisely nothing—I have ready hands waiting in Marylebone to turn that pasteboard into entertainment for His Majesty's pleasure, and apprentices eat whether I can keep them busy or not. Can you, sir, imagine doing your job without cow or pig?"

The butcher made a sympathetic noise. "When Thayer returns, sir, I'll give him your message."

"Thank you. Tell him after the twenty-eighth the pasteboard will do me no good, and I will not pay for what I no longer need."

As Etienne held out his arm for Margaret, the butcher spoke up. "You mentioned the King, sir. What is it you do with pasteboard to entertain His Majesty?" He screwed up his brow as if contemplating a difficult riddle, and Margaret had to admit that if she did not know the Belland family business, it would be hard to imagine how pasteboard might delight.

"I am a fireworks maker by royal patent." Etienne straightened to his full height, for the royal patronage was a point of great pride.

"I see them fireworks over the river from time to time." The man nodded. "I've enjoyed 'em, and taken my little ones down to the bank for the treat. Have you a show these next days?"

A bit of color crept up along Etienne's neck. Margaret knew he did not wish to be unkind, but to tell a random tradesman the details of a royal entertainment would be unseemly. After a moment of awkward silence, Etienne said, "Sir, I am not at liberty to comment, but I promise when next my work rises to the sky, you shall see it from here easily. There will be tricks of light that are entirely new." He lowered his voice, as if sharing some great secret. "Keep an eye out for a pure body of flame, like a comet, flying higher than the top of St. Paul's and wavering there like a bird on the wing."

The man's eyes widened and he looked suitably impressed.

In response, Etienne stuck out his hand and gave the butcher's a firm shake.

"Oh, Etienne," Margaret said, laughing as he handed her into the coach, "you love nothing so much as that newly designed rocket! You tell everyone about it. What if it does not work on the night of its debut?"

"It will work." He slid in beside her. "And I love you far more than that piece of handiwork—or any I will ever make." Leaning over he kissed her, a deep kiss that caused Margaret's flesh to tingle and her hand to rise unbidden to his dark hair. She was increasingly hungry for his kiss in a way that both amazed and frightened her. A year ago no man had ever had his lips on hers, and she had not felt that absence. She'd been bemused and scandalized by the glinting eyes and deep, sometimes moaning, admiration her fellow maids expressed for various male members of the court. The crude jokes courtiers made about the King and the Duke of York and their mistresses had brought a flush of embarrassment. But now when the heat rose in her face over such things, it was caused as much by curiosity and desire as by embarrassment. When Winifred had spoken of the Earl of Tyrconnell getting Margaret on her back last evening, her blushing response had arisen in part from wondering what a man really did when he got beneath a woman's skirts and how it would feel to have Etienne there. Not a thought she'd shared with anyone—not even Simona. Now as the carriage bumped along and Etienne pulled her onto his lap, Margaret wished the distance to Paternoster Row longer.

As they entered the shop, Thomas Bradish stood behind his counter, wrapping a stack of books for a tall, slender gentleman and chatting amiably. "How goes the construction of your theater at Oxford?"

"My patron, Archbishop Sheldon, writes he is impressed with the progress," the gentlemen replied. "I am willing to rely on his word, for if I run back to Oxford to see for myself the vice-chancellor will try to keep me there." The head, sporting a well-curled wig on the golden end of brown, shook dismissively. "And my mind and ambitions are all in the capital at the moment. What is the design of a theater for students—even the brightest in England—when the prize of St. Paul's waits to be snatched by one of us brought on by the dean to advise on the Cathedral's future?"

Margaret moved to browse one of Thomas's shelves. From this angle she could see the book buyer's face. He had striking arched eyebrows, a cleft chin, and a long aquiline nose. But what truly caught Margaret's attention was the way his wide-set eyes burned with the same sort of focused, ambitious passion she saw in Etienne's when he bit his lower lip and watched the firing of a new rocket after weeks of calculations. She was unable to look away until the shopper turned his eyes downward to take money from his purse.

Handing coins to Thomas, the man continued, "London deserves something magnificent . . . the new style churches I saw in France . . ." He paused, face glowing. "The crossing of the nave and transept at Sainte Marie de la Visitation rises all to a tremendous dome, all air and light, that must surely remind every man of the power of his creator. *That* is the purpose of architecture: to elevate the mind. And *that* is what is needed here in London. Not a worn-out Cathedral with a ramshackle tower and south transept roof that has tumbled in."

The gentleman tucked his parcel under his arm and, turning from the counter, acknowledged Etienne and Margaret with an inclination of his head.

"Who was that?" Margaret asked as the street door clicked shut behind him.

"Doctor Christopher Wren, Professor of Astronomy at Oxford and member of the Royal Academy." Thomas moved aside his ledger and ivory pen to make room on the counter.

"That was Wren!" Etienne exclaimed. "I wish I had known. I might have made so bold as to introduce myself. Margaret and I read his writings."

"I ought to have made an introduction. I am sorry. After all, I know the pair of you are nearly as mad for science as Wren himself." Thomas gave his carefully tended goatee a tug. With golden beard, moustache, and hair; gray eyes; a high forehead; and full lips, Margaret always thought that, but for a large mole near his right eye, he looked as if he could be the Duke of Buckingham's lost brother.

"My excuse must be that when Wren extrapolates on something, I forget my manners and sometimes even my name." Reaching beneath the counter, Thomas lifted out a stack of books. "Here is what I promised you, and a bit more. Etienne, I found a treatise translated from the oriental languages on the use of chemicals to color fire. Perhaps some new tricks for your work?" He winked. Then raising his voice, called, "Agnes, Margaret and Etienne have arrived."

Bradish's wife emerged from behind the shop, baby Raphe on her hip and little Ellinor clinging to her skirts. Etienne squatted down and with a wave of his hand, as if he were a street magician, produced a sweet that he held out to the delighted Ellinor.

"Margaret, how good to see you." Agnes said, bouncing the baby as he began to fuss. "Come to the kitchen and I will get you some caudled ale. The streets are so dry. If only it would rain."

Margaret glanced at Etienne. Finished charming Ellinor, he'd buried his nose in the book on chemical agents. "Thank you, Agnes, ale with you sounds considerably more entertaining than reading about alum."

Soon they were seated at a well-scrubbed table, each with a small tankard, while the children played on the floor.

"Thomas says Etienne is going to build you a telescope and has been reading volumes on lenses."

"We share a great love of the skies."

"That may be, but mark my words, this current obsession of his has nothing to do with the heavens and everything to do with you. When we were courting, Thomas used to watch me hem shirts and remark upon the fineness of my stitches, but that did not mean he was interested in sewing."

Margaret looked into her tankard.

"You are clearly as enamored with Etienne as he is with you." Agnes's voice was gentle. "He is a good man—I have known him for years. What's more, he makes a good living. The coach that brought you has *glazed* windows. And you have seen his family home in Marylebone."

Margaret smiled. When she'd first visited the Belland home and workshop, she'd been presented as a friend of Agnes Bradish and the daughter of a tea importer. No one had questioned that. Why would they? On such equal footing, Etienne's parents and younger siblings welcomed her warmly.

Agnes lowered her voice. "Is it because Etienne is Catholic? I know it is a hard thing, and sometimes a dangerous one, to be a Catholic in England. But our Queen is Catholic, as is the King's own mother. The Bellands are careful not to flaunt their faith or flout the rules governing it, and they can afford to pay the fine for failing to attend services in the Church of England." She rose and bustled about, topping off their tankards. Then, reseating herself, she nodded as if making up her mind to something.

"Thomas and I ourselves adhere to the Church of Rome." A slight flush rose into Agnes's cheeks. "I hope this will not spoil our friendship."

"Never!" Margaret replied. "I would be mortified if you thought my opinion could be altered by such a point."

Agnes smiled. "I suspected it would be so. In the months I have known you, you have shown me your heart is as good as your mind is sharp. No wonder Etienne loves you. But perhaps your conscience, liberal in terms of friendship, cannot overlook the serious matter of faith when it comes to marriage. I know, I know, I ought to mind my own business. It is only that you seem to go on so well together . . ."

Agnes reached down to wipe Raphe's nose with the lower edge of her apron as he crawled past, but instead suddenly sat bolt upright, locking wide eyes on Margaret. Glancing down, Margaret realized why: while she had donned a bodice and skirt appropriate to a tradesman's daughter, she wore her own knitted silk stockings in a vibrant cornflower blue and her own high-heeled leather shoes trimmed in gold braid. Items she'd carelessly allowed to peek from beneath her skirts.

Prior to this moment, Agnes, like her husband and Etienne's family, had accepted Margaret as a tea importer's daughter. But the stockings and shoes were a tell, marking Margaret as at very least rich, and more likely as a member of that class called the great.

A noblewoman. Margaret could see the recognition in Agnes's bewildered gaze. As such, Margaret was not someone Agnes might appropriately host at her table, or sit beside as if they were equals. Jumping to her feet, Agnes took two quick steps backward, heedless of the fact she bumped poor Ellinor, sending her sprawling. "Forgive me, Mistress," she stammered, voice full of deference, "but as you are a guest in my home, may I have the honor of knowing your name."

"I am sorry, Agnes." Margaret felt tears gathering. "I did not come here in a false guise for the purpose of betraying your trust. I hide who I am to protect Etienne and for the selfish purpose of seeing him." The first tear loosed itself, running down her face, and her chest constricted. "The conversations we've had, the laughter, the face I have shown you—all this has been as genuine as my garments are false." She wanted to go on, to give the name she'd been asked for, but she could get no air. Gasping, she put both her hands to the base of her throat as the room flashed, then faded to black.

The next voice she heard was Etienne's. "Margaret, Margaret, my love."

She lay somewhere soft, struggling to open eyelids too heavy to lift.

"Shall I get a physician?" The voice was Thomas's.

"No. It has been thus with her since childhood. She has seen the best physicians. They are helpless to affect a cure for these fits. All we can do is wait for her to come back to us." There was a long pause. She felt a hand take her own. "And fear she will not." His voice was choked.

"Do not say such a thing," Agnes scolded.

Again a pause, and then Thomas's voice: "My friend, I think you must be mad. Consorting with a royal Maid of Honour. All that you and your family have built, your life too . . . these are in genuine peril if you are caught."

Etienne gave a hollow laugh. "You sound like Margaret. She is anxious over such things. But I count them as trifles. I worry about only one eventuality: our inescapable separation. About the day that she swoons and fails to rise or the day she is married to another. There is not enough time."

He squeezed her hand, and she found herself able to squeeze back. A moment later Margaret looked up into Etienne's warm brown eyes. "Time enough, my dearest Etienne."

◊

St. Paul's Cathedral

Monday, August 27

I arrive first by design. Standing in St. Paul's churchyard—the largest open space in crowded, chaotic London—I close my eyes. Inigo Jones's portico, with its obelisks, scrolls, and columns—a dressing up commissioned by our present king's father—disappears.

Jones's renovations show his great talent, but they were powerless to revive the crumbling hulk of St. Paul's, worn by time and weather. His flourishes were as futile as binding only one wound on a soldier who is cut in a hundred places. They could not disguise the missing lead from the great roof or restore the spire gone a hundred years. And since then, the patient has sickened further, thanks to

Cromwell's Roundheads, who used the mighty church as a stable and worse. It was they who desecrated the baptismal font and stole marble from the south transept floor.

I am sorry, Inigo, but your columns, your bull's-eye windows, must come down. The time for patching is done. St. Paul's must begin again. I must give London a new Cathedral, with a dome such as has never been seen on English shores.

A hand touches my shoulder, and I open my eyes to find my friend and fellow member of the Royal Academy, John Evelyn. He is a man of exceptional taste, so I am counting on his support as we walk the nave today and Hugh May, Roger Pratt, and I each try to convince the Cathedral's dean and other Royal Commissioners that we know what is best for St. Paul's future.

"Evelyn," I say, clasping his hand in greeting, "when you wrote *Fumifugium*, decrying London for the stinking, ill-planned cesspool it is, why did you not spend some words setting out the disgraceful state of St. Paul's?"

"Too late now, Wren." He laughs. "Were I to compose a hundred pages tomorrow, dissecting the Cathedral's faults, they would be seen merely as a partisan foray in the ongoing war betwixt yourself and Roger Pratt. Tell me: as you stood, eyes tight shut, were you imagining the shimmering new dome you wish to design, or your hands around Pratt's throat?"

"The dome," I reply as he holds open the door of the church so we may enter.

A quarter of an hour later, when I close my eyes again, trying to calm myself, I do indeed imagine strangling Roger Pratt. Then I open them once more and say in the most even tone I can manage, "On and on you go about a new survey. We do not need months of measuring, when the naked eye can see the outward thrust of the roof has pushed the Cathedral's walls off line." I make a sweeping gesture from floor to ceiling. "The walls are failing. It is time for them to come down and better ones to rise in their place."

"The eye is an imperfect tool, Wren. It can be fooled." Pratt shakes his head with the air assumed by those who think themselves superior, to remind others of that fact. "I am surprised that a man whose report to the Commission boldly trumpets the importance of engineering, and who claims great knowledge of it, is willing to be so *unscientific*."

Evelyn casts me a warning look, knowing how the accusation will goad. Then he inclines his head toward the clerk standing beside the dean, taking minutes of this meeting, reminding me that if I lose my temper I will do so on the record.

We stand clustered at the intersection of the nave and transept— nearly a dozen of us, churchmen, Commission members, the architects appointed to report, and a handful of skilled stonemasons. "Have any of you a plumb line?" I ask the tradesmen.

An aging mason draws one from his pocket, handing it to the youngest among them with a firm nod. The youth, not overawed by his sacred surroundings, sprints to the nearest bit of scaffolding— there is so much of it in St. Paul's—and clambers up as if it were a tree in a garden. Our group stands in silence as he drops the line.

"Science," I say to Pratt, noticing that the dean and bishop nod, watching with satisfaction how the clerk takes down my pronouncement. "Shall we send him up another scaffold, Pratt, or are you convinced?"

"Well, if the walls *are* out of plumb, that does not necessarily make them unsound." Pratt purses his lips like a maiden aunt who has walked in on a scullery maid and a stable boy in flagrante delicto. "Perhaps they are *deliberately* so. Our Norman forefathers, whose work has stood the test of time throughout this kingdom, may have chosen to build the walls as we see them to enhance the effect of perspective."

"Ridiculous!"

My mouth drops open. *Good heavens! Evelyn has lost his patience after warning me to hold mine!*

"Is it?" Pratt's gaze falls on Evelyn as heavily as iron. "I will tell you what is ridiculous, Evelyn." His voice rises in agitation. "Wren's obstinate assertion that the tower cannot be repaired but must be taken down to make way for his ludicrous dome. Even if such a—what did he call it in that incendiary report of his? Ah yes, 'noble cupola.' Even if his cupola did not smack of popery, think of the cost!"

"Pratt, I demand an apology for your insinuation that I am a papist." I take a step toward Pratt to remind him how short he is. "My father was Chaplain in Ordinary to King Charles the first, and Dean of Windsor—a man devoted to the Anglican Church. The Roundheads did not doubt it—when their forces entered Windsor, they saw to it that he was deprived of his living and our family possessions were broken to bits because he stood for King and Church of England. Yet *you* have the temerity to doubt *my* conformity!"

Pratt glowers.

"Gentlemen"—the Very Reverend Dean Sancroft holds up both hands as if he would give a benediction—"let us have no more squabbling. You disagree on what precisely? Not that this holy place must be restored to its former glory—you both have a great passion for that project—but merely on the means. You will serve God best by working together."

I hold out my hand to Pratt, not because I am ready to forgive, and not because I believe we will ever work amiably on this or any other architectural endeavor, but because the Dean used the dreaded word "restored." For the moment, then, it sounds as if Pratt is winning, and I would not make my situation worse by seeming obstinate. No indeed, I hope the clerk is recording our handshake.

"I think," the Dean says, "we must have a committee of workmen from the building trades examine the foundations and either establish or decry the stability of this structure."

"Another committee?" *Dear God in heaven.* "How long will that take? And what purpose can it possibly serve? London deserves a glorious new St. Paul's, not a pale, piecemeal, patched one." I bite my tongue the moment the words are out. So much for my judicious handshake. I have now shown my irritation nakedly, and doubtless unadvisedly. But I am not Job, and these constant delays have become unbearable.

Just five weeks after returning from Paris, luggage stuffed with folios so I would not forget the marvels I'd seen, I presented this Commission with my inspired design for a new St. Paul's. That was May the first. Nearly four months have passed, and still the Commissioners equivocate between my beautiful, bold suggestions and Pratt's timid course. My ideas are better. It is that simple. Why do the men standing before me need more time to see it?

When the meeting is over, Evelyn and I repair to a nearby tavern.

"Tell me, Evelyn," I say as soon as I have drained my tankard, "should genius wait upon the slow and imperfect understanding of the average minded? And it is clear, however famous, Roger Pratt is a middling sort with no special understanding of beauty or mathematics. How in the *hell* did he become the most fashionable architect in England?"

"Commissions," Evelyn replies. "Once vast sums have been expended on something or someone, it is in the interest of those who spent them to praise the results."

"Yes, well, that does not answer the question: Should true talent defer to such men? I would argue such deference is not rational, and irrationality is crime in this age of reason."

"Wren, you ought to be an orator, not an architect."

I slam my tankard down. "What galls me most is this will be a matter of money."

"Most things are."

"Yes, and *that* is why I worry. Pratt's way—his infernal suggestion that all the faults in the Cathedral can be bricked over—will appeal to the Commission because it seems the model of thrift, and if there is anything a committee loves better than thrift, I do not know it. But one might as well throw money in the Thames as spend another pound propping up the unsalvageable. St. Paul's must come down, Evelyn. It must come down."

CHAPTER 3

Present-day London

Friday

"Parker, it's Friday night, don't you have anywhere more exciting to be?" Evans stopped beside Nigella's desk, coat over his arm. "Keep this up and you'll be me in another decade."

"You mean promoted?" Nigella took her hand off the phone on her desk.

"Maybe. But I meant you'll be the person everyone suspects has no life, who can't remember if there is anything in the fridge that is still technically edible, and who just got a call from an ex screaming about how you missed your son's birthday. And I don't mean missed sending a gift; I mean missed dinner when you promised to come. So you'll be heading to a pub to slam back enough drinks to wipe the image of your disappointed kid shrugging off your non-appearance out of your head. At least that's my Friday night plan."

"Jesus, sir, you certainly know how to inspire and reward dedication in your subordinates." She shook her head and rolled her eyes.

"You're already plenty inspired. And if you want to spend all weekend with your files, I guess I am not really in a position to judge." He shrugged into the coat. "But take them home. Remember our talk."

"Five minutes, promise. Just want to make a call."

He shook his head. "Night."

Nigella watched him walk away. The call was to Spiffy, the company that owned the van used at the Monument fire. Things had exploded yesterday on one of her major cases, and all the neatly organized "to-do" bullet points on the arson, including calling the cleaning company, had been shoved aside. Today had been more of the same. But it seemed wrong to head into the weekend without at least starting the wheels turning on the van identification.

She dialed the number. A chirpy recorded voice told her they were closed. Not unexpected given the hour, but she'd been hoping, since commercial cleaning crews worked nights, somebody would be on duty in the office. The recorded woman informed Nigella she could press one if she was an existing client with a cleaning emergency. Nigella hesitated. Not being a client wasn't what kept her finger from the button—being the police generally meant you got to push whatever buttons you wanted. What stopped her was the realization that forcing some poor sod to cancel Friday night plans to answer questions about industrial cleaning vans in a nonurgent matter was pathetic.

Seriously, pathetic.

Nigella shoved the fire-related files into her bag and switched off her desk lamp. Then she texted James: *U up 4 taking me to see that public art boat? Or just up?*

She rode the elevator down, waiting for a ping—a newly assigned notification tone, thank you very much DI O'Leary—announcing an answer. Nothing.

At home, she put her mobile on top of her small café table, more often used for work than eating, pulled out the files, and got down to it. She went over O'Leary's lab report, covered over with his own scrawling notes, twice, willing herself to see something he hadn't. It was the same damn pine, same traces of linseed oil. But this time there was a secondary accelerant—petrol. Probably because the suspect needed fire faster and fiercer. After all, St. James's stood in an area that would see a fair amount of traffic, even late on a Wednesday night. The location and timing were bolder than the Monument incident. Slightly less so if the suspect knew about the lack of cameras. Her instinct said he did.

How? Was he connected to the parish? Had he been homeless and slept there?

Her mobile phone shimmied. It must be late enough for night mode, with its silenced ringer—except for official numbers of course. Nigella snatched it up. Not James—her mum. Nigella wasn't interested in being pressured into brunch this weekend, or told about Giles's latest achievements, coupled with broad hints that he'd love to catch up with her. So she left the call unanswered.

The thoughts of brunch made Nigella realize she was hungry. She opened the fridge and was chuffed to see that Evans had that bit wrong. There was plenty of healthy food: carefully prepared midweek, portioned, and put in plastic boxes stacked like little pyramids—biggest on the bottom, smallest on the top. *Just as obsessively placed as your toothbrush.*

Nigella took out a stack, selected a container of salmon and sautéed fennel, purposefully put the remaining boxes back crooked, and slammed the fridge door—vaguely angry because she realized the crookedness bothered her. She ate on the sofa so that she wouldn't have to move her work, relishing her view of the lighted dome of St. Paul's across the river.

Good food, world-class view. All that was missing to make it a perfect Friday night was either a break in a case or James's well-toned body, naked and eager. She'd have to go for the former because the latter remained silent in response to her message.

Nigella had requested high-quality stills of the Spiffy van from the CCTV footage—asking the lads to do what they could to improve the resolution. She slit the end of the envelope and slid out three images. Stone the fucking crows! The van had a corporate ID number, S11, that hadn't been evident in the grainier video. Maybe this was her reward for fighting her "do it now" instinct and putting off the call to Spiffy. Now it would be a shorter conversation: what could they tell her about S11 rather than an entire fleet.

She poured herself a glass of red wine and checked her phone again; a pointless exercise given she would hardly have missed it vibrating in the silent flat.

Well, one could kill a bottle of wine almost as easily as two could. Time for a *Great British Bake Off* binge. Or maybe some vintage *Prime Suspect*—after all Jane Tennison was a personal hero.

She'd drifted off when the buzzer woke her. Before she could answer it, her mobile vibrated. A single line glowed on screen: *Downstairs, up for it. You?*

She buzzed him in, waiting with her hand on the doorknob. Fuck yes, she was up for it. The minute he crossed the threshold, she moved forward to be kissed.

"Better late than never, eh?" He dropped a gym bag, then pulled off his jacket and let it fall to the floor. "I was working out, then back at my studio with the ringer off. How 'bout I shower first?"

"I don't mind a little sweat." She moved in, but he put up a hand.

"What is it they say—Abstinence makes the heart grow fonder? Give me five." He collected his bag.

As he went through to the bathroom, Nigella picked up his jacket to hang it on a peg. But she dropped it again as James began undressing with the door wide open, stuffing his clothes in the bag at his feet, a sight that completely distracted her.

As soon as he was under the shower, she went into the bathroom and began stripping down on the other side of the glass door. "Forget five minutes—how about three?"

"Hell, I only need two."

$\text{\Large ♦}$

He was still lying beside her, post-coital panting, when her mobile sounded. Shrieked really, from the table in the other room where she'd abandoned it.

Nigella rolled toward her side of the bed.

"Leave it." James reached after her.

"Can't—that's the official ring." She sprinted to the living area. "DI Parker."

It was Evans. "It's not a nuisance anymore," he said. "Call the Yard, tell him to get to Temple Church. I'm sending a car. It'll be there in a jiffy." And then he was gone.

"You've got to go!" Nigella picked up James's gym bag and tossed it onto the bed.

"Blimey, talk about wham, bam, thank you, ma'am—or, in my case, sir. I just gave you the rogering of your life and you're turning me out."

"It was a very good rogering, but I've got to go to work."

"I guess that's one hazard of doing a rozzer, eh?" He got up and pulled on his trousers, commando. "But don't worry, you're *so* worth it."

Whatever. Nigella dialed her phone. *Come on—pick up.*

"DI O'Leary," the voice wasn't groggy and there was background noise. Was he at a club or a late night pub? How very un-him.

"O'Leary, it's me. Where are you? Never mind"—Nigella realized she'd asked out of curiosity, not necessity, and that it was none of her damn business—"Evans rang. We've got another one, and by the sound of it, a body." *We both knew someone was going to die. That's why we spent lunch hours and evenings on this burner boy. Or at least I spent evenings . . . you obviously have something more exciting going on.* "Can you get to Temple Church?"

"Yeah, but it's not going to make me popular."

"Nothing to worry about then—you've never been popular."

She was running a brush through her hair when she heard the siren in the distance. James sat on the edge of the bed, tying up his trainers. "No need to wait for me," she said. She knew she was being stupid. Just because they emerged from the building at the same time didn't mean the uniform sent to pick her up would assume they were together or care enough to take note, but still . . .

He stood. "Still want to see that boat sculpture?"

"Absolutely!" She feigned more enthusiasm than she felt, hoping to get him moving. "Text me. Drinks on me to make up for this."

He smiled and moved in for a kiss. Nigella offered her cheek. The siren was much closer. She was eager to head out and have her mind on business. He shouldered his gym bag, and she picked up a lipstick and leaned into the mirror. Normally, she wouldn't have bothered. She heard the flat's outer door shut. That made the lipstick worth it.

Stuffing her tablet into her always-ready kit, Nigella counted to ten, then burst into the hallway. No time to wait for the elevator—she hit the stairs.

Rolling up to the Temple complex's Tudor Street vehicular entrance, Nigella's first thought was *"How?"* How had the suspect managed to breach what was basically a one-entrance, one-exit compound after close of business? Nothing in this old and storied section of London's legal district was open to the public by the time darkness fell. The Temple Gardens closed mid-afternoon and the Temple Church at four PM—she'd asked Siri what the hours were on the way over. And while currently the bright yellow and black traffic gate was raised to allow police vehicles to pass, usually it would have been closed, and the befuddled looking private guard standing near it would have been in his glass guardhouse, monitoring entrances.

Police vehicles filled the U-shaped lot framed by imposing old buildings. A taxi, stopped in the middle, stood out. O'Leary climbed out. He had a jacket on and shiny shoes. When had he started owning shiny shoes?

"You coming?" he asked, turning to welcome her as she hopped from the squad car, then stepping back to let her lead the way.

"Don't tell me: ladies first?"

"DI Parker, I know better than that. This is your ground."

True.

They headed toward a tall, square archway between a red-brick building and a yellow-brick one. Officers spanned the opening, and DCI Evans stood, waiting, at the center.

"We have a death," Nigella said.

"And it's a cracker. Beyond that, we have a sensitive situation. The Right Honourable Sir John Davies found the body. He has a pied-à-terre in the Inner Temple. He is not amused."

Well, that was one way for a case to go from non-priority to top priority.

Evans didn't say anything else, just turned and walked, drawing Nigella and O'Leary in his wake.

The arch opened into a stone courtyard sandwiched between the Inner Temple and the Temple Church. Incident screens formed a ring near the far end, just to the left of a spotlighted stone column at least thirty feet tall, topped by a pair of knights astride a single horse.

"Who's on forensics?"

"Wilkinson, on the assumption this is connected to the Monument fire."

"Speaking of fire," O'Leary said, "I don't see or smell smoke." He was right. No smoke rose from the cordoned area, and no trace hung in the night air.

"How long's the fire been out?" Nigella asked.

"There was no fire—at least not here," Evans said grimly.

Nigella exchanged a look with O'Leary. He was clearly as confused as she. But where Evans was concerned, it was better to look first and ask questions later.

As they got closer to the circle of stretched plastic and metal fencing, there *were* fire odors: smoky notes underlain with the unpleasant, unmistakable panoply of smells—acrid, musky, coppery, charcoal-like, and sulfurous—produced when a human body was consumed by flame.

Evans lifted the flap.

"Jesus," O'Leary said, "or at least meant to look like him."

An immolated figure lay on its back, knees together and slightly bent, feet together, arms outstretched cruciform. And just in case anyone missed the reference, there was some sort of piece of fabric tied around the figure's head where a crown of thorns would be.

Nigella knew what to expect: her hands and feet going cold as ice, a tingling in her limbs, and breathing that grew faster and shallower. But these symptoms and the fear that triggered them no longer paralyzed her as they once had. She simply let her eyes close for a moment, and in the darkness reminded herself:

what you can't conquer destroys you. Then she opened her eyes and looked hard at the body.

It was not evenly charred. The arms and legs were blackened, yes, but where the thin outer layers of skin had peeled and the thicker dermal layer had shrunk and split, traces of underlying yellow fat could be seen.

"Face and arm bones exposed, but no ribs or leg bones—not even shins," O'Leary remarked. "This body could've burned past this stage just on its own fuel. I think our boy stopped it deliberately."

"Agreed," Nigella nodded. "This whole thing's an intentionally crafted tableau—the position, that thing on the victim's head. What *is* that thing?" she asked Wilkinson.

"Man's tie."

Nigella moved forward. She didn't dwell on the split face, the protruding bones, the discolored, literally fried, skin, focusing instead on the band around the forehead. "It's not even singed."

The light, peach-colored silk was in perfect condition. And on it was an outline she knew well. "That's St. Paul's," she said, pointing without touching. "The dome in profile."

"A tie imprinted with London's greatest church, wrapped around the forehead of a victim laid out as if he were crucified. Still laughing at my 'angry at God or the C of E' theory, Parker?"

"I'm not laughing at anything at the moment, O'Leary. How did this psycho hold the body in position while it burned?"

O'Leary walked to the corpse's knees and pointed. It was faint, but as Nigella moved along her side of the body to join him, a stripe where the skin was less burned became clear.

Nigella continued down to the corpse's ankles. "Same here." Her eyes met O'Leary's across the cruciform figure. "You don't think . . .?"

Slowly, grimly, as if they knew what they would find, the two DIs moved to the dead man's outstretched arms. The fingers on his hands were curled as fingers did when burned. Didn't matter—the palms told the tale: there were round wounds, opened up by the heat of the burn.

"If they find fragments of nails in those, I'm asking to be transferred off this case," O'Leary said.

"I think they will. And you know you won't." Nigella looked up at the sky for a moment, trying to think clearly. A drapery on the top floor of the Inner Temple twitched, drawing her gaze. There weren't many residential units left in the Temple, but there were some, and nearly all were occupied by the same sort of personages of power as the senior judge who'd found the body. Could the killer be someone of that ilk? It was an interesting question, but the moving curtain made Nigella realize anyone with a high enough vantage point was being treated to this gruesome show.

"Photograph the hell out of him, Wilkinson, and then get him out of here." She pointed toward where the curtains had moved and a light now shone. "We don't need a bunch of civilians leaking shocking and embroidered details."

"Good catch," Evans said.

The police photographer began snapping away, at first in relative silence, but soon agitated voices could be heard over the clicking of the camera shutter.

"Bloody press is here," Evans grumbled. The DCI headed across to the arch to deal with them.

Nigella and O'Leary stood side by side as the photographer finished and the stretcher was brought in. A half-dozen team members gingerly lifted the lifeless form.

"I want the arm positions preserved!" Wilkinson shouted in warning. "Lose so much as a finger between here and the van, you are going to hear about it!"

No mark on the pavement where the body had lain. Nothing but some bits and pieces, unavoidably left behind, despite the team's care. She knew Wilkinson: someone would bag these fragments of bone, flesh, fiber.

"No chance he burned or was extinguished here," O'Leary said. They'd both known it, but the confirmation was welcome.

"Interview time," Nigella said. "Judge first, if he'll see us."

"What a load of bollocks!" O'Leary shook his head. "This job is tough enough without bowing and scraping."

♦

The Right Honourable Mr. Justice Davies would see them. He was waiting not in the back of some police van, but in his expansive top-floor flat.

"It's just like a BBC drama," O'Leary said under his breath as they stood outside the door to a wood-paneled and oriental-rugged library, where the witness sat ensconced in a leather chair as Evans gave reassurances that all was being handled with alacrity. "All that is missing is the Waterford brandy snifter."

"Not missing," she whispered back. "Look on the desk."

Evans called them forward to be introduced, then withdrew and left them to it.

Nigella didn't bother with the "so good of you to see us" platitudes. Evans had covered that territory abundantly. "Sir John, can you tell us how you came to find the body."

"When I stay here, I always make a point of spending an evening with our Reverend and Valiant Master of the Temple." Then, perhaps seeing the same confusion in O'Leary's eyes that Nigella detected, he added, "that is the name given to the Anglican prelate appointed by Her Majesty as senior cleric at Temple Church. It is a nod to the history of our church, which was the home and chief meeting place of the British Knights Templar from its consecration in the late twelfth century until the Knights were driven out of England in the fourteenth century." He spoke slowly, deliberately, like a man used to passing judgments and explaining complicated things from the bench. But there was not a trace of condescension in his deep baritone as he explained. Nigella liked him immediately.

"The Master's house is just north of the Church. He and I are old friends, so I take a bottle of something special, and we discuss theology, art—anything but the news of the day. This was that evening." He smiled, as if recollecting the better part of his night. "The wine was good, the conversation better, and neither of us has a pressing engagement tomorrow, so next thing we knew it had gone one. We said goodbye and I started wending my way home. I got halfway across the courtyard before I realized there was something lying near the Knights Templar Column."

He paused, collecting his next set of thoughts.

"The ambient light from the column reflects only palely on the stones below, so I had no idea the object was human until I got closer. A quick once-over with the flashlight on my mobile was quite enough for me. DI Parker, I look forward to hearing that the animal who did that to a fellow human being has been brought in and is set down for trial."

"I'll do my best, Sir John. Other than the deceased, did you notice anything or anyone else?"

"He and I were utterly alone. Believe me, when you are standing beside a dead body, waiting for the police, your senses are heightened. And in that time the only noise I heard came from what I presume was some number of inebriated students making their way back after a night out—a place with this much stone does echo."

"Students?" O'Leary asked.

"Yes, there used to be numerous accommodations for scholars of the law scattered among the chambers. They're largely gone now, but some remain as both a tradition and a convenience. They're let to new barristers undertaking Bar courses. I'll have a list of resident students sent round. I'd be tremendously disappointed to think a member of the Bar was involved, but years on the bench have taught me not to make snap judgments."

He looked Nigella in the eyes, his gaze suggesting he was reserving judgment on her as well . . . waiting to see if she was any good at her job.

"We won't take up any more of your time, but if you think of anything—something that bothered you when you saw or heard it, a seemingly random thought that will not let you be— please contact me." Nigella drew one of her cards from the outside pocket of her bag. "The number on the front is my desk.

But this"—she scratched a number on the back—"is my mobile. Do not hesitate to use it. It is not as if I will be sleeping much these next days."

On the way out, O'Leary said, "Impressive. Way to make him feel valued and important without seeming like a sycophant."

"He *is* valued and important. Did you notice his calm, the level of detail in his recall? This man has heard thousands of witnesses. He knows how to be one. How often do we get that?"

The gate guard certainly did not fall into that category.

"Despite what your uniformed friends think, there is no way I just let some arsehole carrying a smoking hunk of former human waltz in here." The guard's pudgy arms closed defensively over his chest. "You have to have a sticker on your car or state your business to get past me."

"I'm sure that you have a well-controlled access system," Nigella said, trying to ingratiate herself. "Our suspect is clever though."

His face hardened into a scowl. Oh God, apparently he thought by saying the suspect was clever, she was intimating he was not. He wasn't, clearly. But there was absolutely nothing to be gained by letting that opinion be known.

"Do you log comings and goings?"

"Don't need to. We have cameras if we need to check up on a coming or going. But we usually don't. Entry is mostly controlled by sticker. If you've a sticker on your windscreen, I lift the gate and in you roll. If you don't, we have to have a little chat."

"So who'd you chat with tonight?"

"Quiet tonight, I'm telling you. More traffic out than in—there are always law types working late, even on Fridays. Early on, I had half a dozen tourists on foot, begging to have a peek round at the buildings and the Church."

"Did you let them in?" Nigella asked.

"You think a bunch of Chinese had a concealed body on 'em?"

He seemed determined to be belligerent. O'Leary gave Nigella a look, seeking permission because this was her ground. She gave a small nod, and he stepped in. "We're not suggesting they did. Look mate, you should have been off shift by now."

The guard nodded.

"You got caught up in this because you were doing your job. And that's what we're trying to do, so that all of us can go home or go have a pint. This is nobody's idea of fun. I was on a date when this got phoned in. We're not trying to blame you. We're trying to get a line on the major wanker who spent his Friday burning some poor bloke and ballsed up all of our weekends. So help us out, eh?"

"I didn't let the tourists in. Sometimes I do, but this wasn't one of those times."

"Other pedestrians?" O'Leary asked.

"Bunch of young suits that live here, returning from a night out, ties askew, loud. One of 'em had picked up a nice bit of skirt. She could barely walk."

God, on top of being uncooperative, he's an arsehole, Nigella thought. *Drooling over some poor girl too drunk to consent to anything, rather than helping her.* She saw a flash of disgust cross O'Leary's eyes. Then he pressed on.

"Anybody besides her staggering so much they needed support?"

Nigella saw what O'Leary was thinking. Perhaps the victim had been drugged or liquored up and brought in under his own power, only to be killed, bound, and burned—not necessarily in that order—somewhere in the complex.

"Other than the blonde looker whose skirt barely covered her minge, nah."

O'Leary offered the guard a "one of the guys" smile, and even though she knew it was both feigned and useful, Nigella's toes curled in her shoes. Then he said, "So drivers—who'd you chat with?"

"Like I said, it was quiet. Couple of takeaway delivery fellows before nine."

Nigella made a mental note. If the body was burned out-side the complex, she found it hard to believe it could have lain unobserved for that many hours, but still.

"Any cleaning crews?" she asked, thinking of van S11 and hoping her failure to press number one earlier that evening hadn't cost somebody their life.

"They come every night. They have the stickers, so I don't talk to them."

"Who's the contractor?" She held her breath.

"Pro something or other. Blue vans." In part, she was relieved. Blue meant not Spiffy. But at the same time, the fact that the witness sat here night after night and couldn't remember the name on the daily cleaning vans was not reassuring. If he didn't have that in his noggin, what else had he missed?

"Somebody, you talked to somebody, right?" O'Leary's voice was a tad desperate.

"Yeah, two blokes. One got angry. He said he was catering something for one of the Right Honourables . But it wasn't on the schedule—if a firm, a resident, or even the Church has an appointment, an expected delivery, or an event, it gets plugged into the schedule." He gestured toward a computer screen on his little desk.

"Sometimes people forget to notify us about a delivery, but not a party, because a party requires a guest list. If we don't have a list, traffic backs up 'cause whatever unfortunate bloke is on duty has to phone the host and clear each guest as they arrive."

Nigella felt her pulse rising. "And no guests tonight?"

He recrossed his arms, clearly unhappy she'd taken over the questioning. "Not a one, and nothing in the schedule. When I told this bloke that, he got worked right up. Swore at me. Then after a bit, he asked if I was looking at tonight or tomorrow. I said tonight because that was when we were both sitting here, and he called me a knob—said he'd told me the food was for a brunch tomorrow."

"Did you let him in?" O'Leary's voice was quiet, his tone flat.

He's as excited as I am, Nigella thought. *Might be our first break.*

"Yeah, because the brunch is listed for Saturday."

O'Leary deflated—so much so that he stooped, leaning his palms on the security console.

"And the other fellow?" Nigella asked.

"Delivering a piece of scenery for that Shakespeare thing going up in the Temple Church next weekend. Those fellows have been coming and going for days."

Nigella's heart was sinking like a stone. But she knew the drill, so she asked the standard follow-up. "Anything that struck you about this delivery?"

And she noticed a fidget. His arms uncrossed then crossed again over his chest. *There was something.*

"He didn't have one of those placards—we issued about two dozen to the theater types. They aren't vehicle specific, but if they are in the window, we don't have to stop the driver."

She had to tread carefully. She wanted to ask, "So why'd you let him in?" but she knew that'd shut him up. So she waited. Sometimes people filled the gap when they were nervous. She began to count to ten in her head, slowly. When she hit seven, he couldn't take it anymore.

"I stopped him and asked why he didn't have his placard if he was delivering scenery for the show. He didn't get angry or anything, not like the other bloke. He just said, 'Bollocks, I'm a pillock. I meant to get it.' Then he asked me if I could do him a solid and let him drop his stuff. Told me he had a key."

He must have seen something in her eyes, because his narrowed.

"He held one up. And he didn't insist. He told me if it would get me in trouble, he'd just come back tomorrow, and there went his day off, but it was his own damn fault."

Oh God, maybe we aren't going to go away empty-handed after all.

"Do you remember what he was driving?"

"White van."

"How was it labeled?"

"Don't think it was."

"And what did this fellow look like?"

"I don't know, just a bloke in his twenties or thirties."

Again, he must have seen something in her expression.

"Listen, sweetie, you may ogle every man you meet, but I'm not that type. A good-looking bird, sure"—he puffed up a bit—"but blokes are blokes, if you know what I mean." This last was directed to O'Leary.

"Cheers, mate," O'Leary said. He gave Nigella his "are we done?" look. She nodded. The witness liked O'Leary better. Fine. Let him wrap up. "If I wanted a look at that camera footage you mentioned, who should I ring?"

"There's a fellow at corporate." He clicked around on his computer, then jotted down a number. "Name's Anthony." He ripped the page off and handed it to O'Leary. "Good luck catching this fucker, and I'm telling you, you're going to see he came in another way, or maybe earlier in the day."

As soon as the door of the guard booth closed behind them, O'Leary said, "What a gormless prick. We need that footage."

"Yeah, but I don't suppose Anthony is at his desk at four AM on a Saturday."

O'Leary looked at his watch as if he didn't believe her. "Feck."

"Worried about that date, eh?"

"Yeah, Ni. You don't date. I do." He paused and sighed. "The timing on this is bad for professional reasons as well. I hate to break it to you, but I don't imagine Anthony will be at his desk at all on a weekend."

It was Nigella's turn to curse. "We're pretty much dead in the water until Monday."

"Let's hope so, because if we aren't, it means that something else bad has happened."

He was right. She looked across the parking area: plenty of squad cars left. "I've got to get with Evans about press strategy, but let me get you a lift home first."

"Don't bother. As a friend of mine once said, that's what Uber's for, and who says I'm going home?"

CHAPTER 4

Whitehall Palace

Sunday, September 2, 1666

"Mistress Dove, what a pensive look you give that bird, although he sings so prettily for you. He wonders, I am sure, as do I, what it takes to make you smile?"

Margaret turned to find the Earl of Tyrconnell in a coat and Rhinegrave breeches of rich russet silk, tidied off with ribbons. The color put her in mind of a male chaffinch. "I smile easily at the birds in the gardens, My Lord. But it is hard to smile at those caged here when there is so little room for flight in their worlds."

"So you would smile if given room to spread your wings." The Earl inclined his head as if this was the most interesting thing he had heard in days. Margaret sincerely hoped it was not.

Slipping a hand in her pocket, she wrapped her fingers around the watch there—a gift for Etienne purchased from the King's clockmaker, Edward East. She planned to slip from the palace tomorrow to give it to him. But many hours stood between her and that happy prospect. So Margaret wandered the long gallery because that was what one did on the Lord's Day after services concluded. She found the ritualized leisure of strolling and gossiping tedious, and now the attentions of the Earl threatened to make them torturous.

"I wonder, do you sing as prettily as this fellow?" Tyrconnell stepped close, putting a finger through the bars of the cage and stroking the canary. The Earl was about the same height as Etienne; yet, because his proximity was unwelcome, it felt as if he loomed over her.

"I am afraid I do not sing, My Lord." Margaret edged away until the bars of the silver cage pressed into her back—something that made her feel even more trapped. "But I play. If you would like, I will play for you now." She had some fear that her musical skills would only charm Tyrconnell, but she was absolutely desperate for an excuse to be further from him, while she still could. To be married to any man but Etienne—the thought made her physically ill, and that in turn made her feel vaguely guilty because the Earl never showed her anything but kindness.

"Delightful idea!" The Earl ran his hand fleetingly along her bare lower arm, stroking her as he had the bird. Margaret's flesh crawled, and she quite unwillingly imagined his full lips pushing aggressively against her own. When he at last took a step back to let her pass, she surged toward the nearest velvet-lined instrument, wondering how she would play at all with throat nearly closed and trembling fingers.

As she struck the first chord, the doors at the end of the gallery burst open. A knot of serious-faced gentlemen entered, buoying Samuel Pepys along as if he were a boat instead of the man who ran the Naval Office, regardless of whoever else was ostensibly charged with that.

Margaret's hands dropped to her lap. Could there be news of the fleet? Yesterday, the Royal Navy had engaged the Dutch amidst fierce gales, and the court had thus far gleaned only the most rudimentary details of the action.

Tyrconnell stepped forward. "Is it the Dutch?"

Pepys broke his stride and bowed. "At this moment, My Lord, peril comes by land, not sea. London is ablaze!" Every eye was on him now, and he clearly felt them, for he took a dramatic pause. "More than three hundred houses are gone, and with this infernal wind whipping the flames, more disappear each minute."

There was a collective gasp, and Pepys, appreciative of his audience's reaction, raised both his hands dramatically. "St. Magnus the Martyr has burned up. And from the Tower, I saw St. Laurence Pountney burst into angry flames, then, as quickly as you may snap your fingers"—he paired the phrase with an appropriate snap of his own—"collapse into a burning heap."

"Fire!" The word—spoken boldly by some, whispered by others—swelled to fill the gallery. Chairs and carefully cultivated poses were abandoned as everyone rushed to the tall windows. Margaret joined the throng, but there was no smoke to be seen. By the time she'd turned from the glass, Pepys was gone— whisked further along his route to see the King. To Margaret's relief, Lord Tyrconnell seemed to have been drawn along in his wake.

🔥

I awaken late, head pounding. *Perhaps attempting to drown my irritation with Pratt in ale was not a good idea.* There is a noticeable smell of smoke in my chamber, and the same wind that carries it brings the telltale sound of bells ringing backwards. Something is afire. But then, in massive, sprawling London there is nothing new in that.

Descending to the dining parlor, I absently ask the innkeeper, "Where is the fire?" as he sets my dinner before me.

"To the east, Doctor Wren. And it is not just a matter of some family turned out into a lane to watch their house burn. Whole neighborhoods are in flames!" He points to a boy carrying plates. "That lad's uncle, who keeps—or, rather say, *kept*—a tavern in Fish Street, was here not a quarter of an hour ago saying it is gone, all gone. Not only his establishment, but the entire street. All is madness in Thames Street and thereabouts! A great mass of people flood the lanes and alleyways, trying to shift what they own to safety." He pauses to fill my tankard, and I contemplate the question of whether small beer will make my head better or worse.

"If I had a cart, I could make a fortune hauling things." He shakes his head, and I cannot help thinking he is more dismayed by this imagined loss of revenue than by the news he has had of destruction. "If you thought to go out today, you might do well to reconsider."

"You need have no fear for me, my good fellow." I take a tentative sip of my beer. "I will give the area that burns wide berth."

Stepping into the street a short while later, I am nearly knocked off my feet by a man pushing a wheelbarrow mounded with household goods and topped with two small children. My landlord did not exaggerate; the road is crammed in both directions. Those coming west are laden with a vast variety of personal objects, while carts fighting their way east are empty, their owners clearly out for the coin my landlord covets. Glancing toward the morning sun, my eyes encounter a wide column of smoke, dark and angry against the cloudless sky. Its massive size makes me curious just how much burns, and for a moment I hesitate.

Perhaps this is a conflagration worth viewing . . . Nonsense man, do you think Roger Pratt wastes time gawking at flames this morning? And Pratt has likely been up for hours. Unless he also got well and truly drunk in the aftermath of yesterday's depressing gathering.

Somehow I doubt that—and like him all the less for it. No he is probably writing letters this very minute to the dean and the members of the Commission, commending them for ordering a structural review . . . soothing them with nonsense about how St. Paul's will be found stout and sturdy.

Resolutely, I turn my back on the promise of an exciting burning spectacle and fight my way toward the Cathedral. Crowds persist even unto the gates of the churchyard, which I have nearly reached, when, dodging to keep from being trampled by a horse, I slam into some poor fellow, sending him sprawling. Turning to offer my victim assistance, I am startled.

"Thomas Bradish, of all the hundreds in the streets, how unfortunate that I should knock over an acquaintance!"

"Better that than a stranger who might be quick to anger," the bookseller replies, brushing himself off. "I've been at the riverbank for a view of things. There's not been a fire like this in my lifetime. The waterwheels under the bridge burn. One fell off and floated away like a flaming raft as I watched! The lofty water house itself is engulfed. If the great engine inside should be stilled, London's conduits will run dry. How then shall this fire be fought?"

"I don't know," I reply honestly. "Thankfully, that is not a worry for an architect, but for your Lord Mayor and all the various men charged with administration of the city."

"It is also a worry for me and my fellow members of the Stationers' Company. We make our living in paper. If our stock burns up, we will be left ruined men."

"A grim thought, but surely premature. It must be a mile at least from the bridge to Paternoster Row."

Bradish nods. "Yes, and the winds seem content to drive the blaze north and south rather than west—God be thanked." He colors. "Though I suppose I am a poor Christian, thinking only of myself when so many have lost everything already. One fellow at the waterfront told me the flames have devoured the meat markets of Little Eastcheap, and another that the poor Fishmongers have lost their Company Hall."

"A hard thing for the Fishmongers." I wonder if their hall smelled like fish when it burned—that would certainly have been something. "I will say a prayer for the members of the Stationers' Company while I am in St. Paul's."

"Very good of you, sir."

"Also self-serving, Bradish. It would be a sad day for me if my favorite bookshop in London was destroyed."

♦

Whitehall Palace

Early hours, Monday, September 3

The voices were strange and out of place. Lying in bed, awakened from a dream of Etienne, Margaret could not determine what they said or where they came from. They reminded her drowsy ear of a holy service. Why?

They were chanting—yes, that was it.

Somewhere, someone chanted as priests did in church. Margaret shook her head to clear it, because that made no sense.

The dormer windows in the sloped ceiling of her room glowed, not with cold, blue, moonlight but with a warm, orange, unsteady light. As Margaret pulled a dressing gown over her nightdress, the door flew open to reveal Simona, disheveled and hair loose, and Margaret could at last make out the chanted words: "God and the King save us!"

"It is the end of the world," Simona said, eyes wild, "just as the almanacs predicted. Such an unlucky year, with 'six-six-six' in its tail!"

Margaret's stomach sank. Then she reminded herself that the prognostications of almanac writers, and the sorts of preachers wisely banned from London by the Bishop as heretical, were neither scientific nor godly. To give into fear inspired by them would be weakness.

"It is not the end of the world, Simona," she said firmly. "And whatever it *is*, it has nothing to do with the nonsense in that book of dire predictions I caught you fretting over. Let's go learn the truth of things."

Snatching up her friend's hand, Margaret dragged Simona to the stairway, where they joined a host of ghostlike figures. The shield gallery below was filled with courtiers and servants alike in various stages of undress. Margaret stopped amidst the throng, transfixed by the odd light dancing on the palace windows.

"We will be overrun!" The voice from behind was tinged with panic. "Thousands press against the guard, shouting for His Majesty."

Can it be an uprising? Is the Restoration to be over so soon?

She heard no gunfire. And a crowd that thought to overthrow a king would surely not call on that king to save them. So not rebellion, but the alternative was also frightening . . . could the fire that the King had assured them would be quickly extinguished still rage?

Earlier that day, Margaret had been with the Queen as word came that the royal barge had been sighted returning from the city. Catherine of Braganza, usually all moderation, had snatched up her skirts and run, eager to hear what her husband

and the Duke of York had to say of the fire, which they had sailed downriver to observe. Catherine's maids and ladies followed, pounding down the Queen's private stairs and out into the late afternoon sun. No had one bothered trying to stop Margaret from dashing along. They'd reached the landing at the Privy Stairs in time to watch the King disembark. His Majesty was furious—his instructions to London's Lord Mayor to pull down houses and create firebreaks had been ignored.

"It seems Bludworth is more afeared of liability to landlords than of disobeying his king," Charles had thundered. Then, sensitive to how they'd shrunk back, he had quickly put on a smile, telling the ashen-faced women, with soothing voice, that he had placed an able man in charge of London's fire defenses in Bludworth's place and ordered a regiment of Coldstream Guards into London. "They will see the proper things are done to make quick work of this fire," he'd reassured them, patting his wife's arm congenially.

Yet now the windows of Whitehall danced with otherworldly, flickering light, suggesting something burned fiercely. "Come." Margaret took Simona's hand again, pulling her through the mesmerized throng.

"Where are we going?" Simona asked as they raced past the door to the Queen's withdrawing room.

Margaret could not find the breath to both run and answer, so she chose the former, not stopping until they stood on the leads. A gale blew, whipping Margaret's dressing gown; pulling it half off before she clutched it back again. Below, the river was alive with a jumble of little lights on boats bobbing up and down on wind-whipped waves. And beyond, downstream, a terrifying sight.

A sob rose in her throat—the outline of London stood in dark relief against a towering wall of fire. "My God, my God," Margaret breathed.

Flames licked the sky above rooftops, and great columns of smoke carried their eerie light even higher. Despite the distance, whiffs of that same smoke—at once acrid and earthy—tickled Margaret's nose. As she watched, horrified, spits of fire, like snakes' tongues, shot out of the undulating mass, stabbing into the heavens, rising higher even than the tower of the Cathedral of St. Paul's.

Like rockets, Etienne's new rockets, only made by the devil himself.

Etienne! Margaret's heart thundered in her chest. She stared at the burning city, striving to find landmarks at the fire's edge. Slowly her fear flowed from her, for Marylebone was well east and north of the portion of the city aflame. The Bellands then were safe, but what of Thomas, Agnes, and the children? Could their bookstore already be afire? And what of the numberless souls whom such a massive fire must hold in its grip? Houses on the bridge burned—so there would be no means for those fleeing to cross the Thames on foot.

Beside her, Simona wept. "Do you believe me now? Revelations says that the beast can bring down fire, and London is all in flames. We are going to die."

"Simona, be sensible." Margaret wrapped an arm around her friend. "We've had ten months of drought and a cold, dry winter followed by scorching summer heat. It is not necessary to see the future to predict fire in such circumstances. Nor must we hear the voice of God and see the end of times in the scene before us."

Simona sniffed. "It is still terrible, though—so very terrible."

Margaret pulled her friend closer. There was no denying the horror stretched out before them. Together they stared at the burning city without speaking—the distant crackling of the monstrous flames eating away at London interrupted periodically by Simona's hiccupped sobs. Then a new sound—a door opening—disturbed them. Simona pressed a hand to her mouth, and Margaret understood the impulse. She felt a sudden desire to disappear, fueled by an irrational fear that some demon had come seeking them. But the figures that emerged were mortal: two men, fully dressed. A torchbearer followed, and Margaret gasped softly when the torch's glow illuminated the King and the Duke of York.

Doubtless they had come to the leads for the same reason Margaret had—the unparalleled view of London. And that view alone had their attention. Margaret felt the impropriety of remaining unseen and spying, but before she could draw Simona away, the wind carried the King's voice to her.

"A sight from Dante, brother. Would God it had stayed on the page rather than invading my capital." The King's tone was one of hollow despair. "The latest messenger to scramble though the crowds reported more than a thousand structures have burned."

It was a monstrous, incomprehensible number: more than three times what Pepys had pronounced to his rapt audience less than four-and-twenty hours ago. It froze Margaret where she stood.

"I have no report of the dead," His Majesty continued. "But I fear they are many, for I am told the flames move like wild horses: thundering along, dodging this way and that, sparing one house and then sweeping away all its neighbors. Rood and Fleur de Lys Alleys, with all their tightly packed houses and shanties, each burned end to end in moments. When an entire lane is gone in an instant, what time is there for escape?"

In Margaret's imagination, flaming figures ran down twisting streets, and the wind that shrieked in her ears became their cries.

"We have no great love for London, brother." Charles's voice was as dry as the sound of flints striking. "It is hard to love a place whose citizens cost your father his head." Suddenly he looked like a man, not a sovereign, eyes haunted by loss, face taut with anger. Then he drew himself up and the bitterness fell away, leaving a king in place of a damaged eighteen-year-old, grieving for his father from the refuge of a foreign court. "But we have a duty to save the capital, to save my people, even those who might wish me ill or elsewhere, and I will have no legacy but this moment if we fail."

"What would you have me do?" York put a hand on his brother's shoulder.

"Take charge of fighting this fire. Bring it to heel before the burning beast eats all—house, church, and hovel."

"It will be my honor."

"And also your burden." The King's voice fell so low that Margaret wondered whether he actually said the words or she imagined them. "You will have authority over all, even the Lord Mayor, and as many troops as we can muster."

The Duke turned from the river. His face, caught in full torchlight, was animated and eager. Margaret took comfort in his look of unshrouded resolve. Surely the flames would be turned back by such determination put into action.

"Give me noblemen as well," York said, "to place at the fire stations, that they might set an example of resolve and duty. And every man must bring a full purse, for if life has taught us anything, brother, it is that money may motivate where duty alone fails."

The messengers arrived, short of breath and smelling of smoke. They came with news for the King and the Council, but were not allowed to return into London without reporting to another solemn assembly. The women clustered in Queen Catherine's withdrawing room, keeping vigil for their menfolk, leapt from their seats to pepper each man with questions, seeking news of this duke and that earl. Confirmation that a husband, father, brother, or son stationed on the fire defenses was unharmed brought heaving sighs and sobs of relief.

There was no relief for Margaret. She could not ask whether Etienne Belland was safe. Tucked into the green damask drapes at one of the Queen's windows, she imagined the narrowed eyes and gaping mouths if she inquired about the royal fireworks maker. Fire or no fire, her interrogation would begin at once, for Lady Saunderson took her duty as shepherdess of the Maids of Honour and preserver of their virtue—which was to say their value to their families—seriously. Yet Margaret would have risked exposure, censure, and punishment had she believed any of the messengers capable of reassuring her. But it was folly to think such soldiers would know Etienne. Just as it would be foolishness to think any gentlemen laboring under York would recognize him, despite seeing him in the background at royal entertainments. He was the sort they would have overlooked quite naturally.

So Margaret stayed silent, listening carefully to details of the fire's progress. And always, beneath the voices in the room, the terrifying thundering sounds that rose from the burning city assaulted her.

By afternoon she was numb and feverish. The latter gave her all the more reason to avoid the sharp eyes of Lady Saunderson and the kind eyes of the Queen by staying in her bower of heavy silk. Worrying here with the others was a terrible thing, but lying, terrified and without hope of any news, in her bed while a surgeon bled her would be worse.

The next soldier arrived, his face and uniform soot smudged. Margaret winced as she noticed that his hands were blistered. "The Royal Exchange is afire, Your Majesty," the man declared. "The stone kings of the past lie among its burning remains. The fire at the waterfront has taken Queenhithe stairs—"

Ladies gasped, for the King and York had only yesterday disembarked at Queenhithe to take stock of the fire.

"—but His Highness the Duke of York is determined to stop the conflagration's westward spread before it reaches Bridewell."

"How many poor souls are locked away there?" the Queen asked quietly. It was in her nature to think of those others might forget, such as the prisoners in Bridewell.

"I cannot not say, Your Majesty, but scores more than were confined there yesterday. The prisons are filling with foreigners, dragged in by their neighbors."

"What are their crimes?"

"Not being English, Your Majesty." He looked distinctly uncomfortable saying it to his Portuguese-born Queen, and gave another bow. "Rumors swirl, as viciously as the firestorm, that London was set alight by the Dutch, the French, or both together. Anyone foreign is seen as an enemy at this terrible moment. Those being taken to prison are the lucky ones." He shook his head. "I was with His Grace the Duke of York when he saved a poor Dutch baker from being hanged.

The man was beaten nearly to death outside his ransacked shop. When His Grace asked what the man had done to justify such abuse, the mob claimed the fellow was part of the plot to burn London. The Duke replied there was no plot so far as anyone knew, and had me put the man on my horse before the crowd could hang him from the crude noose they'd put round his neck."

Jagged lines interrupted Margaret's vision. She clutched the soft fabric of the drape to maintain her balance and bit her tongue until she drew blood, to keep from losing consciousness.

"I and my fellows in the Guard have spent more time these last hours rescuing folk from mobs than saving people from burning. And we've cut down unfortunate souls we were not in time to save." The soldier paused and swallowed hard, and his eyes, already full of weariness, took on a haunted look. "Not just men. We found a woman . . . body desecrated, her little son weeping beside her. The poor lad told me those fleeing thought his mother had fireballs in her apron, but she had only chickens. Her protestations of innocence did her no good, doubtless because she had the same French accent as her boy."

A French accent . . . slaughtered as her child looked on, for being French. Margaret's imagination conjured Etienne dangling from a noose, his long, graceful legs twitching. Every tradesman who dealt with him and all his neighbors knew he was French. Her knees gave way, and the sound of rending drapery brought all eyes to her as she collapsed to the floor.

"Time enough"—that is what she'd told Etienne, what she'd had engraved on the back of the watch in her pocket.

What if time has run out? Margaret thought as Simona knelt beside her and began to frantically fan her. *What if I never see Etienne again? Never hear his voice.* The pain of these thoughts, sharp as a blade, was increased by the knowledge that, should something happened to him, she would not be allowed to show her grief. She had no rights to Etienne, yet in her heart he belonged to her completely, and she to him.

By afternoon there is no sun. It is blotted from the sky by thick smoke. So much of London burns.

But not the one thing I need reduced to ashes.

St. Paul's stands above the destruction, out of reach of the fire's hot fingers. And though the winds blow west, none seem to fear for it. Over my cold, hurried dinner, the innkeeper counsels me to move my valuables to the Cathedral. "Many are taking their worldly goods there, Doctor Wren. It is God's own citadel, and surely he will protect it."

The man's face beams with confidence and admiration. I nearly groan aloud—for if every man and woman in London views St. Paul's in that light, the battle I fight to persuade the Royal Commission to see it differently—to allow St. Paul's to be torn down to make way for the new—takes on the aura of a hopeless crusade.

I will leave London, I think, mounting the stairs to my chamber. It will be easier to ponder the puzzle of St. Paul's without the cries from the streets, the endless roaring of the flames, and the great, strange groaning and moaning caused by the collapse of buildings as they burn. I have a horse in the inn's stable. Did I not plan to use him, I could get a mighty price for him, or so said my friend the innkeeper. "Handcarts that were yesterday charging only shillings to take away goods are now getting five and even ten pounds! Horses—well, Doctor Wren, you could demand a king's ransom, perhaps even forty pounds."

The man has silver in his veins, not blood, I think as I bundle things for my journey. Soon all that remains are my books. Too many books—they are piled on my desk, beside my bed, everywhere. I wonder, would Thomas Bradish hold them for me against my return at his bookshop?

Bradish . . . egads! I stop tying bundles. I promised to pray for him yesterday. As I passed between St. Paul's great fluted columns and opened the Cathedral door, I fully intended to descend into the western crypt, to St. Faith's, which, being parish church for a majority of London's booksellers, seemed the perfect spot for such devotions. But I became distracted by a workman examining a wall and took him round to see some cracks I feared he might overlook.

In my defense, I think, what is a prayer for the safety of paper when balanced against the importance of a true assessment of the deficiencies of St. Paul's? And those cracks would have been easy to miss, partially obscured as they are by the newly installed choir stalls. *Another bit of slapdashery, that choir.* It was meant to look Gothic, but the new stalls are poor imitations. Each time I see them, I wonder what the originals looked like—the ones pulled out by Cromwell's men for firewood.

Firewood: that is what St. Paul's is fit for. How sad then that stone does not burn.

But it does. Or at least it collapses. Among the fire gossip bandied about by my fellow lodgers was talk of churches burned to collapse; of bones once neatly entombed revealed and smoldering ghoulishly; of stained-glass windows shattered into shards by heat greater than any oven. More than nine parishes are gone—left as shells or rubble in the wake of the advancing flames.

It is as if I have been struck by lightning. My flesh tingles all over.

I sit on the edge of the bed in a trance. When I rise at last, I take the steps on the inn's staircase two at a time and dash out the door, at a run, into streets filled with acrid smoke.

I stop to wet a handkerchief and clutch it to my nose and mouth, but it does little good. All around me people pass through the gloam, not pushing wheelbarrows or carrying pots, pans, children, and chickens as they were yesterday, but staggering, shrouded in ash like ghosts, or smudged black with soot. If the state of these sad souls was not unsettling enough, the persistent and nearly deafening sound of the conflagration is like nothing I have ever heard: it is as if some giant demon howls and thunders, his lamentations punctuated by the crashing collapse of buildings I cannot see. If I were of faint heart, I would quit my errand. But I am not. Great art requires sacrifice. So, though my pace is slowed by crowds, I push resolutely onward.

The door of Bradish's shop is bolted. I pound until my fists ache, until at last it opens.

"Doctor Wren," he says, face astounded as he lets me slide inside, "I do not open today. My wife and children are packing. We will quit the city. I would stay behind if I could arrive at any plan for saving my inventory and thereby my livelihood. But, alas, my brain fails me."

"My good man, do not despair; such an idea has come." I slap him on the shoulder. Then I lean in and whisper it—not because there is anyone about who might hear me, but because such an odd combination of the devious and the sacred feels as if it should be secret.

The wheels of his mind turn like the gears of a clock. I see them reflected in his bright eyes. Watching his drawn features relax, then harden again, this time with determination, I feel a surge of joy.

"Quick man!" I urge, wanting to have him in motion—wanting the wheels of my fate to turn as quickly as those in his mind did. "There is not a moment to be lost. The fire has reached Watling Street and Sopher Lane. The Cutlers' Hall is gone, the Dyers' too. Run to your great Hall while it is still there; rouse your brethren."

He turns this way and that, as if too agitated to know where his own door is. Then he throws his arms about me, heedless of the improper familiarity of the gesture. "Bless you, Doctor Wren. You are an angel sent to save us! I will owe you a great debt when all this is over—all the Stationers will."

"Nonsense," I reply, letting him hold the door for me and then watching him secure it, "you owe me nothing." I feel a sudden pang. *Stone is but inert, even where it has been consecrated, and paper is only paper . . . but where it is a man's living . . . or rather say the living of many men . . .* Bradish will not be in my debt; I will be in debt to him and his fellow Stationers. All London will. Will that console these men at least in part?

I push such considerations away and return to the matter at hand. "And, my friend," I say as I slap him on the back by way of parting, "as the best deeds are those that go unheralded, pray keep my role in this rescue to yourself. It will be far more pleasing to me for you to have the credit with your fellow Stationers."

He disappears at a run.

CHAPTER 5

Present-day London

Monday

As soon as she hit her desk, Nigella checked for messages. Friday's crime had been all over the papers. She'd read *The Telegraph*, *The Sunday Times*, and *The Guardian* while avoiding the tabloids, where coverage would have been more salacious and inaccurate. No use getting her blood pressure up. Even the papers she'd read used screaming headlines like "Gruesome Murder outside Mother Church of the Common Law" and "Man Burned Alive Friday Night." *A bit precipitous, that last conclusion,* she'd thought. No autopsy yet. But when had that ever stopped a reporter?

Still, reporters had their uses. Each had ended their coverage with a plea: "Police are seeking the public's assistance in identifying the victim, a male, approximately six foot, wearing a peach-colored tie featuring architectural drawings of St. Paul's Cathedral." The papers had not been told where he'd been wearing that tie. And each plea finished with a telephone number.

No useful messages on the contact line, sod it—just the usual crazies and psychics offering their help. Nigella hoped it wasn't going to be that type of a day.

Evans came out of his office. "Two things: First, Sir John's secretary sent this list of law students living in the Temple complex over yesterday." He held it out.

"Wish I had the power to get that kind of cooperation on Sundays." She took the sheets.

"And second—"

"Morning!" O'Leary got off the elevator, messenger bag over his shoulder, carrying a box."

"—and second, since we're spearheading this thing, being the jurisdiction with the fatality, the Yard has agreed to temporarily station DI O'Leary here. Loaner desk is in the corner."

So it *was* going to be that type of day. Nigella stood up. "I'll show him."

"Aw, I don't get to share your desk?" O'Leary followed her toward the far edge of the room. "You can't decide if my being here is a blessing or a curse."

"It's better to have the whole team at one location."

Nigella's phone trilled and she sprinted for her desk. "DI Parker," she gasped.

"Good, you're in." It was Chief Medical Examiner Dr. Gwen Phillips.

"So are you." Nigella wanted to add that it must be a woman thing—always first to arrive, last to leave, overkilling it to make certain you were seen as being as competent as male colleagues who did less. "You can't have autopsied already."

"No. We just put your friend on the table and discovered something while undressing him that I think you'll want to see."

"Be right there." Nigella hung up. "O'Leary, forget about unpacking. That was the medical examiner. Let's go see our victim."

The gray-tiled morgue was considerably colder than the hallway they entered from, and more brightly lit. Dr. Phillips stood at a steel table, stooped over the crown of a head she'd peeled the skin back from. Nigella couldn't see the victim's face, but she could see the subcutaneous bruising. Another body— maybe their victim—lay on a second table, shrouded in a crisp white sheet. The gentle humming from the wall of refrigerated cold lockers for preserving the dead was the only sound until the hall door clicked shut behind O'Leary.

Dr. Phillips looked up.

"Your boy is after this fellow." She draped the sheet back over the exposed head. "But what I want to show you is with his personal effects, such as they are." She moved to a small, wheeled stand beside the body on the second table. The stainless-steel tray atop it was remarkably empty—just the peach tie, lying face up with dozens of St. Paul's outlined on it.

"When I said 'undressing,' I might have exaggerated. Our victim was stripped before he was burned. We haven't found a single fragment of clothing, not even stuck in a fold or crevice. And no jewelry. Just the tie."

"It's a signifier—meant to send a message," Nigella said.

"Oh, it was meant to send a message, but not just symbolically."

Phillips held out a box of latex gloves so Nigella and O'Leary could take some, then she flipped the necktie over. The back was covered in tiny, precise, black, block lettering.

"Holy shite." O'Leary breathed.

Phillips handed over the tie, and Nigella read the message aloud:

IT IS FITTING THAT THE PHOENIX CARVED ON THE SOUTHERN TRANSEPT LOOKS LIKE A BIRD OF PREY. NOT ALL WHO RISE IN THIS WORLD DO SO ON THEIR MERITS OR DESERVE THEIR HONORS.

THIS FOOL DIED FOR ALL SINNERS WHO MISTAKE CELEBRITY FOR GENIUS.

"BIG COMMISSIONS GO TO THE BIG TALENTS"— THAT'S WHAT HE SAID.

AH WELL, TASTELESSNESS IS THE EIGHTH DEADLY SIN. YOU MIGHT SAY I REDEEMED HIM, BUT I AM NOT GOD, BUT DISCIPLE. I SEE WITH THE EYES OF THE FEW THE TRUE GOD

WHO LIVED, AND DIED, IN THE FALSE GOD'S SHADOW. THE HAWK, NOT THE PHOENIX, INSPIRES ME. AND BY FIRE RESURGAM.

"I shall rise again," O'Leary said. "That's what the Latin means. Why did our first real break have to be the rantings of a madman?"

"Better than nothing, and ten minutes ago nothing is about what we had," Nigella said. She turned to Phillips. "Thanks for not waiting to call."

"Read it again, O'Leary," Nigella said once they were buckled into the car, tie in a plastic evidence bag on O'Leary's lap.

When he'd finished, she said, "Between the references to a transept, the deadly sins, and God, it looks like your theory that there's a religious motive moves to the top of the list."

"Maybe," he said. "But much as I'd like the credit for getting it right out of the gate, I'm not so sure I deserve it. I meant religion with a capital 'R'—but the killer isn't talking the language of traditional Christianity, either mine or yours. He uses 'gods' plural, and bad taste is most certainly not a sin in any Christian doctrine I'm aware of. Good thing too, or poor sods like me who've never owned a tie as nice as this would be going to hell for sure." He paused for a moment, staring at the writing through the plastic. "Damn! I wish he hadn't used block letters, because whether he meant any of his 'god' references to be capitalized might help us decode this."

"Back to basics," Nigella said. "Who, what, when, where?"

"Plenty of 'who,'" O'Leary replied. "Those who rise in this world." He held up a finger. "The victim who the suspect has decided can't discern between ability and celebrity." Up popped a second finger. "Then we have several self-references to the nutter-in-chief. Finally we have a pair of gods, one true and one false." All five of his fingers were now raised, and O'Leary looked at his hand as if expecting it to clarify something. Then he shrugged and dropped it into his lap.

"In terms of 'what,'" he continued, "we've got nothing much—just some 'big commissions,' a hawk, and a phoenix. We know feck all about the commissions or the inspirational hawk, but we know the phoenix is carved on a transept, presumably at a church—"

"The only place referenced in the note," Nigella interjected. "That's our starting point, because that place is somewhere solid. Maybe the site of his next crime."

"And if not," O'Leary said, "standing there might help us to understand the bastard's motivation. We have three crime scenes now. So besides figuring out where this south transept is, we need to grab a whiteboard somewhere and see how the Monument, St. James's Piccadilly, and Temple Church intersect."

"Hey, we're the most exciting thing that happened this weekend—we warrant an incident room and our own white-board," Nigella replied.

"I guess we get to share a desk after all." O'Leary offered her raised eyebrows and a slanted smile.

"It's a table, but whatever floats your boat."

He was arranging the things that had never made it out of his box at one end of a conference table in the brightly lit space with three glass walls, while Nigella stood at the large wall-mounted whiteboard she'd subdivided into squares. The "who, what, and where" they'd identified were already neatly noted inside a box labeled "Tie," and a bullet-pointed list of leads occupied a second square. Consulting her open laptop, Nigella prepared to tackle her "Connections" block.

O'Leary stuffed his empty box under the table, stared at the board, then leaned back—so far back Nigella thought any second he'd end up lying on the floor. Instead, he popped bolt upright. "We've missed a 'where.' The transept isn't the only one on the tie."

"It is. We've reread the killer's note half a dozen times."

"I didn't say the note." He clicked something open on his own laptop. "I said the tie. The whole thing is slathered edge to edge with a place. You recognized it at first glance—St. Paul's. Wren's greatest work, Wren's Monument, Wren's church in

Piccadilly. That's not a coincidence, Ni—it can't be—that's a pattern."

"Brilliant!" Nigella wrote "Sir Christopher Wren" in the connections box and starred it.

"I love it when you call me brilliant. Let's see if the pattern holds?" O'Leary typed, clicked, and scrolled. Nigella held her breath. "And boom, the Temple Church website has our answer: 'After the Great Fire of London in 1666, the church, though undamaged while eighty percent of the city's churches were destroyed, was refurbished by Sir Christopher Wren.' Don't you love the internet?"

Yes, she did. But . . . Nigella laid down her marker. There was something nibbling at the edge of her consciousness. Sitting down, she pulled out the red accordion folder containing the notes on the Temple Church murder. It was slender, but they had the initial incident report and pictures. Fanning the photos out, she plucked out one taken from a distance. And she knew what was bothering her.

"Our killer didn't leave his burnt offering at the Temple Church."

"What are you talking about? It was *in* the church court-yard." O'Leary stared at her as if she was daft.

"Hear me out. At the first incident, our wooden man burned directly against the base of Wren's Monument. In our second, he stood just beside Wren's church, giving it the finger in case we needed help seeing the relationship—"

"This bloke really hates Wren," O'Leary interjected.

"Maybe, but maybe not, because what I was about to say was that in this latest incident, our suspect—who we know places everything deliberately—put the dead man at the foot of a column, not beside a church."

"Maybe Wren did the column."

A ping emanated from Nigella's laptop. "Yes! We've got digital footage from the Tudor Gate cameras."

O'Leary raced round the table, column forgotten, as Nigella opened the file from the guard station and began fast-forwarding. She watched images of cars rolling out while monitoring the progressing time stamp out of the corner of her eye. The Chinese tourists came and went. Once they were gone, a mid-sized SUV rolled up, and soon its driver was leaning out, gesturing angrily.

"Must be the caterer," O'Leary said, leaning in from the chair he'd grabbed beside her. "Though notice it's a personal vehicle."

"Yeah," Nigella froze the footage and took a screenshot.

They rolled through a lot of nothing.

"Christ, that guard's job is boring. Is that him picking his nose? Can't say that I blame him," O'Leary remarked as the time stamp moved past eleven PM.

Minutes later a white van pulled up. The window rolled down, but the driver remained out of sight. He didn't lean out, even when the guard began talking to him. The only part of him that could be seen was a forearm and a hand.

"He knows about the camera," O'Leary said.

"He sure as hell does."

The gate lifted and the van rolled out of view. Nigella stopped the playback. "Since the driver is hiding, let's get a better look at that vehicle." She clicked open the file from the second camera—the one that pointed down Tudor Street.

"It was 11:17 PM," O'Leary said, sliding to the edge of his chair.

Nigella fast forwarded to eleven fifteen PM and then let it roll. A white van came into view. No visible markings, just as the guard had said.

But as it got closer . . .

"Stop." O'Leary was so eager he reached for her trackpad. "Look." His finger hovered in front of the screen. "There's a line there. It's an edge, by Christ. I think the bastard has put something over markings on the vehicle."

Nigella moved the van closer, frame by frame.

"You're right. He's covered something. This is our boy—it has to be." She rewound. "Oh, it's him alright. He's masked the front plate."

"Back one, too, I shouldn't wonder—thorough bastard."

"We need a rear view." She switched files, reversed the van back to the booth and let it roll away in super slow motion. She froze a frame showing the back of the van.

"Camera's set at driver level," O'Leary said. "We can't check the rear plate."

"That's not what we're doing." Nigella used her mouse to zoom in and then slid to the outer edge of the van's right-hand rear door. She squinted hard at the grainy image, then gently zoomed out. Three blurry spots became clearer—one letter, two numbers, S11. She let out her breath audibly. "O'Leary, it's Christmas: that's the Spiffy van!"

He had the phone in his hand before she could even reach for it.

They rolled up quietly. Their target, a terraced house in Basildon, looked completely unremarkable. There was a noticeable absence of flowers along the walk, so while their suspect had a thing for fire, he apparently didn't have one for gardening. They parked three houses away, and the police van stopped even further off. They'd dropped a couple of officers at the corner, and Nigella wanted to give them time to get round back, assess escape routes, and block them.

Nelson Taylor, thirty-seven years old, with Spiffy for twenty of those years and never a complaint from a client, currently crew head of team S11: could this guy really be their suspect?

"Vans are garaged centrally," Spiffy's VP had told O'Leary, "but they're individually assigned to crew heads." A secondary set of keys was kept in the office in case the crew head called in sick or someone needed to service the vehicle.

At first, she and O'Leary had fixated on the key in the box because, as he'd said, "Given how careful the suspect is, why would he use his own damn van?"

But then they'd remembered Occam's razor—the simplest theory is the one you test first.

So now they were going to pay Mr. Nelson a visit and run him in for questioning.

The radio crackled, "In position, and guv'nor, there's a garage back here."

"It is Christmas and Easter," O'Leary said.

"Team two, did you copy that?" Nigella asked. "Unload half your officers, then move round to the rear, open that garage, and let me know what you find. We go in sixty."

She set the timer on her phone.

"Why is it that a minute feels like an hour when you're waiting to collar a murderer? O'Leary unbuckled his seat belt.

"Here's hoping you're right, because if this is our killer, nobody else dies." The phone buzzed and they swung open their doors and made for the house.

Nigella pressed the buzzer and knocked. Nothing.

"Shite!" O'Leary said, his body tense as a tripwire.

"Don't get impatient. Taylor works nights." She said it as much for herself as for him, because her heart sank with every passing second. She pounded again. *Is that a noise?* Nigella listened intently. *Yes, footsteps!* The door swung open, revealing a groggy, red-faced, slightly overweight man.

"Nelson Taylor?" She kept her tone pleasant and nonthreatening.

"Yeah, what's all the pounding about? I'm trying to sleep?"

"I am Detective Inspector Parker, and this is Detective Inspector O'Leary. We have a warrant to search these premises." She flashed the nick, but Taylor didn't look at it; he just stared directly at her, mouth agape. Didn't turn, didn't run, didn't argue—just stared, utterly dumbfounded. And that threw her. Unless he thought he was utterly brilliant, and unless the house was absolutely clean, there should have been a more dramatic reaction. Nigella's instinct said they'd got it wrong.

The radio clipped to her waist crackled to life: "Team one, we have a van in the garage. Do you copy? I-D, 'S' as in Sierra, eleven." Nigella's doubts were wiped away, replaced by pure adrenaline.

O'Leary pulled out his cuffs. Nigella put a foot in the door, to keep it from closing. Still Taylor didn't move.

"Nelson Taylor, I am arresting you on suspicion of murder. You do not have to say anything. But it may harm your defense if you do not mention, when questioned, something which you later rely on in court. Anything you do say may be given in evidence."

"What the bloody—are you people insane!?" The voice wasn't so much angry as confused, but finally, as Nigella reached for him, Taylor twisted and tried to run. O'Leary had him in less than three steps. Pinned him to the ground and cuffed him.

Taylor struggled between them on the way to the car. "You're making a terrible mistake," he shouted, "I'm not a killer—I'm an office cleaner." By the time they had him in the back of the vehicle, he was crying. Nigella felt not one modicum of pity.

They didn't take him right to the interview room. They were waiting for initial forensics on the van. "One trace—there has to be something," O'Leary said, pacing. "I don't care how careful he was—there is always something."

Nigella didn't respond. She knew what he was doing; she'd done it herself often enough. There was some part of every police person's mind that felt certain that saying something over and over again would make it so. One of the phones on the conference table rang, and they both jumped.

"DI Parker, this is central messaging. We've had a call on the Temple Church victim identification. A Ms. Juliet Lindstrom, who works at the law firm of Griffard, Gibbons and Smith, believes she may have pertinent information. Human Resources phoned it in. They'd like someone to come round."

They are going to get their wish. "Address?"

"Twenty-four Monument Street."

Nigella put down the phone. "O'Leary this isn't just Christmas and Easter; it's also our birthdays. Either that or we are both going to be pushed onto the tube tracks and die, because we've got someone who wants to talk to us about a possible ID on the victim. So what say we let Mr. Taylor contemplate his sins and go and see her? You are not going to believe where she is."

🔥

"You're right, I don't believe it," O'Leary said as they rode a sleek escalator up from the main reception at GG&S to a floor full of meeting rooms. "If the Monument was any closer, it would be in the lobby."

Ms. Lindstrom arrived in conference room 1A red-eyed, accompanied by a woman of a certain age, who, despite a severe hairstyle and no-nonsense suit, kept patting the younger woman on the back. The two DIs rose and introduced themselves.

"I am Mrs. Kay from HR," the older woman said, pulling out a chair for her companion and watching her perch on the edge of it. "Would it be alright if I stayed?"

"Absolutely." A comfortable witness was a better witness. Nigella seated herself across from the pair with O'Leary beside her. "Ms. Lindstrom, we'd like to thank you for coming forward. Any potential information you may have on the identity of the gentleman killed Friday is of the utmost importance, both to finding his killer and to contacting his loved ones."

Ms. Lindstrom's eyes began to fill. "I didn't read about the murder in the papers. I don't like violence." She let out a little sob. "But today at lunch, Margaret said, 'Can you believe the guy they found dead Friday was wearing that tie—the same one that Andrew Smyth was showing off last week when he was chatting you up?' She read me the description of the tie and—" The witness put her hands over her face.

Mrs. Kay spoke up. "Mr. Smyth is one of our solicitors. Ms. Lindstrom is a part-time receptionist."

"I see. And"—Nigella hesitated, but it had to be asked—"is Mr. Smyth in today?"

"No," Mrs. Kay replied, "as soon as Juliet came to my office, I checked. No answer on his mobile either."

"Ms. Lindstrom, can you tell me when you last saw Mr. Smyth?"

The girl took her hands from her face. "I didn't work Friday, so it had to be last Thursday. Mr. Smyth stopped by reception at lunch." She paused to wipe her eyes. "He was always coming round, trying to get me to go for a drink. And on Thursday he was showing off his tie."

"His tie?" O'Leary interjected. "Seems an odd way to recommend himself to the ladies."

"I study architecture at UCL, so he thought I'd like it. He went on a bit about Christopher Wren . . . how important he was. Then he asked me if I'd go with him to St. Paul's sometime and give him my impression of Wren's masterpiece."

"What color was the tie?" Nigella asked.

"Light peach, just like they said in the paper, and the line drawings were sort of rust-colored, so they looked vintage."

"Did you accept Mr. Smyth's invitation?"

"I sidestepped it," Ms. Lindstrom replied. "Instead of answering, I asked him where he got the tie and he said from an online museum gift shop. He went on a bit about how talented Wren was and how the size of his commissions clearly proved it, and then he was called away." She took a gulp of air.

Nigella, on the other hand, exhaled deeply. The witness's remark parroted almost exactly the quote from the killer's note: *"Big commissions go to the big talents"*—that's what he said." Apparently Smyth had a thing for that phrase. Nigella's mind stumbled for a moment: *How could Nelson the office cleaner know Smyth well enough to talk to him about art?* But she was getting ahead of herself, tripping over her own feet. *Focus. Finish the interview.*

"If he got it at a museum gift shop, there have to be thousands of ties like it, don't there?" The young receptionist's voice was pleading. "It doesn't have to be Mr. Smyth you found. It could be anybody who owned the tie."

"Absolutely." Nigella didn't believe that, not given the eerie parallelism between Smyth's remark and the note on the body; the fact he wasn't at work; and that his work was mere steps from the scene of the first crime. "Thank you again for contacting us, Ms. Lindstrom. I don't think we have any other questions.

"Mrs. Kay, if you wouldn't mind staying for a moment."

The older woman nodded. "Juliet why don't you take the rest of the afternoon off. You need a cup of tea, a hot bath, and some quiet." Ms. Lindstrom nodded gratefully. "Nice girl," Mrs. Kay said as the door swung shut behind Juliet. "Bright, good worker. We won't have her for long once she attains that degree."

"And how about Mr. Smyth? Nice man?"

"Truth be told he was a bit of a lad. Constantly hitting on my girls—not just Ms. Lindstrom either. We had to replace his secretary more than once. Not easy to work for." Mrs. Kay shook her head censoriously.

"High opinion of himself?"

"The solicitors of Griffard, Gibbons and Smith are hired because they are some of the best and brightest." Mrs. Kay paused. "In your experience, Detective Inspector Parker, what sort of egos do such men have?"

Got it.

"Can we find out if Mr. Smyth was in on Friday? And is there any sort of system that might help us determine when he last left the building?" Nigella asked.

"I'll check with security. And I suspect you'll want emergency contact information. That I can get you immediately, if you'd like to come upstairs."

"Thank you. And a home address too, please." It would be easy enough to send someone round to make sure Mr. Smyth wasn't there, sleeping one off, Nigella thought. "One final thing: where would we get a picture of Andrew Smyth?"

"Our directory on the firm website includes photos." Mrs. Kay spelled out the address, then stood.

They took Smyth's contact information back to the nick. Preliminary report on the first sweep and swab of the van was in. There were obviously fingerprints and some hair and skin cells because it was used daily by humans. It would take a while to cross-check them against Nelson Taylor and the rest of his team. Hopefully there would be something left belonging to someone else. But no smoking gun, or as O'Leary rather indelicately put it, "No smoking body pieces."

"God, what I would have given for them to have popped it open and found a furniture dolly and straps." Nigella sighed.

The report on the garage and a garden shed wasn't encouraging either: no tools for woodworking, no wood shavings, no evidence of linseed oil.

Nigella slapped her hand down on the table.

"Come on, Ni, you didn't honestly expect the suspect who managed to pull off these three incidents to whip up the wooden men in his own backyard. And if he'd burned Smyth there, the local fire brigade would have been called in by at least half the neighborhood. I mean the smoke, the smell . . ."

"Yeah, I know. It's never that easy. Only just once, wouldn't you like it to be?"

"I've got a fairly long list of things I'd like in an ideal world, Ni. So if you find one, let me know. For now, time to go see Mr. Taylor. Let's walk in there like we know more than we do and see where that gets us." O'Leary slipped his jacket on and straightened his tie. Glancing over at Nigella as she buttoned the center button on her black and white houndstooth blazer, he said, "How is it that your suits always look like they're just back from the cleaner, and mine look like this?" He gestured to a bit of lining hanging down below the bottom edge of his jacket.

"Because I don't sleep in my clothing? Speaking of suits, let's take Smyth's photo with us and get a reaction." Nigella opened the GG&S website and clicked the "Our Solicitors" tab. There was Andrew Smyth: white shirt, blue jacket, striped tie, dark hair combed aggressively back, smiling like he owned the world.

She hit "Print," and O'Leary picked the image out of the tray as they went past. "Not your typical solicitor."

"What do you mean?"

"Look at the size of that neck and that tan." O'Leary held it out. "The solicitors I've met are generally mealy white like me, and more on the bookworm end of builds."

Nigella took the picture from him. The thought flashed through her head that the physique on their possible victim reminded her of James. "You don't hang around the financial district much, do you?"

"No call to—can't be a serious investor on a Met salary."

"Smyth's built like a banker, broker type. A lot of hypermasculinity among the high-flying finance and business boys. Fair share of vanity too. If I had to guess, the tan is spray and the hair has been touched up."

"Well, one thing's for certain," O'Leary said. "I look at that smile and I understand why Mrs. Kay didn't like him. Not that likeability is a requirement for living your life without being brutally murdered and partially incinerated."

"Maybe Nelson Taylor thinks it is."

As soon as their suspect arrived in the interview room, Nigella switched on the recorder. Stating the time and date was habit, as was repeating the official caution. Then the meat of things began.

"Mr. Taylor, do you recognize this man?" She slid the picture across the table.

Taylor leaned forward, looked at the photo, then sat back, pushing it away. "I mean he looks like a bloke who would work in an office, and I clean a lot of offices. But no, sorry."

He maintained eye contact. He didn't mumble. Seemed very much like a man giving an honest answer and genuinely trying to cooperate. *Shit.* Over-cooperation could be as much a cover as avoidance behaviors . . . but there hadn't been as much as a single twitch when he'd seen Smyth's face. *Stick with the facts. Right now they are stacked against Taylor.*

"Listen," Taylor said, plunging onward, "I don't understand why I'm being held. Nobody'll answer my questions."

"You are here on suspicion of murdering this man." She slid the picture back toward him. Willing him to give her a tell.

"I'm not a killer, and how could I kill someone I don't know? Ask anyone: I'm a stand-up fellow. I was employee of the year last year at Spiffy. I call my mum every Sunday. I don't play the pools. I don't owe anyone money—"

"Mr. Taylor, would you like a solicitor?" Nigella felt the need to repeat the offer because Taylor was starting to babble.

"What for? I haven't *done* anything! I don't want a solicitor; I want to get out of here before I'm late to work. They wouldn't let me call in. I don't want to be absent without calling in."

"We'll make certain that Spiffy knows you aren't coming."

"I don't want *you* to let them know! What'll they think, me being arrested?"

"Mr. Taylor, does your work for Spiffy involve lifting things?"

"You mean like *stealing*? Now you think I'm a thief too!"

"No, Mr. Taylor, I mean lifting heavy objects."

This brought him up short. He took a deep, gulping breath and seemed to calm down. "Not really. I mean, when we bring in the floor polishers, they have to be got off the truck, but we have a ramp. And all the buildings have elevators. Supplies come in industrial sizes, but they're broken down at headquarters because nobody needs a fifty-five gallon drum of cleaner."

"And you're assigned a van?"

"Yeah, I'm a crew head, which means I drive and I'm the one who has keys to the van."

"The van we found in your garage?"

"That's mine, number eleven."

"Was the van at your home all weekend?"

"We're allowed to take them home—"

"Was the van at your home all weekend?"

"No. I picked it up this morning so I'd be ready for tonight."

This is going to be his story? He's stone-faced enough to unflinchingly look at Smyth's picture, but now his whole plan is to make it look like the box keys are the ones at issue? Nigella glanced at O'Leary. He looked as incredulous as she felt.

"I am curious, Mr. Taylor, why would you do that? Why not just take it home with you after work Friday?"

"Because I didn't work Friday. I've been on vacation. Not one of those caravan holidays either—Mallorca."

"You were in Spain." Nigella kept her voice even.

"Got home Saturday. Bryan Air. I know folks complain about 'em, but I paid bugger all for the seats and I thought they were fine."

"When did you leave the UK?"

"The Saturday before. Had near a full week on the beach."

Damn, Nigella thought. That would explain the complexion. Why the hell had she just assumed ruddy? Looking more closely now, he did look sunburned.

"Anyone vacationing with you?"

"Yeah, my missus. She's with Spiffy too, in payroll. That's how we met."

"Where was van S11 during your holiday."

"Garaged with the fleet. I'd have been in some trouble if I'd left it out in Basildon and someone'd had to run out to get it, wouldn't I?"

Nigella looked at her mobile as if it had vibrated. Oldest trick in the book for having a word with a colleague without tipping Chummy off and letting him relax. "Mr. Taylor, if you'll excuse us for a minute." She rose and O'Leary followed.

"It's not Christmas anymore," he said as soon as the door shut. "Spain, sod it all. I'm in the wrong business. I should've been an office cleaner, and then I could've spent last week on a beach with my missus rather than running round after an evil bugger who lights people on fire to get attention."

"You love chasing evil buggers, which is why you never take the vacation you have coming and go to Spain. Not to mention, you'd sunburn worse than Chummy." She sighed. "I suspect it'll be easy to verify the trip, what with hotel and airline reservations. It'll take some time to check, but unless you've got an argument against it, I say we release him."

"Let him go. And let's focus on who could have used that van in his absence, 'cause it may not be Christmas anymore but I'm hoping we can hang on to Easter."

Watching Taylor walk away was hard. Not because Nigella believed he was guilty, but because she sensed he wasn't—wasn't someone likely to converse about architecture, wasn't acquainted with Andrew Smyth, wasn't in the damn country at the time of the murder—and that left the investigation miles behind where she and O'Leary had thought they were when the van was found in Basildon.

Nigella looked at the whiteboard from where she and O'Leary sat dejectedly at the conference table. *Don't dwell—move forward. Make order out of chaos, and you'll feel better.*

"Let's call Smyth's next of kin." They had brought two numbers away from GG&S—the first for a brother who also worked in the City, in finance, and the second for the family home in West Sussex.

"Let's not," O'Leary replied. "This day's gone pear-shaped enough without having to call some poor unsuspecting mum and dad and tell them their son is a pile of char. Besides, Smyth's family—assuming it's Smyth—is going to want to know how he died. We should have the autopsy by tomorrow. Both of us believe he was killed, then burned. Well, let's have that all neat and official, so at least we can tell his family that he didn't suffer."

"Yeah," she said. "Want to order takeout and start on Sir John's list? Or we could research the Temple column or mysterious phoenix transept—"

"Ni, I'm done. There is nothing on that list you just rambled off that has to be done tonight. Let's go home. Or let's have dinner, only not here in the shadow of that damn overwhelming whiteboard."

"You go ahead." She was hoping to get in touch with James, both figuratively and literally. She hadn't seen him since the night of the fire. All weekend, nothing. Not even in reply to her text on Saturday afternoon. Nigella had a rule: she didn't text again if a first text remained unanswered. She never wanted any man to feel she was attached enough to badger. But after a day like this, when she needed something to take her mind off work, maybe she'd break her rule.

O'Leary grabbed his messenger bag, then hesitated at the door. "You sure?"

"Under the circumstances, I wouldn't be a particularly amiable dinner companion." When he gave her a wry look, she added, "Even less so than usual."

Out he went. As Nigella watched him waiting for the elevator, she almost relented. But if she started relying on O'Leary for companionship outside of work, that might give him the wrong idea.

At that moment her laptop pinged: a message from Gwen Phillips. She sprinted to catch O'Leary as he stepped into the elevator. The look of unabashed pleasure on his face as she put her hand on the door to keep it from closing made it clear she'd been wise to skip dinner. "Autopsy results are in," she said. "I'll see you tomorrow, eight AM, at the morgue." Then she removed her hand and let him go.

CHAPTER 6

Whitehall Palace

Tuesday, September 4, 1666

The fire drew closer. The air at Whitehall was dry and hot, as if fanned from an oven. Beads of sweat gathered on the back of Margaret's neck and glistened on the faces of the ladies surrounding her. It was not only the heat that turned them pale and clammy: through the walls of the palace the conflagration sounded like a thousand shrieking souls, shaking the chains that bound them in hell.

There had been no darkness the night before. Margaret knew this for certain, for she had lain awake, watching the hands on Etienne's watch, rubbing the inscription on the back as if the gift were a talisman and holding it could keep Etienne safe. No darkness, but now neither was there proper light, for the smoke blotted out the rays of the sun. It felt to Margaret as if it could be any time or no time at all—a nightmarish state of purgatory perfect for those sitting without occupation in the Queen's apartment, waiting for whatever would come next and at the same time dreading it. They hoped for word from York or from the King, who had left for the city at five in the morning—an hour previously unknown to Charles II save as the end point for all-night revels.

"The Queen Mother departs for Hampton Court!" Frances Stuart entered at a run, her cheeks and eyes bright. "She declares she will not wait for the fire to lick the doorstep of Somerset House."

Near the door, Katherine Boynton staggered dramatically and, when that did not bring anyone running, let herself fall to the ground. She was largely ignored because, unlike poor Margaret, everyone knew Katherine fainted for attention.

"Shall we begin packing, Your Majesty?" Frances asked.

All held their breaths—they could not flee Whitehall while the Queen remained, but most were eager to go, a fact they'd discussed in lowered voices while the Queen was at her Mass.

"I will not stir until the King decides that is to be our course," Catherine replied with a serenity that did little to foster the same in Margaret's breast. Looking entirely deflated, Frances sank down between Margaret and Simona. As Margaret reached out to squeeze her hand, the door flew open again, coming to a stop against Mistress Boynton's prone body, causing her to sit up with a grunt.

A sweaty, soot-smeared Earl of Tyrconnell entered, coughing as he came. And even as he turned to the Queen to bow, his eyes strayed to Margaret. "Your Majesty, word from the Duke of York. Although we intended to stop the fire before it crossed the Fleet, and made a line at the bottom of Ludgate Hill for that purpose, we have been confounded. Flakes of fire as large as hawks, and as good at flying, over-soared us, reaching Salisbury Court and establishing a new fire there."

"Heaven preserve the Duke." The Duchess of York clutched her sister-in-law's hand. On the opposite side of the room, York's mistress began to weep.

"And us too," someone murmured.

"Your Grace, take heart," the Earl said to the Duchess. "Your good husband is not afeared. Though any lesser man would be, for the flames behave as if they are not of this world." Tyrconnell straightened like an actor on stage, voice—rough from hours of inhaling smoke—rising, hands flying.

Some part of him enjoys the drama of it all, Margaret thought. *Relishes the idea of bringing us to our knees in awe at his words.*

"Great cones of fire spin like whirlpools. Patches of flame jump from the main body, twisting and turning to follow fleeing men like sensate demons. Horses run, manes blazing, screaming as if they bear devils on their backs." He finished with his gaze on Margaret, seeking admiration for his eloquence in the face of danger, but Margaret looked away, shuddering. She wondered how many men suffered as the horses did.

Burning is a terrible way to die, worse even than hanging.

"Despite such sights, the Duke does not falter. We do not falter," Tyrconnell continued. "We double our efforts, fighting the fire both in front and behind. And His Grace sends Your Majesty a request."

"Whatever aid is mine to give, York will have it," the Queen replied unhesitatingly.

"His Grace has ordered all foreign persons seized by the populace handed over to the Guard so that they may be protected from slaughter. Many persons have been surrendered and must be made safe. His Grace asks if those of the better sort—ambassadors and their households, persons known to members of the court—might take shelter at Whitehall?"

"Of course!" The Queen rose, sliding off her signet ring and holding it out to the Earl. "Send them under my seal. Or only let them ask for a member of my household, and they shall be seen to."

"Gracious Majesty"—the Earl bowed again—"the Duke will be grateful, and those who are in peril even more so. Now I must return to the lines, but before I go, I would solicit prayers for all who labor there." His eyes fixed on Margaret. "And I am bold enough to hope there may be some here who will say a few words to the Almighty on my behalf, look pale, and wonder where I am once I am gone."

Margaret knew she *ought* to feel moved. Tyrconnell was a brave man returning to do his duty in the face of grave danger. But she merely wanted him gone, and doubted she would have another thought for him once he was. All she could think about was Etienne and his family—of whether they were and would remain safe. Guilt warmed her cheeks, but the Earl clearly thought her blush had another cause, for he smiled. As the door closed behind him, Winifred Wells tittered and Lady Saunderson beamed. Under other circumstances, the latter would surely have rushed to pen a letter full of breathless matchmaking anticipation to Margaret's mother.

At least the fire will delay that. But not even London burning may prevent an offer from the Earl, and if he offers, you will have to accept.

She did not have long to dwell on such thoughts. Everyone began talking at once, making plans to receive those that the Duke would send. Having selected ladies to alert the guards, and others to canvas the court to discover who could offer space in their lodgings, the Queen paused. "His Grace needs to think of the fire, not of finding victims of violence. Let us lighten his burden by getting such as we can out of harm's way before they are taken up by the mobs. Mistress Stuart, bring me my little desk. I will write to the various ambassadors offering refuge." Her glance swept the room. "The rest of you must write offering protection to those of foreign birth with whom you are acquainted."

It was as close to a command as the Queen had ever come, and hope leapt in Margaret's breast. She rose. "Your Majesty, shall I collect the letters and coordinate their dispatch?" Simona gave Margaret a look—guessing why she volunteered—but Margaret pressed onward, shamelessly. "If the missives are organized by city ward, each messenger will be best used."

"How very clever you are, Mistress Dove! Ladies, let it be understood throughout the palace that all those wishing to send for someone should seek out Mistress Dove."

Less than an hour later, Margaret watched a mounted messenger depart at full speed, carrying a note to Etienne. *Soon,* she thought as she bundled missives for other couriers, *soon I will know if he and his are safe. And if they are, I will make certain they remain so.*

It was a victory, yet Margaret's heart ached, because she recognized its cost—inside the walls of Whitehall there could be no hiding who she was from the Bellands.

◊

"Why did you not come at once?" Margaret pounded closed fists against Etienne's chest. They were in one of the palace larders, surrounded by hanging meat and barrels of provisions but otherwise blessedly alone. Many hours had passed since Margaret dispatched her message. Droves of people had arrived to take refuge, but not the Bellands, so that when they finally came—five of them wide-eyed and asking for her at the gate—Margaret's relief unleashed a great and irrational anger.

"I was not at home." He placed one of his hands over hers stilling them. "So your letter lay unopened."

"I ought to have addressed it to the family." She had considered doing so—but it felt like an acknowledgment that Etienne himself might already be lost. The odor of smoke from his clothing nearly overwhelmed Margaret, and the edge of her anger flared again. "Where were you? Wandering London watching it burn? Your obsession with fire will kill you one day!"

"I went into the city to see if I could be of any use." She felt a tremor move through his body, and the heart beneath her hands raced. "I saw terrible things. I joined York's men near Bridewell Gaol. Hundreds upon hundreds fled the surrounding warren of haphazard houses in panic. The Duke and the King did all that they could. I saw His Majesty knee deep in water, directing the pulling down of buildings as York manned a pump. But the heat was too great, and it drove us back. Then the fire swept forward, and we ran for our lives. Heaven help those who could not run."

Again the shudder, and this time so fierce that Margaret forgot her vexation. Unclenching her hands, she reached up and took his face in them tenderly. "Tell me."

"Bridewell burned." His smoke-hoarse voice caught, and he turned his head so that she could not see his eyes. "If I live five score years, I will not forget the sound of those calling for help and then screaming in agony."

The soldier who first reported attacks on foreigners reported many had been taken to Bridewell. Had Etienne been snatched from the streets for his accent, he might have been inside dying instead of outside fighting the flames. The back of Margaret's anger broke. She pulled his head down and kissed him fiercely. "You are here now. And here you must stay."

"While other men risk themselves to save London and its citizens?"

"They have that luxury—you do not. They are hanging Frenchmen in the streets. You can help no one if you are strung up.—And only think of the loss to your parents . . . and to me." Reaching into her pocket Margaret drew out the watch that had been with her for days while Etienne was not.

"I got this for you so that you can carry me with you always. Do you see what it says?" Margaret flipped it over, pushing it toward him. "'Time enough.' I know that you do not believe that, that you count our days and the hours as if they would end tomorrow. Well, if you go back into London, they may well end tonight. Why would you do that? What do you think you can do that others cannot?"

He closed his hand around her gift, giving her another kiss before tucking it into his waistcoat. "I am good with black powder, my love. You know I am. Such skill is needed. Sailors bring barrels of powder ashore to blow up the houses lining the banks of Tower Ditch."

Margaret gasped. "That is madness! Surely as many may be killed creating a firebreak in such a manner as that break may save!"

"More than half a million pounds of gunpowder are stored in the Tower," Etienne's voice dropped to a whisper.

Margaret drew her breath with a shudder.

A year ago such a figure would have meant little to her, but she had a better knowledge of, and a truer respect for, black powder thanks to what Etienne had taught her about firework manufacturing. A single rocket wrongly fired could kill or maim the men standing round it. The amount of powder at the Belland workshop when a large display was being prepared could, if accidentally ignited, flatten not only that establishment but the dozen houses nearest it. Not that they told the neighbors that, Etienne had joked.

"If the Tower explodes, what remains of London will be gone," Etienne said grimly. "Thousands fleeing the city will perish in a single instant. Those on the river will die as the boats there—including the naval vessels—are obliterated."

Cataclysmic illustrations from Simona's doom-saying books sprang to life in Margaret's imagination. She saw the bridge fall into the Thames and be swept away; the beasts of the royal menagerie housed at the Tower in flames, shrieking in pain as they ran among the rubble of what were once prosperous streets; the walls of Whitehall on fire. Why had she been so quick to laugh at her friend's claims of Armageddon?

"The exploding of things is an unpredictable science, but I know how to calculate the time it will take a line of powder to burn and reach a rocket, or in this case a barrel. No one in the city is better with a fuse than I," he said softly.

Margaret buried her face in Etienne's doublet, smelling his familiar smell through the noisome fire odors that clung to it; struggling, as his arms closed around her, with what she might say to keep him at Whitehall that would not sound as selfish as she felt at the moment. She did not want to make him less than he was, but the alternative—letting him race back into the peril of the flames and mobs—was a thought too terrifying to entertain.

In the silence that stretched between them, Margaret became aware of noises in the kitchens beyond. It was far too late for meal preparation, yet she distinctly heard voices and hurried steps.

Etienne must have heard them too, for he kissed the top of her head, saying, "Let us discover what goes on before we are discovered ourselves and become the subject of gossip."

Gossip. Would there never be a time, never be events extraordinary enough, to wipe away that worry?

"Promise me you will not return to London tonight. I could not bear that. If they still have need of you tomorrow, I will stand on the leads and watch you go. But give me this one night of blessed certitude that you are safe."

He nodded, then took a step toward the door.

"Wait!" Margaret snatched up a platter of cured meats, then swung the larder door open. "You there," she barked at a kitchen maid running past, "I need wine. We cannot let those taking shelter as their Majesty's guests go hungry and thirsty."

The girl stopped in her tracks, staring at Margaret as if she were daft. "Mistress, have you not heard? All the court will shortly be seeking shelter, not offering it! His Majesty has arrived back, and York with him. He orders all to make ready to leave for Hampton Court at dawn."

Above stairs, all was chaos. Courtiers ran this way and that, shouting at servants. Many Margaret and Etienne passed, male and female alike, wept openly. As they drew near to the Maids' lodgings, Frances Stuart ran up to them. "My dear Dove," she sobbed, pulling Margaret into an embrace, "if St. Paul's has been lost, can anything be sacred, anything safe?"

"St. Paul's? What do you mean?" Etienne asked over Margaret's shoulder. "I saw the Cathedral not two hours ago—yard unbreached, walls untouched."

"Well, sir, it is gone now." Tears streamed down Frances's cheeks, dropping onto the silk of her gown, where they spattered like the rain London so desperately needed. "His Majesty saw it go from the royal barge. Saw lightning lick its roofline like the tongues of an evil cat; heard it groan as if in pain. And then there was a great noise—one of the officers of the Guard says it sounded as if every cannon in England fired at once—and the center of the church blew apart, leaving a fiery pit yawning like the mouth of hell."

"*C'est bizarre,*" Etienne muttered, looking puzzled.

"'Odd' is not the word I should have chosen, sir." Frances peered at him searchingly. "*Vous êtes français?*"

"Yes," Margaret responded quickly. "This is Monsieur Belland, His Majesty's fireworks maker, summoned to the safety of Whitehall because he is a Frenchman."

"French or English, I think we will none of us be safe here much longer, for the fire is but a scant half mile away."

🔥

Margaret crept back into her rooms, exhausted. The stress of frantically packing for the Queen had been exacerbated by smoke that made breathing painful, and by talk among the ladies of the desperate efforts to stop the fire before it escaped the city proper. Few had faith its westward progress could be halted, even though the man charged with holding Temple Bar was as true a friend to the King as ever lived. "Alas, ladies, mortal men are but paltry players and pale warriors in this battle with nature," the Queen said as they took their leave. "Trust God, sleep lightly, and be ready to go if you hear the bells."

As Margaret entered her apartment, the robust snoring of the senior Monsieur Belland provided a momentary distraction from the gruesome combination of fire and wind noises that had become a constant background for life at Whitehall. Margaret crept past the family on their pallets, wanting to wake Etienne but resisting the urge because he needed his sleep and because she feared where giving into her instinct, when her heart was so desperate, might lead. Alone in her bedchamber, she struggled to undress herself, unwilling to summon a servant. Then she crawled into bed. A few moments later, the door creaked open, and she saw the outline of Etienne's figure in the half-light.

"May I lie on the floor beside you?" He leaned his head in but did not cross the threshold until she nodded.

"I do not think I will sleep," she whispered.

Reaching up, he offered his hand, and as she took it, he began to sing softly: a French lullaby. She had not known he could sing. Her last thought was that he had a beautiful voice.

Waking in the dark, she could not at first say what had disturbed her. Outside, the sinister orange light was brighter than ever. Had the fire arrived? Margaret's heart rose to her throat until she realized there were no summoning bells, only the now familiar sounds of the conflagration. Then, as her pulse slowed, Margaret realized one noise was absent: the howling of the wind that had echoed unceasingly for five days. Leaping from bed, Margaret tripped over Etienne.

Sprawled on the floor, tangled together, they covered their mouths to stifle the laughter that came as a pleasant surprise but might awaken the others. When she'd finished shaking, Margaret whispered, "Come."

Out on the leads, Margaret's night dress barely fluttered. "Oh Etienne, the gales have blown themselves out!"

It was not the end of the fire—London still lit the sky—but it might be the beginning of the end. And that bit of hope was intoxicating. Joining hands, they spun until they were too dizzy to continue. Then Etienne put his arms around Margaret and they stood, looking not at the glowing city, but up into the sky, where a few pale stars shone through noticeably thinner smoke.

God's hand is in everything—man and animal, stone and star, rain and wind. Perhaps this morning, particularly in wind, or the lack of it.

"Do not go to Hampton Court this morning." Etienne interrupted her thoughts, pulling her even tighter. "Let them go, and stay with me."

Margaret knew what he was really asking, but it was a question without a practical answer. That had always been clear, but never more so than in these last few hours. For Etienne's parents, so comfortable with Margaret when she was a tradesman's daughter, now treated her with awkward formality—bowing as they thanked her again and again for giving them refuge. Etienne's youngest sister, who had joked easily with Margaret at Marylebone, could no longer find her tongue, confronted with the fact Margaret was a lady of the court, with peerless lineage and fine gowns. And more difficult than experiencing all this was watching Etienne's eyes fill with pain as he observed it. He knew that there was no going back to how things had been. That she could never again sup with the family or sit in the workshop and watch the apprentices.

No, if she were really to stay behind when the court moved to Hampton, it would be an act of rebellion, a choice that would make them both outcasts and see them fleeing not only London but England. They would be pursued relentlessly. Margaret was a valuable asset, and her family would not merely let her go. Instead, her father would surely seek a warrant against Etienne. Should they be apprehended, her handsome love would be tried and punished for her "abduction," however willingly she had accompanied him. Even if she and Etienne managed to evade capture and took up residence in France, or perhaps the New World, their actions would have grave consequences. Etienne's family would pay the price for their audacity. Merry as King Charles might be, he needed the support of his nobles and would be willing to punish harshly if one complained of damage and sought redress. The Belland's royal patronage would be lost, and other property might well be confiscated. Margaret could never wreak such damage on the family, and deep in her heart she knew, despite his suggestion that they defy propriety, Etienne could not survive the guilt of inflicting such destruction upon the parents and siblings he loved.

So Margaret sidestepped the question, forcing herself to keep her tone light. "I do not believe anyone will leave. So we will stay here together until it is safe for you and your family to go home again."

"Is it very wrong to hope that such a period will stretch to weeks?" Etienne asked.

"If it is, we are both of us wrong together."

CHAPTER 7

Whitehall Palace

Thursday, September 6

Margaret cast Etienne a sidewise glance where he bent over the drawings for their telescope. Normally such a labor would have elicited the look of eager attentiveness that she so loved. Not today. Instead, Etienne wore no discernable expression at all. His face was rigid, a mask, one that had slipped into place the night before and that Margaret felt powerless to dislodge. She reached out a hand, tentatively touching his where it rested beside the ruler. Without comment he shifted away, and her stomach contracted.

Damn the Earl of Tyrconnell. Damn him for destroying a day that began with Etienne and I wrapped in each other's arms.

The Earl had come directly to Margaret's apartment from the fire lines, interrupting a late supper with the Bellands. Sweated over and smelling of smoke, His Lordship had expected a hero's welcome, and he'd deserved one. But as he'd bowed over her hand, kissing it and making effusive statements meant to reassure her of his safety, a blushing Margaret had watched a spark of understanding flare in Etienne's eyes, and found herself wishing Tyrconnell had not returned.

When the Earl at last swept from her rooms with a flourishing bow, he'd taken Etienne's smile, witticisms, and tender looks with him. Perfect politeness replaced intimacy. And for the balance of the evening, Etienne had treated her with a ruthless deference that, whether intentionally or not, wounded Margaret deeply. When he failed to arrive to lie at her bedside that night, Margaret sought him. They'd stood on the leads, where the day had begun so differently, this time too far apart to touch, and Etienne had asked directly. Honesty was bedrock between them, so Margaret had told him the truth: the Earl sought to make her his wife.

"Perhaps there is some way to create a telescope with two eyepieces." She struggled to keep her tone playful. "Such a device would be a first, perhaps worthy of presentation at the Royal Academy. But more importantly, it would mean we will not have to take turns when looking at the stars."

"I will let you go first"—he drew another line on the page with his metal drafting pen, then met her eyes—"as befits your rank." A slight inclination of his head, so formal that Margaret's eyes pricked. "Or perhaps I will make a wedding present of the telescope to you."

"Etienne . . . I do not care for him." She'd said it last night on the leads, but she would say it a thousand times if necessary.

"Does that matter?"

"It *ought* to matter, but perhaps I have misjudged you." Anger flared inside Margaret. "How *dare* you cast yourself as the only sufferer here? You will not be forced to marry anyone." *And you do not face the prospect of exile to an Irish estate! It will be like returning to my childhood, being the canary in the cage until and unless my husband choses to take me out and stroke me.*

"Margaret, I—"

A frantic knocking interrupted, causing Margaret to overturn the bottle of ink on the table between them. She snatched up their sketch to get it out if the ink's way, desperate to preserve at least one dream.

"Sir! Sir!" a female voice cried from beyond the door. "Take care—strange men have followed us from Marylebone!"

"That's our maid, Charlotte." Etienne dropped his pen.

Fear surged through Margaret, reminding her of what was really important—not their argument, not the paper she had a moment ago been so eager to save. Letting the drawing drift to the floor, she scrambled to place herself between Etienne and the door. "Hide! I will answer!"

The worst of the fire was over, but the danger to foreigners was not. Flames had destroyed more than three-quarters of the city, leaving seventy thousand Londoners homeless and furious. King Charles had ridden to their great camp and declared the fire an act of God. But his words had not assuaged the masses because the Almighty could neither be reached nor punished. They longed for—they *needed*—revenge. So the idea of fire as foreign plot continued to flourish, and a new rumor ran wild among the tents at Moorfields: the flames were not an end, but a beginning, precursor to a full-fledged Dutch and French Invasion.

"A great horde of Londoners march back toward the smoldering ruins, crying out that fifty thousand foreign soldiers are coming to finish them," the exasperated Duke of York had railed, as he had set out to stop the crowd. "Because they believe such nonsense, I, who have not slept in days, shall get no rest." Dozens of innocents had been beaten and slaughtered before York stopped the riots, and no one at Whitehall believed the violence was over.

Dear God in heaven, has it breached the walls of the palace itself?

"Please, Etienne." Margaret tugged hard on his sleeve as the pounding began again.

"No, Margaret." Etienne gently picked her up and set her aside. "If danger arrives, my family's presence brought it, and it is mine to deal with." Then, before she could impede him again, he opened the door. Charlotte darted in, followed by a serving boy carrying a brace of rabbits.

Half a dozen glowering men remained just outside. Margaret recognized their leader as the butcher from Warwick Lane, the one who had been so helpful and obliging about giving a message to Etienne's pasteboard supplier on the day they'd last visited Bradish's bookshop.

"That's him—Belland!" The man pointed accusatorily.

"Yes, I am Etienne Belland, your servant, sirs." Etienne's voice was calm, and his hand did not tremble where he placed it on the doorframe to make certain the men did not enter. "What may I do for you?"

"You've done enough, villain! And *to* us not *for* us! Can you bring back my shop and livelihood? Can you unburn the streets, businesses, churches, homes, and company halls that lie in rubble and are picked over by crafty creatures willing to burn their hands to steal the remains of what once belonged to others?"

Margaret's chest tightened. The implication of the butcher's words was clear.

"I am heartily sorry for your losses." Etienne's voice was grave. "But you have come to the wrong place if you seek their cause."

"I think not," the butcher snarled. "You told me yourself all London would see your next show. That it would have rockets flying higher than St. Paul's and hanging in the air. Well, as I fled for my life with my littlest on my shoulders, I saw them—saw your infernal spears of fire shooting into the sky and wavering there like evil birds on the wing. You might have gotten away with much—including murder—if you had only held your tongue, but you are not only a blaggard but a braggart."

He stepped forward until a mere hand's breath separated him from Etienne. "I accuse you, Frenchman, in front of these men, of having destroyed London and ruined us all under the pretense of making fireworks for the King, a crime you'll pay for by swinging from a gibbet."

Margaret swayed where she stood, expecting the men to rush Etienne, wondering if she screamed, who would hear, and who come running.

"Why then, you will hang an innocent man, for I reply to you, with God as my witness, that I make nothing but innocent things that do no harm and for which I have a patent from the King."

Margaret's frantic mind twisted, caught between pride in Etienne for being so calm in the face of mortal danger and crushing fear that it would take more than sangfroid to save him. She wished desperately that there was some weapon at hand—even as she realized she likely would not know how to use it.

"If you are innocent, why are you hiding? What should you fear?" The man's lips curled back like a mad dog's, and he reached for the front of Etienne's coat.

Margaret forgot that she had no weapon. Stepping forward, she pushed the butcher's hand away, taking satisfaction in the way his eyes widened. "Mister Belland does not hide—he is my guest. And as for why he or any person not born on England's shores might wish to make themselves safe, consider your own behavior: entering a royal palace, unsummoned; making accusations and threats. Little, puffed-up men like you have killed scores of innocent people these last days—striking them down with iron bars, stringing them up without trial. Perhaps"—she narrowed her eyes and lifted her chin—"you would have been better served by using your fury to fight on the fire lines as the man beside me bravely did."

The butcher stepped back, cowed, despite the fact he was more than a head taller than Margaret. Those around him shrank back likewise, snatching off their hats.

I am myself a weapon, she thought in wonder. And it was true, for faced with a courtier, richly attired and imperious, the men suddenly recollected they had overstepped their proper places.

Etienne began to close the door, but Margaret, emboldened, stopped him with a gesture.

"Before you leave"—she made sure to meet the eyes of each ruffian in turn—"be warned: Mister Belland and his kin have friends in the highest places. Repeat the nonsense you have spoken here, and an order will be issued suing each of you for slander." Then she reached out and pushed the door closed herself with a satisfying click.

"You were magnificent!" Etienne crowed, catching her under her arms as her knees gave way. "I have said it before and I say it again—your surname should be 'Hawk' not 'Dove.'"

What a marvelous thing it was to hear him speak to her again as if the Earl had never come between them.

I would rather have my name be Belland than either . . . and never more so than at this moment. Margaret would have spoken it aloud but for the two servants who cowered not ten feet away.

She took a few deep breaths, then shifted her weight back onto her own feet and stepped away from Etienne, straightening her skirts as she did. "You are safe now," she said to the trembling pair. "Take those hares to the kitchens, and tell them Mistress Dove and her guests will have them for supper."

Halfway to the door, Charlotte turned back with a bob. "Begging your pardon, Mistress, but Monsieur Belland—I nearly forgot on account of having my wits frightened out of me—a lady came to the house in tears, looking for you. When I told her it was not in my power to say where you were, she begged me to give you this." The girl retrieved a bit of paper from her pocket.

Etienne unfolded it, then looked at Margaret, eyes wide with anguish. "It is from Agnes Bradish—Thomas is missing."

🔥

Agnes's face was streaked with tears. She'd thrown her arms mutely about Margaret and Etienne when they greeted her at the palace gate, and now, having taken a seat at Margaret's table, her silence continued.

This is what it feels like to love and to fear. Margaret watched her friend struggle to gain sufficient composure to speak. *I recognize the pain of it and feel it in my bones as I might not have only days ago.*

At last, with a deep swallow, the bookseller's wife began. "I have not seen Thomas in three days. He is a man governed by love of family"—her voice cracked, and she took a great gulp of air—"so something terrible must have happened to keep him from us."

"Perhaps you have merely crossed paths." Etienne infused his voice with reassurance, but his eyes brimmed with concern. Fearing Agnes could see that as clearly as she, Margaret rose and poured some wine to fortify her friend.

"Where did you see him last?" Etienne asked as Margaret set the glass before Agnes.

"In front of our shop as he put us in the back of a cart he paid far too much to hire." Agnes took a deep drink, then began to cry. "We'd been arguing all morning. I told Thomas we must leave London together. That he was more important than saving books." She paused to wipe furiously at her eyes. "He insisted they were not merely books, but our future—his, mine, the children's. 'You have worked as hard as I these years to build what we have,' he told me. 'How shall we survive but as paupers on parish charity or in a debtor's prison if Bradish and Son is lost?'" She paused to wipe her eyes again, then straightened in her chair.

"I am not a woman easily defeated, so I turned my argument, trying to convince him we would not be safe without him. The streets were clogged, and I pointed out that bad men as well as good fled the city. A woman and two young ones alone might fall prey to anything, and at very least, all that we packed, including our strong box, would likely be taken. I thought I had him with that. He stood quiet a long while"— she smiled slightly through her tears—"well, a long while for Thomas, for he is a loquacious man. Then he said, 'You are right. I have wracked my brain for an idea to save our stock, without the faintest trace of a plan arriving. If I cannot protect our livelihood, at least I can protect you.'"

This seemed sound logic to Margaret. "But he changed his mind? Why?"

"There was a terrible pounding at the door. On and on it went, until it could not be ignored. Thomas went to see about it. After some minutes, when he did not return, I crept forward to the shop just in time to see him holding the door for someone before sprinting away."

"He left without a word?" Etienne looked as puzzled as Margaret felt.

"I know! It was so odd—frightening. I don't mind telling you, I was angry. I would have run after him, but I could not leave the children. The noise of the fire was upsetting them, and Ellinor was coughing from the smoke. Then, perhaps an hour later, Thomas was back and no longer talking of coming with me. He bustled about, saying he had no time to argue—that a man far cleverer and greater than he had found a way to save not only our inventory but also that of our friends in the Stationers'

Company. He told me a cart to move our books would arrive soon, but as I and the children were the most precious things in the world, we would go first—to his sister's in Marylebone, not far from your home, Etienne—and if the cart was late back, then he would work all night.

"The next thing I knew, I was craning to see him through the crowd as the cart rolled away."

"When was that?" Etienne asked.

"Late afternoon Monday. I did not worry when he failed to arrive Tuesday morning—working all night might have turned into working through the morning too." She looked at Margaret and shook her head ruefully. "Men always underestimate how long things take. A certain amount of bravado is in their natures, even the booksellers among them." Her ragged smile faded. "But by Tuesday afternoon . . ." Her voice trailed off, and she took another swallow of wine. "It is but an hour's walk from our shop to his sister's home. Even with roads clogged by discarded goods and some closed by fire, surely he should have been with us by then. I tried to go back into the city—"

"Agnes! What were you thinking?" Etienne's outburst did not cow Agnes. She gave him a defiant look.

Margaret, remembering how frantic she had been over Etienne's initial delay in arriving at Whitehall, understood both that look and Agnes's actions. "Etienne Belland," she said, offering him a glare echoing Agnes's, "it is unbearable enough to feel hopeless without heaping helplessness upon that. Had I been my own mistress on Tuesday, I would surely have searched for you. And you are a liar if you say you would not have gone looking for me."

"But I am a man—"

"A man in danger of angering a pair of women in no mood to be lectured. Go on, Agnes."

"The guards would not let me in the gates." Agnes shook her head. "No amount of begging—not even bribery—would move them. Only this morning, very early, was I finally able to creep inside the walls." She covered her hands with her face. There was no noise, but her shoulders shook violently for some moments. Then, removing her hands again: "I did not go very far. I did not have to. There is no Paternoster Row, no shop, no husband—only a charred blackness that stretches as far as the eye can see. Dear God in heaven, London is a wasteland."

Etienne looked a question at Margaret. When she nodded fiercely, he took Agnes's hand and said, "We will find Thomas for you."

🔥

As they emerged from Whitehall into King Street, it was as if nothing had changed. Margaret knew it was merely a trick of perspective, a result of the buildings around them obstructing her distance view, but for a moment she allowed herself to pretend that the horror they'd observed from the leads and the evil orange light that had illuminated the palace windows for four days had been imagined. Then she squared her shoulders, reminding herself that pretty delusions served no one—least of all Agnes Bradish.

In the Strand, St. Martin-in-the-Fields stood, gardens green over its rear wall. The New Exchange, home to luxury merchants frequented by the members of the court, hugged the road, all solid stone and confidence. But there were signs of the fire in the piles of possessions that lay at the sides of the street, often accompanied by huddled protectors—most so weary they did not raise their eyes as Etienne and Margaret passed.

Then, without warning, London was gone.

They stopped in their tracks. Etienne gave a low whistle, and Margaret took his hand, not caring who saw. The flatness took her breath. Acres—no, not acres, but miles—of rubble, all in shades of black and gray, lay before them, smoking.

"'Seest thou these great buildings? There shall not be left one stone upon another, that shall not be thrown down.'" The passage from the gospel of Saint Mark came unbidden to Margaret's tongue. Then she shook her head firmly. "No! I do not believe God took the city as punishment. I cannot believe that, any more than I believe Dutch agents felled London with fireballs."

"Or that a French fireworks maker did so with his rockets." Etienne's voice was flat. "And yet some believe each of those things." He shuddered as if a great coldness went through him, despite the fact that already the heat radiating from the ruins sent beads of sweat down his face. "Margaret, this is a sight that will surely ruin not only the livelihoods but the minds of many. I do not understand why the air is not alive with the wailing of the grieving and the mad." He crossed himself. "Yet listen to the quiet. If I could not hear my own voice, and yours, I would swear I had been struck deaf."

Margaret closed her eyes. All London's sounds had been lost with her buildings. There were no voices—no wailing, no shouting out wares for sale, no chatting, no admonishing children—there were no cattle lowing on their way to slaughter; no dogs barking; no wheels on cobblestones or rattling of carts; no creaking of well pumps and slamming of doors; no church bells.

"There is not so much as the song of a sparrow," Margaret whispered in both wonder and horror.

Etienne touched the spot where he had strapped on a knife before they left Whitehall. "We must be careful, my dove. None but the desperate and the criminal will be found wandering such a ghastly landscape."

And perhaps the souls of the dead. Oh Thomas, are you dead? Margaret wondered.

"Which are we?" The levity was Margaret's desperate attempt to defend against the hopelessness that threatened to overwhelm her. But Etienne did not smile.

"I fear we may be another category altogether—fools. Or at least *I* am a fool for letting you come. I must take you back to the palace."

"Etienne, I am not going back! And you do not *let* me come or go anywhere. You are not my father, and if you were, you would find me ungovernable. Or haven't you heard? I sneak away from my duties to the Queen to spend time with a Frenchman."

This time he did smile. "Lucky man. Well then, keep your eyes and wits sharp. I may wear a knife, but that does not mean I am good with one."

Margaret put her hands on her hips and cocked her head. "So, how are we to find Paternoster Row when the streets are gone?"

"Landmarks." Etienne drew a map from inside his coat and a compass from his pocket. "With few buildings to impede our view, we can see those that survived quite clearly. We stand just inside Temple Bar. There is the Tower," he pointed east. "Praise God and all his saints that it was not blown to bits. And that"— he gestured north—"must surely be the tower of St. Bride's Church, leaning so solitarily. We will employ triangulation."

"I knew there was a reason I loved you."

"Science, eh? I wish I had divined earlier that it was the way to a woman's heart." He shook his head.

Margaret offered him a look of mock severity. "Who exactly would you have wooed with it in my stead? But yes, your scientific mind is one of your greatest attractions. And I believe it is with the tools of science and by the observations of the rational mind that we will find Thomas."

If we find him. Etienne's eyes said the words, though his tongue was still.

They set off. As the street disappeared, swallowed by eerie mounds and valleys of stone, timber and ash, Margaret winced at the stinging heat of the ground, placing each foot down only to jerk it up again as quickly as she could. Watching Etienne do the same, she let out a half-stifled laugh despite the grim circumstances.

"What?" Etienne asked, pausing but continuing to move his feet up and down as if he were a puppet dancing in place.

"We look like birds hopping about."

Again and again, they were forced to turn, their way blocked by stone, fallen timbers, and sunken cellars and cesspools belching smoke and sometimes flame. The pathos of the destruction increased whenever they happened upon an object that had survived while all around had burned to ash. An abandoned but obviously much-loved rag doll in the corner of an unburned garden was Margaret's undoing. The sobs that rose in her throat could not be smothered, but as Etienne tried to gather her into his arms, she pushed him away. "You must not indulge me," she snapped, furiously swiping away her tears. "Agnes, Ellinor, and Raphe will not be helped by crying."

A short distance later, they stumbled upon half a horse, its larger bones bare, its smaller ones turned to dust. Margaret could not take her eyes from the skull of the poor thing as they picked their way round it. As the grisly remains were left behind, she became increasingly aware of a putrid, cloying odor. Despite the sweet note in it, it was worse than anything she had ever smelled. Worse even than the noisome odor of the Fleet River, where sweepings from butchers' shops stewed in brackish water with dung and God alone knew what else on hot summer days. The scent grew overwhelming, until it filled not only Margaret's lungs but her mouth, bringing with it bile she forced herself to swallow.

Stopping to consult the map, Etienne retched. Drawing a handkerchief from his pocket, he passed it to Margaret who gladly pressed it to her face. "That is the stench of death. Perhaps all London's rats have burned up. Have you noticed? We've not seen a one."

"I'd be happy if 'twere only rats, for none would miss them. Or even if the dead were only poor beasts like that horse," Margaret replied softly. "But I fear we smell worse, for men and women must surely have been overtaken by death in the city's winding fire-filled alleyways."

Not Thomas, please God.

"Children too." The words caught in Etienne's throat.

Margaret laid a hand gently on his arm as her stomach knotted. Etienne never could pass a babe without crouching down to make a playful face. This habit had oft slowed them when they were together in London, for children were ubiquitous in the city—or they had been. The thought of London's youngest residents, lost, frightened, dying . . .

As the fetid air became thicker and more swollen with heat, Margaret's limbs grew heavy. She fixed her eyes on the ground, fearful of stumbling as she struggled to draw sufficient air without gasping audibly and alarming Etienne. But it was Etienne who suddenly and convulsively caught his breath, drawing Margaret's eyes upward.

The high altar of St. Paul's stood in the morning light. Wreathed in smoke, it might have been mistaken for a religious vision had it not been surrounded by mounds of debris. Atop that rubble, a lad ran about, playing. Margaret rubbed her eyes in disbelief as they moved past where walls full of magnificent stained glass should have stood but no longer did. But the boy remained, wielding some manner of ancient sword and cavorting thoughtlessly atop the remains of a holy site all had expected to endure until the Second Coming. Where was his respect for God? For the dead?

Balling her hands into fists, Margaret opened her mouth to shout. But the voice was sucked from her when a flash of fire drew her gaze left, down the remnants of the nave, to a massive pit with tips of flame licking hungrily from it. The edges of this lake of fire were ragged, and along that precipice, a great iron band that must once have held a heavy door twisted up and away from the hinge still holding it to the stone floor, as if metal could writhe in pain and try to flee. Mutely she tugged on Etienne's sleeve, pointing.

"The western undercroft must have exploded with tremendous force," he said. "Fascinating. I wonder . . ." His words trailed off into a firm shake of his head. "I forget our errand. Come," he said, leading her through the shadow of the now-missing nave. "What is left of Paternoster Row will be just on the other side of this holy wreck."

Nothing was left.

Or it seemed so at first. Then Margaret spotted a curled bit of wrought iron protruding from the debris.

"Etienne, Thomas's sign! Here is the bracket that used to hold it—I am sure of it!"

Their friend had been prodigiously proud of the sign commissioned from a painter in Harp Alley. Emblazoned with a stack of colorful books, spines decorated in gilt and topped by a globe with England facing forward, it had been enormous, as had the elaborately curled brackets required to suspend it over the street. Agnes had gleefully needled Thomas about its size, telling him that the creaking as it swung kept her awake on windy nights.

Etienne pulled out his knife and carefully shifted the ash and rubble around the bracket. He jumped back as if burned when a piece of the sign itself was uncovered. Blackened at its edges and riven with fissures, the center of the fragment remained bizarrely unburnt and bore the single word "Son."

Margaret swallowed the lump in her throat. It was part of the inscription—"Bradish and Son"—their friend had requested, although precious few in London could read, to make sure that all knew his shop would be his son's legacy. No legacy now but soot and wreckage.

Etienne reached toward the fragment but quickly drew his hand back, blowing on his fingertips. "We ought to have brought a stick."

In silence they crisscrossed the site, stooped like old beggars as Etienne raked the debris with the tip of his blade. Most of what they saw was indistinguishable, but occasionally an object stopped them in their tracks—a misshapen fragment of the blue and white porcelain vase that formerly held pride of place on the Bradish mantel; an iron pot Agnes had served stew from when they'd stayed to sup; the ivory handle of the pen Thomas habitually used to mark his ledger. This last Margaret picked up, employing the handkerchief Etienne had given her. It scorched her fingers, but she did not care. Such a tangible memento of Thomas belonged with Agnes.

"That pen was always on the counter," Etienne said, "so we must stand amidst the ruins of the shop itself." He paced back and forth, shifting things, nodding periodically in unfathomable satisfaction. "I see no evidence of books," he said, looking up at last. "Agnes said Thomas intended to move their stock. I believe he succeeded."

"On what evidence?" Margaret demanded, incredulous. "Paper burns. If bits of porcelain drape like fabric—clearly the effect of a heat great enough to soften them—how can you believe a single scrap of paper would survive? An absence of paper proves nothing."

"Ah, but I was not searching for paper. Most of Thomas's books were leather bound. Leather is hard to burn. It may curl, shrink, and blacken, but burn clean away . . . that I have not seen. This resistance to flame is why we use leather gloves when we fire rockets. And why I put that cumbersome leather vest upon you when I showed you how we assemble them." He paused, smiling at the memory. "Should something explode or ignite when it is not supposed to, leather offers protection to a man who might otherwise be quickly immolated."

"So no remnants of curled-up leather bindings, no books. Etienne, you are brilliant!"

"As brilliant as Robert Hooke of the Royal Society, whose writings you devour? Can I hope to compete with him for your esteem?"

Margaret looked Etienne up and down, as if assessing him. "Hooke is very clever, but you are far more handsome. Is your vanity sated?"

"It would be better satisfied with a kiss." The corners of his mouth turned up teasingly.

Margaret let him have a kiss, then stepped out of reach. "And now, Monsieur Belland, let us get back to the business at hand. Because if Thomas succeeded in moving his books, the next step in our investigation is to determine where."

CHAPTER 8

Present-day London

Tuesday

Nigella tapped her foot impatiently outside the medical examiner's office. Elevator doors opened to reveal O'Leary. "It's 8:05," she said. "I don't operate 'better late than never.'"

"You're in a pissy mood," he said. "I'm going to overlook it, though, because the prospect of standing over a charred victim isn't thrilling me either."

Nigella would have been better satisfied if her mood could be accounted for by the grim spectacle laid out on the table, with Dr. Gwen Phillips waiting beside it, or even by O'Leary's tardiness. But she'd gotten out of bed this morning "in a pissy mood," as O'Leary so charmingly put it, because it had been a long, lonely night. Still no reply from James, even though she'd broken down after her second glass of good red and sent a second text.

Phillips began as soon as they joined her. "As we suspected, our friend was dead before he was set alight. Not a trace of soot in the lungs, no fluid-filled blisters on the skin, COHb saturation in the normal range. I could go on but I won't bore you: fire didn't kill this gentleman."

"Do you know what did?"

"My answer is going to surprise you—Rohypnol overdose. In fact, given the quantity of the drug in his system, I'd call it Rohypnol poisoning.

"You mean somebody dosed him to death with roofies?" O'Leary asked.

"Yep. He would have gotten loopy first—staggering, responsive to suggestion and obedient to commands without knowing what he was doing—and then he'd have blacked out."

"Maybe Smyth was clubbing, bragging about his big . . . um . . . talent and commissions, and our suspect decided to turn him into a charred representation of the eighth deadly sin. It's easy enough to get that shit on the street, and clubs are full of it," O'Leary said.

"Maybe, but remember people also take Rohypnol by prescription as a sleep aid. Your victim didn't have to be partying, and your killer may not have obtained the drug illegally," Phillips responded.

"So the victim was killed by a fatal dosage of a drug we most commonly associate with date rapes, and then burnt," Nigella said. "What about the time between death and when he was set on fire?"

"Significant. Victim was certainly past primary flaccidity and well into rigor mortis before he was lit. I mean he has the grimace." She pulled the sheet back from the body's head.

"God, I hope there is some way to identify this victim without making Smyth's parents look at that," O'Leary said. "We may know it wasn't a reaction to pain or terror, but it sure as hell looks like one."

Phillips pulled the sheet back up. "Get dental records. But back to the time of death, I'm convinced rigor had advanced from the small muscles to the larger ones. Given the precise positioning of the body into the form of a crucified Christ, with the slight knee bend being sustained even during the burn, I think he was posed and allowed to become rigid."

"How long would that take?" Nigella asked.

"Generally, for the large muscles to be affected by rigor, I'd say six to twelve hours, but given his build—because even in this state it is pretty obvious that our victim was a gym rat—he'd rigor faster. So on the short end of that. If he was somewhere cold, that shortens the time even more. And we have no idea what he was doing right before he died. If it was anything strenuous, that would speed things up as well."

"He was likely a lawyer," O'Leary said. "How strenuous is that, really?"

Dr. Phillips ignored him. "On the other end, I don't think he was dead as long as a day. If secondary laxity had kicked in and his muscles had started to become flaccid again, we wouldn't have this perfect pose."

"Bottom line?" Nigella asked.

"Best estimate, he was set alight between four and eight hours after death.

"The next question is, how was he extinguished?" O'Leary said. "Nobody here believes he burned himself out."

"Right, and I don't believe any of us think high-pressure fire extinguisher," Phillips said. Nigella and O'Leary nodded. Had an extinguisher been used, they would have expected residue and also for bits to be broken off—burnt people got brittle, a blast of something high pressure left damage. "And there's no evidence of water."

"So we're back to basics," O'Leary said, "nature and availability of fuel, availability of oxygen, ability of the burn to lose heat to the surrounding air. Let's start with fuel."

"Traces of linseed oil to aid with ignition, basically to get the body sufficiently engulfed for the skin to split and transdermal fat to become the fire's primary fuel. Ultimately, I found some cotton fibers in a pattern suggesting your killer created a wick—something as simple as a bedsheet, twisted and wound around the victim—to help the fat feed the flames." Dr. Phillips pulled the sheet back to the victim's waist. "But as you can see, there is still fat unconsumed. So the fire didn't run out of fuel."

"Then we were looking for means of suffocation. How about something environmental? Deliberate deprivation of oxygen?" O'Leary asked.

"Your murderer would have to place the body in a very confined space, preferably one in which airflow could be controlled. That would be tough," Phillips replied.

"But not impossible," O'Leary conjectured. "I mean, you could do someone in an old fridge laid on the ground and just flip the door shut when the body was crisped to your tastes."

"You know O'Leary, sometimes you scare the shit out of me," Nigella said. "If I ever find a body in an old fridge, I'm driving to your place with an arrest warrant."

"You'll never get a warrant on that evidence, DI."

"I'm thinking something much simpler," Phillips said. "Fire blankets."

"Those tiny little things that hang in the kitchen?" O'Leary asked incredulously.

"They come bigger. And they're not expensive. You can get one online that is approximately six foot by four foot for under twenty pounds—I checked."

"So, to be safe, you spend fifty and cover your burning man in a pair of fire blankets and let him go out. Sod it!" Nigella paced away from the table, then rounded and stalked back again. "Fire blankets as a lead are no better than bloody Scots pine! Please, Gwen, tell me you have something else for us."

"Actually, I do have goodies." Dr. Phillips smiled and lifted the sheet near the corpse's feet to reveal a little stainless steel tray. "I pulled these from the hands."

Nigella looked into the tray and saw three fragments of what appeared to be dark metal in a nearly square shape. "Are those—"

"Nail remnants," Phillips answered. "Iron. Not a modern style. Of course you'll have to have them tested to see if they are old or just look old style. But either way, they are unusual. These aren't the sort of extruded wire nails lying around in everybody's toolbox or garage."

O'Leary gave a low whistle.

"I like to save the best for last," Phillips said.

🔥

Back in the car, the neatly bagged nails were a temptation. But it was time to finish follow-up on the body. A positive ID would focus their efforts on Andrew Smyth's movements on Thursday and Friday. While they'd been in with Dr. Phillips, Nigella had received the report from the security folks at GG&S: Smyth had gone to the company gym after work on Thursday, a door that required swipe access. Beyond that, there was no trace of him. Within standard business hours, employees didn't need to swipe into or out of the firm's floors. And getting out of the building just meant strolling out past a security desk—at least before midnight.

"Let's go to GG&S, see if they have camera footage of Smyth leaving Thursday, and talk to his secretary," Nigella said. "Christ on a bike, O'Leary! That's a pedestrian! Do you always drive like this?"

She'd let him have the wheel to leave her hands and eyes free to check email, but now she wasn't sure being updated was something worth dying for.

"Naw, Ni, this is payback for that coffee you put in my lap the day of the Monument fire." He winked.

"I'm going to call Mrs. Kay and get things set up. Try not to run any lights or wrap us around any poles."

Turned out Smyth shared a secretary with two other mid-level attorneys. Mrs. Kay ushered Nigella and O'Leary to her desk, introduced them, and then went off to make certain someone was pulling the camera footage.

"Was Mr. Smyth at his desk when you left on Thursday?" Nigella asked.

"He actually stopped by my desk as I was gathering my things." She blushed slightly.

So presumably not a work-related conversation. But they could spare her the embarrassment of probing it, because that didn't seem relevant.

"And did you see Mr. Smyth on Friday?"

She hesitated and colored again.

Nigella's senses sharpened.

"He wasn't in." A rather long pause. "I don't want to get into any trouble."

"Why would you get in trouble because your boss took a day off?" O'Leary asked.

"He didn't. Not officially. I got a text from him Thursday night." She looked down at her hands, then up with a rather pleading look. "You don't have to tell anyone here about what I'm going to tell you, do you? I mean, I need this job."

"To the extent that you have broken your employer's rules, but not the law, we're not interested," Nigella assured her.

"I got a text from Mr. Smyth, asking me to cover for him on Friday because he was going to make a long weekend of it. And I told him sure because he reviews my performance."

"What did 'covering' mean?"

"You know, like if one of the senior lawyers comes looking, I say he just went into a meeting with someone or popped out for lunch. Oh, and I move things around on his desk as the day goes on, pick up any notes left for him and put them in my drawer." She touched her bottom drawer.

"Sounds like you've done this before."

Again the eyes went to the hands in her lap. "Yes, well, Mr. Smyth likes to save his vacation for a real holiday." This time when she raised her head and met Nigella's gaze, her eyes were defiant. "He is not easy to work for—not like my other two. A lot of girls have had to be rotated out of this position. So his being out makes my life better."

"I can imagine." Actually Nigella didn't have to. A woman didn't move up the ranks in the police service without running into a male cop or two, often a senior officer, who got either mouthy or, worse, handsy. She remembered one from her rookie year whom she'd mentally christened the Octopus. "Did you hear back from Mr. Smyth after you agreed?" she asked.

"Just a couple of words. Hang on." The secretary pulled out her mobile, opened a message thread, and handed Nigella the phone.

Nigella noticed the little circle at the top identified the sender not as AS, but as BB. "BB?" she asked.

The young woman lowered her voice: "Blowhard boss."

Geez, Smyth really didn't have a lot of fans.

His text to her was dated after nine PM on Thursday:

Pamela, got an offer I couldn't refuse 😣 from a lady. Taking a long weekend. Cover, yes?

Her reply was perfunctory:

Of course Mr. S. Enjoy your weekend.

His parting shot continued the swagger:

You're the best. I see big Xmas bonus in your future.

"He didn't come in on Monday, did he?" Nigella asked.

"No. I was kind of angry that he didn't bother to text. But . . . I kept covering. And I haven't seen him yet today."

You aren't going to. You're never going to see him again. Wonder if, other than relief, that will trigger any emotion at all?

Mrs. Kay was waiting for them in HR. "I have the footage you wanted." She held out a flash drive. "Both entrances Thursday at five PM, through Monday morning."

"Thanks." Nigella pocketed the drive.

On the way down in the elevator, O'Leary said, "Time for next of kin. Let's talk to the brother."

"Spare the parents." She nodded.

The elevator door opened. O'Leary put his arm across to make sure it didn't close again, and waited for Nigella to get out first. "That and the fact that people tell siblings things they might not want mum and dad to know."

"That is the common wisdom."

"How *could* I have forgotten you're an only child, Ni, when it explains so much. Let's pay Peter Smyth a visit," he said as they stepped into the crisp autumn air. "We want to be able to see his reactions, don't we—uncensored."

She pulled up the contact information on her phone. "No need to move the car. This Smyth works just a couple of blocks from our dead one. Bit of a relief, that. Not sure I could take any more of your driving."

Peter appeared to be Andrew's older and very successful brother. He received them in a spacious office along the outer edge of a floor. "You said this was about Andy," he said, opening the conversation as soon as they were seated. "And everyone thought I'd be the inside trader." It was clearly a joke, but it felt wrong given that they were police and given what they knew and he did not.

"When was the last time you spoke with Andrew?" Nigella asked.

"Midweek last week. We met after work to drink and watch footie."

"How did he seem to you?"

"Like he always does when we hang out: ready for a party. We're both work-hard, play-hard types. Can I ask what this is about?"

"Bear with me for a few more questions, Mr. Smyth. Did your brother seem concerned about anything? Did he mention, for example, quarreling with anyone at work?"

Someone angry over a big-talents, big-commissions comment could well be a competitive coworker, Nigella thought.

"Nope. He was in high spirits, beyond the booze and the fact our team was winning. Told me he might have a weekend away with a pretty lady coming up. Honestly, he's more of a talker than a Lothario. But, when Mum called to complain that he missed phoning Sunday, which was my parents' anniversary, I assumed he'd got his bit of ass. Of course I told Mum he was out of town on business."

O'Leary looked at Nigella with eyes that said, *"dead men can't call their mums."*

Nigella drew a long breath. This part never got easy. "Mr. Smyth, your brother was not at work on Friday of last week nor on Monday of this one. He isn't in today. I am sorry to say, we fear he may have been the victim of foul play."

"Foul play—you're pulling my leg, right? I mean just the phrase sounds like something from a BBC2 mystery my mum would watch."

"Mr. Smyth, did you read the papers this weekend?" O'Leary asked in a low, even tone.

Peter nodded.

"We believe your brother, Andrew, may have been the victim in the Temple case," O'Leary said. "We are seeking to make an identification."

All the color drained from the banker's face. "Jesus. There's no way. Why would Andy be at the Temple on Friday night when he was supposed to be out of town, romancing some receptionist?"

"Well, let's hope he wasn't." Nigella saw no point in correcting him over the location of the death, or anything else. Let him have his last moments of denial—they were a refuge, and she was about to destroy it. "Do you know who Andrew's dentist is? Because, under the circumstances, dental records would be very helpful in ruling your brother out or confirming that he is the victim."

Peter Smyth sat frozen. Then he started as if awakened from a sleep. "I want to see him. If it's my little brother, I'll know." His voice cracked. And Nigella felt herself split in two as she always did in such situations—head remaining professional, focused; stomach feeling sick.

"No, Mr. Smyth, you don't," she said firmly. "Not yet, at least. If we make a positive identification from dental records and you want to see him after that"—she paused for a long moment—"you have every right to."

The last of his certitude crumbled, and the defiance in his eyes transformed into a mingling of despair and desperate hope.

"Do you have a contact for your brother's dentist?" O'Leary asked with marked gentleness.

"I don't." There was a tinge of panic in the voice. "It would be in his mobile, but if the body had been found with a phone, you wouldn't be here. He may still see the old fellow who did all our teeth in Sussex. I can give you that name."

"I am sure that will be sufficient." Most people had the sort of dental work that helped in identification—fillings, teeth pulled—before their thirties anyway, Nigella thought.

They left Peter Smyth slumped at his desk. They were about halfway back to the car when O'Leary said dryly, "Only in this business can you feel this done up before noon."

She knew what he meant. Standing in the street, Nigella suddenly saw Andrew Smyth lying, obscenely blackened, on the table at the morgue. The realization hit her like a gut kick:

even destroyed, his profile was undeniably similar to that of his grieving brother. She couldn't make herself feel better, but she had an urge to try to lift up O'Leary because she knew, for all his cheeky humor, he had natural compassion that years of policing had not eroded.

"Listen," she said, "let's have lunch or something before we go back. Shake off all the shit we've seen and heard this morning, and start fresh after."

"Don't feel like eating. But I have an idea." O'Leary pulled out his mobile. A few finger strokes later, he looked up. "Let's go to church. That's better than lunch for restoring the soul, and look." He held his phone so she could see it. A stone phoenix looked out at her over a headline: "St. Paul's Reveals Restored Phoenix."

"We can kill two birds with one stone, find a little peace and have a look at one of the killer's clues. I mean the note on the tie mentions a phoenix on a transept, and here's one staring at us from Christopher Wren's greatest work. That doesn't feel like a coincidence."

Fifteen minutes later they stood at the edge of Carter Lane Garden, across the street from St. Paul's Cathedral, shoulders nearly touching, heads thrown back. Far above, over the columned portico covering the south transept entrance, a phoenix spread its wings. "That's our bird," O'Leary said. "And right beneath him, in nice big letters, in case we were wondering if we're in the right place: 'Resurgam.' What did he say, our suspect—that the bird looks hungry?"

"He said it looked like a bird of prey."

"He got that right. That thing looks angry at the very least. I guess I would, too, if my feet were on fire. But seriously, we've got stone flames, Ni. Let's go inside, find a plaque or a docent; we need to know everything about this bird."

Pulling out her mobile, Nigella tilted it and snapped a picture of the phoenix, stepping off the curb as she did. O'Leary's hand at the back of her blazer snatched her back so hard that she fell into him. His other arm closed around her protectively as a lorry sped past. One more step, and it would have taken a chunk out of her, or worse.

"Jesus, Ni," he said, releasing her, "pay attention or I'm going to have to insist you hold my hand when we cross the streets."

"Thanks."

O'Leary's body trembled. He raked a hand through his hair, leaving it sticking up. Instinctively, Nigella rose on the balls of her none-to-steady feet and gave him a quick kiss on the cheek to reassure him—then instantly felt a desperate desire to lighten the moment. "I owe you. Next time I have the chance to save you from being maimed or killed, I will."

"Very gracious." He tried smiling but missed the mark. "Now come on: look both ways, and let's get in there and play police detective."

CHAPTER 9

Whitehall Palace

Saturday, September 8, 1666

Thank God for the Duke of Albemarle!
Margaret knew she was not alone in her appreciation for the Captain-General of the kingdom, but was certain the reasons for her enthusiasm were unique.

Yesterday she and Etienne had staggered out of the burned city—drenched in sweat, shoes ruined—far later than Margaret had anticipated. She'd changed quickly, then gone to attend the Queen, expecting to be upbraided for having missed the early afternoon rituals of Her Majesty's day. But no one had admonished, or even noticed, Margaret. Everyone was too busy speculating on when the Duke, called back from aboard the *Royal Charles*, might arrive. And as they calculated the hours, the Queen's ladies rhapsodized about how comforting it would be to have such a phlegmatic, able man in charge of keeping order in ruined London.

Yesterday, George Monck, Duke of Albemarle, had been her savior. *Today,* Margaret thought, examining herself before the mirror, *he will be my unwitting accomplice.*

Monck would shortly call upon King Charles. When he rode out again—heading for Gresham College, where the Exchange and Guildhall were temporarily reconstituted by royal command—the Duke's large retinue would be increased by two.

"Are you certain this is a good idea?" Etienne asked, staring at Margaret in her breeches, knitted stockings, and man's wig.

"No. But we haven't a better one. 'Twas you who said, as we stood in Paternoster Row, that the best way to discover where Bradish took his books would be to speak with another member of the Stationers' Company. And you who lamented that, with their shops burned and Hall gone, members would be hard to find. Well, such an important trade will surely be represented at Gresham today when Monck meets with the Alderman and merchant companies. All we need do is hang to the rear of things, and when the Duke rides on to survey the city, question whichever Stationers we can find."

"A sound plan . . . unless we are caught, which we very likely will be. Then you will be locked away as a madwoman, and I will, at the very least, be beaten out of town."

"Pshaw! How are we to be caught? You look every bit a nobleman."

He did. Margaret and Simona had borrowed his garments from the wardrobe of Prince Rupert, who was away with the fleet. Etienne wore them with the natural grace of a gallant, and Margaret wished fervently they were his rightful garb, for if he had a title to match his beautiful suit, she would be married by autumn's end.

"And while I may not be the most convincing gentleman"— she struck a pose with her hand on the hilt of her borrowed sword—"who will look closely at us, two among many, when everyone's thoughts are on what is to be done in the aftermath of this tragedy?"

Etienne still looked dubious. "Perhaps the Duke will not call us out for frauds, but surely you will be missed here."

"Nonsense. Her Majesty will accept Simona's assertion that I have taken to my bed—my health suffering from days of stress and smoke—and not give me another thought. This is one of the few times that being perceived as an invalid will be an advantage, not an aggravation. Besides, the ordinary order has been upset. No one knows where anyone is or what they are doing. Nor do they care with graver matters at hand. The King worries about shortages of food and small beer, and the overwhelming task of rebuilding London. The Queen frets over those living in squalor at Moorfields and organizes charity for them. Who shall think of Margaret Dove under such circumstances?"

"I will," Etienne replied gruffly, straightening the falling bands at her neck.

Their horses were ready. When Margaret had ordered them, in the name of the Duke of York, the stable master had not even blinked, merely bowed and took the command as genuine. *How daring I have become,* she thought now, standing at the edge of the courtyard, reigns in hand, watching Monck arrive. *And how delightful it feels.*

As soon as the Duke entered the palace, Margaret signaled Simona. Her friend opened a door, and half a dozen servants streamed into the courtyard, bearing refreshments for the Duke's men. Margaret hoisted herself to her saddle under the cover of this distraction, throwing Simona a grateful smile. She got a worried shake of the head in return. *Poor Simona, I must give her that bracelet of mine she admires when this is over.* Margaret did not have another thought to spare for her friend as she carefully kept her horse at the edge of the courtyard—not far from the party, but not yet a part of it. It was not until the Duke returned, remounted, and the riders began to make their way out of Whitehall that Margaret and Etienne cautiously joined the rear of the group.

The ride to Gresham College was the most dangerous part of their errand. Passing as noblemen among noblemen—this was a feat much more difficult than passing as such among the common sort, who would be in no position to question them. Margaret and Etienne had agreed to speak as little as possible, and only to each other. And to stay at the very back of the party, where they could see the others but were not likely to be seen by them.

Perhaps, she thought as they traveled along the northern edge of what had burned, *we need not have worried so.* The attention of all was on the barren and destroyed landscape. To see the Thames, not merely a glimpse but its whole long bank, from such a distance emphasized how thoroughly London's jumble of buildings had been wiped away. A sadness beyond tears welled inside Margaret. *Which is just as well,* she thought, *because one of the Duke's gentlemen can hardly be seen crying.* And then she heard a throat clear as a rider in front of her choked back a sob.

"Look," Etienne whispered hoarsely, pointing toward the distant ruins of St. Paul's. "The crypt still belches smoke. I cannot imagine what sustains a fire there when the rest of the great church lies quiet."

Gresham was soon reached. "I have always wanted to cross the threshold of this great temple of science," Margaret confessed as they reined in their horses short of their destination. "But not under such circumstances. Exploring the place where the Royal Society was founded should be a happy occasion."

"Why have you never gone?" Etienne asked as they watched the rest of their party dismount at the College's steps and go inside. "Lectures at Gresham are open to everyone. I have been to several."

"How many women did you see?" When he remained silent, she nodded. "Perhaps you have not noticed, Etienne, but *everyone* generally means every *man.* Men keep the best things for themselves. Not only the great things, like the work of performing experiments and passing laws, but the little things like riding astride." She patted her horse's neck.

"I am sorry," he said softly, reaching out to cover her hand where it lay on the animal. "Marry me and it will not be so with us, I swear."

He had never asked directly.

Margaret's heart swelled, but the feeling was painful rather than joyous. "Etienne, I believe you, truly. But that changes nothing. The world will no more allow me to be Mistress Belland than the next professor of astronomy at Gresham." Margaret turned her eyes from him. She heard two sharp, shallow intakes of breath. The hand resting on hers was gone.

They sat on their horses, thighs nearly touching, in unbearable silence. Then Etienne cleared his throat. "So you would displace Doctor Wren and teach students about the stars?" His tone was too somber for the jest to be convincing, but Margaret blessed him for trying.

"I would settle for meeting Wren and asking him to have a look at our telescope drawings."

"We did meet him, remember, at Brandish's bookstore? And poor Thomas felt so badly that he neglected to introduce us . . ." He trailed off, the mention of Thomas's name bringing frowns to both their faces.

"We will find him, Etienne." This time it was her hand reaching across the gap between their animals and momentarily finding his. "He will rebuild his shop. And the next time Doctor Wren visits, Thomas will introduce us."

◊

"Bradish, missing?" George Tokefield, Clerk to the Stationers' Company, stood before them, darkly circled eyes filled with concern, while on every side bankers and tradesmen conversed. Buildings might take years to rebuild, but the business of London was quickly resuming.

"I saw him last at the entrance to St. Faith's early Tuesday, My Lord."

Etienne, despite having just introduced himself as an earl and Margaret as a baron, appeared momentarily confused by the clerk's use of the honorific. But at least he did not physically jump as he had when the clerk, old enough to be his father, bowed during those introductions. "St. Faith's?"

"Yes, it is . . . was . . . our Company parish. We had just sealed the doors with wet clay, having expended many hours filling the space with bound books and reams of paper in hopes that sturdy stone walls would hold them safe.

"Before scattering to save our families and ourselves, we stood shoulder to shoulder in prayer." He gave a sad, small shake of his head and licked his dry lips. "What waste of breath. Neither God nor the crypt's walls safeguarded our wares. The walls, being merely stone, could not be moved by the pleas of mortal men, but I shall wonder till I die what we poor Stationers did to offend the Almighty to harden him against us."

He gave another little half bow at the end of his recitation of these facts, and Margaret marveled internally, much as she had the day she'd driven the butcher and his mob from White-hall with stern words and looks, how rank was both sword and shield. Etienne's French accent was as noticeable as ever, yet although that fact had endangered him as a tradesman, it was of no consequence now. The Stationers' Clerk still bowed and showed deference because a nobleman was a nobleman and not to be questioned. Accent or origin did not change this. After all, Prince Rupert, whose clothing Etienne now wore so gracefully, was German.

"And where is St. Faith's?" Etienne asked.

"Beneath St. Paul's, My Lord."

"So it is reams of paper that burn so fiercely!" The words burst from Etienne with unseemly satisfaction. Margot under-stood: the puzzle in his mind—one that had been vexing him since they'd stumbled upon the ruined altar and the massive, flaming, hole in the floor of the Cathedral—was solved. But Tokefield could not know that. He looked aghast.

"We saw flames rising from the bowels of St. Paul's as we rode over, and wondered what fed them." Margaret offered, making her voice gruff and holding her breath to see if the man would notice she was not what she seemed. He didn't. "Is everything lost then?"

"Yes. I do not like to complain of it, Your Lordship, when every man, every trade, has lost more than can reasonably be counted. But we—the men of paper and books—are ruined, and with us English publishing. And, cruelest irony, I shall be able to put a price on what was destroyed, for I took the Com-pany accounts to my house in Clerkenwell."

Tokefield paused, resting three fingers on his chin. "If Bradish has run off leaving his wife and babes, I pray he does not act out of misplaced guilt."

"Guilt?" Etienne cocked his head. "You say he labored alongside the rest of you, and doubtless he gave his best efforts, for if ever a man trades and lives as one ought it is Bradish."

"Bradish is an honorable fellow, My Lord." The man bowed. "But while a scoundrel will seek to avoid blame owed him, the best men have been known to shoulder guilt where they are not at fault."

"An astute observation."

"It was Thomas, My Lord, who came up with the plan for moving our stock to the crypt. Monday afternoon, he arrived at our Hall, out of breath, declaring to those of us gathered that we ought to pack St. Faith's and seal every crevice. 'If we can only keep out such sparks as come,' he said, 'then even should the mighty Cathedral burn, the materials of our trade will lie safe, waiting to be uncovered when the flames have passed.'"

Odd, that is not the story Agnes told. She spoke of Thomas returning from she knew not where, crowing that a way had been found to save their books by someone else—someone cleverer than himself.

"We took up his idea at once, sending word to our members, collecting clay from the banks of the Thames, taking money from the Company strongbox to hire carts. And all the while, men embraced Bradish and blessed him for the scheme. Perhaps when it failed, Bradish believed he was at fault, or he feared his fellows would blame him. Though I assure you"—the man's hands fluttered in agitation—"no Stationer would."

"Of course not," Etienne replied soothingly. "Did Bradish say anything of his plans as you parted ways?"

"If he did, I did not hear it. I was eager to be out of London."

"Is there someone who might know more?" Margaret asked.

"Archer," the clerk said, his eyes lighting up. "He was with us at St. Faith's, and he and Bradish are close as brothers." He glanced about, then raised a hand and called, "Archer, quick, sir—you are wanted!"

A wiry young man with his hands wrapped in linen broke off his conversation and joined them.

"These kind gentlemen are concerned for the welfare of our friend, Thomas Bradish," the clerk said with an obsequious bob of his head. "It seems Bradish cannot be found."

The younger man looked stricken. "He is not in Marylebone with Agnes—Mistress Bradish?"

"Is that where he was going?" Etienne asked.

Again a bow—or rather two, as Archer seemed to feel one was owed each of them. "Yes, Thomas was headed to his sister's, to join his wife and little ones. He told me so as he embraced me on the steps of St. Paul's. When I said I would try to reach my lodgings to collect my best suit, he slapped me on the shoulder, joking that perhaps I ought to have worn it." A smile touched the corners of the man's mouth. "He reached in his pocket, took out his favorite pen, and said, 'Observe my foresight.' Then, tucking it away, laughed and said he might go back to his shop once more, nonetheless—just long enough to get Agnes's prized blue porcelain vase as a surprise for her.'"

Margaret no longer saw the stationer's earnest face, but rather a melted fragment of blue and white porcelain lying among ash and rubble. *Oh Thomas, why did you not collect the vase and take it to Agnes?*

"He is like that, is Bradish—always thinking of others. In fact, the last thing he said before I ran off was to take care in the streets, for more burned than did not, and the way was like to be treacherous." Archer took a hitching breath, eyes looking beyond them to some past moment. "The smoke, the flames—you cannot imagine.

"Road after road was blocked, by fire or the Guard. I got lost, gave up going to my lodgings, and sought only escape." He gulped for air as if the building in which they stood was filled with smoke as the streets had been. "I was trapped in a blind alley by a fallen beam. Had I been alone, that would have been my end, but others were there. Together, we moved the thing and got away, though not unscathed." He held out his bandaged hands. "I cheated death," he whispered. "What if Thomas did not?"

In the street, Archer's question hung over them like a pall.

"If Thomas fell between St. Paul's and Paternoster Row, we will not find him, though the distance is short," Etienne said bleakly. "Like paper or wood, mortal man burns." He began to cross himself, then, recognizing such a gesture might mark him as a Catholic, let his hand fall. "'For dust thou art, and unto dust shalt thou return.'"

Something about Etienne's conclusion—beyond its morbid nature—bothered Margaret. Thomas had returned to his shop, she felt sure of it. Why? The reason danced outside her grasp, teasing her. Frustrated, she kicked the dust of the road, causing her horse to sidestep nervously.

She straightened her shoulders. "Let's ride to St. Paul's. Thomas was last seen on its steps. After that, our friend's movements are conjecture. Even if we discover nothing pertaining to him, there will be consolation in watching you happily examine the ruins of St. Faith's. You are eager to have a closer look at that crypt now that you know what fueled its explosion."

"I do not deny it. Tokefield mentioned sealing the door with clay. In principle such a method ought to have worked. As the Cathedral grew hotter, the clay should have hardened but not burned, protecting the door beneath. Yet the crypt blew open as if a barrel of black powder ignited inside it. Who would not be curious in such circumstances?"

🔥

The boy with the ancient sword was gone. In his place, at least half a dozen souls wandered the ruins of St. Paul's, gawking.

Or perhaps doing worse.

Riding over, they had seen people scavenging, and witnessed an altercation between a man digging through rubble and a second who sought to chase him off, claiming the ruins were his home. Blood had been drawn before Etienne had separated the two by shouting and riding his horse at them.

They drew up where the Cathedral's western end once stood. All that remained of the great portico were broken columns lying like fallen trees. As she clambered from her horse, Margaret's foot touched upon a stone declaring the portico to be a gift of King Charles I—every letter of the inscription still legible.

A fallen monument to a fallen king, lying amidst a fallen city. How shall we ever recover?

A handful of soldiers, doubtless some of the eight hundred summoned to London by the secretary of state, were passing. Etienne called to them as boldly as if he were indeed an earl, charging one with looking after the horses.

As Margaret and Etienne passed a partial wall and entered the roofless nave, a middle-aged man ran up. "My Lords, if you are looking for an astounding sight, we have found a long-dead bishop, stiff as a board, his red hair and beard unsinged!"

Red hair meant whoever they had found—bishop or no—was not Thomas. If Margaret was to look at dead bodies, she did not wish to do so idly. "Have you found any other dead?" she asked gruffly.

"A dog, stiff as a board, with skin like leather!" His voice was hopeful.

Margaret suppressed a shudder. "I meant other men."

"An old woman, but she is not interesting to look at, being burned like a log. You'd do much better to see the bishop! His teeth are better than mine."

"No thank you," Etienne's voice was icy; he had clearly had enough of this fellow hawking the dead as if they were wares. As he raised a hand to drive the man off, a boy ran up.

"Father, I've found another come out of his coffin! And just as wondrously shriveled as Bishop Redbeard, except his hair is golden." The lad was so excited he stumbled over his words. Noticing Margaret and Etienne for the first time, his eyes grew large, but he was certainly not overawed, for in the next instant he plunged onward. "He has a tiny beard, and a moustache like yours, sir." He pointed at Etienne.

Etienne blanched. "Show us this fellow."

The boy scampered off eagerly, heedless of the uneven terrain and the dangerous, burning pit that had to be skirted.

Surely there were hundreds who came to the Cathedral seeking shelter from the flames, Margaret told herself, following. *Any one of them might have met his end here. It is silly to let the prickling of my skin convince me it is our friend.*

The boy stopped near a tomb, the heavy marble of its broken sarcophagus cleft into odd-shaped pieces. One fragment bore the words, "resteth the body of Thomas Kempe, Bishop of London," and another a date: 1489.

Please, God, let it be Bishop Kent we are led to see, Margaret thought as she carefully edged around the last portion of the chasm that had once been St. Faith's. *But a moustache like Etienne's . . . and a small beard . . . no man in the fifteenth century wore such things.* The paintings of her ancestors at the family estate and the portraits of Richard III and Henry VII at Whitehall all showed clean-shaven men.

Clear of the smoldering pit, Margaret's eyes fell to the boy's feet. The remains of a man with skin the color of a roasted suckling pig, rather than any shade she had ever seen in human flesh, lay on the stone floor. One desiccated arm—spindly as a child's—was raised across his forehead, as if he would ward off his horrible fate. Margaret's stomach contracted. She reached for Etienne's hand, and then stopped, remembering she was dressed as a man. The deceased wore the dark and modest suit of a successful tradesman, not the robes of a bishop, and even wizened his profile reminded her of Thomas's.

"Stay here," Etienne commanded. But she could not, she *had* to know. Not just hear it from Etienne, but *know.* An instant later, looking down on the poor remains, she did—for there, beside the sunken socket of the right eye was a large mole.

My God, Thomas dead. Poor Agnes . . . how shall we find the words to tell such a terrible truth?

Beside her Etienne cursed—something Margaret had never heard him do. Putting out an arm, he gestured her backward. She gladly obeyed. She expected him to follow. Instead he circled the body, shooing the boy out of his way. Stopping, Etienne nudged something with his toe. He stooped and picked up an iron bar, bent at one end into a hook.

"Why would a clergyman have a pries bar?" their guide asked.

Why would Thomas have one?

"Looks like a grave robber, thinking to steal from the dead as the church burned, got his comeuppance," the man continued, his voice infused with a self-righteous glee very much at odds with the fact that he himself was seeking to profit by showing off the dead.

"Quiet, fool! I know this man!"

Their companion shrunk back as if slapped, but did not leave.

Handing the bar to Margaret, Etienne squatted next to Thomas's head. He tilted his own one way and then the other: lips thin, eyes animated in the same way as when he and Margaret discussed science or the stars. It was a gaze of raw curiosity. Then he let his eyes fall closed, and his lips moved silently.

Prayer done, Etienne rose and stared down at the body again. "It appears he still wears his purse." He bent to retrieve the item but recoiled as his fingers got close.

"Allow me, My Lord." Their companion bent without compunction and, after a moment's difficulty with the strings tying it in place, handed the pouch to Etienne. The leather, Margaret noticed, was contracted and shriveled like poor Thomas.

Etienne hefted it. "Still full." He took a hard look at the man beside him and at the boy still hovering nearby. Margaret sensed he was weighing them as he had Thomas's pouch. Tucking that relic of their friend away, Etienne drew out his own purse, pouring a mound of coins into his palm. "See to it that these remains are borne to an address in Marylebone, and all this"—he held out his hand so that the man could better see the money—"shall be yours."

The man nodded eagerly, hand opening. Etienne placed two coins on the dirty, empty palm.

"That should be enough to hire a cart," Etienne said.

"My Lord, you are generous."

"I will be, when the body arrives. And if you find anything pertaining to this man when you move him—if anything should fall from his pockets or lie beneath him—bring that to me as well, and I will pay extra for it. Pay far better than anyone you might think to pawn such objects to."

The man licked his lips. Etienne turned from him and took a step toward Margaret, then turned back.

"One last thing, and mark me well: I do not wish my friend made into a spectacle for others to point and gape at. See that he is covered respectfully as you bring him through the streets. If I find it has been otherwise, you will have none of the monies I have promised, but a sound beating instead."

"Why the workshop and not some place of Christian burial?" Margaret asked as they stumbled out of the ruined Cathedral, her words slurred and tears streaming down her face.

"Because the back of Thomas's head appears to be broken open, and that"—he pointed to the ash-covered crowbar she clutched—"lay beside him."

CHAPTER 10

Present-day London

Tuesday

The Cathedral had a historian—of course it did. In fact, it had a "Chief Historian," which suggested it had more than one. This fellow was a cleric, elderly, with a warm manner contrasting with his spartan dress and perfectly erect posture.

"So you need to know about our phoenix," he said. "If you'll indulge me, I'll start a little further back than its creation because, well, historians just can't resist delving into the past."

He motioned to the chairs opposite his desk and waited for Nigella and O'Leary to sit. "St. Paul's has always been this city's most revered landmark. The predecessor to this incarnation of the Cathedral was a place where dead monarchs lay in state and lord mayors prayed on the day of their installations. But Cromwell's Roundheads didn't care about that. They stabled horses in the nave, smashed windows, let a patchwork of huts and stalls surround and even invade St. Paul's until Our Lord Jesus would surely, had he been alive in the flesh, have strode through, casting the merchants out on their ears." He smiled—broadly.

He'd lay out a bob or two to watch his Savior kicking some Roundhead and merchant butt, Nigella thought. She found herself liking the heck out of him for that.

"By the time we got our King back, and the Church had the Cathedral restored to it, old St. Paul's was a pitiful place, falling to bits in parts, and one of those parts was the south transept."

He raised a bushy white eyebrow as if to say, *"See? I told you I'd get there."*

"It had needed roof repairs since before the execution of Charles I. Work was finally started after the Restoration. A Royal Commission was established by Charles II, and a great many plans were discussed to restore the whole of the church. But then, of course, the Fire happened." He leaned over his desk, his voice growing gossipy. "And I do mean *the* Fire, not one of its predecessors, because this Cathedral has experienced a goodly share of conflagrations. *The* Fire, the Great Fire of London, ended all talk of patching up. There was nothing left to renovate. The Cathedral didn't just burn—it exploded thanks to the fact that London's booksellers had, however unwittingly, packed it tight with fuel.

"This was a shocking thing for the people of London you understand—even in the midst of the Great Fire, with the city in flames for four long days and nights, nobody believed St. Paul's would be lost. And then it was gone. *Poof!*" He half threw up his hands, like a children's magician, to emphasize the statement.

"It wasn't the only thing of course—eighty percent of the walled city of London, some of it six centuries in the making, was gone. More than seventy thousand people were left homeless when over thirteen thousand homes burned or were pulled down for firebreaks. Taking into account their rents, historians value the lost houses alone at nearly four million pounds sterling. Can you imagine! And that in a time when Samuel Pepys, Lord love the man for his record keeping, paid his cook only five pounds per annum."

O'Leary gave a low whistle.

"St. Paul's was one of eighty-six churches destroyed by the Great Fire, or so badly damaged they had to be pulled down. Thirty-five of those were never rebuilt. But there was never a question of leaving St. Paul's as a ruin. London simply could not exist without its great Cathedral, and fortunately for us as we sit here today, Sir Christopher Wren was given the commission for its design: a life-changing commission that most would say he executed with divine inspiration." The historian sat back in his high-backed chair with a satisfied sigh.

"And the phoenix was part of Wren's design," Nigella said.

"That, young lady, is a common misconception—that Wren designed every inch, every decorative flourish."

O'Leary had a hard time keeping a straight face. "Young lady" wasn't a term anyone associated with the mature, competent Nigella, least of all Nigella herself.

"Wren asked for a phoenix to represent St. Paul's rebirth, but Caius Gabriel Cibber envisioned and created the sculpture. Our bird wasn't his first collaboration with Wren; he sculpted the western panel on the Monument to the Great Fire—the one with our beautiful Lady London weeping while King Charles II and his brother stand by, waiting for her to rise again, knowing she will. Some people consider that allegorical panel the most exquisite piece of art to emerge from the wreckage of the Fire. Utter nonsense, of course—this Cathedral is that."

"Has anyone ever told you that the phoenix looks like a bird of prey—a vulture or the like?" O'Leary asked.

The cleric used two fingers to slide his glasses further down his nose so that he could peer over them at O'Leary. "No, Detective, they have not. I would say he is a fierce bird, but if one would rise from the ashes, rather than lying down in the face of such tragic destruction, ferocity is surely a useful trait."

"It is a useful thing in police work as well," O'Leary replied. "We have a homicidal arsonist on our hands, Father, and for some reason he brought Cibber's phoenix to our attention." O'Leary pulled his phone from his pocket. Nigella watched him open up a note. "*It is fitting that the phoenix carved on the southern transept looks like a bird of prey. Not all who rise in this world do so on their merits or deserve their honors.*' That is what our killer wrote—and not just anywhere, on the back of a tie bearing Sir Christopher Wren's line drawings for this place. Based on the balance of his note, our killer thinks someone has been or is being honored without deserving it. And we need to sort that before some other poor b-b . . . bloke"—Nigella had the distinct feeling O'Leary had been about to say "bugger," then decided it was not a church-worthy word—"ends up nothing but a pile of charcoal that we can't let his own brother see."

"It's the case from the weekend papers then," the older man said softly. "We prayed for your victim this morning."

"And I am a man who believes firmly in prayer, even though mine take a different form than yours." O'Leary leaned forward. "But praying is not our job, DI Parker's and mine. Our job is finding this killer. So could it be that this sculptor Cibber was an unworthy artist? You say his work at the Monument is considered significant. Our suspect has a chip on his shoulder about people who mistake celebrity for genius. Was Cibber a celebrity?"

"I do not believe anyone would call him that," the historian said.

"Can you tell us about the creation of the phoenix?" Nigella asked.

"I can try. There is no consensus on the exact date of its creation. We know the design was imagined after 1675, nine years post-fire, when the foundation stone for a new cathedral was finally laid. And there is a legend suggesting the impetus for its subject matter came from an on-site incident with Sir Christopher Wren several years prior to that."

Wren again. Always Wren. Except for the Temple fire, Nigella reminded herself. They *had* to look at the history of that courtyard column.

"Could you point us in the direction of a few concise reference books on the Cathedral's destruction and rebuilding?" she asked.

"I can do better. We have a library and archive containing every substantial history of this Cathedral. It includes a number of very rare volumes, and I believe one of them discusses the Cibber and Wren collaborations. Let me lend you that book and a more modern history of the rebuilding. If you will just wait . . ."

When the historian returned, he held out a parcel wrapped in brown paper. "I trust that you will handle these with the same care that you do evidence. Keep them as long as they remain useful to your investigation. And come back anytime. The archives and I are at your disposal." He looked directly at O'Leary. "We will pray for you, but more worldly assistance is also within our means—after all, the Lord helps those who help themselves."

As they reached the doorway he added, "Oh, and I've included a third book—a volume from before the Fire—on the mythology of the phoenix. I thought it might help. Please be particularly conscientious in your handling of that book. Even vellum is not eternal."

🔥

"So, is it going to be a history afternoon? O'Leary set the parcel on the conference table and began to tear open the brown paper.

"Books can wait. Gwen's nails are our best lead." Nigella dangled the evidence bag aloft. "I'll run these to the lab."

"You sure?" O'Leary held up a small leather-bound volume, elaborately worked and with gold on its spine. "How can an Oxford alumna resist this gem about the legend of the phoenix?" He threw her a crooked smile. "Bet it hasn't been opened in a hundred years."

He held the book out and Nigella took it like a mum retrieving a toy from a child she needed to get back on task. Once she had it in her hands, though, she couldn't resist turning the volume over and running a finger over the beautiful embossing. Setting the bag of nail fragments on the table, she opened the book. "Look at that typeface." Gently she began flipping through. Something fell out.

"Notes?" O'Leary asked as Nigella put down the book and picked up what appeared to be several tightly folded pages. "I'll bet some dull doctoral candidate is searching for those."

Nigella unfolded the yellowed sheets. "Not unless it's a doctoral candidate who uses quill and ink."

The writing was from a bygone era, small and full of looping flourishes. The first line jumped out at Nigella, raising the hairs on the back of her neck. "*'Not long ago we abandoned our dangerous pursuit of the Phoenix,'*" she read out.

"What did you say?" O'Leary looked at her as if she'd gone crazy.

"It's not what *I* said; it's what's written here. That's the first line."

"If you're not having me on, then I'm creeped out."

"Holy shit, listen to this:

Not long ago we abandoned our dangerous pursuit of the Phoenix. Abandoned it even though a man died and a mighty edifice fell, not by act of God, but by the actions of a man's hands. We were wrong to do so. And I have resolved to confront the Phoenix.

My dearest Etienne argues that there is nothing to be gained; that a man willing to do that which we now believe incontrovertibly the Phoenix has done will not simply bow his head and admit his guilt. And perhaps he is right. But eight days ago I saw a poor, muddled man hanged most horribly for starting the recent fire that swallowed London, a fire that His Majesty the King, and all the Court believe to have been an act of God.

On the ride back to Whitehall, I knew. Knew that in such circumstances, where accident has been made crime, to allow an actual crime to pass disguised as just a part of that self-same accident is beyond me. I cannot bring the Phoenix to justice, but I can be as the conscience he does not have, speaking his deeds into his ear and into God's.

However, cognizant that the blood of Thomas Bradish, bookseller, father, and good friend, is already upon the Phoenix's soul, I leave behind this, a reconstructed summary of our labors, Etienne's and mine, safely tucked away in Lord Anglesey's library. Should the worst befall me, I hope some good soul may find these pages and know what we discovered. Perhaps the finder will be better situated to make demands upon English justice.
Lady Margaret Dove
3rd November 1666

"Am I the only one covered in gooseflesh?" O'Leary asked. "She's talking about the bleeding Great Fire, Ni. About a crime committed during it. Those are case notes in your hand."

Nigella touched the words "fire that swallowed London." Sixteen-sixty-six . . . O'Leary was right. Lady Margaret, whoever she was, meant the Great Fire.

So what? Ghosts from the past don't solve cases; police work does.

"O'Leary we don't have time for a cold case more than three hundred and fifty years old."

"I am not sure about that. I think we were *meant* to find them."

"You realize that you sound like a superstitious fool."

"Maybe to a lot of people, Ni, but not to you. You've got a bit of it in you as well—the sense that in this crazy job blending science, smarts, instinct, and luck, things happen for a reason. Everywhere we've turned this last week, we've run up against the Great Fire, and Wren, the man who rebuilt London after it. So maybe those notes were set in our path to help us along it."

The pull of the pages was strong. Who was Lady Margaret and who was her "dearest Etienne?" How had a woman so obviously a member of the royal court come to be investigating a murder in the aftermath of London's Great Fire? Nigella flipped through the remaining sheets. The handwriting was minuscule and would require hours to decode. Taking the time to do that now was irrational, and Nigella didn't believe in giving in to irrational impulses. So she made herself put the notes back in the book and shut it.

"Iron nails are solid evidence, O'Leary. Whispers from long-dead amateur investigators are the stuff of fairytales and fiction. I'm heading downstairs."

Nigella impressed on the fellows in the lab just how interested they ought to be in her nail remnants, then caught the elevator. She could hear O'Leary's voice as soon as the doors opened; he was doing his nut.

"Understand this: you—not just your employer, you *personally*—will be complicit in the deaths of any new victims." She dashed for the incident room, reaching the doorway as he bellowed, "I'd take this all the way up the damn chain of command. Have your publisher sign off before you run that ugly little item. Make sure he knows we're not going to sit still for this, so he should plan to spend money on lawyers." O'Leary paused for a moment, looked up at Nigella, and glowered. The veins in his temples were showing.

"Hang on a minute." He put his hand over the telephone mouthpiece. Nigella thought he was going to say something to her, but instead he took three very deep breaths. Then he uncovered the receiver. "How about this—" the voice now was smooth, bargaining rather than bullying— "give us some time, and I'll make sure you get something exclusive? We both know this sort of sensational stuff makes great headlines." His expression closed as he listened intently. "Hey, I'm not saying we will absolutely ask you to quash what you've got. All we want is time to try to predict which is more dangerous: publishing it or failing to. And we need the original. A 'no' on that is a deal breaker." Another pause. "Deal. Have someone run the note to Wood Street, 'Attention Detective Inspector Parker.' If it ends up you don't get to run the note, you'll get any photo we release twelve hours before everyone else. Plus I'll throw you something lurid and exclusive as a thank-you. If we don't release a photo, you'll get two exclusive shocking bits."

He put the phone back on the cradle gently, then with a sweep of his arm knocked it to the floor.

"What the hell was that?"

"That, Ni, was me making a deal with the devil—or with London's most popular tabloid, which amounts to the same bloody thing. You will not believe what they have. That arse, that fucking, sick, twisted, son of a bitch who burns people for jollies, wrote them a little note. Actually he wrote *us* a note and decided their pages were the best way to make sure we saw it."

"Not good."

"Not good? Under-fecking-statement of the century! Would you like the highlights?"

She became aware of a jumble of scrawled sentences on the pad in front of him.

"He's angry at us—the police—because we're not 'allowing his artwork to be seen.' I believe I got that phrase down exactly. He's just gutted in fact. He put hours of creative labor into producing his 'art'—again his damn word because I'm pretty fecking sure that neither we nor ninety-nine percent of the population of London would describe what's left of poor Andrew Smyth as art—so why haven't the papers run pictures?"

"Fuck my life." She shoved the nearest chair, sending it shooting across the floor. It collided with the whiteboard wall with a satisfying crack.

"That's more like it, Ni. It gets worse. He's demanding we submit his "portfolio" to art critics—he names a bunch of academics—and hand over pictures to the newspapers."

"We ought to publish a reply telling that cocksucker we will give him a one-man show—inside Frankland Prison," Nigella said.

"He closes with a threat. I'm afraid I didn't get the wording, it was so smarmy . . . something about his preferring to be known for the quality rather than the quantity of his work. The gist was, if we don't meet his demands he is going to have to dramatically up his output."

How much time did you buy us?"

"Until Friday. Then we have to either let them run it or hope the juicy stuff I promised if they don't will continue to seem like a good bargain to them."

Two days and whatever was left of this one. Not a lot of time, but she wasn't sure she could have done better.

"Nobody's going home tonight. As soon as that note arrives, I'll loop Evans in, the official response to burner boy is his call," Nigella said, taking a deep, determined, breath. "Meanwhile, let's get back to catching this bastard. We've got footage of two entrances at GG&S. Let's find Smyth leaving that damn building."

Nigella chose the back entrance for herself, because people who didn't want to be seen usually took the less public route. The footage was high resolution. Apparently the building's poshness extended to its cameras. A couple of people ducked out

for a smoke. The office cleaners arrived. One man in a cleaning jumpsuit trailed in a bit late. She stopped the replay, but he
appeared to be the real deal.

Nigella had just started fast-forwarding again when O'Leary
slapped the table.

"I've got Smyth! 7:19 PM. I'm telling you it's him leaving the
building, and he's *not* alone!"

Nigella rolled her chair over. Two men moved across the
lobby. One walked. The other staggered along with his arm over
the first man's shoulder. The guard looked up, said something,
and then laughed. Nigella couldn't see the face of the man assist-
ing the other, but she presumed he responded, because the guard
laughed again.

O'Leary froze the feed. "The fellow staggering has the
right build for Smyth." He put the image back in motion. The
semi-incapacitated man turned his head over his shoulder to
say something to the guard. O'Leary slapped the table again in
excitement. "It's Smyth. He looks steaming drunk, but someone
on Rohypnol would. He was drugged in the building."

"Workout clothes," Nigella said as the men moved out the
door. "Smyth's wearing workout clothes. He swiped into the
building's gym just before six PM. And now we know he left
the building about an hour and twenty minutes later—without
his suit."

"We need street footage! I'll call Mrs. Kay because GG&S
will doubtless have outdoor security cameras," Nigella said,
picking up the phone still sitting on her side of the conference
table, "and less red tape than London's finest.

"For the record, City Police are London's second finest."
O'Leary replied as Nigella dialed.

She shook her head at him. "How about you pick up that
phone you knocked to the floor and make arrangements. We're
headed to GG&S, sirens blaring."

"Time to hit the gym, eh?" O'Leary flexed an arm playfully,
but he had muscles. Not body-builder, beach-show-off muscles,
but hardworking ones. She remembered them vividly, braced
over her in bed, and banished the thought.

The fitness center was small, but state of the art. A building security guard swiped them in, asked the single occupant—a skinny twenty-something on a stationary bike—to collect her things and go, and then stood officiously outside.

Nigella and O'Leary went straight to the locker room, forensics trailing behind.

The third locker they tried was full. On the top shelf a pair of neatly rolled socks lay beside expensive cuff links. At the bottom, a pair of shiny brogues shared space with a gym bag. And hanging neatly right in front of them was a dark suit and a French-cuff shirt.

O'Leary expertly patted the jacket, then slipped a hand in. "Keys"—he drew them out, handing them to Nigella—"and wallet." He flipped it open. "Look at that gold stamp. It's a Bond Street wallet. Bet this thing costs more than I spend on groceries for a month. And sure enough"—he slid the first credit card from its slot to reveal the name Andrew G. Smyth—"it belongs to our victim." He patted around a bit more. "That's it."

"Bag it all," Nigella said to the team. "Dust the locker. We have no chance of getting prints off what remains of the presumed Andrew Smyth, but I want to know if we've got more than one set of prints in there. Remember our killer took Mr. Smyth's tie."

She and O'Leary walked back to the equipment room and stood looking at each other.

"You might voluntarily leave the gym in your workout clothes," she said at last, "but not without your wallet. That confirms what we suspected from the way he staggered on camera: Smyth was drugged right here."

"Bottle of water?" O'Leary speculated. "I mean nobody is throwing back a pint on the treadmill. Though that would be what it'd take to get me on one."

"What about covering the taste?" Nigella said.

"Does Rohypnol have a strong taste?" he asked. "I've never tried it. But I always thought what makes roofies such a favorite of club-creeper rapists is that they aren't easily detectable. And hang on . . . it didn't have to be water." He beckoned her back to the locker room doorway. Humming away in one corner was a vending machine containing everything from electrolyte-enhanced water to biliously colored sports drinks.

"The team has this covered," Nigella said. "Let's grab that additional security footage, head back to Wood Street, and see if that ugly note has arrived covered with 'star-reporter' finger-prints."

As they rode up in the elevator, Nigella pondered the absence of a mobile phone from the suit pockets. Of course, given Smyth's secretary had received a text from it at nine PM–ish that wasn't a surprise, but she wondered: had the killer forced Smyth to text before dying, or did the suspect know Smyth well enough to send those texts himself? The elevator doors opened, and still lost in thought, she stepped out into someone carrying a stack of folders.

"Nigella?"

It was James. What were the damn chances? Probably not as slim as her gut reaction suggested, Nigella conceded, eyes fixed on his eager and smiling face. After all, while there were finance firms stacked on top of each other in this part of the City, only two of London's top law firms had headquarters within sight of Monument Station. And though she might not have known much—or cared much—about James's work life, Nigella hadn't missed his constant string of complaints about commuting from Spitalfields to Monument Station. They'd struck her as particu-larly whiny because, whether by bus or train, it was under fifteen minutes travel time. But James frequently grumbled that there were two Silver Circle law firms on his doorstep in Spitalfields, and if he could just snag a job at one of them, then the time he "wasted" commuting could be "used creatively" instead.

"I didn't realize this was your building," Nigella said awk-wardly. She really couldn't think of anything else she was will-ing to say with O'Leary at her elbow.

"Yeah, this is where I slave away for pay. Hey, I'm sorry about going MIA this weekend. Family thing. Out of town. Short notice."

"You haven't introduced me to your friend, Parker." O'Leary looked mightily entertained. He stuck out his hand. "DI Colm O'Leary, Metropolitan Police."

"So you're the copper who calls at inconvenient times." James grasped the proffered hand and pumped it.

Nigella wanted to kick him in the shin. Or kick O'Leary. Or kick both.

"Being a detective isn't the best profession in terms of relationships," O'Leary said, maintaining a look of utter seriousness.

"I'm sure, Colm. You said Colm, right? But Nigella's worth it. I bet your missus feels the same about you."

O'Leary laughed. "Not sure any woman feels that way about me other than my mum."

"James," Nigella said, "DI O'Leary and I need to get a move on. We have a dead body and a killer on the loose."

"Catch you tonight?" He leaned in to give her a kiss, but Nigella sidestepped him.

"'Fraid not, mate," O'Leary answered with a smile. "Parker's told the team, nobody goes home tonight."

"Tomorrow then," James replied. Then he headed off down the hall.

"O'Leary, you tosser —you enjoyed that." Nigella crossed her arms.

"Of course." He cast a glance after the retreating James, "He's nearly as much of a workout king as our departed Mr. Smyth. If I were seeing someone ten years younger, you'd be throwing out jibes about men, sexism, and the objectification of younger women. But heck, Ni, I gotta hand it to you: Who doesn't want a nice younger piece when they can get it?"

"Five years, O'Leary. The gap is five. And it happens that James and I met at a gallery. He is a serious artist."

"I'll bet he is."

They picked up the flash drive containing footage from the front cameras. The first few blocks of the drive back to Wood Street passed in silence—at least on Nigella's part; O'Leary appeared to be keeping up a steady stream of conversation, but she was too steamed to listen.

Nigella wasn't sure why she was so irritated, or even at whom. At O'Leary? He'd teased her, but hell, he always did that, and she gave as good as she got. At James's territorial display? *Either he's less cavalier than his failure to text this weekend suggests, or just testosterone charged enough that he has to lay claim to me in front of a potential male competitor.*

She didn't like being laid claim to by anyone. James wasn't her husband or boyfriend; he *was* a nice young piece, as O'Leary had said, and she'd always been perfectly up front about that. Her mind skipped back to the moment O'Leary had pulled her out of the road earlier in the day: the feel of his arm around her, the implicit caring in the whole incident. Then her thoughts jumped to his quip about nobody thinking he was worth it outside of his mum. It was a great laugh line and showed a willingness to self-denigrate in front of her metaphorically chest-beating lover, but was it something more? *Christ, the last thing I need is guilt on top of an unsolved arson-murder. I mean just because I told the man he wasn't the love of my life doesn't mean I made him all low-self-esteem. Does it?*

"So what's her name, this woman you're seeing?" She interrupted O'Leary mid-sentence without having the least idea what he'd been saying.

"What? Is this 'show me yours 'cause I showed you mine'?"

"Yeah. You had a looky-loo at James, so who is the woman you won't be getting home to tonight?"

"Her name is Amy, and she doesn't have a key to my place yet. Does James have one to yours?"

"You know better than that. Did you have one? What does Amy do?"

"Primary school teacher."

"Perfect! She loves kids, you love kids." Nigella remembered how toddlers used to draw O'Leary's gaze when they were out together; how a baby in a highchair had once stopped him in his tracks, leaving her to arrive at their restaurant table alone.

"She's terrific. So let's park the car, watch that new footage, and solve this damn case before she gets tired of waiting for me to have my nights off."

Upstairs in their incident room, an envelope lay on the conference table. Nigella knew it was from the tabloid's "star reporter" before she slit it open. Who else would write "Attention: Detective Inspector Parker" in bubble letters more appropriate to the notebook of a girl in year nine at school?

No bubble words inside. Just the same, grim block lettering the killer had used on the back of Smyth's tie. "What a grisly piece of work." Nigella shook her head as she finished reading his latest note aloud. "I'll kick this up the chain of command, shall I?"

Evans began talking before she could cross the threshold of his office.

"Had a call from the Commissioner this morning. His wife's a friend of Sir John's. Wondered how we're getting on, blah, blah. We're under an unforgiving official spotlight on this one because our victim happened to be found by a nob of consequence. And now you hover in the door, looking like bad news. For the love of Christ, Parker, don't tell me you're at a dead end!"

"It's not that, sir." *Though in another couple of minutes you may wish it was.* "We have more leads than there are legs on a centipede. We've IDed the victim—just waiting for dental records to confirm—and we think we have our killer and the victim together on film the day before he died."

"But? Because nobody looks like you do right now, Parker, unless there is a big fat *but* coming."

"This." She handed him the note. "Delivered to a certain largest-circulation tabloid."

Evans scanned it. "Should've retired last year. Wouldn't have been at full pension, but still. When do they run it?"

"O'Leary bought and bullied us some time. Not before Friday—if at all. He negotiated an out."

"I don't want to know what O'Leary promised to buy them off." He grabbed a couple of heartburn chewables from a dish on his desk that should have held candy, and popped them in his mouth. "How far do I cave in to this nutter's demands?"

He tapped the note on his desk half a dozen times. "This isn't about pride. It's about practicality. We don't want to encourage the suspect to kill again. And we sure don't want him killing more people faster. But if we publish any of the stuff likely to assuage him, we could have a public in terror and newspapers coming up with Jack the Ripper–like bullshit to fan those flames. Even if we could be entirely certain publishing the note would placate the killer without starting panic in the streets, there are always unintended consequences. We don't want other crazies thinking they can make the papers if only they do something barbaric enough."

"A string of copycat body burners, sir, and I'll join you in retirement."

"Parker, you'll never retire. And neither will I. Not until they force us out. Get back to your desk and do what you do best. I'll handle this damn note. I'll also throw a couple of sergeants your way. Use them as extra arms, legs, and ears. But keep the brainwork for yourself and the Yard—he seems like a decent cop. And don't worry about overtime. This thing went from work-from-home to work-round-the-clock pretty damn quickly, didn't it?"

🔥

"Ni!"

Nigella jolted upright in her chair. Had she drifted off? How was that possible when she'd consumed at least six cups of coffee since leaving Evans's office hours ago?

"We're both knackered. We have to sleep," O'Leary said. "This case doesn't get solved tonight. If we run ourselves into the ground, we don't do our best work, and that does our suspect a favor."

"What time is it?" she asked.

"2:45 AM. And look at the whiteboard—we've crossed off a hell of a lot."

Their most significant progress had been the discovery that after the potential suspect shepherded Smyth out the front door, he'd led their victim into the parking garage of a nearby building. Moments later, a white Vauxhall Corsa hatchback had pulled out. Given the distance, there'd been no way to visually confirm who was driving it. But it was the suspect, without question, for one simple reason—something had been taped over the plates. At that time of the day, the driver couldn't hope to navigate the city with masked plates, so Nigella and O'Leary posited he'd have uncovered them sooner rather than later. They drew a circle on the map and submitted a request for urgent review of footage from every CCTV camera in the radius from the time the car emerged until thirty minutes later. The reviewers were gathering and running plate numbers for all white Corsas. They were also keeping an eye out for a man fiddling with plates on one.

But that was a hell of a lot of footage, and it would likely take days to get results. When they did, there would be dozens, if not hundreds, of Corsas to follow up on—they were a popular car.

O'Leary stood and stretched. "It's time to either hit the cots or hit the road."

Nigella glanced surreptitiously at her mobile. James had texted half a dozen times since they had run into him at GG&S. She wasn't so much interested in sex at the moment as in ferreting out if he knew Smyth. James, without knowing it, was poised to be her new man on the inside.

"Right, we knock off. I don't live that far. I'm heading home."

"Way to rub my nose in your fancy digs, Ni. I'll sack out here. See you in the morning. Maybe you could bring a colleague a breakfast sandwich?"

"You're pushing your luck, O'Leary."

"Always, Ni, always."

As soon as she was out of O'Leary's field of vision, Nigella texted James. Not as much of a longshot as it might have seemed. The tenor of his texts suggested a man waiting for an answer. Sure enough, by the time she'd reached the car, she'd heard he was headed to her place.

He was outside when she arrived.

"Thought your partner said nobody was going home tonight. You leave poor O'Leary at the station all alone?"

Crap, he was jealous. How annoying. She didn't answer, just swiped them in.

"He's not bad if you like that Irish look," he quipped as they rode the lift.

"He's a colleague, James, not a pinup. I mean, do you judge other artists by their looks?"

"Only if they are as hot as you, or hotter."

She opened the flat door. "So when you find someone hotter, you're off. That's entirely fair." She flicked on the lights, tossed her keys into the basket on the credenza, and set down her bag. James reached for her, but she pushed him away. "Tonight we talk first."

"You're not mad at me for having it on with your fellow rozzer are you?"

"If you mean do I wish you'd kept things professional when we ran into each other in a professional setting? Yeah, I do. But that is not what I want to talk about. Wine?" She knew she could murder a glass of Amarone. A pricey choice, but carpe diem; or maybe "drown the day" would be the more appropriate phrase—she'd have to ask O'Leary if there was Latin for that.

"Sure."

While she poured, he took a seat on the sofa.

"Tell me about life at Griffard, Gibbons and Smith. How long have you been there?"

"About four years." He took a glass from her. "Seems twice that. You have to think of time spent at Griffard in dog years. Why?"

"My case involves someone there."

"Really? Do tell!"

"Do you know a solicitor named Andrew Smyth?"

"Randy Andy? Yeah. I've had the—um, what is an appropriate way to put this?—misfortune of working with him on a couple of matters. Have one with him now. Talk about a pompous prat. The things he'll throw a paddy over."

Nigella held her glass to her nose, swirling it. The department had not officially identified the victim. That wasn't what worried her. She knew in her bones the body was Smyth. She was less certain whether James could be trusted. Leaks could ruin a career. *If they can be definitively traced . . . The name of the victim isn't your most confidential piece of information, and if James is going to be useful, he has to be tested.*

"He won't be pitching a fit over anything anymore," she said. "He's dead."

"Shit, now I feel bad for complaining." He took an enormous swig from his glass. "Okay, I don't, but still. Shit! How? When?"

"He's the man found outside Temple Church."

"The one someone burned to a crisp. Oh my God." He took another slug, then held out his glass for more.

"Yeah. It's pretty clear from everyone I've spoken with, including yourself, Smyth wasn't winning popularity contests—"

"Not sure I'd say that." He pointed to the chair opposite. "You mind sitting down? With you looming over me, I'm starting to feel like a suspect." He waited for her to settle in. "I bet you've been talking to people who worked for Smyth. But if you talked to the club, the boys who matter—at least in their own minds—you'd find he was liked well enough. A majority of the solicitors on the rise are of a pattern. And he fit right in. They only fall out when someone gets a case or a promotion that puts him ahead. We in the lower order—receptionists, secretaries, clerks, legal assistants like me—don't like most of them because we don't matter enough to be treated nicely." He drained the rest of his refilled glass and twirled it between his fingers. "There are exceptions, but Smyth wasn't one."

"Anybody with a particular grudge against him?"

"Plenty of secretaries left because of him. Plenty of legal assistants joked about slashing the tires on his fancy car. Is that the kind of talk murderers indulge in?"

Some of them. "Do me a favor: the identity of the victim is not public. Let's keep it that way."

"Sure."

"And can you keep an ear out? People talk more freely around their coworkers than around cops."

"You want me to play detective. Sounds like a good time." He appeared to be recovering from the shock of knowing a man burned to a crisp, because he set his glass on the side table and patted the seat next to him as if he expected her to jump up and move to it.

He really doesn't know me at all.

"Are we done talking?" He patted the cushion again.

"Not quite."

"Here comes the lecture. Listen, Nigella, I'm sorry I let your texts go. I had this thing in Surrey, and between my old man asking me if I've given up on 'the art thing' yet and my great-aunt insisting I look at her latest 'work,' it was complete rubbish. I couldn't think of anything clever or sexy to say."

"That wasn't where I was headed. Remember our talk about how figural sculptures are out of fashion? Well they're popular with my killer. You know anyone doing male figures?"

"Like the ones in that boat I swear we're going to see this week?"

"Yeah, but not androgynous—distinctly male, as in they have obvious genitalia."

"Ooooh, and are they well hung?" He was trying to be seductive, but Nigella found the comment utterly disgusting.

Note to self, Nigella thought: *Next time I need to find someone more mature, even just for sex.*

"Any idea who'd carve something like that out of wood?" she asked.

"Then burn them? Flaming wooden men—if someone is doing that, I don't know him. But that's provocative. Sort of on the performance-art side of things. Do you have pics?"

Nigella cursed herself for leaving her laptop at work. "Not with me."

"I'd be happy to come by the station. And not just to be helpful. It might be fun to spar with your friend O'Leary again. Are you sure he's not an admirer of more than your detecting talents?"

She thought of O'Leary on his standard issue police cot and made up her mind to hit the Caffè Nero nearest the station on the way in tomorrow and get him breakfast.

"Not at all. He's dating a Primary school teacher."

"Hmm." He looked unconvinced. "That's not as much fun as dating a copper. Primary school teachers don't have hand-cuffs." He held up his wrists with an unappealing wink. "How about it, Nigella? Drain your glass, take me to the other room, and restrain me. Tomorrow I'll come by the station on lunch and give you an opinion on your sculptor's work."

"Only if you behave professionally."

"With my artist hat on, I always do."

CHAPTER 11

Marylebone, London

Monday, September 10, 1666

The Bellands remained at Whitehall, and their apprentices were paid to be idle. So the workshop was theirs alone—Etienne and Margaret's—a place to be scientists: investigating not the stars, or the chemical coloration of rockets, but death.

"You do not have to be here," Etienne said, preparing to uncover the remains of Thomas Bradish on one of the long wooden tables ordinarily used to shape pasteboard for filling.

"Yes, I must; just as you sat with me as I told Agnes. That which is hardest is best done together."

Telling Agnes had been the worst moment of Margaret's twenty years. Done on the Lord's Day, it had not felt like His work. Nor had any amount of prayer since soothed Margaret or erased the image of her friend's eyes at the moment the dreadful truth was uttered.

And we may have more ugly words to speak . . . If Etienne is right, we will have to tell her Thomas's death was not merely an act of fate, but an act of man—no, the act of a monster.

"Besides," Margaret continued, picking up her pen, "who will take notes?" She turned her eyes to the page, eager to keep them there and away from the desiccated form Etienne must examine. "You have many talents, my love, but a legible script is not one." She heard a rustle of fabric accompanied by a sharp intake of breath. Then Etienne retched.

"And the man who brought him insisted he found nothing around or beneath the body?" Margaret asked, hoping that by keeping Etienne talking she could prevent him from losing his dinner.

"Yes. I made sure to show him my purse, but he swore he had nothing else to sell." He took several deep breaths. "I will begin with the pockets."

"Only a rosary," Etienne declared a few moments later.

Another trinket for Agnes. Will she find some comfort in it or in prayers said upon it? Or is she beyond comfort? Margaret wrote "rosary," watching the nib of her pen on the paper. *Pen . . . pen . . .*

"Thomas's ivory pen!" The moment of clarity was so abrupt that Margaret made an ink blotch on her page. "That's what has been bothering me! Thomas showed his favorite pen to Mister Archer on the steps of St. Paul's, yet we found it in the ruins of his shop. Thomas definitely returned home after the crypt was closed!"

"Good Lord, Margaret, you're right!"

"You needn't sound so amazed."

"I am not amazed at your intelligence—never that—but rather at my not thinking of this. Having made his way home, why did he abandon his plan of making for Marylebone? Why return to St. Paul's?"

Margaret wrote the questions down.

"Time to take a closer look at his head." The dread in Etienne's voice was palpable, yet Margaret, her curiosity proving stronger than her aversion, could not resist glancing in his direction.

Thomas had been turned on his right side, and Etienne stood with one leather-gloved hand on their friend's left shoulder. Etienne's face was ashen, his expression vexed. "I wish the hand was not so inconveniently placed." Thomas's right hand hovered, like a wrinkled crone's claw, just inches from his head. Etienne reached out a gloved finger, trying to move it without effect. "He is frozen like stone. But never mind." He tilted the body further forward, and stooped. "Yes, as I thought, there is a hole in the skull."

"Could such an injury have been suffered in a fall? Perhaps as the Cathedral caught fire and Thomas ran to escape, he slipped and cracked open his head on the floor."

"Perhaps," Etienne peered at the fractured skull, "but . . . if one falls on one's back, surely it is the rear of the skull that meets the ground, and this hole . . ." He paused and Margaret feared he'd lost the thread of his thought. Then with a start, he blurted out: "Will you lie on the floor for me?"

As Etienne eased the ruined body onto the table facedown, Margaret stretched out on the workshop's floor.

"Ah, the glamour of being a woman of science. Etienne Belland! Do not dare touch me with those gloves!"

"Sorry." Etienne blushed sheepishly, pulled off the gloves, and laid them aside. He squatted beside her, and Margaret shivered because the tilt of his head, the curiosity in his eyes as he slid his hands under her skull, cradling it with his fingers, all reminded her so closely of his posture and demeanor when he'd knelt beside Thomas at the Cathedral.

"Sit up, please. It is as I thought. The area of contact was a rough circle, perhaps three inches in diameter at the back of your skull." He offered a hand to help her rise. "Thomas's wound falls outside of that portion of his skull that would've struck the ground in a fall."

"People do not fall tidily," Margaret reminded him. "What if Thomas did not collapse directly onto his back?"

"Possible, but that is how he was found, and as we must begin somewhere, I think we ought to start with the hypothesis that he did, and see where that takes us."

Returning to the body, he pulled his gloves back on, and Margaret watched in sickly fascination as he stretched out an index finger and began to probe the edges of the cavity in the skull. "There are no bone fragments readily apparent. Is that not some evidence he was struck with enough force that they were pushed into his brain?"

"With the pries bar?" She cast a sidewise glance at the sinister iron rod lying further along the table.

"Well it *was* found beside him. I wonder would it do such damage?"

"Etienne, do not even consider bashing me in the head for scientific purposes. I will concede for sake of argument that the bar could inflict such a wound."

"But, I can tell from your tone, my dove, you are not unequivocally convinced he was knocked over by a blow."

"No. Something still bothers me." She watched as Etienne turned the body to a more respectful faceup position, trying to see it not as Thomas, but as a puzzle to be solved. "You hypothesize that he was struck a mighty blow from the right rear." She paused and bit her lip, closing her eyes and trying to imagine the events as if they were the scene in a play. "Given the location of the blow and its skull-shattering force, wouldn't Thomas have fallen on his side, not his back?"

"We must make an experiment," Etienne replied. "Come and stand behind me and bring the pries bar."

"I am no more willing to strike you than to be struck by you."

"You are not going to strike me. You are simply too short, my dear, for your hand to reach the spot on my head that we need."

"I will bring a stool then, foolish man, not a pry bar." Margaret lugged one of the apprentice's seats to behind him and climbed onto it. "Now, what precisely do you wish me to do?"

"Shove me here"—he touched a spot on his skull—"hard as you can. I will let my knees collapse, and we shall see which way I fall."

Margaret shoved and Etienne crumpled.

"You were quite right," he said cheerfully from his prone position, "I am on my left side with my left arm trapped beneath me."

"Not the position in which Thomas was found." Margaret looked down at him. "Therefore he must have moved once he fell . . . or been moved."

"Hmm. How are we to know if he moved himself or was merely turned over by some passerby or by his attacker, eager to be certain he was dead?" Etienne sat up, looking toward the table. "What, if anything, can the body tell us about that?"

Margaret's gaze followed his and locked on Thomas's arms—the one raised and partially obscuring his face, the other, which Etienne had complained of, impeding a view of his wound. Yes, there was a story there. Hopping down from the stool Margaret made a fist and drove it into Etienne upper arm with all her might.

"Ouch! Have you gone mad?"

"No, but I think I may have just proved that Thomas was alive when he fell. Look at what you've done."

Etienne glanced to where his left hand had risen reflexively to cover the spot where he had been struck. "You've lost me."

"Look at Thomas's right hand. It looks for all the world as if he was clutching his wound—something you've just proved is a very natural reaction."

Etienne's eyes lit up. "So as horrifying as the prospect is, we have evidence Thomas did not die instantly. And if he were alive, he might have rolled to his back, trying to get up."

"Or hoping to see his attacker. Lie back down as you were, only this time put your right hand on the spot where you were struck." As Etienne repositioned himself, Margaret quietly slid the pries bar off the table, hiding it in her skirts. "Now, try to get up." As he began to roll toward her, Margaret drew the iron bar from behind her, lifting it high into the air.

"What are you doing?" Etienne shouted, his left arm rising to shield his head and face.

"Look at your arm. You've done just what it appears Thomas did. His arm is raised as if he would fend off another blow." She dropped the bar to her side. "I'd call that a successful experiment."

"I'd call it terrifying."

"I am sorry." She held out a hand to him. "Perhaps you'd better have a closer look at that left arm."

"We need to get his coat off."

"Let's cut it away." Margaret grabbed a pair of shears from one of the workbenches, and set to cutting the sleeve. "My goodness," she said as she clipped away the shirt beneath and Thomas's flesh became visible. "The covered skin is the same color and texture as the uncovered."

"He dried. He did not burn. His clothing would not have provided much insulation, so his unexposed skin would be subjected to virtually the same withering heat as the exposed portions." Etienne eagerly tore away the remaining fabric of the sleeve. "Look, the skin on his forearm *is* split."

"So a second blow fell. How terrible." Margaret's voice cracked, and her lungs seized. It was not her infirmity leaving her breathless, but a sadness so deep it was paralyzing. There could be no question of a merciful fall anymore. Thomas had been maliciously wounded, helpless and doubtless terrified. "Men ought to die in peace. Whatever we tell Agnes, let's spare her knowing that he survived the first blow."

Etienne nodded solemnly. "I think the body can tell us no more." He draped the coverlet over it. "We have come to a conclusion our friend was murdered"—the word jolted Margaret, even though there was no denying its accuracy. "We know how. But we are left in an unsatisfactory place. A murder demands justice, and we cannot see that administered without knowing who struck Thomas down."

"Logic suggests that unless it was an unprovoked act of savagery, and surely such things are rare, his attacker had something to gain," Margaret said. "Cutpurses are an epidemic in London, but we have a purse and a rosary to rule out robbery. If not for his money, then why was Thomas killed?"

🔥

"Wren, you devil!" Evelyn swings open the door to the room at Gresham where we have been working these last days and strides in, shaking a finger at me. "You've been to see the King this morning."

"Of course I have." I straighten from my drawings and smile. "Doubtless Hooke began working on his ideas for a new London as the city was still in flames. Surely it is wise to beat those with better political connections but less talent to Whitehall."

"Careful my friend, lest I think you consider me one of that number." He moves to the table opposite mine, glancing down at his own nearly finished plans for a resurrected city.

"You are a very great talent, Evelyn, which is why it was even more important to beat *you* to the palace."

"You are a man entirely without scruples."

I look past him, out the window to the interior courtyard, neatly divided into four triangles by paths I have walked lost in thought so many times these last days, considering whether I am indeed unscrupulous. Asking myself and my God whether there is a difference in His eyes between a premeditated sin and an impulsive—nay, better say an accidental—one? As my qualms over what I have done, both planned and *ex tempore*, have ebbed and flowed, the answer to my friend's question is the one thing that has become clear to me.

"No," I reply, meeting his eyes once more, "I am not a man without qualms. I am simply a man possessed, as by a demon, with a vision of what London can be when it rises like a phoenix from the ashes."

"You certainly work as if you are possessed. You even sleep here." He casts a disapproving glance at the accommodation of sorts I have assembled for myself in the corner: a cot, a mirror, a basin, a chamber pot, a scattering of books, a stack of folded garments.

"Where else should I sleep? I was burned out of my lodgings."

"You know very well you might stay with us at Sayes Court."

"In Deptford? I thank you for your offer, but that is more than four miles. And with the need to secure boat crossing of the river, thanks to the bridge being unusable, it is a hard four miles. That, my dear Evelyn, is why your model is behind mine."

"And you, it seems have seen and seized opportunity in that."

"It is very rich to hear you speak of opportunity, given you are a Privy Counsellor with the King's ear. You mustn't be greedy, Evelyn. It's one of the seven deadly sins. You have so many advantages that, as a sportsman, you ought not begrudge me the small benefit of a head start."

My friend makes an exasperated noise and shakes his head, but smiles. "You realize, Wren, whereas I am only vexed, the rest of our fellows in the Royal Society will be furious. Your model should have presented for review. You will be chided."

"But not chastened. Tell me, do you plan to submit your model?" I gesture to his nearly completed scale representation of the chief points of his plan. "You need not answer, for I know you are no fool, and only a fool would allow such an important work to be delayed and diluted by committee."

"Well, now that you have set the precedent . . ." He smiles again, then leans forward, hands on table. "So how did it go?"

God love him for always being my eager audience.

"His Majesty was, and I say this in all humility, wildly enthusiastic." I take a flourishing bow. "You may expect to see my plans at your next meeting of the Privy Council."

"Wren, you and humility are not well acquainted, but still, I am glad for you. You have made your thrust; you must expect me to parry. I shall pick nits in Council."

"If you intended to so, you should not have helped me find the weaknesses in my plans these last days."

"My plan is also strong. I pretend no humility in saying so. You are a man of grand dreams, Wren, but I shall prevail in the details."

He may be right. Evelyn has been to Rome, the most admired city on the continent. He has seen Pope Sixtus V's renewal of it, walked its beautifully paved and organized streets, and stared up at the soaring Dome on St. Peter's—a thrill I can only imagine. And he has practical experience in the construction of roads and sewers, having been Royal Commissioner for both. Evelyn was dissecting and critiquing London long before I turned my eyes from the study of the heavens to the study of earthly docks and dwellings.

But surely, surely, vision is what matters most.

I can help King Charles raise a city on London's rubble that will make Paris, and perhaps even Rome, forgettable. Kings desire such legacies . . . so do I. I glance at my plans, at the dome of my new St. Paul's, and hear a single word in my head is if whispered by an angel: *Resurgam.*

"Agnes, I am sorry to make you go through this." Margaret reached out in a rustle of silk and covered her friend's hand where it clutched a handkerchief in her lap. Agnes sat rigid in a high-backed chair with heavily scrolled arms that suggested Thomas's elder sister, in whose withdrawing room they were gathered, could afford to follow the latest fashions. Silent tears rolled down her face—an image strikingly contrasted by a baby's joyful babbling. Etienne had little Raphe in his arms and circled the room, bouncing the boy to entertain him.

"No, no, there is more pleasure than pain in remembering Thomas. After all, memories are all I have, and if, as you say, he was taken from me not by God, but by some evil person, then I owe it to his memory to help you discover who."

"We will do all we can to see justice done," Margaret said. "Proverbs teaches, 'Destruction shall be to the workers of iniquity.'"

Agnes sat in silence for some moments, brow furrowed. "I am sorry, but I can think of no one who profits by Thomas's death. We had no vast fortune, just a comfortable business, and now that is gone. We live moment to moment on the charity of his good sister, and if we did not have that . . ." Her voice trailed off, and she pressed the handkerchief to her nose and mouth.

"We keep thinking"—Margaret nodded in Etienne's direction—"that Thomas's death must have something to do with St. Paul's. Not only because he was found there, but because his last hours all come back to that place: from packing the crypt to returning for some purpose we have yet to divine."

Margaret paused, watching the wax drip down the side of a candle on the mantel, and thinking how much better the world would be if a blue and white vase sat there and Thomas sat beside Agnes.

"Agnes, could someone have discovered during those hours at the crypt that Thomas was Catholic?"

"His closest friend, Archer, knew already, but Thomas was very careful. We both were. We attended services at St. Faith's occasionally as a sort of disguise, and he never failed to mark important Company occasions there. And truly, Margaret, in a time of flame and terror, do you think anyone would care so deeply about religious nonconformists that they would delay their own escape to kill one?"

Margaret blushed scarlet—knowing she was one of the *they*. "People were beaten and killed for being foreign as they fled the city—accused of starting the blaze."

Etienne stopped behind her, resting a hand on her shoulder. "But Thomas was not foreign. And while Catholics have, after the fact, been lumped with the foreign-born as possible conspirators in a fire our King ascribes to God, it is hard to imagine how one would be picked out in the midst of the conflagration. I have a French accent, but there is not a Catholic one."

"There is something or someone we are missing." Margaret slapped the dark, barley-twist-legged table beside her in frustration. "We know Thomas passed hours at the Cathedral with his fellow Stationers, but we can none of us imagine why they might want to kill him—"

"No, the Company men are like family," Agnes agreed.

"—and we know, thanks to his ivory pen, that he left St. Paul's, but have no way of knowing who he met on his way to your shop; if someone was waiting for him there; or if, when he returned to St. Paul's, he did so alone."

In motion once more, Etienne gave a deep, exasperated sigh, which set little Raphe giggling. "What about the other end of things?" Etienne asked. "Agnes, you told us before Thomas left the shop on the day you parted, someone knocked."

"Yes."

A moment that she and Etienne had spent with the Stationer's clerk clicked into place in Margaret's mind. "I know who it was!"

"You know? You know who knocked at Paternoster Row?" Etienne looked at her incredulously.

"Not in the sense of having a name, but the man who knocked was the author of the plan for securing the Stationers' goods inside St. Paul's."

Agnes looked astonished, but Etienne nodded.

"Agnes, you told us that as the pounding began, Thomas had agreed to leave London, admitting that he had no idea how to preserve your shop or its contents."

"Yes."

"Yet George Tokefield said that Thomas arrived at the Company Hall with a fully formed plan for putting the Company's wares in the Cathedral vault."

"Damn him!" The words burst from Agnes with furious force. "Damn the man, whoever he is. He might as well have murdered Thomas himself. Had Thomas come with me that day, he would be alive."

"Think, Agnes, think." Etienne set the baby in her lap. "When you entered the shop and glimpsed Thomas leaving, who else did you see?"

Agnes closed her eyes, holding little Raphe tight. "Thomas held the door for . . . that professor . . . the one who bought so many books on French architecture. His name sounds like a bird." Her lips grew thin with concentration. Then her eyes snapped open. "Doctor Wren."

Margaret and Etienne left Agnes with Thomas's rosary and went out into the street. "I may have fooled the Stationers at Gresham, but I do not believe I can pass as an earl with Doctor Christopher Wren," Etienne said as they climbed into his family carriage. "And even were that not the case, how are we to find him?"

"He will find us—or rather me."

"What?"

As the vehicle jolted into motion Margaret enjoyed his look of amazement, relishing the idea that Etienne thought her a seer, because generally he was the magician, lighting the skies. Then she smiled and said, "Wren was at Whitehall yesterday. I recognized him outside His Majesty's apartments. Under other circumstances, I would have mentioned it, but spotting a Royal Society scientist is a rather a trivial thing given the serious matter that occupies us. Or rather say, it seemed trivial—now it seems fate."

"Fate toying with us. We've missed our opportunity to speak with him because we did not know we needed to."

"Fate is kinder than you think." She took his hand. "I told you Wren will find me, and so he shall. Yesterday, he presented the outline of a plan for rebuilding London. The King was effusive in his praise of it to Her Majesty, and promised she should hear the whole of Wren's presentation herself when he returns with additional drawings. While we wait for that event, I will make my interest in architecture better known to the Queen."

🔥

This man has the talent to make London the wonder of the world. Margaret's gaze followed Wren's hand as it swept from the rendering of a new piazza surrounding a rebuilt Exchange to a stunning Grand Terrace along the Thames, where ships could dock on the doorsteps of Halls built for the city's prominent Companies. She was utterly dazzled, so swept up in Wren's narrative she nearly forgot her true purpose in being present—until he mentioned St. Paul's.

"It is only fitting that the greatest church in London should sit like a jewel at its center. See, Your Majesties, how the new St. Paul's Cathedral, topped by a dome that will bring it into this century, can be glimpsed in all its radiant, faith-inspiring glory, not only from the whole length of Fleet Street but from this royal palace as well." He gently touched the miniature dome, its whiteness sparkling in the candlelight, then gave a little bow to indicate he had concluded.

The Queen offered a smile. The select group of ladies surrounding her applauded. Margaret joined them even as she wondered if she would ever be able to look at St. Paul's, even in a beautiful new incarnation, without seeing the lake of fire it had become . . . without seeing Thomas's shriveled body on the table in the Marylebone workshop.

He is in the ground now. Etienne saw to that. Margaret had never been to a Catholic Mass, but she'd gone to the one said for Thomas—face covered, hand on Etienne's arm. And she'd watched, transfixed, as Agnes fingered the beads of the rosary they'd found on her dead husband.

As Wren carefully moved his model to one side of the table, a second gentleman moved his own to the now-vacant spot in preparation for addressing the gathered courtiers. Margaret recognized him as a member of the Privy Council. He, too, they'd been told, had a vision for the next London. But she did not have the luxury of hearing John Evelyn's presentation. As Wren answered a few last questions from the King, she leaned forward and whispered to the Queen, "Your Majesty, if I might be excused. My heart beats so quickly . . . the plans were, perhaps, too exciting."

She felt guilty for preying upon the Queen's compassion. But as Margaret rose in response to Her Majesty's nod, and dipped low in a parting curtsey, she reminded herself that her true reason for begging leave was far more worthy than her false one.

Margaret had chosen her spot carefully, down the Queen's back stairs in the passage leading to Pebble Court. She did not have long to wait. He was smiling and humming as he came.

"Doctor Wren."

He stopped two paces past her and spun round. He was surprised, clearly, but there was something more—because surely the confusion in his eyes ought to have faded once he recognized her as a lady of the court.

Odd.

"Forgive me, Mistress, I did not notice you. My mind was on my work."

"To produce a plan for an entire city so soon after it burns, I would assume, sir, your mind has been continually upon your business these last days."

"I saw you in Her Majesty's chambers."

Something about the way he said it made Margaret's senses thrum like the plucked string of a harp. It was as if he were answering an unspoken question rather than recounting a fact. *Some part of his mind remembers me from a glimpse at Bradish and Son.* She felt it to be true. And not on instinct alone, for this evening she had sat off to one side and directly behind another of the Queen's ladies, a spot where it seemed very unlikely Wren would have noticed her.

"Indeed, sir, I was fortunate to be privy to your dreams for a new London."

"Plans, not dreams, please. Dreams so often come to nothing. Did you like them?"

"Very much. I was particularly struck by your design for St. Paul's." Margaret paused, searching for a way to sum up how Wren's eyes had changed when he'd spoken of the Cathedral, how he had suddenly shifted from broad strokes, to a collection of minutia. "You have considered that sacred place in such detail. I believe, sir, that the Cathedral is a burning passion for you."

A slash of color crept up the side of his neck. "Oh, I would not say *burning*"—he gave an awkward laugh—"particularly in light of recent events. But yes, I have given St. Paul's a great deal of thought because I've had the honor of serving more than three years on His Majesty's Commission considering how it could best be restored or rebuilt."

"The Cathedral is beyond restoring now, so perhaps you will be trusted with the rebuilding, and we will see your beautiful dome rise over a once-again-bustling London."

Instantly, his eyes glowed with the same ambitious passion she'd seen in them that day in Paternoster Row. And again she could not look away, which was just as well because his reaction to her next statement was important.

"It is still impossible to believe St. Paul's is gone, and with it our mutual friend"—Margaret paused a beat; was he holding his breath or did she only imagine it?—"Thomas Bradish."

Wren's face went pale, making the red that now climbed as far as his ear more pronounced. "Who?" The question burst forth in a tone more angry than inquisitive.

Why react in such a violent manner to a harmless statement? Why pretend not to recognize the name? He has something to hide. Margaret's heart pounded such that she could hear a swooshing of blood in her ears, but she was not cowed—she was excited.

"Thomas Bradish, the bookseller," she replied, pausing to breathe with deliberate steadiness, trying to slow her heart before she saw telltale flashes of light. "I apologize if I have upset you, Dr. Wren. Perhaps this is the first you have heard of his demise. But he is dead, and his sad remains were found in the ruined nave of St. Paul's."

He took a small, almost stumbling step backward. Then recovered himself, placing a hand, rather deliberately Margaret thought, on his hip and striking an indifferent pose. "I am very sorry to hear that a gentleman has died, Mistress, but you are mistaken if you believe *I* knew him." The red on his neck bled into his cheeks.

"Perhaps you do not remember the name, Dr. Wren, but I know you were a patron of his shop in Paternoster Row, for he spoke of you, and your purchases are in his ledger."

Wren's smile wavered—twitched. The lie about the ledger had paid off. "I bought books from so many. They are a great indulgence of mine. Perhaps I did buy some from your friend. What did this fellow, Bradish, look like?"

My goodness how he scrambles . . . like a courtier who has misspoken before the King and turns somersaults to redeem himself.

"He was about your height, sir, with gold hair and beard, and a mole just here." She placed her index finger just next to her right eye. Wren flinched as if she had instead touched his face. "His was the shop with the globe-topped books upon its sign."

Wren put a hand to his chin and cocked his head as if thinking, but his eyes were piercing, not thoughtful—fixed upon her as if she were a serpent. "Ah, that gentleman." He shifted from foot to foot. "I did indeed buy books from him; and a very honest tradesman he was. As he was *your* friend, may I offer condolences. I am sorry to hear he was lost in the fire."

"Yes, well, he and all his fellows in the Stationers' Company were at St. Paul's putting their worldly goods into the vault of St. Faith's . . . but then you know that."

Margaret took a breath, intending to attribute the plan to him—to call it brilliant if ill-fated. But the words froze in her throat. Wren's eyes had narrowed, and he advanced on her rapidly, hands at his sides clenched into fists.

"Why do you say that?" he growled.

Margaret took a step back, mind searching for a path of retreat. "Only that doubtless you are as well informed as we." She widened her eyes, hoping to look innocent and girlish. "All the court has heard the story of the crypt—how the poor Stationers moved their paper there to no avail; how the crypt burned, turning the floor of the great church into a lake of fire." Not a single muscle in his face relaxed, so she babbled onward. "Have you walked the ruins of St. Paul's while considering your plans? They must be something terrible to see." She gave a playacted shudder.

"All such terrifying destruction will be wiped away." Wren paused in his advance, and the hands at his sides relaxed slightly. His eyes burned once more. "And in its place I will create such beauty. The cathedral I build will be a fitting tribute to your friend, to all who died in the fire. It will comfort their loved ones and salve the wounds of those, like the Stationers, who lost so much."

Margaret did *not* feel comforted, because while his passion for architecture rang true, so much of what he had said was still, inexplicably, false. *Men with clean consciences do not bellow, bully, or lie.*

For so long she had wanted to meet Wren, to discuss telescopes, microscopes, the current experiments of the Royal Society. But now, with the hair on the back of her neck on end, Margaret only wanted him gone, and blessed the fact that their unequal ranks meant she had the power to send him.

"I will not keep you, sir." Margaret meant to say it commandingly, but her voice cracked, and Wren's eyes narrowed again. He took a further step toward her.

Margaret began to extend her hand, both as a means of stopping his advance and a reminder of her rank, then snatched it back. For the thought of his lips brushing her knuckles was horrible. And what if he grabbed her hand, pulled her into the darkness of Pebble Court?

"Why would one of Her Majesty's ladies know a bookseller in Paternoster Row?" The question echoed off the stone of the passageway.

"You forget yourself." Margaret summoned her self-command, speaking as she had to the butcher who'd come searching for Etienne. But unlike that fellow, Wren did not flinch, bow, or scrape.

"Perhaps." He tilted his head. His gaze was so searching that she could barely stand still beneath it. "*If* you are who you say you are. But I have seen you somewhere else, and I think you are not. I think your dress is as false as your smile."

His tone was no longer just suspicious; it was dangerous. Panic welled inside Margaret. *If I turn and run, will I make it to the top of the stairs?* Yet surely up would be better than out into a dark and deserted courtyard. She gathered her skirt in her hand, preparing to bolt. As she did, one of Wren's hands rose, reaching for her arm. But before he could grab her, a breathless Simona raced down the stairs.

"There you are! Her Majesty calls for you." Simona took Margaret's free hand.

As she was pulled along, Margaret cast a backward glance at Wren. The menace in his eyes had given way to abject confusion, and his mouth hung open like a man struck momentarily dumb, mad, or both.

"How did you . . . ?" Margaret asked as they gained the top landing and Simona reached for the door.

"Etienne."

Of course. Etienne.

Margaret had forgotten, as Wren became threatening, that Etienne was listening, halfway up the stairs. Now he waited on the other side of the door, and as Simona left them with a shake of her head, and Margaret began to tremble is if she had a palsy, he said, "My God, Margaret, what if Wren is not only scientist but murderer?"

CHAPTER 12

Present-day London

Wednesday

"Real coffee? Ni, I love you." O'Leary reached for the takeaway cup.

"Breakfast too." Nigella handed him the bag. "I must be going soft."

"Your kindness will not go unrewarded. I have things for you." He pointed to the rolling chair next to his. Then, reading the question in her expression. "I slept like shite. There's only one thing we police types do when we can't sleep, right? So first, for your viewing pleasure, I have the only person who dropped anything in that damn tabloid tip box between when it was emptied Monday night and when their intrepid non-reporter called."

He opened a tab to reveal a figure carrying a floral umbrella and wearing a belted, checked, trench coat, approaching the box with purposeful but unhurried steps. They dropped something in the slot, then moved briskly away.

"At first glance, I thought woman accomplice. But size and the way the figure moved seemed wrong, and those are men's shoes." O'Leary froze the image and pointed. "I had a moment of sleep-deprived excitement over that little discovery, thinking the suspect had been sloppy, but let's face it: we're not going to trace him using standard lace-up oxfords."

"Yeah." Nigella said. "A glimpse of his face—now that would be a lead. But that's why the clever bastard carried the umbrella. He thinks about camera angles. He thinks about choosing clothing that's memorable so that nobody remembers the person wearing it. He thinks, period. I'd be impressed if his attention to detail wasn't killing this investigation." Nigella shook her head. "Still, good work. What else do you have?"

"Greedy! Just let me take a bite of my breakfast. I did some reading on the column next to the Temple Church. It's called the Knights Templar Column or Templar Statue after the church's history and those knights on the top. It may look Gothic, but it's modern. Its design was modeled on the marble columns inside Temple Church."

"Now you're just showing off."

"Point is, it was put up in 2000."

"So no Wren connection. There goes our best idea for how the fires locations are linked."

"Not so fast. There is a handy informative sign in Temple courtyard, and also, thanks to technology, on the internet. The column was placed at the spot where the Great Fire was allegedly extinguished and"—he reached for his yellow pad—"'the church was saved and in it the old gothic order survived. The column thus contrasts with Sir Christopher Wren's monument in the City, which stands where the fire started and marks the arrival of the new classical order.'"

"Holy shit, that's blinding! So the placement of Smyth by the column alludes to the Great Fire and also to a shift in artistic styles in the direction of Wren."

"Bet you're glad you brought me breakfast now."

"Keep this up and I may buy you lunch." *Only not today,* she thought. James would be popping by today.

"One more thing. Lab boys called. Dr. Phillips's instinct was right—the nails are old, really old. Based on mineral content, shape and some additional sciency stuff, we're talking eighteenth-century old."

"Really?"

"Yep. So what time do you think the Tweedles will be back at it?"

As promised, Evans had given them two skippers. Nigella had assigned one to follow up on Sir John's list and the other to verify Nelson Taylor's vacation. Although both were competent cops with actual names, O'Leary had immediately dubbed them Tweedledum and Tweedledee.

"I had texts from both while I was in line at Caffè Nero. Their plates are full for the morning; time for us to fill ours. What say we focus on figuring out who could have accessed Taylor's van while he was sunning in Spain? Spiffy S11 is still our one irrefutable link to all three incidents."

"Spiffy on speaker, got it." O'Leary asked for the vice president they'd spoken to before, then, pleasantries over, pushed the "Speaker" button and set the receiver in its cradle.

"We have a few additional questions about access to your vans and their keys."

"Of course, Detective. We're all sick over the fact that anything related to Spiffy might have been involved in a crime."

"The spare fleet keys, how easy would it be for someone to take one?" O'Leary asked.

"Without somebody knowing about it? Impossible."

"Detective Parker here. Why impossible?"

"The box is behind the counter in the office. Anyone wanting a key has to speak to the dispatcher."

Didn't sound particularly impossible to Nigella. "We'd like you to check with whoever worked the desk starting the Friday before last and going through this past Monday, to see if anyone borrowed the key for S11."

"That'd be Emma. Hang on." There was a sharp, annoying crack as the VP set the phone down on something hard. Then they heard a door and some muted voices.

"And to think, police interviews on BBC cop shows look glamorous and dramatic," O'Leary said.

Nigella put a finger to her lips.

"Detective Parker?"

"Yes, still here."

"Emma says nobody asked for S11."

"What about after hours. Could someone take the keys while she is not on the desk?" O'Leary asked.

"The office is locked after eight PM weekdays and on week-ends. Building access is electronic. Crews can get in the main doors with their IDs, access the supply room or the locker room. But the office is office staff only off-hours."

"You said electronic; does that mean there is a record of entries?" Nigella asked.

"Yes. And we make certain the staff knows that." He low-ered his voice. "Our people are good people, Detective, but our margins aren't huge. We can't afford for supplies to go missing."

"Can you check the entries for us?"

"I don't have to. For the reason I just alluded to, my secre-tary prints a report any time there is anything odd, so I can fol-low up. In the last two weeks, there's only been one report, and it had to do with an employee who dropped her watch and was searching. No questionable swipes into the office."

O'Leary grabbed the receiver and said their goodbyes while Nigella sat cursing under her breath.

"We have a van we know was rolling around the city with our killer in it, but he didn't get the keys from that blasted box, so how was he driving it?"

"Copy?" O'Leary posited. "Maybe Emma has a boyfriend or husband, and she made him one or let him hang out at her desk? Maybe Taylor or his girlfriend from payroll made one for some reason?"

"What, and just left it lying around where the suspect hap-pened to find it?"

"You got any better ideas?"

"I've got nothing," she said disgustedly. "Well, not exactly nothing, because either way the suspect has to know someone who works at Spiffy. And that means someone at Spiffy knows him—maybe knows more than they're saying."

"If this were a BBC drama, we'd interview them all, and someone would crack," O'Leary said.

"You have to stop watching that stuff, O'Leary."

"Can't, addicted. Though I'll admit part of the fun is yelling at the TV about how it doesn't happen that way. I mean can you imagine if clever Endeavour Morse had to sit and wait weeks for DNA test results? That'd make for scintillating viewing."

"Let me text Tweedle two—"

"Which one is he, 'dum' or 'dee'?"

"O'Leary, call a cop with the City Police dumb, however you spell it, and you're asking for it. Let me text two and ask him to find out if Taylor took his keys on vacay." She was one sentence into the text when one of the phones on the table rang.

"DI Parker."

"Detective, this is Sarah Ellis, Vicar at St. James's Piccadilly. I don't believe we've met. I tried to reach Detective O'Leary at the number he gave me, but was redirected here."

"DI O'Leary is right beside me if you need to speak to him."

"I'm sure you can help me, that is, if I even need helping. It's just that one of the regulars who sleeps here came to me this morning, troubled. He was here the night of the fire, and the next day I told all our guests it was important they think back and let me know if they remembered anyone around who didn't belong, or anything odd. So today this gentlemen told me that a week or so before the fire, someone new was hanging out with the lads in the alley and sitting with them where they panhandle."

"Reverend Ellis, is this fellow there with you now?"

"No, but I know where I can find him."

"Would you do that for us? DI O'Leary and I can be there in twenty minutes."

"I will."

"Shall we come to the rectory?"

"I think Neil would be more comfortable in the church itself. He has a favorite pew."

"Thank you, Vicar, we'll be there directly." Nigella hung up and rolled her chair away from the table. "Come on O'Leary— we're off to St. James's. This is the most regularly I've been to church in ages."

"Your ground, your interview," Nigella said as they approached the gate.

"If I'm in charge, we hit the takeaway first." O'Leary popped into the Caffè Nero next to the church and came out with a large coffee and a bag.

"You just ate! I don't know how you keep that figure."

"Wiry is in my genes, but this stuff's not for me."

The Vicar met them inside the church door. "I have to warn you, Neil is nervous. He's had some not-so-pleasant encounters with the police."

"Sorry to hear that," O'Leary said. "The next time that happens to Neil or any member of your flock, I want you to call me."

The Vicar smiled, then gestured down the center aisle. Despite how developed the surrounding neighborhood was, a surprising amount of sun shone through the windows at the far end of the church. It was magnified by an abundance of white paint, including on a lovely, vaulted ceiling touched with gold. Four rows from the front, a man sat near one of the square wood columns that supported the balcony.

As the Vicar joined him, O'Leary slid into the pew just in front and Nigella followed. "My name is Colm O'Leary," he said, turning over the back of the bench. "Pleased to meet you."

The homeless man pressed against the bench behind him, eyes open wide. "There's two of 'em," he murmured to the Vicar. "You didn't say there'd be two."

"Oh, I'm sorry; this is Detective Inspector Parker," O'Leary gestured toward her with the bag of food. "Thanks for agreeing to talk with us. It's pretty early for this sort of thing. I've just finished my breakfast. Wasn't sure if you'd had yours, so I brought you this." He held out the bag. "Didn't know what you'd like, so I got the bacon and the sausage."

The man reached out tentatively, pulled back, and then reached out again, taking the bag. He didn't open it, just tucked it inside the oversized parka he was wearing, a coat far too warm even for brisk autumn weather.

"Oh, there's this too." O'Leary held out the cup. "Hope black is okay."

This time there was no hesitation.

"Now, Neil, the Vicar tells us there was a new bloke hanging round before the fire."

"Youngish fellow."

"Is that what made you notice him? Or is it just rare to see someone new?"

"Oh, people come and go, and we get some that are young. Sad that. Whole lives ahead of 'em, but they're on the street—drugs mostly, or family troubles. They have a certain look about 'em, though, that this bloke didn't have: sort of broken, empty eyed, or sometimes desperate." He paused for a moment and looked around the church, whether searching for words or recoiling from this much social contact Nigella couldn't guess. But she took her arm off the back of the bench separating them, to give him more space.

"This bloke's eyes were like yours, or hers. No troubles in 'em."

Nigella fought the urge to laugh. On very little sleep, with a murder case that wasn't getting solved, the last thing she felt was untroubled. Then she realized Neil meant the deeper sort of worry experienced by someone who didn't know where he would sleep or whether he would eat, and her cheeks warmed in embarrassment.

"And he didn't seem like he was living on the streets. He had the clothing—layers for the weather, some of it patched. Not as neatly as mine." He raised a knee to show off a square patch carefully stitched. "But it was off. Sort of a put-on, if you know what I mean."

"Sorry, I don't," O'Leary said.

"He was too clean for one. I don't mean face and hands, but when he reached for something his wrists were clean. I don't care how often you hit a shelter for a shower. Even if you sleep here"—he stroked the surface of the bench next to him lovingly—"the street leaves a layer. And he wasn't wary. He was like a puppy, friendly to everyone, sidling up to Joe and me because we've been here longest. Wanting to know stuff."

"What sort of stuff?'

He shook his head almost violently. "It wasn't the *what* really, not mostly. I mean when someone new moves into this patch, they always want to know where the best places to panhandle are and whether we get bothered or roughed up by . . . you know."

"The cops."

"Which ones are mean, how often they come round. And questions about St. James's, like is it really open all night? That's a common one 'cause there's not many churches in London as welcoming as St. James's. Someone new comes into this part of the city, they mostly can't believe it.

"I think that's why I didn't notice—I wasn't sure until after, and even then I had to think about it. If he'd asked the same questions, and then stayed . . ." Again he stared out into the church again.

"You mean you think it's suspicious that you haven't seen him since the fire?" O'Leary urged.

"No, I mean he never slept here. He asked all about sleeping here. Couple of weekends he was here for breakfast. But he never slept here—so why did he want to know how late it was open and if the police came round more after dark?"

Good question, Nigella thought. *Damn good question.*

"And another thing, that last day he forgot his money."

"How do you mean?" O'Leary tilted his head.

"When some of us keep company, say, outside the takeaway place at the corner of Piccadilly and Swallow, we always divvy up the dosh. And that last day he didn't take his share."

"When was this?"

"Before the fire."

"Can you be more specific?"

The man shook his head "no"—or rather it started that way and transformed into a shaking fit of sorts. The vicar put a hand on his shoulder.

"Neil is not a man who lives by calendars, Detective," she said. "And that's just fine, Neil." She nodded reassuringly.

"Yes, it is," O'Leary said. Though there was no chance he meant it.

"Neil," the vicar said, "there was something else you mentioned. Remember? About the cameras."

The man shuddered.

"Always watching. Man can't take a piss without wondering who is watching him take it out," he mumbled. "Lots of us older ones don't like the cameras. Young ones, they grew up with everyone watching. Do you like that?" He peered at O'Leary. "Do you like watching me take a piss?"

"Actually, the camera footage is not monitored in real time. The police only look if we have a reason to, say, because a crime's been committed."

"I think you like it. Not you maybe—you seem like a decent sort—but the others. What was I saying?"

"Young people grew up with CCTV."

"Right. Somebody has been watching 'em since forever. When younger blokes come to stay, they mostly have a fuck-you attitude toward the cameras. I've seen 'em flip 'em off and drop their drawers and show their bare arses to 'em. I've even seen some of 'em shoot up right where there are cameras. I'm not giving you any names." He narrowed his eyes.

"I'm not asking," O'Leary replied.

"But this fellow was crazy worried about 'em. I remember walking back here from the bins behind that French bakery where folk pay more than two pounds a cookie—can you believe that?"

"Barmy," O'Leary agreed.

"You're telling me. Anyway, it was one of the lads' birthdays and we were looking in the bakery's bins for something sweet to celebrate. Walking back, every couple of yards this bloke was asking, 'Can they see us now? Where are they?' But then when Joe started to raise a hand, he yelled, 'Don't point.' So I says to him, if you don't like 'em looking, then you'd do best to stay close to St. James's. Vicar won't let the fuzz have cameras there. And he got real excited, kept mumbling something. Then I told him, the buildings on Piccadilly and Jeremy streets still have cameras, so there's that. But none in the churchyard proper and none pointing directly at St. James's."

"What about the little street that runs alongside, Church Place?" O'Leary asked. "You talk about that?"

"Yeah, I told him—sorry, vicar—that it's my favorite place to relieve myself 'cause no cameras period. It's like being in your own lavatory. And you aren't suddenly lit up by some bugger's headlights 'cause Church Place is just for walking. When we got back here, we thought he'd stay for a cookie and to divide up the bronze, but he disappeared."

"He didn't take his money and then you never saw him again." O'Leary closed the loop.

Neil leaned forward. He was so close that Nigella smelled his decaying teeth. "I think I *did*. I think I saw him at the concert." He sat back and turned to the Vicar. "Is it time? Where are the programs?"

"Don't worry Neil, it's not time and I have the programs in my office. We host lunch concerts here each Monday, Wednesday, and Friday. Neil is a big help with those."

"And this fellow came back for one of the concerts?"

"Not this one." He looked at the vicar.

"No, that's right, Neil, because this one hasn't happened yet."

"Not Weber. I don't like Weber." Neil shook his head vigorously and then tipped it back and looked at the ceiling.

"Was it Shostakovich?" The vicar touched Neil's arm to get his attention.

"No, the Frenchman. The girl with the straight hair playing the cello, playing the work of the Frenchman."

"Saint-Saëns." The vicar shifted her gaze to the detectives. "That was last Wednesday, one week ago today."

"You saw the man on the day the girl with the straight hair played her cello?" There was an undercurrent of excitement in O'Leary's voice.

"He was the same, but different. He had a tie on. He had shiny shoes. And he wasn't friendly. He didn't say anything to me. Walked right past."

"You didn't talk to him?"

"No."

"Neil, do you think if you sat down with a police artist"—
the man recoiled visibly, pushing up against the pillar to his
left as if he would disappear into it—"if I sent a nice lady artist
around—you don't have to come in, she comes here, and the
Vicar could be with you—if that happened do you think you
could describe this man to her?"

He nodded.

As the door of the church swung shut behind them, O'Leary
pumped his fist. "That man saw our suspect the day of the fire!"

"He saw a fellow who asked a lot of questions, back in
another guise."

"Come on, Ni, it's textbook—you know the psychology on
these firestarters. Plenty of them get off on the ritual of planning and fixate on the location of the act."

"All right, it *is* promising, especially given the guy's interest in cameras. But need I remind you, we had a van in a man's
garage, and it turned out he was totally innocent."

"Or not. Remember what you said this morning, there is
a good chance someone at Spiffy knows the suspect, and that
someone could be Nelson. Maybe all the Spiffy connection
needs to finger the killer—if they are not affirmatively covering
for him—is a sketch of Neil's weekends-only homeless bloke."

"That was odd, wasn't it? Sounded like someone playing at
being homeless in his off-hours." Nigella pulled out into traffic.

"This bloke is a lot of things in his off-hours: would-be artist, pretend-homeless, murdering SOB. Kind of makes you wish
he worked more, doesn't it?"

"O'Leary, you just said something important." In her excitement, Nigella whipped the car around a corner so sharply that
still-unbelted O'Leary slid into his door. "Our suspect works.
Presumably in the same building Andrew Smyth did, maybe
even the same firm, because he drugged Smyth in the gym and
walked him on out of there. When we get our sketch, we're
having a Tweedle run it round to GG&S."

Back at Wood Street, Evans snagged them as they got off the
elevator. "Got an art toff willing to have a look at the nonhuman photos."

"Those'd be my first choice," O'Leary said.

"You get away with that sense of humor at the Yard, do you?" Evans handed Nigella a piece of paper. "She's at the Slade."

"Right, sir." As Evans walked away, Nigella instinctively looked at her mobile, checking the time. The last thing she wanted was James running around Wood Street asking after her. She'd text and tell him to make it after one. O'Leary saw the glance. "Tube, I think," she said briskly. "All of London is trying to get to its desk at this point. Nothing worse than wasting time in traffic."

As they exited the Euston Square station twenty minutes later, O'Leary said, "There *is* something worse than sitting in traffic: standing sandwiched between a bloke whose music is on so loud you can hear it through his headphones and a crazy old geezer clearly due for his yearly bath. You know the phantom feeling, like someone is going for your wallet, that you get every thirty seconds when you're close to a rough sleeper?"

"I'm a woman, O'Leary. Whenever I'm on the tube, I get the feeling, not always phantom either, that some bloke old enough to be my dad has his hand on my ass."

Katherine Rowan, Senior Lecturer, Sculpture, ushered them through a student gallery to her office—a small space full of light and dominated by a modern, minimalist desk. Clothed chicly all in black and with an interestingly asymmetrical bob of blonde hair, she was younger than Nigella had expected, which pleased her. It always pleased her to sit across from a woman in her prime succeeding in a male-dominated profession.

"Professor Rowan, it is good of you to help out in this delicate matter," she started.

"Katherine, please. I understand you're in a terrible situation. Someone claiming to be an artist murdering a man and putting him on exhibit . . . I guess it shouldn't surprise me, but it does."

"Why shouldn't it surprise you?"

"Don't you find, Detective Inspector Parker, that any profession pursued as a passion can lead to dark places?"

"Call me Nigella. I suppose that's true."

"Surely you've seen cops stretch or break rules. Well, in the arts there's also a greater-good mentality. History is littered with artists so convinced of their genius that they were willing to flout conventions and break laws. Think of the men who dug up graves to study human anatomy in order to render it better in their work."

Nigella nodded, pulling a folder out of her bag and laying it on the desk. "This is our suspect's nonhuman work."

Katherine Rowan spread the photos out, then circled her desk. "What the fire does to the wood is visually arresting," she said. "If only the poses weren't so literal. I mean there are better and less trite ways to communicate 'fuck you' than with a finger in the air. If he could make his positioning as interesting as the fissures the flames create . . . and these rough patches. Now that is provocative. If he improved his overall shapes, or maybe put several figures in dynamic opposition, he could really be on to something."

"So, he's good?" O'Leary asked incredulously.

Nigella realized this was a question she'd never asked herself. She joined Rowan looking down on the pictures. "Yes, he is," she replied.

"And," Rowan added, "if he develops in the right directions, he could be great. Memorable. An artist people want to own and talk about decades from now."

Jarred, Nigella felt the thread of connection between them snap. "The only direction this fellow is headed in is to a maximum security prison."

"Of course." Rowan colored. "You asked me to consider him as an artist."

A door opened in Nigella's brain. "I did, and you've made me realize: I've been looking at him *only* as a murderer. But art matters intensely to this suspect. He absolutely sees the fruit of his crimes as art, even when he takes his work to grisly extremes."

"Any insight I can give you into the art end of things I'm happy to provide," Rowan said.

"If we wanted to identify this artist, how would we go about that?"

Rowan put her hand on her chin and stared down at the pictures. "He's clearly studied. I doubt he studied here, because I'd remember a figural sculptor who used fire." She paused, finger tracing the curve of the coiled form from the Monument fire. "Of course, this could be a postgraduation development. With your permission, I'd like to make a copy of a few shots and show them to fellow lecturers—discreetly—see if any past students come to mind. The person you're seeking may not have studied in London, but it's probably easiest to start here. I'd talk to the head of graduate sculpture at the Royal College of Art. And there is Camberwell College at UAL. I can give you contacts at both."

"That would be helpful."

"Studio space is another possible direction. Lots of co-op space in Spitalfields—that is the hot place to work right now."

"Our suspect is smart—too smart to make these where anyone can see them," Nigella replied.

Rowan nodded. "But he might do work that leans stylistically toward this: other types of human forms."

It was Nigella's turn to nod. "We can't thank you enough. There is one more thing." She hesitated because this was the hard ask, and she liked Rowan. "The killer is demanding feedback. Says he'll kill until he gets it."

"So Chief Inspector Evans mentioned." The professor's tone was suddenly dry, remote.

"I understand if you don't want to make a public comment—"

"That could be career ending, whatever my good intentions."

"—but might you be willing to give us a quote we could use in a message to the killer? The most I would say is that the comment came from someone who had shown appreciation for his wood-based work. No attribution."

"I have to think," Rowan replied softly. "Wouldn't you? We work twice as hard to get where we are. I'd throw that away if I was certain it'd save a life. But I'm pretty sure you can't tell me anything in this case is certain."

◊

"DI Parker," the uniform at the desk called out as they entered, "you've an artist waiting in 10A."

In all the crazy, she'd never actually texted James to say she'd be delayed.

"Maybe it's our killer come to turn himself in," O'Leary quipped.

"No, I asked James to come by and look at the photos."

He raised his eyebrows.

"He sculpts and attends scads of shows of up-and-coming artists."

They started down the hall. O'Leary held his tongue until they were out of the desk sergeant's hearing—barely. "So hunky James wants to help. Sure he hasn't stopped by for a quickie?"

Nigella spun to face him. "We've been friends a long time, O'Leary, but that doesn't mean you get to make leering jokes about my private life. You want to haul out that locker-room shit, go back to the Yard."

"It would be locker-room if I was snickering behind your back, or, you know, talking about your ass"—his arms crossed over his chest—"cause, yeah, that is what lots of male cops do. But, damn it, I defy you to name a single time—one—when I've leered at you or any other cop." He narrowed his eye until they were as fierce as his voice. "I won't mention your sculptor again. I won't mention the cat, or your mum, or anything personal if that's the way you want it." His left hand swung away from his chest, pointing accusatorily. "But you know damn well that means treating you differently than other cops, because cops are family, and families don't just talk work."

How did this escalate so quickly?

O'Leary *was* one of the good guys. There had been dozens of the other sort over the years—trying to intimidate or embarrass her, harassing, and yes, even assaulting—but not Colm. *And you do talk smack with other DI's: joke about their drinking, their mothers-in-law, the girlfriends' birthdays they forget.* Those other cops joked back, and she never bristled. So why the hell did O'Leary have such a knack for getting under her skin?

"You can talk about the cat as much as you want." She pointed back at him. "But my romantic life is off limits, and I won't comment on yours."

"Only one of us *has* a romantic life," he snapped. "I'll leave it to you to sort out which. I am heading upstairs. You don't need me in 10A, and I sure as feck am not interested in being there."

He stalked off. Nigella counted to three, then continued to the interview room.

"Detective Inspector Parker." The corner of James's mouth twitched mischievously. Then his face changed. "You look angry."

"Stressed," she said taking the seat across from him. "Hell of a morning. Just back from the Slade."

"That's my alma mater. They can be pretty elitist—even within their own ranks—and God knows they put on a superior air within the art community. I can't imagine they'd try that on with a cop, though."

"It's not the Slade, just the fast-moving nature of this case, and the fact that even so, it's not moving fast enough. Nothing is fast enough when you have a killer on the loose."

"Well, I'm here to try to help, so let's see those pictures."

Nigella watched his face transform until there was not a trace of the cavalier or mischievous left.

"This stuff is elevated—the kind of work I'd like to see in some of those exhibits we go to. I mean compare this to the pedestrian shite we saw at *What's Next—Ten British Artists to Keep an Eye On*—"

"You don't find the gesture of flipping off St. James's a bit obvious?" Nigella realized she was channeling Katherine Rowan as she interrupted his rhapsodizing.

"No, it's brilliant. Direct, not pretentious. It demands people think about the role of God and man in the C of E. Don't you think?" He turned his eyes to her, his gaze demanding validation.

"Could do," she replied. She didn't want to get into a big art discussion, and surely his opinion was legitimate, even if it didn't feel that way after hearing Rowan's. "So, as a member of

the London sculpture scene, have you seen work even tangentially similar?"

He shook his head. "If there'd been this type of work at any
of the openings I've attended, I'd have dragged you to see it.
This stuff deserves recognition."

"How about in the studios of London's art set—seen anything that hints at this?"

"The artists I know best have space in the same co-op I do. I
haven't visited every workspace in my building, let alone in the
other collectives—and there are loads of them in Spitalfields.
That being said, I haven't seen anyone doing work that puts me
in mind of this."

It would have been too much of a coincidence had he replied
differently, she told herself, smothering her disappointment.

"Would work like that take a long time?"

"Most art takes time—hell, just the thinking part can involve
months. A lot depends on circumstances. Sort of like your work.
I'll bet how quickly you solve a case depends on the breaks you
get. And maybe inspiration—I mean, I presume there is inspiration in police work."

Nigella nodded.

"Art's the same. Sometimes I wake up in the middle of the
night and can't sketch fast enough. If I'm really inspired, all that
slows me down are physical limitations—like sleep and having
to be at work. Other times, an idea that seems brilliant when it
catches me in the shower takes months to translate and ends up
being rubbish."

"That's very much like stringing evidence together," Nigella
said.

"Every artist's pace is individual. But I think it's safe to say
this guy is putting at least weeks and probably months into these
sculptures. I mean they're large, so just the chisel work alone
would physically take that."

*So when the killer says he will up his output, there is reason to
believe it will be flesh, not wood.* Unsettling thought.

He picked up one of the pictures again—the front view
of St. James's man—took a giant breath and let it out in a

cheek-puffed-out whoosh. "You'll never see Ethan Fox do anything like this, for all the fuss made over him at this year's *Ten British Artists to Keep an Eye On* exhibit"

"Thanks for coming by James." She held out her hand for the photo. "I don't want to use up your entire lunch. An artist has to eat."

"Would a cop like to eat with him? We could grab something round the corner."

"I wish I could." *Liar, the last thing you want is to be seen walking out of the building and grabbing a bite with someone who came in as a witness.* "But I need to stop this crazy before he kills again."

"Think you can?" It sounded as much like a dare as a question.

Jesus, Ni, now you're getting paranoid . . . doubting yourself, thinking Handsome doubts you.

"Guess that depends on the breaks, and if I get inspired."

Nigella counted to a full thirty after James left the interview room before heading to the elevator. She expected to find O'Leary in a sullen mood. But he was leaning in the incident room doorway, beaming. "Ni, we have the car."

"What?"

"You know that long list of Corsas we were dreading? The team watching the video had about fifty in the target zone, then a bleeding miracle occurred: a camera in White Hart Yard caught a bloke popping out of one and messing with his plates. By the third time through, they were sure the driver was pulling something off. The cop who called was so excited that I didn't understand him the first time he said it. Or maybe I just couldn't believe our luck."

"Are you telling me we have a plate?"

"A Surrey plate. They're running it now. Fancy a trip to Surrey?"

He held up his hand for a high five and she gave it to him.

"You know I do!"

"Want to go in full team like we did at Taylor's?"

"No. We're just going out to ring the bell and pleasantly ask a few questions, right? Maybe have a look round. No search warrant to delay us; no need to touch base with the local CID. We're out there—wherever 'there' is—on preliminaries."

The phone on the conference table rang, and O'Leary sprinted to it. He scribbled something down, then said, "Bless you."

"That a standard Met phrase?' Nigella joked.

"It's a standard 'Colm O'Leary channels his Irish gran when chuffed' phrase. We have an address."

"So put on that coat that makes you look Endeavour Morse," she said, "and let's go."

◊

"O'Leary, this is definitely one of your quaint BBC mystery villages. I am thinking *Midsomer Murders*, or even Christie. What is it called again?"

"Betchworth. Straight through the main of it, and then left by The Dolphin." He pointed through the windscreen. "I can't get over the fact this street is called 'The Street' as if there were only one road that mattered in the world."

"A few hundred years ago in a place like this, that'd be about right." Nigella took the turn.

"Pretty river view." O'Leary gestured right. "No, don't you look, Ni. You drive."

"Then why point it out?"

A short while later, he gave a low whistle. "Look at some of these places. London commuters? Weekenders? If our quaint little village isn't careful, it won't remain Miss-Marple-land for long. Do you think our suspect is some rich GG&S solicitor with a posh, gated place, maybe a wife who rides to hounds? Slow down." He peered out at one of the fancy iron gates. "Nope, not yet."

Normally the question of who their suspect was would have been settled nicely by running the license plates. But nothing was normal in this case. O'Leary had informed Nigella as they crossed London Bridge that the older model white Vauxhall Corsa was registered to a Linda Shotton of the address they were now approaching. It sure hadn't been Linda Shotton caught on camera steering a drugged Andrew Smyth out of a building in Monument Square. Any more than it had been Nelson Taylor who'd pulled up to that same square in a Spiffy van one dark night to light a wooden man on fire.

The gap between road and river widened, and traditional farms and cottages started to dot the way, taking over from sprawling, showy modern estates. Nigella couldn't help thinking they were more appealing.

"Should be there, on the left." O'Leary pointed.

A cattle gate hung open at the entrance to a longish drive. A brick cottage with a touch of half-timbering sagged under a tile roof. It was ringed by an overgrown garden out of a fanciful children's story. The drive split at the corner of the garden fence, with one fork ending near a front walk, and the other petering out near an old barn.

"Pleasant but cautious," Nigella reminded O'Leary, pulling to a stop by the front gate. "If the car wasn't stolen, whoever lives in this house is one hell of a vicious killer, or knows one."

No one responded to her knock. O'Leary stepped into the bushes and peered through a window. "Ni, the owner of our white Corsa is a gran. There is a floral couch with an afghan in there." He tugged on the lower sash.

"What are you doing?"

"Nothing because it's locked."

"Nothing even if it wasn't, because we don't have a warrant."

"I wasn't going to climb in. Just wanted to stick a hand in and see if it was dusty. It looks dusty." He readjusted the angle of his hand above his eyes. "I'd say this lounge is frozen in 1977. Fancy a look?"

Nigella joined him. There couldn't have been a stick of furniture or bit of decor that was less than twenty-five years old, and some of it, judging by a very ugly sixties-style lamp, considerably older. The television had a big, tube-containing back protruding from it. The sitting room absolutely said "afternoon tea with your elderly aunt."

"O'Leary, you sure this is the right place?"

"That's what the map on my phone says, and if that's not enough for you, there's that mailbox with the house number. Let's have a look through some other windows." They set off round the house. "If this place is deserted, at least we've had a nice drive."

As he leaned up to the next window, Nigella's gaze wandered in the direction of the barn. She tapped his shoulder. "Not deserted. Someone's been enjoying a bonfire."

Just outside the garden fence, a lawn chair sat next to the remnants of a large fire. They made a beeline for the spot. "All neatly raked, ringed in stones, grass cleared back," O'Leary observed. "Pleasant place to sit and admire the stars, providing Andrew Smyth wasn't smoldering here."

"Let's have a look in the barn."

"You hoping for a white Corsa by any chance?" he asked.

There was no getting in the barn. O'Leary shook one of the two large locks on the front door. "Either this is a high crime district, or there's something in there someone likes to keep private."

"Well, if this place is shut up much of the time, whoever owns it may be trying to prevent vandalism or keep it from becoming a drugs and drink den for local youth." Nigella walked to the first shuttered window. "Locked from the inside." Every window was the same, and the back door was padlocked as well.

"So we've got no one home to question, no way to really nose around, nothing that gives us grounds to get a warrant, but is it just me or does something stink? O'Leary asked.

Stink. The word made Nigella realize there was an odd odor on the autumn breeze. "Do you smell Christmas, O'Leary?"

He looked at her like she was insane, then sniffed. "There is something . . ." He walked back toward the fire circle with Nigella following. "Something sort of spicy."

"Cinnamon," she said connecting the scent with a name. "And look, there's a half-burned stick of it." She squatted beside the pile of ash and burned wood bits.

"Last time I checked, having a particularly nice-smelling bonfire wasn't grounds for a warrant." He put his hands on his hips. His eyes passed over the barn. He backed up further. "Something's not right about that roof."

"Where?"

"About three-quarters of the way back—that moss-free area. The shingles march along in a nice, neat pattern except for there."

Nigella saw what he meant: the horizontal alignment of the top two or three rows was out of kilter. "Looks patched." She stood up. "We need gloves from the car, and we need to get up there."

"Wasn't there a ladder lying round back?"

Once at roof level, they moved cautiously. O'Leary slipped slightly but recovered himself just as her hand shot in his direction. "Do you need a warrant to look around if you fall through?" he asked.

"If your neck is broken, you won't be looking at anything." Nigella stopped edging forward. "These shingles are the same as the others, but I still think it's been patched. The spacing is wonky, and look: some are broken." She leaned down carefully to touch a partial shingle. The edge that was rough looked considerably less weathered. "This little repair job is recent. She looked closer. "Rectangular nails! Don't we have a bag of those at the nick? Warrant be damned, let's pull one."

O'Leary took out a Swiss army knife. A bit of grunting and twisting, and he straightened up, holding a nail.

"Good man."

"I've been trying to convince you of that for years. If the lab says it's arguably a match to what came out of Smyth's hands, we found it lying in plain view—"

"And we get our warrant!" Nigella smiled.

"What about the Corsa?" O'Leary asked as they climbed into the car. "Want me to put out an alert?"

Nigella tapped the wheel absently. "Police only. Fellow officers on the lookout, but no public help because that lets our suspect know what we're up to."

"It'd be nice if we weren't the only ones lacking a clear picture." O'Leary glanced at his watch. "Early dinner? If we hit one of the village pubs, maybe we can delicately pursue this lead without publishing half-pagers."

Nigella did a drive round before selecting a spot. The Dolphin looked lovely, but that wasn't her criteria—she was seeking the pub that looked most local. The Quarryman seemed like the right call, not a single shiny, new Range Rover parked anywhere near it. She and O'Leary snagged a table and ordered the special, some sort of game casserole topped with mash. As soon as it arrived, O'Leary turned on the charm.

"Smells great." He smiled up at the middle-aged waitress. "Glad to get some hearty fare. So many places these days, I go in for a pint and a bite to eat, and find myself in a fancied-up wine bar with fusion cuisine—whatever that is."

"Or they want fifteen pounds for bangers and mash," she replied sympathetically. "Lots of lovely old places being made over so-called high-end."

"New isn't always better. Like those houses we saw driving in." O'Leary shook his head. "Same problem where my people come from in Ireland: weekenders, tourists, coming, wanting an authentic village experience, then tearing down the things that make a village authentic in the first place."

"What part of Ireland?" the waitress asked.

"West coast of Clare," he said.

As the waitress moved away, Nigella realized she hadn't known that.

"You still have family in Clare?"

"Yep. Right up against the Burren. No trees, but views for miles. My gran is there, and she had nine children so I've got plenty of aunts, uncles, and cousins."

"I always think of you as a Londoner."

"I am, Ni. Born in London, and so was my mum. Sometimes, against their better judgment, the Irish and English intermarry. Waitress is headed back, you're up."

"How is everything?"

"Delicious," Nigella said. "I'm curious, are there a lot of Shottons round these parts? My aunt was at school with a Shotton from Surrey, and I thought from Betchworth."

"There were—been here long as my family—but not any-more."

"Bought out?"

"Nope, the Shotton place is still in family hands, but nobody's lived there regular gone on seven years. Not since the cancer got Linda."

"That's a shame. I'll have to tell my aunt. Don't think it was Linda she was at school with though. Maybe a daughter?"

"That'd be Sybil. She went off to University. Married a boy. Never came back."

"If she doesn't use her property, I'm surprised she doesn't sell it," O'Leary chimed in. "A house needs to be lived in."

"You'll get no argument from me on that. Poor Linda knew Sybil would have no interest in the place, so she left it to a grand-son. Suppose she hoped he'd move in, but he lives in London. Comes round now and again. Nice young man. No trouble to the neighbors, though he's let the garden run wild. His gran would cry to see it that way." She looked at O'Leary's half-full glass. "Another pint?"

"Absolutely."

"You do realize we're on duty," Nigella said once the wait-ress was out of ear shot.

"By the time we wend our way back to London, we won't be. Besides, we ought to be celebrating because we've got a lead on our suspect: Linda Shotton's London grandson, and he is driving an aging white Corsa."

CHAPTER 13

Whitehall Palace

September 14, 1666

"It makes no sense. Why would Christopher Wren, Professor of Astronomy at Oxford, member of the Royal Academy, kill Thomas Bradish?"

"You heard his lies, Margaret."

"Yes, and I saw his eyes, which were more frightening. Wren *was* determined to conceal any connection with Thomas and refute the idea that he knew of the plan for the Stationers to use St. Faith's. I am not denying that. But to assume the reasons behind his deceit are arson and murder . . ." Margaret cast Etienne a deflating look as he walked beside her among the aviaries of the Volary Garden. It was the perfect place to speak privately, being accessible from the accommodations of the queen's maids and generally deserted at such an early hour.

"Dove, you said yourself last night, an innocent man would not respond as Wren did."

"Wren clearly feels guilty about something, but it need not be murder." She paused to let a peacock and several peahens cross the path. "And his feelings need not be rational. Remember, George Tokefield suggested Thomas had fled London because he was guilt ridden over the destruction of the booksellers' ware. Perhaps Wren, as the actual author of the plan for

St. Faith's, feels a similar responsibility, and when I told him Thomas had died, feelings of remorse overwhelmed him."

"Overwhelmed him such that he claimed not to know Bradish?" Etienne shook his head dismissively. "Tell me, did Wren look pained or chastened for a single instant? No. He exploded as if I'd lit a short fuse on one of my rockets. That reaction is *evidence* of a sort, Margaret. If you are willing to accept that his bluster was a defense, why then are you so unwilling to believe he raised it because he is guilty of Thomas's death?"

Margaret plucked boxwood leaves from the nearest hedge, crushed them, and brought them to her nose, drinking in their soothing odor. It was one of the few remedies suggested to her over the years for "nerves" that actually worked. "Because calling a man a taker of a human life is a serious thing. And where is his motive—what could Dr. Wren gain by killing Thomas? He was angry when we spoke, even threatening, but he did not seem unhinged. Surely, only a madman kills without reason."

They continued walking in silence. Just past a large statue of a Greek goddess at the far corner of the garden, they came to a cage full of doves. Etienne stopped, absently making low cooing noises through the bars. "How much more beautiful and lively you are than your namesakes," he said. "How I wish you might never be caged."

"Etienne Belland"—Margaret gave a quick look round to make certain they were alone before rising on her toes to kiss his cheek—"this is no time to worry about my future. Keep your sharp mind on the problem at hand."

He turned to her, and she knew by his eyes her admonition had been wasted. "Are you going to tell me there is 'time enough,' Margaret?" Etienne pulled out the watch she had given him, showing her the back as if she herself had not ordered the engraving there. "I wear the sentiment, but I do not believe it. Do you? Would all the time from now until death be enough? And we haven't that. We have only until you are Countess of Tyrconnell. If you wish to know how I will feel on your wedding day, you have only to recall Agnes's grief in losing Thomas."

His comment felt like a slap—a self-indulgent one. "Etienne, would you rather have me dead? Thomas is *dead*."

"*Mon Dieu*, no, Margaret!" His eyes widened, and a bit of color rose to his cheeks as he raised both hands in protest. "Never think such a thing. I only suggest that between now and the graves each of us must one day fill, there ought to be more to life than unwelcomed captivity."

"Only a man would say such a thing. Look around you! Whether daughter, wife, or mistress, women have little control of their lives. How can a man who is so bright not see this? We are married off to suit the purposes and ambitions of others."

"Not always. Many of the couples I know, my parents included, married for love."

"Because you are a tradesman."

Etienne blushed.

"I do not say it as degradation, merely as explanation. There are many benefits to being a member of a great family—some measure of security and influence among them—but those privileges come with duties, to King, to order, and to the family that elevates you. You are *so* certain that it is right for us to be together, so willing to chance the consequences of that decision. But I tell you, if things were reversed and you were a Duke's heir, you would feel the weight of expectations and family name, and while you might love me, you would marry another."

"I will not concede it." He shook his head violently. "But I accept that were I a woman, with no standing under law, and subject to the rule of thumb, I would be less quick to risk the anger of my father or eventual husband."

He thinks of Lady Scroope, Margaret thought, *of the bruises on her arms last evening that even careful dressing could not hide.* Bruises that would yield no consequences for her husband who had set them upon her—so long as she was not beaten to death.

"Please do not think I censure you," he continued. "I am only angered by the thought of you as the possession of a man who will not know you are a scientist and a seeker of stars."

"No matter whose wife I am, Etienne, I promise I will always look to the stars and wait for your next volley of fireworks." She took his hand, squeezed it, then let it go.

"Now let us focus on the pursuit of justice for Thomas. Perhaps we ought to approach my talk with Wren from a different angle, from the direction of what rang true—his comments about St. Paul's."

"You saw his drawings. Are they equal to his passion for them?" Etienne asked.

"They are a revelation. Not a single angle, window, or door in his reimagining is like the Cathedral that towered over the city before the fire. Even the stone is to be different. If built, I believe Wren's St. Paul's will erase not only the ugly ruins that lie at Carter Lane and Old Change, but the memory of the Cathedral that went before for all that it took hundreds of years to build and stood completed hundreds of years more."

"If it is built . . ." Etienne tapped a closed hand against his nose and stared past her. "*If* it is built . . . And he said *plans*, not dreams—he sounded adamant about that."

"Etienne, your mind hops about randomly like the caged birds surrounding us."

"Margaret, what must you have if you will build an enormous cathedral? Not plans, we know Wren has those."

"Stone, scaffolds, tradesmen—"

"Before those. I will tell you what comes first: land. If you would build a church, you must have a place to build it. Dr. Wren may not have had anything to gain from Thomas's death, but he surely benefits from the fact that old St. Paul's lies in heaps of rubble fit only to be carted away."

"You sound like one of the mad mob that insists London was burned by Quakers or *Frenchmen*. Surely you are not accusing Dr. Wren of firing London!"

"No. That was an act of God. But man is an opportunistic creature. Remember, St. Paul's didn't just burn—it exploded. The King saw the fireball from his barge. Why did it do so? Because the western crypt was packed with fuel in the form of books and paper. Who urged the Stationers to pack the crypt?

Wren." Etienne paced forward at such a rapid rate that Margaret had to run to keep up.

"And that paper caught fire despite the fact, as Tokefield told us, the vault doors were locked, coated, and sealed with Thames clay." Stopping beside an enormous cage full of His Majesty's tropical parrots, Etienne spun to face her, cheeks flushed. "That detail has gnawed at my mind since we heard it. Sealing with clay should have worked, Margaret. I know as much or more about how to burn things or how to keep them from burning as any man now alive. Packing that paper tightly inside thick stone walls and sealing every crack that might permit fire or air to reach it with clay *should* have worked. Even as the walls of the nave fell, the lead of the roof ran like a river, and the choir and reredos burned, the paper in St. Faith's ought to have lain safe, waiting to be uncovered. But instead we found the lake of fire. I think someone deliberately breached the seals and the door itself—perhaps with a pries bar."

In her mind's eye Margaret saw the pry bar lying in the Marylebone workshop. Before it was used on Thomas, had it been applied to the doors of St. Faith's?

"And I think whoever broke the door did so to introduce flame into the crypt and turn it into a bomb."

"It is a sound theory from a scientific point of view, Etienne. But would Wren really have taken such drastic, sinful action? He was already on the Commission advising on the restoration of St. Paul's. He told me he'd been a member for years."

"For *years*. How long can a man wait where he has a burning passion?"

"Good men do not become violent merely out of frustration, do they?"

"Good men and bad alike can and do. I suppose it might depend on whether, in addition to frustrated, Wren felt aggrieved. If you ran away with me tomorrow, I'd expect to be challenged to a duel by the Earl of Tyrconnell even before your father swore out a warrant for my arrest. Both men feel entitled to you, and therefore they would take bold and even violent actions to regain you. So I wonder, did Wren feel *entitled* to be the architect of a new St. Paul's, and was he frustrated in that ambition?"

"The first question must remain rhetorical because a man's feelings are his own if he chooses to stay mum," Margaret replied. "But the second . . . if there is one thing I know from my residence at court, it is that committees of every sort are officious things." She trailed her fingers along the bars of the parrot cage, setting several of the birds squawking. "So there will be minutes of the Royal Commission's meetings. They are the next piece of our puzzle and may help us to divine if Dr. Wren was tempted to act criminally."

"You mean whether he is an arsonist and a murderer," Etienne said.

"Murderer, murderer, murderer," chanted the brightly colored parrots.

♦

"Incroyable," Etienne murmured in a mix of awe and disbelief. They stood in the library of the Earl of Anglesey's Drury Lane mansion: a cavernous, deep green room, bathed in natural light, luxuriously furnished, and lined, floor to ceiling, with bookshelves. "How can one man own so many books?"

Margaret smiled; his reaction closely resembled her own on her first visit. And there had been many visits since. Those at court of a bookish bent all frequented the Earl's library, for it was regarded as the greatest in England, and, by the Earl's instruction, was accessible to those of quality who applied for admittance.

"They say Lord Anglesey acquired his taste for books at Oxford. He is certainly a voracious collector. Theology, history, medicine, poetry, plays, architecture, music—he has them all. And this is but half of his collection." Margaret took a seat in an armchair on one side of a dark wooden table and waved Etienne into its twin across from her. The Earl's librarian had scurried away to get the folios of Commission minutes Margaret had requested. "Anglesey has at least this many volumes at his estate. And I suspect, with the possible exception of treaties of law or copies of the public acts, the vast majority are far more interesting than the notes we've come to see."

"That depends on what the minutes show us of Wren," Etienne replied, laying out paper, ink, and pen in a manner suitable to a personal secretary—which is how he had been introduced.

The librarian returned. "These, Mistress, are copies of the most recent business of the Royal Commission for the Exploration of Strategies for Repairing and Upholding St. Paul's."

Etienne shot her a significant look. "Repairing, eh?" he muttered once the librarian left them. "Under no possible imagining could that great dome of Wren's be called a repair."

Margaret opened the leather folio. The date at the top of the first page was so startling she reached out and touched it. "Oh, Etienne, the Commission stood in the nave of St. Paul's less than a week before it burned. What a reminder that God and not man is the chief architect of life." She began to read aloud.

When she had finished Etienne laid aside his pen and said: "I am surprised Wren and Pratt did not come to blows." He shook his head. "Any renovation of St. Paul's was an anathema to Wren. What words did he use?" He glanced at his notes. "Ah yes, 'unsatisfactory' and 'piecemeal.' If ever a man made both his ambitions and frustrations plain, Dr. Wren has done so."

A great shiver ran through Margaret. "Etienne, I think you are right: Wren made certain the Cathedral burned. That means he was there the evening it took fire. And that, in combination with his strange behavior when I spoke of Thomas, suggests he also murdered our friend." Saying the words conjured a rage in Margaret such as she had never known. "May the Lord have mercy on his soul"—she spat the words as if they were a curse— "for I intend to have none."

She expected Etienne to second her vow. Instead, he picked up the two pages of notes he had just penned and began tearing them to pieces.

"What are you doing?" She reached out to stop him, but he would not be halted.

"Destroying the evidence of our pursuit of Thomas's killer," he replied calmly, as if there were nothing shocking in the act. "Our investigation has no hope of a useful outcome, so what else is there to be done?"

"Confront Wren!"

"Shh." He put a finger to his lips as if the name had power to summon the man. "To what end? Do you think a man who would fire a church and kill a man will be shamed into owning his acts by an accusation?"

"No, but I know what he looks like when he lies—how the red creeps up his neck, how his voice changes. If he speaks false, I will know."

"What will you do then?" Etienne leaned forward, looking searchingly into her eyes. "Who will listen to you rather than dismissing your tale at once as another ludicrous conspiracy theory—and you must concede our conclusion is so outlandish that it sounds like one—like those already plaguing His Majesty and the men charged with governing a ruined and lawless London?"

"I will go to the Queen. She is a good woman. She knows I am no idle gossip. She will credit what I say, and advise me."

"Perhaps Queen Catherine will believe you. You know her; I do not. But I cannot imagine what she could advise that will see this man"—he reached out a finger and touched the name on one of the scraps before him, then laid his hand over the pile—"charged with burning St. Paul's Cathedral. Their Majesties, and indeed all those who want calm in London, fervently desire discussions of fire-starting conspiracies to stop. They will not, I think, be eager to feed them with tales of deliberate acts of arson. Setting Wren down for trial would do just that."

"But," Margaret sputtered in anger and confusion, "why have we investigated these events, tracked them to Doctor—"

"Do not say the name aloud." He shook his head in warning.

"What shall I call him then? The Phoenix, because he wished to make St. Paul's rise from ash? That mythical bird did not fire himself so that he might rise. It was merely his destiny to burn."

"Yes, the Phoenix, we will call him that. And perhaps our Phoenix believes building a new St. Paul's as he imagined it—as he fought to do for many months—is *his* destiny."

"It is if we do nothing! Where is the justice in that? And where the satisfaction? Even if my words to Her Majesty do not result in his arrest, surely they will stop the Phoenix from getting the commission for which he killed—a tremendous punishment to such a greedy, ambitious man. Her Majesty can take my evidence to the King, who has the power and influence to see the commission to design St. Paul's goes elsewhere."

Etienne looked pensive. "That is not an unreasonable conclusion, but, as you've just said yourself, to convince their Majesties you will have to present evidence—that means laying out all we have done. Such a recitation will have consequences for you, my dove."

Etienne was right. Telling Queen Catherine how she had sneaked from the palace and lied about being ill would be humiliating and would change the Queen's opinion of her. And doubtless Margaret's actions would result in dismissal from the court. She shrank momentarily from both prospects, only to be caught in a rush of shame. *What is my good name when a man has been killed? And if they send me from the court to live under the cold gaze of my angry mother, surely that is no worse than my childhood.*

Margaret took a deep breath, ready to say she was willing to do what was necessary, whatever that cost her personally. *You will never see Etienne again.* The thought caused the words to die in her throat. No medical torture from her childhood could compare to such a punishment.

But Agnes will never see Thomas. Is your selfish love more important than justice for that?

"Margaret, what are you thinking?" Etienne's voice summoned her back to the Earl's library. As his beautiful dark eyes met hers, she had a new thought: there would be consequences to him as well. Margaret could not hope to convincingly claim she had gone into London alone, had retrieved and examined Thomas's body with no assistance. But if she revealed the identity of her partner in the investigation, Etienne would lose the trust of the Queen and King, and the Bellands would likely lose their royal patronage. All that two generations of his family had built might be wiped away by her words. *You promised yourself you would never destroy Etienne, your private fire, your beautiful magician.*

Margaret's stomach fell. "I will not go to the Queen," she conceded. "Thomas, or for that matter Agnes, would not want our lives destroyed in pursuit of an uncertain-at-best official justice. Wren may well have the commission for St. Paul's. Given his magnificent plans, it seems likely. But even as he supervises stonemasons and woodworkers, I want him to be haunted, to look ever over his shoulder, wondering who knows what he did. He is not entirely impervious to guilt. I learned that when I questioned him. Well then, let me amplify it—set guilt and fear like twin worms inside him until he is eaten by them. Let me at least have the satisfaction of accusing him."

"It is too dangerous! To a man with one death upon his soul, another will seem a small matter. Call him an arsonist and a murderer, and he may kill you."

All my life I have been pushed and cajoled with threats of an early death. Would one seem a blessing now when I am so close to being separated from the man I love and consigned to long years with another? No. The answer was immediate and stark, and Margaret realized that "time enough" meant every possible moment. She was not willing to sacrifice one.

"You will save no one by your actions." Etienne pressed into the hesitancy he sensed, moving his hand from atop the destroyed notes to cover hers. "If we stood in the nave of St. Paul's as the Phoenix raised his pries bar, if I thought I could stop that bar from striking Thomas—I would not falter, even at the risk of it falling on me. Nor would you. I know your heart, your courage. But nothing we do now can save Thomas. Nothing bring him justice. Perhaps then we ought to leave justice to God, to have faith that the Almighty will weigh the Phoenix's sins and mete out punishment."

"Vengeance is mine; I will repay, saith the Lord." Margaret closed her eyes, saw Thomas shriveled and ruined. Swallowed

hard, and saw him alive, behind the counter of his shop, laughing with Etienne, Agnes, and herself. Thomas and Agnes could never be happy again, but if she left justice to the Lord her God, perhaps she and Etienne could be.

"Burn the notes." She gestured to the fireplace, lit against the autumn morning's chill. "When we return to Whitehall, I will burn those I took when we examined Thomas. I will be content to know the truth and to know that God knows it. Our pursuit of the Phoenix is over."

His face relaxed into the smile she loved.

"We will tell Agnes that we could not discover Thomas's killer, that perhaps we were wrong, and he only fell," she continued. "There is mercy in that, and mercy is a worthy quality."

He nodded, and together they watched the torn bits of their notes curl in the flames.

They were just outside the door of the great house, heading for their carriage at the bottom of the stone steps, when a man dismounted in the courtyard and crossed it at a run. Noticing Margaret, he paused in his swift ascent of the stairs to bow.

"Mistress, such news! They have arrested a young Frenchman at Romford in Essex. He was fleeing England. And what do you think? He has confessed to firing London!"

🔥

October 1666

I am curious about Robert Hubert. I have been since they brought him by farm cart, manacled and shackled, from Essex to London and locked him away in the White Lion Gaol. He claims to have been part of a conspiracy to burn down London, yet every man of intellect, from His Majesty to my fellows in the Royal Academy, knows the city burned by the perfect combination of weather and a poorly tended hearth.

I cannot help but think, however, some are not sorry for this confession nonsense. Hubert makes a convenient scapegoat to soothe those—and there are tens of thousands of them, some still at Moorfields, others in cellars or shanties where their homes once stood—who insist the city burned by mischief. The more daring of these conspiracy mongers have wandered from blaming foreigners to blaming our King. A dangerous enterprise for them, but hardly good for Charles II either. So Hubert's confession—or rather confessions, for he has made several, each different—may prove a useful occurrence.

Just as the Fire itself was useful to me. I look out the carriage window at the continued nothingness of London and cannot suppress a smile. I travel to the temporary home of the Criminal Court to see Hubert tried. Interrupting work on a detailed illustration showing how the pattern on the floor of St. Paul's is to be laid, in the hope that seeing Hubert will rid me of the distracting swirl of questions that have dogged me since his arrest. Chief among them: Why do people confess to things that otherwise cannot not be proved?

But crimes that are unproven in a court of law are still crimes . . . still sins. My smile fades. The thought is reminiscent of those that awaken me at night these last weeks, that rouse me from dreams of a man with hair of a certain shade of gold, leaving me clammy and shaking.

Only stone was meant to fall. Stone that feels no pain and has no family.

My plan went well at first. I spent a long day on the steps of the Cathedral—an iron pry bar and a bottle of my landlord's wine for company—waiting for the flames towering to the south and the east to burn close enough to provide cover for my inspired deed. Over those hours, I watched scores of people scurry through the churchyard gates, laden like beasts of burden. Some left their precious bundles in the yard. Others boldly staggered—carrying chests, tables, all manner of goods—into the Cathedral itself.

As they departed, I was glad to see them go. I would have been gladder still had they not come at all, for, as a rational man, there was no way for me to deny their impending losses. The family heirlooms; the bolts of wool, silk, and linen that the Mercers Company leaned against the church's outside walls, loose ends fluttering in the wind like flags; and yes, the paper and books the Stationers locked away in St. Faith's—all represented livelihoods. And I was sorry that livelihoods must be left in ashes so that London could be rid of the hulking shell of St. Paul's.

But you knew then and know still that sacrifices are necessary for great art.

As I sat choking on smoke, day became night. When at last a boy came running down Ave Maria Lane, a dog in his arms, crying, "Cheapside burns, Cheapside burns!" as if he were the watch, I made certain to carry his news inside with me. Shouting it as I passed down the Cathedral's central aisle. Counting on the warning to clear out those souls still kneeling in prayer. I even stopped beside an old man, dozing in a pew, shaking him awake and admonishing him to make haste to be away, lest he be turned to ash and bone.

You did what you could to keep people from dying. It is the same thing I tell myself when I wake from one of my nightmares, but it never entirely satisfies because I know it is a lie. *You lifted that pries bar.* I shake my head to dislodge the thought and focus my attention on the rubble along the roadside. My eyes are drawn to a stone cross and half an arched window in a partial wall—the ruins of a parish church. My breathing slows, as these holy remnants summon the thought that has sustained me these last days whenever guilt nips at me like a sharp-toothed rat. *You had a sign—a sign from God—that you were meant to do as you did; and you will repay any losses caused with a cathedral that will stand for all time, to His glory and the delight of all Londoners.*

Again the view out my window fades, the interior of my carriage falls away, and I am returned to that night, and specifically to the moments when I feared, as I have never feared anything, that I had tarried too long in the Cathedral and would die.

The roof above me and the scaffolding around me were in flames as I sprinted down the nave. As I burst out of the Cathedral, gasping and sweating, into air so hot I felt as if my flesh was alight, a flash of eerie and unnatural lightning broke above me, drawing my eyes to the heavens when they ought to have been on my escape route. I missed a step and tumbled down the others, landing prone in front of the church portico. Turning my dazed head, my heart raced—lead from the roof streamed past me in rivulets like liquid mercury. If I did not rise, I would surely be scalded. I scrambled to my feet, only to be confronted by a wall of flame higher than a two-story house.

There was nothing for it: I could perish where I stood, or I could try to breach that horrible, dancing wall.

Wildly, I raced back and forth along the flaming curtain like a menagerie animal along the bars of its cage, searching for a gap. When one appeared at last, I darted through, beating out the embers that caught on my coat, glad that they singed my hands, telling myself that fire could purify as well as destroy.

Out of immediate peril, a new fear gripped my heart: *you've failed. Your clever plan and risk of your own life will achieve nothing, even as your inadvertent sin damns you.*

Stopping to catch my breath, I turned back, eyes drawn reflexively to the mighty edifice of St. Paul's, ready to mutter a beseeching prayer. A great roar, more deafening than the crashing and shrieking of the fire that gobbled up all of London around me, stopped the words in my throat. The ground beneath my feet shook, and the center of the Cathedral exploded up and outward into a fireball so large that for a moment my bewildered mind thought the sun had fallen to earth. The air around me was sucked toward this new inferno, and I laughed like a madman as my carefully curled wig went with it, and my garments wrapped round me. A ghostly vortex of dust, smoke, and flame rose high above what remained of the church, expanding, restoring the air to where I stood. And in the swirl of it, hundreds of sheets of paper floated down. A single page from a book landed directly at my feet. It was in Latin, and as I stooped to pick it up, a word struck me with force: *Resurgam.* It was a sign.

I knew in that moment that I would survive and that St. Paul's would rise again in accordance with my vision for it.

My carriage jolts to a stop. I climb from it and wend my way into the makeshift courtroom, squeezing into a corner of the area provided for select spectators. *Does this young, palsied watchmaker who has confessed want celebrity?* I wonder as I look about to see who else is in attendance. Does he wish to be remembered for all time, which, judging by what I read and hear of him, would be otherwise unlikely? And is infamy the same as fame in his mind? Because if convicted, he will hang. I cannot believe being hated by every man, woman, and child in England, and being cursed and pelted with stones and dung on his ride to London, is the sort of recognition a sane man would seek.

Does he believe he burned London . . . or did he say so under torture?

A chilling thought. If I were to be found out, if some soul fleeing St. Paul's saw me cracking Thomas Bradish's pate, I am convinced mere words would never be enough to make me confess. But could I endure pain in the name of art and survival? I hope that is a question I need never answer.

The Lord Chief Justice of the King's Bench, John Kelynge, takes his place, robed and bewigged, and the prisoner is led in. I have only to hear Hubert answer the first question to lose interest in him. His words are a rambling, circuitous mess. Within moments, it is apparent to all present that his latest story is a wild change from his last confession. He is confused and witless. That such a man inspired so many serious questions in my sharper mind suddenly seems incomprehensible. I must stop worrying about the nature of guilt and the price of fame.

I turn my attention to Justice Kelynge. His expression as he listens to the accused prattle on is openly incredulous. The chary look in the Justice's narrowed eyes reminds me of someone . . . All my newly found peace and confidence drain away.

There was something in her eyes, that Maid of the Queen's.

It has been near a month since she surprised me, but I cannot forget the woman, how her gaze suggested she did not believe me when I said I knew nothing of Thomas Bradish. The pit of my stomach forms into a familiar knot, tied there by the uneasy feeling I have been powerless to banish, that she *knows*.

How much? Whom has she told? Whom will she tell?

I've taken the trouble to learn her name: Margaret Dove. And she is, as she insisted, a Maid of Honour to Her Majesty. This fact undercuts my initial instinct from that evening below the Queen's stairs—that I knew her face from elsewhere. As Mistress Dove stood talking of Thomas—as she'd said, "He and all his fellows in the Stationers' Company were at St. Paul's . . . but then you know that"—I was *certain* I'd seen her in Bradish and Son's only days before the fire. But I saw a tradeswoman, not a courtier.

Am I going mad from guilt?

No. Whatever guilt I feel over Bradish, it is not so overwhelming as to lead to a loss of wits. And it is outweighed by the deep conviction that I will, at last, have the commission I've so long sought, to give London the cathedral it deserves.

The man before me at the bar is clearly mad, however. I watch him twitch, moan, and mutter as Justice Kelynge instructs the jury. They do not take long to return a verdict: guilty. Guilty despite the fact I sense not a single one of the gentlemen sitting around me, nor the judge, believes a word Hubert has said. He is guilty of nothing but lying.

And yet, Robert Hubert will hang.

Whitehall Palace

October 26, 1666

"I cannot understand it. Both the Earl of Clarendon and Justice Kelynge told His Majesty that Hubert is a poor mad wretch, more interested in telling those around him what they wished to hear than stating the truth. For heaven's sake"—Margaret threw her hands up—"he even claimed to be Catholic when all know him to be a Huguenot."

She paced back and forth in front of Etienne, heels clicking furiously on the wooden floor of her apartment. He and all the Bellands were living in Marylebone once more, but thanks to his considerable sojourn at Whitehall, Etienne's face had become well known to the guards and inhabitants of the palace. So he now came and went with ease—a situation Margaret had been counting on when she'd sent him a note as dusk fell.

"Margaret, hold still. You tire yourself unnecessarily."

"My agitation is quite necessary, I assure you!" she replied stubbornly, although colors flashed before her eyes, and she knew she risked collapse if she did not take care. "The House of Commons Committee clearly doubts the verdict. Why else call the baker, Farriner, before them and ask if the fire at his premises could conceivably have been an accident?"

"Farriner testified an accident was out of the question," Etienne replied. "He swore he'd checked every room and the state of his hearths before retiring."

"Well, he *would* say that, wouldn't he?" Margaret felt guilty for the anger and impatience in her voice. Etienne was as convinced as she that the condemned Frenchman was innocent. "It is not a coincidence that three of the five people signing the indictment against Hubert came from the baker's family! A fire starting on Farriner's premises burned down the largest city in England. Farriner does not wish to be blamed for all that loss. But it is sin to let an innocent man hang for it!"

"Is it certain then that the King will not intervene?" Etienne placed himself firmly in Margaret's path, and Margaret, rather gratefully, came to a stop, leaning her clasped hands against his breast.

"That is what Her Majesty says." She shook her head sadly. "The Queen was distraught this afternoon. She told those few she permitted to wait upon her that Justice Kelynge had suggested the young man is feebleminded and quite probably beyond understanding the fate that awaits him. But His Majesty does not like the idea of riling all London by setting aside the verdict of a duly constituted jury. Her Majesty refused her supper in favor of retreating to her chapel to pray for Hubert. But *I* think"—Margaret's eyes locked fiercely upon Etienne's—"she ought to have said a few prayers for her husband's soul, for he is a coward in this matter."

"Margaret," Etienne hissed. "Talk like that could see you in irons."

Turning from him, Margaret sank into a chair before the fire to hide how much her knees shook. "Etienne, we are cowards too."

"If you refer to the matter of the Phoenix, our decision was sound."

"There is sound, and there is *right*. I am not sure they are the same in this case. And I fear I must do a grim thing in order to discover the truth of the matter."

"What is that," Etienne asked, eyes wary.

"Witness Robert Hubert's execution."

"How will that help?" Etienne gazed down at her, his eyes full of utter confusion.

Margaret struggled to put her swirling thoughts and feelings into words. "I am not sure it will. But Etienne I begin to fear my failure to report the Phoenix's crimes to Their Majesties will haunt me for the rest of my days. The thought of living every moment under a heavy yoke of unresolved guilt and sin . . ."

"Margaret, seeing one man hanged will not put the noose around the neck of the other. You just said yourself His Majesty is loath to start riots and stoke rumors by setting aside the jury verdict in Hubert's case. Well, if you decide to take our conclusions regarding the Phoenix to His Majesty, King Charles will have far more to lose than gain by crediting your words and placing Wren before the bar."

"Ah, but that decision will be on His Majesty's soul and conscience, not mine. He will answer to God for allowing the Phoenix his liberty or, worse still, rewarding his murderous actions with the commission for St. Paul's. I shall have done my best to seek justice."

He nodded. "I can understand how handing the decision to another, and in this case one whose God-given place it is to rule over us all, might salve your conscience, but—"

She reached out, taking his hand where it hung at his side. "But my soul will be made lighter at a mighty price to both of us, love," she whispered, as if afraid her words might be overheard. "I understand that Etienne. And that is perhaps why it is so important for me to be sure action is absolutely necessary."

By witnessing an execution?

"I know it sounds irrational, but much of life, and certainly men's thoughts and fears—as was amply demonstrated during and after the Fire—are irrational. I may be a woman of science, but I too have instincts and feelings defiant of reason. If there is even a chance that witnessing Hubert's end will clarify my duty in acting or failing to act in the matter of the Phoenix—"

"Do you know what that means, Margaret, to watch Hubert's final moments? Truly, do you? While many—perhaps most in London—view hangings as spectacle, I know your soul . . . you look away when the gibbets along the banks of the Thames are full."

"So do you, my love." She laid a hand on his shoulder. "You have no more stomach than I for dead men displayed in cages."

"And this will be a living man, killed before your eyes."

"Will you take me?"

"If you are certain, yes, I will."

◊

They arrived in Tyburn just past noon, under a weak sun in a gray sky. "You told me there would be thousands," Margaret said as the carriage rolled to a stop some distance from the triple tree gallows with its horizontal beam supported by three legs. Looking out of the carriage, she was surprised that although the wooden stands, constructed by villagers for whom hangings like this were a money-making business, were full, much of the ground around them was empty.

"There will be more people than this space can hold, but for many it is not enough to merely witness the hanging. They want to be part of the procession—jeering, joking. Men of business shut their doors on execution days as if they were holidays. Woe betide any of my apprentices if I spot them in this crowd."

"Shall we get out?"

"Not yet. There is a chill today." He reached across, tucking the blanket on Margaret's lap around her more securely. "We will hear twelve bells when they have reached St. Giles in the Fields, and even then they will be a half-hour's walk away. We need not step out of the carriage until the accused's cart is within sight."

Etienne had proposed, and Margaret had agreed, that they would sit atop the carriage rather than venturing into the crowd. "We will see well enough from there, or likely too well—I doubt either of us shall ever forget the sights of this day," he'd said.

Margaret closed her eyes, half wishing the wait were shorter because her mind did nothing but fill the time with terrible imaginings, and half wishing the cart would never arrive. At length, she heard the bells, and then the crowd, more like the rumbling of thunder or the growl of animals then human voices. She shuddered because the noise so closely resembled the unearthly sounds heard during the fire.

Opening her eyes she said, "Let's go up."

Etienne rapped on the carriage roof. As the footman opened the door, the driver unlashed a ladder from the equipage's rear and leaned it against the vehicle. Etienne climbed first, spreading a blanket on the roof and then reaching down to offer Margaret a hand.

Sitting, legs dangling, Margaret could at last see the crowd, a massive, sprawling thing moving in surges and jolts. At its front, walked an officious-looking man flanked by a half-dozen uniformed guards.

"That is the chief warder." Etienne pointed.

Next came a wooden cart. At first, Margaret only saw one man inside—a bulky fellow, wearing a leather jerkin and a flat, wide-brimmed, black hat, crouched at one side of the open bed. But as it drew closer, she spotted a second man across from the first, hunched so low that his head barely cleared the cart's rim. He was dressed in black, and a hemp noose hung from his scrawny neck. "That must be Hubert. What has happened to his eye?" An angry red gash marked the man's pale forehead above one of his eyebrows, and blood streamed from it.

"He's been pelted along the way." Etienne bit off the words. "Something thrown found its mark."

"Whosoever hateth his brother is a murderer: and ye know that no murderer hath eternal life abiding in him." The words of the apostle ran through Margaret's mind as fluidly as the blood ran down the side of Hubert's face.

The cart stopped beneath the crossbeam of the scaffold, and the burly man pulled the smaller one to his feet. Hubert was wound all around with the noose's tail. His face, already ashen, contorted at the sight of the beam upon which he would die. He looked from it to the man who had hauled him up, then glanced wildly around like an animal cornered by hounds. The crowd fell silent.

"What are they waiting for?" Margaret whispered, shuddering.

"They expect the condemned to bow," Etienne murmured.

But instead, Hubert slumped into the large man, who thrust him roughly upright again with a sneer.

Jack Ketch, the man in the jerkin with the ferocious face must be the executioner.

Margaret had heard of Ketch. He was spoken of with fear, even at court. People said he had a way with death. They whispered his wife bragged of it, of how he could make death the quickest or slowest thing imaginable; make men drop or dance according to their deserts and for the entertainment of an appreciative crowd.

Ketch shoved Hubert again, then motioned, as if the Frenchman were a child too young to understand words, urging the condemned to speak. Instead, Hubert dropped his head to his chest, and the crowd snarled.

Even the faces of the women and children contort as if they are demons.

In all her life, Margaret had never seen anything like it. She recoiled, pressing herself against Etienne, finding even the arm he slipped around her insufficient shelter.

Shaking his head and rolling his eyes, the executioner mimed a shrug to the jeering crowd, then climbed from the cart. A set of steps was pushed into place, and a priest climbed into the cart. Margaret recognized the cleric from Whitehall: the Queen, it seemed, had sent her own confessor to offer comfort to the dying man. This evidence of her mistress's compassion, when all around seemed entirely devoid of it, brought tears to Margaret's eyes.

The shouts and cries of the crowd faded. There was a palpable prickling of expectation, and near silence as the priest began to offer a prayer. When he stopped, Hubert spoke at last, his voice rising to a panicked shriek, his words French.

Beside her Etienne pressed a fist to his mouth.

"What did he say," Margaret asked.

"He recanted." There was pain in Etienne's voice, and glanc-ing at him sideways, Margaret saw that his eyes too were wet with tears.

"Surely the priest will tell the warder, will translate and . . ." Margaret let the sentence trail off. A jury had convicted Hubert based on his own confession, and whatever he said now came too late.

The crowd began to roar again in anticipation. Margaret pressed her hands to her ears to muffle the noise. She wanted to roar too, not for blood, but for justice; to rage at the travesty playing out before her. Climbing back onto the cart, the execu-tioner drew Hubert to its center, directly beneath the scaffold crossbeam. Unwinding the rope from around the Frenchman with the finesse of a showman, Ketch threw it to a lackey sitting on one of the scaffold's supporting beams. This man secured the rope while the crowd hooted.

Feeling the noose rise behind his neck and realizing why, Hubert's mouth dropped open. In his tortured eyes, Margaret saw the scream that she could not hear over the noise of the once again raucous crowd.

Ketch jumped down, drew a short black whip from inside his vest, and walked to the cart horse's rear flank. Silence fell over the blood-crazed crowd.

Be done with it! The voice in Margaret's head shouted. She struggled to breathe, as if her own neck were in a noose. Ketch raised the crop in the air, and then paused, enjoying a moment that ought to have been nothing but awful for any Christian man. He nodded at the man who held the horse's head to release it, then down the crop came, cracking with a cruel, sharp thwack.

The cart surged forward, and Hubert staggered along in it until there was no more cart. Then he hung in midair, twist-ing, turning, legs thrashing. To Margaret's horror, his motions were mimicked by many in the crowd, including children, who capered about, holding a fist at one side of their necks and cocking their heads as if they hung from a noose. Even those who did not mimic jeered.

"Die, dear God in heaven, let him die." Margaret was unaware she'd said it aloud until Etienne's arm around her tightened. And still Hubert lived, his tongue lolling, his bulging eyes full of unspeakable terror. A great burst of laughter sounded as the front of his pants became wet. It seemed as if it would never end, but at last the poor man's body was still, moved only by the breeze. Margaret, who had lowered her eyes to his twitching feet to avoid witnessing any more of Hubert's fear, hazarded a glance at the dead man's face and gasped—it was blackened and badly contorted.

Ketch cut the body down, letting it drop like a sack of flour, as if it had never been a man. A surgeon stooped over the remains. As soon as he straightened, declaring Hubert dead, Ketch began to strip the Frenchman beginning with the rope.

"What is he doing?" Margaret cried.

"The dead man's effects are part of his pay. He will sell them, and without doubt, since so many believe that Hubert was the burner of London, Ketch will make a mighty sum." Etienne put his fingers into his mouth and gave a low whistle, recalling the attention of the servants. "Margaret, it is time to go. Margaret?"

He touched her shoulder, but Margaret could not reply, for an angry horde of spectators had broken through the line of guards surrounding the executioner and his victim. Despite Ketch's solid, muscular figure and fearful reputation, members of the crowd wrestled the corpse from him. Once they had it, they attacked as bears might claw a dog that came within reach at a baiting, howling as they did.

So many swarmed that soon, blessedly, Margaret could no longer see Hubert's body. Momentarily freed from the horrible spectacle, she turned to Etienne. "Let us be gone." She lowered a foot cautiously onto the first step of the ladder, only to be distracted but a great cheer. Glancing across the frenzied mass, she saw a severed arm waved in the air, bloody and ragged where it had once joined Hubert's body.

Losing her footing, she slid helplessly down the rest of the ladder, scraping her back viciously and landing in a heap on the ground. Jumping from the roof, Etienne scooped her into his arms and thrust her into the carriage. They were in motion the moment he joined her, before he could even secure the door.

"They ripped him apart as if they were wild beasts," Margaret sobbed. Then scrambling to her knees on the carriage seat, she opened the window and vomited.

"I will never forgive myself for bringing you to Tyburn," Etienne said as she fell back onto the seat. He held out his handkerchief.

"I fear that is true, but not for the reason you think." Margaret wiped away the bits of sick that clung to the edges of her mouth. "For having seen an innocent man hanged for a crime he did not commit—that no one committed—I cannot allow a genuine crime to pass unremarked. I have been weak, allowing my wish to continue my life as it is to keep me from doing what I knew to be right. Whatever the danger or cost to myself, I must confront the Phoenix with his murder of Thomas and his firing of St. Paul's."

"No, Margaret. No."

"Yes. I cannot bring Wren to justice, but I can act as the conscience he does not have, speaking the words of his crimes to him in a way that will fix them forever on his soul."

"If someone must risk his wrath, I shall. I could not bear for you to die at his hands." Etienne's voice broke, and he paused and bit his upper lip. "I hold my own life less dear than yours and less dear than I once did, for I have come to accept that it is already foreshortened. Not in years perhaps, but in moments of joy, all of which will end when we part. Under such circumstances, I do not fear death."

Margaret closed her eyes until the flashes of colors that had begun to narrow her vision turned into a swirl of images—not from the hanging of Robert Hubert, but from her own life. The happiest were recent, and all involved the man sitting across from her. Opening her eyes again, she took both his hands in her own.

"I do not fear death either, and I know it well, for I have been threatened with it all my life. I have been told if I rode too long, got too excited . . . if I did much of anything worth doing, death would claim me through my weak heart. Well, here I am. And I do not believe death will have me this time. But if I am to live many long years, I must do so with a clear conscience."

He would not meet her eyes, so she released his hands and put her own on his cheeks—turning his head until he could not avoid her gaze. "I promise you, Etienne, if you let me do this myself, I will spend those years with you."

CHAPTER 14

Present-day London

Thursday

Nigella arrived in the empty incident room at seven AM. O'Leary had said he planned to be in early when she'd dropped him home after their trip to Betchworth, but he had a fairly flexible understanding of that term.

Spotting an envelope in their inbox, she slit it open, hoping for the police artist's rendition of their suspicious homeless man. Not the sketch; a dental records match. No surprise, but the confirmation would occasion a lot of pain for Peter Smyth and his parents. *What a shitty start to the day.*

The thought was hanging like a cartoon bubble over her as Evans stuck his head in. "I was up last night thinking about your damn killer's demands. I can't see a way forward that doesn't leave us looking like we're praising that arsehole. Just running pictures of his wood figure from St. James's as part of an article saying that crime may be linked to the Temple murder won't satisfy him."

"Nope," Nigella agreed.

"And doing more is obscene." Evans tugged at the knot in his tie, and then, aware of the gesture, said, "Not half seven, and I'm reduced to tie loosening. That breaks all kinds of records. Parker, if we're not going to give our killer the artistic evaluation he wants, we both know what comes next."

"More bodies."

"We don't like more bodies. For our sakes—and for the sake of the folks walking around right now enjoying an autumn day who will *be* those next bodies—"

"I've got to catch this bastard before corpses are piled up like firewood." She shivered at her own word choice.

As Evans moved off, still looking disgruntled, Tweedle Two slipped into the incident room.

"What did Taylor say about his van keys? He take 'em on vacation?"

"Sorry, guv'nor, not following." His eyes held that special mix of confusion and terror common in officers unable to answer a senior officer's question. "You asked me to confirm Taylor was in Spain, and he was."

"I asked you to find out about the keys to his van. Please tell me you didn't wait to do that until you'd checked airline tickets."

"I . . ." The skipper stopped talking and just stared. Then he pulled a pad from his pocket and flipped through the pages. "I have a list of all your instructions here, guv'nor. I've got nothing about keys."

Nigella had a bad feeling. She pulled up her messaging app. There it was, the half-finished, unsent sentence containing her request to ask about keys.

"Oversight on my part, Sergeant. I need you to get on with Taylor, find out if he ever made a copy of his van keys, and if so, who has them. Also, where his keys were while he was on vacation."

"Right." He snapped his notebook shut. "He's probably asleep with his phone on silent, so I'll get out to Basildon."

Nigella watched him go and then sat glowering. She wasn't angry at Tweedle Two. She didn't like slipping up; it cost them time they didn't have. But being angry at herself didn't feel like enough under the circumstances, not on a morning like this, with every step that felt like "next" stymied . . . and with goddamn O'Leary more than "missed the train by that much" late.

And just at that moment, he sauntered in. Without thinking, Nigella picked up the nearest thing—a stapler—and threw it at him.

He dodged and it fell with a thud.

"What the hell, Ni?! That's not a customary greeting at the Met."

"You're not at the Met now, O'Leary."

"And to think I was just telling folks at the Yard it wasn't half bad working over here . . . that is, *after* I chewed out a couple of people." He held out an envelope. "Got a call this AM asking me didn't I want the sketch that had been setting on my desk since midday yesterday. Wish I'd known about your stapler-throwing tradition, because I'd have used it to get the attention of the Skip, who wasn't clear on the fact that my Met desk is not my desk at the moment, and stuff sitting on it's in limbo."

As she took the envelope, he shook his head. "You thought I'd stopped for breakfast."

"Well, you're known to be tardy." She knew she sounded churlish but couldn't help it.

"Ni, compared to you, the whole world is tardy. But this morning I beat you here. I was sitting right in that chair when I got the call."

"Sorry."

"Yeah, well, do me a favor and maybe stop assuming I'm a fuckup."

"I never assume that, O'Leary. You're one of the best they've got over there." She stood, offering him the chair back, even though there were several others empty.

"Backhanded compliment, but I'll take it. Go on—have a look."

The man in the sketch wore a hoodie, hood up. A bit of dark brown curly hair peeked out at the front. The unshaven face was better than average looking. He had brown eyes, lips that were neither thick nor thin, a decent jawline. All in all, a nice-looking man, late twenties or early thirties, without any distinguishing characteristics, stared out at her from the page. As Nigella stared back, she couldn't help thinking he seemed vaguely familiar.

"Does this guy look like someone we've seen?"

O'Leary leaned over. "At the risk of being a victim of further stapler violence, he reminds me of that fellow you're dating."

James? Did he look like James? Jawline was similar, hair too, but not the eyes.

"Maybe a little, but . . . naw. Damn it, I am not sure whether to blame Neil or the artist, but we've been given such an everyman, I am afraid he's going to look familiar to everybody."

"You're not wrong," O'Leary replied in disgust.

Nigella sighed and flipped to the descriptive sheet attached to the sketch.

"We've got a tattoo, or at least we might have. Our homeless friend thinks that he saw a bird on the underside of one of this guy's arms, about midway between wrist and elbow."

"What do you bet it's a flipping phoenix?" O'Leary said.

Or a dove. James had a dove tattoo . . . *"My dove"—that's what Etienne called Margaret.*

Sitting in bed last evening, Nigella had found herself irresistibly drawn to Lady Margaret's notes. She'd begun deciphering the difficult, antiquated hand. The first page started with a short description of Margaret and Etienne, laying out their credentials so that a reader might judge their credibility. But what shone from the prose, confronting Nigella in every line, was Margaret's warmth of feeling for Etienne. Their mutual love and respect could not be missed and made Nigella uncomfortable. *I'd rather know who the Phoenix is,* she'd thought.

"Speaking of phoenixes," she said, laying the sketch on the conference table and swiveling to face O'Leary, "I started on those three-hundred-year-old case notes before passing out from exhaustion last night—"

"Without me?" He looked hurt.

"Yeah, sorry. Aren't you the one who's always saying history is *my* thing?"

"Those notes aren't just history, Ni. I said it before: we were destined to find them. They relate to this case, even if we can't see how. So if you're going to do anymore bedtime reading, let's do it together."

"All right, the notes will be our reward for a day's work well done. But I am *not* calling them bedtime reading, because the closest you'll ever get to my bed again, O'Leary, is a seat on my sofa with all the lights on."

"All the better to read by."

"Now let's take our handsome-but not-really-distinctive fellow to GG&S."

Nigella was backing out when her mobile rang.

"It's Tweedle Two," she said before hitting the hands-free. "Go ahead, Sergeant."

"Guv'nor, Taylor had a house sitter while he was in Spain. Needed someone to feed the cat."

"And let me guess, the house sitter had the keys."

"Whole set."

"O'Leary and I are on our way. Good work. Now get yourself back to the nick. There's a sketch in the incident room—man in a hoodie. Make a copy and head to GG&S. Ask Mrs. Kay who to show it to—discreetly Sergeant, discreetly."

"That one is definitely Dee, not Dum," O'Leary said. "Off to glamorous Basildon. I'm betting we don't get a warm welcome given last time we were there, we hauled Taylor away in cuffs."

O'Leary was wrong. Taylor was completely cordial. He took them through to the kitchen. "Hope you don't mind. I haven't cranked the central yet, so the kitchen's the warmest room. Tea?"

"No thanks." Nigella and O'Leary took seats at the table. As if on cue, a ginger cat leapt to the tabletop. "So this is the cat who needed sitting," Nigella said, reaching out a hand to stroke it.

"Yep, that's Mr. Snuggles." Taylor reddened. "I didn't name him; Sheila did—Sheila from payroll."

"Does Sheila live here as well, then?"

"Moved in about six months back. I don't mind saying it's been the best six months of my life. That's one reason we went away—anniversary. Anyway, we couldn't leave Mr. Snuggles with no one to look after him."

"Mr. Nelson"—Nigella drew the sketch out of its envelope and laid it on the table—"do you recognize this man?"

"Looks kinda like Nicholas." He picked up the sketch and peered at the face more closely. "I've never seen him dressed in a hoodie, or unshaven. But still, it really does look like him—sort of."

"And Nicholas is?"

"My house sitter: Nicholas Hawksmoor."

And just like that we have a name. Nigella felt her breath quicken. And she felt something else as well—a touch of relief that the name wasn't "James." So, subconsciously at least, she hadn't quite dismissed the resemblance or the bird tattoo coincidence. *How unnerving.*

"Where'd you find Nicholas?" O'Leary's question snapped Ni's attention back to Taylor.

"Don't remember exactly. I put a note up on the bulletin board at work—"

Nigella noticed O'Leary was taking notes. Good man.

"—used one of those free house-minder websites, and Sheila had the idea of putting up a notice at her old college, looking for a student interested. All them places had my phone number. We had a couple of calls, and I got coffee with the ones that seemed worth it, to check 'em out in person."

"You had coffee with Nicholas?" Nigella asked.

"Right here. He was the only one who offered to come out. That's one of the reasons I hired him. And he was cheaper than some of the others. Gave me a reference: fellow in London. Nicholas told me to wait until after seven to call 'cause he worked long hours. Bloke was enthused. Said he came back to a happy dog and a house that didn't look like someone had thrown a party."

"I don't suppose you'd have that name and number?"

"Naw. Six months ago I would've. Bit of a pack rat by nature, but I'm trying to be more tidy, for Sheila."

"Do you remember the name?"

"Christopher something or other."

"What about Nicholas—did he tell you what he did besides pet-sitting?"

"Graduate student, I do remember that. He told me house sitting was a much more pleasant way to make pocket change than being a barista at some coffee place near campus."

"Which campus?"

"UAL, I think, or maybe that just sticks in my mind because that's where Sheila went—she studied graphic design before transferring and switching to accounting."

University of the Arts London! An art school, and our killer is an artist. This identification felt real, but so had the last, and he was now sitting across from her as a witness.

"Did Nicholas have any tattoos?"

"Can't say as I noticed. He was a friendly sort, and Mr. Snuggles warmed right up to him, sort of like he has to your friend there."

The orange cat had climbed into O'Leary's lap and rolled onto its back, seeking the DI's attention.

"Once you decided to hire him, how were the keys handled?"

"Nicholas suggested he take mine and drop 'em through the mail slot after he visited Mr. Snuggles that last Saturday. So that's what we did. I hid 'em in the back garden the morning we left, Sheila took her set, and when we got back, mine were lying on the mat inside the door."

The cat rolled too far, landing with a thud on the floor. O'Leary leaned down, scooped it up, and put it back on his lap.

"Mr. Taylor, do you have contact information for Nicholas?"

"Yeah. I have him in my mobile because I'd definitely hire him again."

Not if you knew what we do.

"Mr. Taylor, I have a couple of strong suggestions. O'Leary, can I have a sheet off your pad?" Nigella laid the paper on the table between herself and the witness. "First, change your locks." She wrote that down. "Do it today. Second, once Detective

O'Leary and I leave, do not call Nicholas again—ever—and do not take calls from him. Third, if Nicholas shows up, do not open the door, and call 999. When you reach the emergency dispatcher, tell them you have a dangerous man on your property and give them my name. Tell them that I am looking for this person in connection with a violent crime. Will you do that for me?"

Nelson Taylor nodded, eyes wide. Nigella added her name and number to the bottom of the short list and slid the paper over.

"Mr. Taylor, we have reason to believe that your house sitter used your keys to retrieve your van, then used your van in the commission of three crimes, one of which ended with a man brutally murdered. Do you remember the picture I showed you at the station? That is the man that we believe Nicholas murdered and then set on fire."

"Oh God," he gasped. "I think I'm going to be sick."

"I don't blame you. Detective O'Leary and I have been queasy over this case ourselves. So the minute we leave, you're going to put the kettle on, and while you're waiting for it to boil, you're going to call a locksmith. Now mind you, I do not believe Nicholas will come here—there is no reason for him to—but this is definitely a case of better safe than sorry."

Taylor nodded vigorously.

"Before we go, I am going to ask two favors. First, I'd like Nicholas's number, and then, while we're all sitting here together, I'd like you to ring him."

"Ring him? What am I supposed to say: 'Hey, you seemed like a great bloke, and the cat liked you, but the police are here and they say you're a murderer'?'"

"No, you are absolutely not to say that. If he answers, you're just going to tell him you have a friend who needs some house sitting, and would it be all right to pass his number along. Tell him your friend's name is Mary."

She'd call Nicholas later, as Mary, attempt to set up a meeting. It was a long shot, but worth a try.

"You can put the call on speaker, and we will be right here with you," she said soothingly.

Nelson Taylor swallowed hard. Nigella thought he was going to balk, but he took the mobile phone from his pocket. "You want the number first?"

"Yes, please. O'Leary, stop petting the cat and write it down."

Taylor read it out, a 020 exchange: London, pretty much anywhere in London. Then he put the phone in the middle of the table and pushed "Call." No answer. Interestingly, the voicemail was nothing more than a computerized female voice repeating the number back and suggesting the caller leave a message. They didn't.

Nigella stood up and stuck out her hand. "Thank you so much, Mr. Taylor."

As Taylor released her hand, his mobile vibrated and the screen lit up. He picked it off the table, then passed it to Nigella as if it were made of molten metal. "It's a text from Nicholas."

Sorry I missed your call, Nelson. What's up?

"May I?" Nigella asked.

He hesitated. Clearly having a text exchange with a likely killer was freaking him out.

"I'll just say exactly what you planned to if he'd answered."

He licked his lips. "All right."

The response was immediate: *Sure, pass along my number.*

Back in the car, O'Leary said, "We have a name, we've got a mobile number—things are about to get ugly for Nicholas Hawksmoor."

"God, I hope so." Nigella backed out of the drive. "O'Leary, are you picking cat fur off yourself and dropping it in my car?"

He collected a particularly large clump and set it on the dashboard. "Consider this me getting even for your stapler toss."

"Well, stop, and get on the line with the nick. Tell them to run a records check for Hawksmoor. And get them started on tracking that mobile. He may have location services turned off, but we can still triangulate from the towers."

When O'Leary got done giving instructions, he said, "This boy's an artist, right? How about I google his name along with the word 'artist'? Maybe he'll have a website or be mentioned in conjunction with some art-exhibity place." He fiddled with his phone, then cursed. "Hate to tell you this, Ni, but we do *not* have a name—or rather, we do but we're being played. Nicholas Hawksmoor was a late-seventeenth- and early-eighteenth-century architect. One guess who he worked with."

"Christ! Not Christopher Wren."

"Exactly. Wren took this Hawksmoor bloke on as a clerk in 1679. He worked with Wren, then with some other high flyer, and by the eighteenth century he was building stuff on his own, including half a dozen London-area churches."

"That clinches it: the house sitter is our killer. And he is no more Nicholas Hawksmoor than you are."

He laughed.

"What the hell is funny?"

"I just asked for a records check on a bloke who has been dead a couple of hundred years. Imagine the shit we're going to get if anybody back at Wood Street learns our big lead of the morning is a dead church architect?"

She groaned.

"But listen, Ni, this is still a big break. We've got that phone number, and we know, thanks to Taylor's reaction, that the suspect can be recognized from the sketch."

♦

O'Leary stretched, interrupting Nigella's thought: *The last person to sit with his head this close to my knee was James, and he was naked.*

"Refill on the coffee?" He rose, reaching for her cup. They'd knocked off around seven, feeling they'd made genuine progress but not wanting to jinx things by crowing about it, and O'Leary had ridden home with Nigella for an evening of seventeenth-century note reading.

"I'd say it's about time to switch to wine." Nigella had just finished reading Margaret and Etienne's autopsy notes aloud, and her experienced detective's mind, full of dead bodies, had brought the details to life.

"Tell me what to open," O'Leary replied, gliding into the kitchen and pulling the corkscrew from a drawer. "I am glad we didn't get to the part about finding that poor burnt-up stationer until after we finished our curry, or I'd be off Indian for months."

"And I am glad you've never asked me to stand in for a victim hit with a pries bar."

"Why? Do you think I'd insist on a greater level of authenticity then Monsieur Belland?"

"You really can't speak French at all." Nigella grinned at his genuinely awful pronunciation of "Monsieur."

"Nope. Yet another reason I am not a successful ladies' man. This red okay?" He held up a bottle extracted from her wine cooler and, when Nigella nodded, opened it and poured.

He still knows where everything is. And he's the only man you've ever allowed to learn that in the first place.

O'Leary returned to the sofa and handed both glasses to Nigella. "I don't like my chances of lowering myself to the floor without spillage. And we both know how you feel about your white carpet."

"Hang on," Nigella said. "In all fairness, I think it's your turn up here." She set the glasses next to the pages on the side table and uncoiled her legs from beneath her.

"Clever, you're tired of reading aloud, so you're putting me in the spot with the better light."

"If you mean tired of your quips when I make an error, yeah. Let's see how easily you get on, shall we?" She picked up her glass and sank down, cross-legged, without spilling a drop.

"Looks like it's suspect interview time—after a fashion. Let's see here . . . what the heck is a Pebble Courtyard?"

Fifteen minutes of joint decoding later, Nigella set her empty glass down. "The Phoenix is Wren—*the* Christopher Wren— has to be."

"Yeah. Jesus. I think it does," O'Leary replied. "I mean he *is* Mr. St. Paul's. I don't know about you, but if we finish these pages and I'm convinced the famous Sir Christopher Wren was a remorseless killer, I'm never going to look at that view in quite the same way again." He pointed at the dome shining across the river.

"I am glad Margaret and Etienne are long dead," Nigella said. "It'd be hard for them to swallow how revered their suspect has become. Or maybe they lived long enough to know it . . . I wonder." She linked her fingers, stretched her arms palms upward over her head, and yawned. "Should we try to finish tonight?"

"That's your third yawn." O'Leary slid the aged pages into their folder. "Three yawns and I'm out. It's a rule that's served me well."

"Guess you're right." Nigella raised a hand to stifle yet another yawn. "We want to be on our game tomorrow. And even if Wren is the Phoenix, it's not like we disinter him and slap the cuffs on."

O'Leary laid the folder of notes down with a shake of his head, "Maybe it's the second-generation cop in me, but I still hope Wren gets his if he is guilty—even if it is just a kick in the reputation administered by some bushy-browed historian."

Nigella picked up both glasses and took them to the sink. "I am still disappointed our skipper didn't get an identification at GG&S."

Tweedle Two had reported back just before the end of the day. He'd shown hoodie-boy to the folks in HR, Andrew Smyth's secretary, and a couple dozen lawyers on Smyth's current cases. Several felt the man looked familiar, but none had experienced the sort of "aha" moment Taylor had. O'Leary thought the problem—besides the fact that sketch-guy wasn't all that distinctive—might be the two-day beard and clothing. "I'll ask the artist to clean Nick up," he'd said—they'd begun calling the killer "Nick," even though they knew he wasn't.

"Should get location data on the suspect's phone tomorrow. And the lab on the nail we nicked." She started washing the glasses. O'Leary came to stand beside her picking up a towel.

"If the nail's a link, we tear that sweet little barn and cottage apart." He opened the cupboard and put the first glass away with the same ease that he'd found the corkscrew.

She handed him the second glass. "Given the hour, you're welcome to sack out on my sofa. I've got an extra phone charger and a toothbrush." She felt suddenly embarrassed, possibly by the realization that she'd once allowed things to get to the point where he'd kept his own toothbrush there. Part of her was glad O'Leary's face was hidden behind the cupboard door, but another part wished it wasn't, so she could gauge his reaction.

The door swung shut. He wore his teasing smile. "This your plot to make certain I'm at work on time? Or make that on 'Nigella time' because, honestly, woman, I'm one of the first officers in at the Met most mornings."

"That doesn't speak well of the Met."

"No, *you* don't speak well of the Met—not ever, if you can help it. But despite your ulterior motives, I'm tempted by your hospitality. It's a long ride to my place."

"I'll get you a pillow." Nigella dried her hands.

"Throw in that eiderdown your gran made, and it's a deal. You know, the one that so doesn't go with your decor."

Nigella didn't answer, just pulled the cover and the pillow from her linen cupboard and tossed them on the sofa.

Tucked in her own bed, she could hear O'Leary's breathing slow as he slipped into sleep before she had even turned out her light.

A phone shrilled. Something felt off about it. Struggling to consciousness, Nigella grabbed her mobile from the bedside, hit the button, and pressed it to her ear. "DI Parker," she said—to a dial tone. And still the ringing sounded. *Not my ring.*

In the next room she heard O'Leary croak, "O'Leary here, go ahead." There was a pause. "Aw, sweet Jesus. Get barriers up!" Two more beats of silence. "On my way, and I'll let Parker at City know."

Nigella looked at the clock: it was just 12:42 AM. No wonder it had been hard to wake up—she had been asleep less than an hour. She swung her legs out of bed and stood just as O'Leary, in his tee and boxers, appeared at the door. "Christ Church Spittelfields, and Ni it sounds like—"

Another ringing. This time it *was* Nigella's mobile. "What do we have, guv'nor?" she asked.

"Good guess," Evans responded. "Or maybe not, because lately when your phone rings at night, it's me with bad news. This one is on Met ground."

"I know," she replied. And then, thinking he might deduce that O'Leary was with her, added, "O'Leary's been in touch."

"Good man. I'll let you get out of there then." Evans hung up.

O'Leary had disappeared. Nigella stripped out of her pajamas without worrying where he'd gone or if he'd pop back while she was semi-clothed. He stuck his head in as she pulled a comb through her hair.

"Sounds like we have a change up: two objects and only one on fire."

"Either of them human?"

"Yeah. And apparently another disturbing display." O'Leary paused, "Officer who called sounded unhinged. And he's not the type to come undone at a crime scene."

"Fuck, I hate Nick," Nigella said picking up her bag. "Let's get there."

They rolled up, all sirens and lights, abandoning the car on Commercial Street, which was blocked in any event. Blocked, but not deserted. A massive wall of police barriers stood on the steps of Christ Church.

O'Leary paused and took it all in. "How the hell did he have the balls? On the steps of a church at the crossing of two major streets that wouldn't have been deserted—not even gone midnight. That's not just bold, Ni—it's crazy."

"Yeah," she replied, staring at a group of sobbing women huddled beside a uniformed officer. They looked to be in their mid-twenties and out for a hen night: a bit of fun that had certainly taken a turn for the worst.

"Let's get in there," O'Leary said. They only got a few feet up the steps before a burly officer accosted them, or rather O'Leary.

"Just so you know before you step behind the barrier, we've got a dead bloke wrapped in wire and flamed," he said, "with a bleeding wooden angel standing watch. All the boys were hoping he was wood too, but we knew he wasn't, from the smell."

"Right, this has to be the same killer as our ongoing case with City. We need the same forensics. Ring and tell them to get Wilmerson."

"Wilkinson," Nigella corrected.

"What she said. Tell them to wake him whether he's on call or not. Then tell our team he's taking lead, and if they don't like it, they can lump it, because he was at the Temple fire."

He turned to Nigella. "You ready."

Never, and always.

The scene was surreal by any standards. Her eyes were caught first by an angel, petite and decidedly feminine. Like the figures that had come before, she was naked and had rough patches. But she was unburned. She stood glistening under the beam of one of the church's spotlights, with wings that appeared to be of velvet and burlap stretched out to her sides. Her arms reached to the heavens but her eyes were cast down. Had they been real, her gaze would have fallen on the crime's victim: naked, partially burned, curled tight, arms clasped around his own coiled legs, and encased in an orb of wire mesh.

"His legs are pressed right up against the wire," Nigella said grimly. "Nick trussed this poor soul like a sacrifice so that muscle movements were limited during the burn."

"Let's hope," O'Leary said in a low voice, "Nick the prick had the decency to finish him off before setting him alight."

In her head, Nigella heard screaming: not a man, but two little girls screaming in fear and pain. She curled her fingers into her palms until nails bit flesh. That always made the screaming stop. Then she focused on the corpse again.

The victim had areas of unburnt skin, particularly where his legs folded against his torso. Some of his hair was intact. Under the lights, its color was jarringly close to O'Leary's auburn. "He didn't burn for long. That likely means he *was* dead, because I don't think this burn would have been enough to kill him."

The burly cop rejoined them as she was speaking. "He was dead when we got here. I checked him myself before I called you, guv'nor." He nodded at O'Leary.

No wonder he'd been unhinged on the phone, Nigella thought. Checking those remains for vitals . . .

"Wilkinson on his way?" O'Leary asked.

"Yes."

"Witnesses?"

"At least a dozen. But most were drawn by the fire and didn't see this stuff being set in place." He pointed to the group of young women Nigella had noticed. "They saw your killer arrive."

"Then they're the ones we speak to tonight. Commandeer a room in that pub on the corner. I don't want to make those ladies answer questions standing on the street with the smell of a dead bloke hanging in the air."

The officer headed off. "The rest of you, out." The suited forensic folk and stray uniformed officers didn't question, just moved to the other side of the barricades.

"I figured we need a little time alone with our thoughts and Nick's handiwork."

Nigella nodded. "Corpse or angel?"

"Corpse. My ground, so the rough stuff falls on me."

She didn't argue, just moved up the steps to the shining feminine form. Pulling on a pair of gloves, she gingerly touched a wooden shoulder. Her glove glistened. Nigella sniffed. "Linseed oil, so maybe he meant her to burn. Maybe he meant her to catch fire from the victim."

"If he'd wanted that, why put him two steps down?" O'Leary replied, looking up.

From this angle, his hair looked even more like the victim's. Nigella shivered.

"Heavy-gauge wire around wrists and ankles. Casing is standard chicken wire. Hold on! What's this?" He leaned in, then dry heaved. Little wonder, Nigella could smell the malodorous combination of smoke and burnt flesh where she stood. With his face so close to the dead man, O'Leary must have been choking on it. He took a great gulping swallow of air and held it, reaching two gloved fingers through the wire and into the curl of the dead man's body—where the skin was still intact. Extracting what looked like a crumpled ball of newspaper he held it toward her.

Nigella came down the steps and took it. As O'Leary rose, she began gently pulling it open. She saw the headline first: "Is He Number One Among *Ten to Watch*?" Uncrumpling a bit further, she glimpsed an image of a steel clothespin. Nigella nearly dropped the paper on the steps in her hurry to shove it back at O'Leary. As soon as he had it, she doubled over. Unlike her fellow DI, she didn't just heave, she vomited—something she had not done at a crime scene since she was a rookie.

"Ni? What is it?" She felt O'Leary's hand on her back.

"I think I know who the victim is," she replied, carefully keeping her eyes from the desecrated form. "Ethan Fox. I've met him. He's an artist from the *Ten British Artists to Keep an Eye On* exhibit I attended last month."

"You sure?"

She straightened up. "How the hell can I be *sure* in his current condition? But that paper in your hand—I think it's coverage of Fox. "And"—she looked straight up into the night sky and took a deep breath—"he had hair just the color of yours. So does the victim."

O'Leary made no reply. She could hear the sound of paper—presumably of him flattening out the clipping. "It *is* about Fox," he said at last. "Poor bugger is grinning in this picture like his whole brilliant life is in front of him." He paused. "It should have been."

She knew what he was thinking, because she was thinking it too: *we failed him.*

He touched her shoulder, and their eyes met. His were harder and brighter than a moment ago. The armor was on. It was time for Nigella to put hers on too. "Let's interview those witnesses," she said.

The back room of the pub was warm, but the young women shook. The one sitting nearest Nigella had mascara running down her face but, unlike the others, wasn't crying anymore. That's probably why O'Leary started with her.

"Becky," he said—the burly officer had given them all the names before leaving to finish collecting statements—"I understand you saw the fellow responsible for all this arrive."

"I did—we did—or rather saw him on the steps. A car was at the curb with its flashers on, and he was setting something down." She stopped and bit her lip. "He smiled at Agnes and me, then he pulled the cloth off like he was a magician, and there was this angel. And he said, 'Behold, beauty for the beautiful.'"

"He spoke to you?"

"Yeah. And he gave an elaborate bow. We all laughed. We figured he was an artist or a busker setting up."

"What'd he look like?"

"I don't know." Then, as if seeing or sensing O'Leary's disbelief, "He had a hoodie on, and he was wearing a mask, which is another reason I thought he was a performer."

"What kind of a mask?"

"Like a carnival mask, one of them black and silver ones with lace and feathers. And then he bounded down the stairs and took something else out of the back of his car. A big shiny ball."

"Shiny how?"

"Wrapped all in shiny paper."

Like a fucking birthday present.

"What kind of car?" O'Leary asked.

"White hatchback."

The Corsa.

"So he took this ball out of the back of a white car. Did it seem heavy?"

"I don't know. I didn't touch it!" Becky recoiled, as if O'Leary had struck her.

One of the other girls, the one wearing a sash proclaiming her the bride-to-be, used both fists to wipe her eyes, then leaned forward. "He did this staggering thing as he lifted it out of the back. Then he put it down and sort of rolled it up the steps. He was really leaning into it. I thought it was an act. I laughed. I *laughed*." She burst into tears.

"You couldn't have known—none of you could have." O'Leary looked from young woman to young woman. "This is a horrible, extraordinary thing. DI Parker and I have been police officers for years, and this is still shocking to us."

"Did you say 'Parker'?" a third girl, with too much rouge on and hair bleached nearly white, spoke up.

O'Leary had introduced himself at the beginning of the interview but skipped Nigella, and she'd felt no need to jump in and embarrass him.

"Yes, I am Detective Inspector Nigella Parker."

Every one of the girls reacted—eyes widened, mouths gaped.

"He mentioned you!" Becky pointed accusatorily at Nigella.

"Hold on," O'Leary said. "You sure?"

"Yeah!" Becky leaned forward, hands on knees. "After he got the ball up the stairs, he turned to us and said something about this being the real show, the real moment of magic—"

"No, he didn't say 'magic,'" the blonde interrupted. "He said 'creation.' I noticed, because I was all like whaaat?"

"And then he lit the ball on fire, turned, and said: 'If you enjoy the show, please tell Ms. Parker.' Then he gave another bow and went off. That was a bit confusing because it wasn't like there was some lady standing by, handing out surveys. But I forgot about it right quick 'cause I was focused on watching the ball—we all were. He promised a show, so I thought something brill was going to happen. But when the covering burned away, there was a man in there! And he started burning too. And we were screaming, and people started running."

If you enjoy the show, please tell Ms. Parker. The bastard was taunting her.

O'Leary looked at her sideways. He seemed to have lost his place in the interrogation. He just sat. Then Becky said, "No one at work tomorrow is going to believe this," and his trance broke.

"I'd like to ask you ladies not to talk about what you've seen."

Becky's eyes remained hard and bright. She had obviously just realized she was at the center of the biggest story in London.

"The press may contact you," O'Leary continued, "and I can't order you not to talk to them, but I want you to remember that you met a killer this evening, a dangerous man who might not like tales told about him."

This was a complete falsehood; their suspect craved press—craved attention. But it was in the interest of their investigation not to have wild talk. There would be quite enough of that as it was, come tomorrow, without these witnesses getting in on the act.

"Oh my gawd! Are you going to give us police guards?"

"That won't be necessary. The police have no intention of giving out your names, and our killer has no way of knowing who you are." O'Leary paused, giving the wide-eyed young women a chance to think *"unless you put yourself in the spotlight."* "I want to thank you for your help," O'Leary continued. "Walker will round up some officers to run you home." He gestured to the burly officer who had just returned.

They filed out with a clacking of high heels.

O'Leary sprang up and started pacing. "Sending nasty notes to us via tabloid isn't enough. That todger has decided to dedicate his work to us." O'Leary paused and leaned both hands on the table, looking Nigella squarely in the eyes. "And while we are tracking him, he is tracking us. I don't like it; I don't like that he knows who you are."

"I'm not hard to find." She shrugged. "Neither are you. We are the investigating officers. My name was in the papers when we were seeking information on Smyth. I doubt there's tracking involved. I'm not worried, I'm angry. He made a bunch of young women watch a man burn, for fuck's sake."

The door cracked and Walker's large head came round it. "Sorry, guv'nor—Wilkinson's calling for both of you."

There were even more people standing around the steps of Christ Church. And civilians had been joined by the press with their lights, cameras, and microphones.

"Is it true you've got another burned body?" one of the reporters yelled. Every eye in the crowd and every camera swiveled to them, but they didn't stop moving.

Passing behind the barriers, Nigella noticed the angel was gone. Wilkinson was crouched by the body, tipping his head this way and that. "Something interesting?" she asked.

"Many things," he replied, standing. "But I sent for you because when we lifted the angel we found this." He reached into his jumpsuit and drew out an evidence bag containing a piece of paper. Moving to stand in a spotlight beam, Wilkinson began to read:

ANOTHER FALSE GOD FALLS. MET AN OLD SCHOOLFELLOW FOR DRINKS. I FIND HIM MORE INTERESTING NOW THAT I HAVE TRANSFORMED HIM THAN WHEN HE WAS ALIVE. CERTAINLY MORE INTERESTING THAN HIS OWN SCULPTURES. BUT THEN, I ALWAYS HAD THE BIGGER TALENT, EVEN IF HE GOT THE BETTER PRESS COVERAGE.

O'Leary gave one of his low whistles, and Wilkinson paused. "Mean something?"

"Means, as far as I am concerned, Parker's identified the body," O'Leary replied.

"There's more. And it's about to get personal," Wilkinson glanced back down at the paper.

HE IS MY OFFERING, PLACED ON THE STEPS OF ONE OF LONDON'S MOST BEAUTIFUL CHURCHES, ACCOMPANIED BY AN ANGEL. DETECTIVE O'LEARY, I THINK YOU ARE A MAN WHO APPRECIATES BEAUTY IF NOT ART. MY ANGEL IS BEAUTIFUL, ISN'T SHE? BUT PERHAPS NOT AS BEAUTIFUL AS DETECTIVE PARKER, WITH HER PORCELAIN SKIN AND THOSE LONG, GRACEFUL LIMBS. I'VE SEEN YOU TOGETHER. HAND AND GLOVE. 😉

Wilkinson looked at both of them. "There is no signature. But there's a creepy wink emoji. What the hell does that mean?"

"Out," O'Leary barked. "Still think he's not tracking, Ni?" he asked as the last cop disappeared. "He could be out there in the crowd, could have watched us walk up the steps together."

"So? Plenty of arsonists hang out to see the cops examine their work."

He locked eyes with her. "Evans needs to take you off this case."

"That's bollocks. If detectives were cut from cases just because a suspect taunted them, lots of crimes would never be solved. Remember that thief who hit the jewelry salon in Mayfair? That boy had your number and never stopped heckling."

He continued to stare, eyes angry and unrelenting. A dark thought crept into the edge of her mind. "O'Leary if you go to Evans and suggest that he pull me, if you stab me in the back—"

"You think this case is worth dying for then?"

"Every case is worth potentially dying for, and we *both* fucking believe that, or we wouldn't be in this line of work." She spat the words at him.

He ran his hand over his forehead up into his hair in the way he did when he was upset, and the gesture took the edge off her anger. It was hard to be furious at someone so obviously concerned for you. Nigella put a hand on his free arm. "You're blowing this way out of proportion," she said softly. "Nick hasn't threatened me. Unless intimating that you think I'm beautiful is a threat."

He shook off her hand.

"Well, I sure as hell don't feel comfortable with it."

"With what?" Nigella threw up both hands. "With you, Nick, or anybody thinking I'm beautiful? With Nick knowing who we are?"

"He knows more than *who* we are." O'Leary lowered his voice. "He knows *how* we are together."

"What's that supposed to mean? We're colleagues, O'Leary. That's it. That's all."

He turned his gaze from her to the balled-up figure of Evan Fox.

"Nick is no fool," Nigella continued. "He knows cops care about each other, and he is playing the oldest game—rile up the male member of any team in defense of the female member. But I don't *need* a defender." Her voice became as hard as his eyes had been. "I hate chivalry, and you know it, because at its base it's just a nicer label for sexism, and I've got no fucking patience for that. So can we please quit the argy-bargy, let forensics in here, and get back to finding this monster?"

"Fine." He didn't look at her. Instead, he walked to the barrier opening and bellowed, "Forensics! Walker, I want that corner cleared! Tell everyone if they want to watch a crime drama they, should go home and turn on their tellies." Then he stamped off to speak with the press.

For the next two hours, they worked together but separately. "What do you say to nine for a start tomorrow?" Nigella asked as the last barrier came down and they were left standing on the steps near the discolored spot where the body had lain. "We've got to have at least four hours of sleep if we don't want the day to go balls up." She started down the steps. "You coming?"

She knew from the look on his face he wasn't.

"I'll get Walker to give me a lift," he said.

"Sleep well."

He rubbed the back of his neck, then buried his hands in his pockets. "Not until this case is over."

The first thing she did when she got back to her flat was fold the eiderdown. In their haste to get to the scene, O'Leary had left his watch on the side table. Nigella picked it up, felt the weight of it, then flipped it over. Somehow she expected engraving on the back, but there was none.

"Time enough, my dearest Etienne". But he wasn't Etienne, Nigella reminded herself. And she wasn't Lady Margaret. She slipped the wristwatch into her bag so she could return it. As she climbed into bed, her mobile vibrated—a text. James, not O'Leary: *how was UR night?* Well, she sure as hell wasn't going to answer that.

◊

Present-day London

Friday

Evans rang while she was brushing her teeth.

"Parker, the papers are not good. 'Horrified Crowd Watches Body Burn.'"

Nigella used her free hand to rinse her toothbrush, but kept silent.

"I can't even take consolation in the fact the Met is bearing the brunt of the current bruising, because we both know it was just luck that poor bugger roasted on their ground, not ours. Besides, that O'Leary's a good cop. He was here when I got in this morning, looking like hell."

Coming from Evans, that was high praise. He associated looking done in with doing the job right.

"He didn't mention me, did he, sir?"

If O'Leary had beat her to the office to spread hysteria regarding the killer's note, she would make him pay.

"You mean like, 'Where the hell is Parker when we have another dead man?' No, it was me asking that."

"Speaking of our dead man, sir, we have a hunch on who he is." Nigella hoped the inexplicably early O'Leary was running down contact information for Ethan Fox. "I'm confident we will firm up identification by the end of the day."

"Tell me, Parker, does knowing *who* he is make him the last victim? Because that is what I really want to hear. You've got more leads than a drunk has favorite pubs, but where exactly are you with this case?"

"We've got a phone number, we've got a face. It's only a matter of time until we nick our man."

"Don't say, 'It's only a matter of time.' Do you realize it's not two weeks since we stood in Monument Square at what we all thought was a crazy nuisance arson? Time is killing us here—or, more precisely, killing Londoners, and that is getting laid at our door."

Nigella could imagine the look on Evan's face. "Guv'nor, we're tightening the circle, but the smaller it gets, the more frantic our killer is going to feel. So the body on the steps of Christ's Church may not be our last."

"You want to tighten something, make it a noose and get it around this bloke's throat, because this morning it feels like it's around mine. Hoist this fellow, Parker, so we can all hang from his legs until he strangles."

His phrase reminded her of Margaret Dove's comments on the execution of the man accused of starting the Great Fire, sending a shiver up Nigella's spine.

"I'm going to hang up," Evans said, "because my coffee is cold, and presumably you want to get in here."

Nigella was a block from her flat when her mobile rang again.

"Detective Parker, it's Katherine Rowan." Nigella could picture the art professor with her black turtleneck and asymmetrical blonde hair.

"You saw the papers."

"Yes, but that's not why I'm calling. This morning I emailed a mentor—an emeritus professor—the image of the burned sculpture found outside St. James's. He called me moments after I hit "Send" and said, 'Katherine, that boy applied to the Slade.'"

"Professor, that's good news, and given that you've seen the papers, you know I need good news. What else did he say?"

"He saw a submission packet maybe four or five years ago. The work in the portfolio was wooden, figural, and had been rubbed with different agents to enhance or distress it. He distinctly remembers seeing one miniature figure that had been burned."

"Did he remember a name?"

"No, sorry, but he is nearly ninety. What he did remember is things got heated during the candidate's interview."

"Heated?"

"On the topic of British Baroque architecture. He said the candidate was—and these are his words—'an extremely zealous devotee of Nicholas Hawksmoor.'"

A month ago that phrase would have sounded odd. The idea of anyone getting heated up, let alone violent, over art or architecture would have surprised her. *Not anymore.* "Does Hawksmoor have a large following?"

"Small but cult-like. Fixated on his restoration, for lack of a better word."

"Restoration to what?"

"They'd say his rightful place in this history of British architecture, and they have a solid argument. Hawksmoor's been conspicuously overlooked in discussions of British Baroque for going on three hundred years, despite the fact he created alongside Christopher Wren and John Vanbrugh. Hawksmoor worked on famous English landmarks like Blenheim and St. Paul's, but you'd be forgiven for not knowing that because you won't find his name on the little historical plaques there. It's really only in the last decade that he's been given serious attention in academic writings. Most of the honors and credit for the architecture in that period have been heaped upon Wren. Have *you* heard of Hawksmoor?"

"Just yesterday," Nigella replied dryly.

"Of course, the latest victim was found at Christ Church," Rowan replied softly.

"Excuse me?" Nigella had been thinking of her interview with Nelson Taylor.

"The crime last night, the papers said it took place on the steps of Christ Church in Spitalfields. That's a Hawksmoor Church. One of half a dozen he designed for a Commission charged with constructing fifty new London parish churches."

"Professor Rowan, our killer has used the name Nicholas Hawksmoor as an alias. That definitely sounds like cultish devotion."

There was a period of silence on the other end of the line, ending at last with a deep intake of breath. "Detective Parker, I've been wondering since I woke up if there would have been a dead body at Christ Church if I'd given your killer the feedback he wanted."

"There would've been. Don't blame yourself, and don't fall into the oldest trap in the book—the one that takes down a lot of good cops—the trap of believing you can control a killer.

You can't. I can't. Nobody is responsible for what this killer does except him."

"That may be, but it will take me a while to shake the feeling of complicity." Her voice caught. "So if there is anything I can do to bring this monster to justice, call me."

O'Leary looked up as she entered the incident room. "Parker."

She couldn't remember the last time he'd called her Parker.

He was wearing what he'd had on when she left him at Christ Church. Nigella glanced sideways at the cots; one had been slept in.

"You told me that you'd get a lift home," she said.

"Did I? Well that was last night and this"—he held up a piece of paper in his hand—"is now."

"Is that a warrant?"

"It sure as hell is." He stood up and shrugged into his rumpled blazer. "That nail from Surrey was gold—or rather iron of the same approximate age and composition as the nails from Smyth's hands. Feel like cutting the locks off a barn door while we wait for the coroner's report on Evan Fox?"

She did. But she wasn't sure she felt like an hour in the car with O'Leary under present circumstances.

"Local DCI wasn't in, but he rang back ten minutes ago. He's on notice. Offering help as needed. Told him we'd call when we got close so that we can use their forensic folk. They may not be Wilkinson, but surely they're capable of bagging things up for Wilkinson."

"I see you're getting his name right this morning." Nigella hoped the joke would elicit a smile. It didn't. "How about you drive, and I'll catch you up on a call I had from Professor Rowan."

He tilted his head slightly. She assumed it was because he knew she was trying to placate him. But then he took a couple of steps forward, reached out, and with a single finger touched the corner of her mouth.

"Some toothpaste there," he said gruffly. "Can't have officers in sleepy old Betchworth laughing at London DIs, can we."

"Nope," Nigella said. She could still feel the pressure of his finger like a phantom touch even though he was halfway out the door. *"He knows how we are together"—that's what O'Leary said last night. Well, if Nick knows that, he knows more than I do.* She shoved the thought ruthlessly away and followed her fellow DI to the elevator.

The ride was better than Nigella anticipated. O'Leary kept his eyes on the road and his comments on her Rowan report minimal. She phoned Fox's agent. He was horrified by the possibility that his client might be the dead man from the papers. But he was also calm and organized. Nigella suspected he'd definitively fail to locate Fox by noon. "If you reach him, nobody will be more relieved than I am," she said. "If you don't, I'll need names—relatives, partner . . ."

"Partner . . . Oh God, Marjorie," he replied. "I can't let her see him like *that* . . . if it is him. Detective Parker . . ." There was a pregnant silence. "If someone has to identify a body . . ." She heard the swallow she couldn't see.

"Someone will," she said gently.

This time the silence stretched long enough for her to wonder whether she had lost the signal as they made the turn out of the Betchworth commercial district onto the road along the Mole River.

"I'll do it," the agent said at last. "Nobody's lover or mum should have to see that."

"You're a very good man," she said sincerely.

"I wonder, what's it going to take to get you to say that about me?" O'Leary asked as she pocketed her phone. It should have been a joke, but his tone suggested it wasn't.

Nigella didn't get to make a reply—the car swerved abruptly, and the next thing Nigella knew they were off the road, bumping to a stop. "What the bloody hell—"

"That!" He pointed. Ahead, where the low brick wall between the road and the river gave way to metal railings. Two police cars were parked, lights flashing, and a tow truck was backed up to the river. One of its operators stood at the water's edge while, with a grinding sound, a white hatchback emerged from the water, rear-end first.

"Is that our Corsa?" Nigella swung her door open. She didn't get far before an officious constable stopped her.

"Sorry, ma'am, I can't let you get any closer."

"I am not a 'ma'am,' I'm a DI with the City of London Police"—Nigella could see the rear plate on the car—"and that vehicle is the subject of an all-points."

Another car came to a stop nearby, unmarked but with lights.

"Guv'nor," the constable said to the man who got out, "lady says something about this car being subject to an all-points."

"DCI Grosvenor," the man said, joining them."

"O'Leary, Scotland Yard. We spoke this morning." O'Leary stuck out his hand.

"Down from London already. You don't waste time."

"I suspect you don't either when you have a killer on the loose. This is DI Parker, with City. We were on our way to execute our warrant when this operation of yours caught our eye. Wednesday night we put out an all-points on a white, older model Corsa linked to two homicides."

"We haven't had a chance to run the tag yet," the constable said with a tone equally defensive and apologetic.

"Well," Grosvenor replied, "looks like you won't need to run it now. You sure it's your car, O'Leary?"

"It's ours," Nigella chimed in. "I recognize the tag."

The car was now four wheels on dry ground.

"You want it towed to the city?" Grosvenor asked amiably.

"No need," O'Leary replied. "We'd be obliged if you handled it—I'll give you the name of the lead forensic officer on our investigation, and your fellow can report to him."

Grosvenor nodded.

"Mind if we give the vehicle a once-over before we get on our way?" O'Leary asked.

"Not at all.

Officers opened the car's doors as they approached, releasing a whoosh of dark river water. "All the windows are rolled down," Nigella noted.

"Fits with it being ditched," O'Leary replied.

"I take it we don't need to dredge for a body," Grosvenor said.

"Nope." O'Leary shook his head. "Would've been a dream come true if you'd hauled it out to find a man in his late twenties or early thirties strapped in the front seat."

It would have indeed, but Nick's too smart for that.

The car was clean. Not a soggy registration, random piece of clothing, or scrap of paper under a floor mat to be found; nothing but some debris from the river in the sodden interior.

"That's disappointing," Grosvenor opined as he walked them to their car.

As soon as they were back on the road, Nigella replied, "Not disappointing, because nobody strips a car down like that unless they've done something criminal."

"And I think it's good news he dumped it out here. Means he doesn't know we've been on his property," O'Leary said. "Also means he likely slept there. Hard to imagine him getting a train from Betchworth in the middle of the night."

Nigella opened her browser. "Nothing before six thirty. God, I hope he was less thorough cleaning up after himself at dead nan's house than he was with her car."

They nosed around enough to make sure Nick wasn't on the premises, then headed to the barn. O'Leary raised the bolt cutters, then let them drop. "One of the few advantages we have is that we know about this bolt-hole, but Nick doesn't know we know. So let's not tip him off."

Nigella nodded, and pulled out her lock picks. "So, we tread lightly, touch little, and if we bag anything, try not to leave a trace."

"Yep, and you're the right officer for that," O'Leary replied. "Keeping things neat—if there was a medal for that, you'd be wearing it."

The jibe cheered rather than irritated. Joking was a sign he might have started forgetting to be angry.

Workbench, tins of screws, tool belt, and expanses of empty space—it was all pretty standard stuff for a barn or garage.

Then O'Leary spotted something against a wall. "Look what we have here." O'Leary pulled the giant roll of heavy-gauge plastic upright. "Not something everyone keeps lying about."

"Not unless they're going to do a hell of a lot of home painting or have hobbies that create scraps you don't want the police to find," Nigella said.

"I think you mean shavings," O'Leary replied. "Or at least I hope you do, because the alternative to wood shavings is scraps of Andrew Smyth. Let's do the house."

They picked the lock on the back door and started in the kitchen. Nigella cracked the fridge. Empty. Not sort of empty, entirely empty. She put her hand on the top shelf. "It's not even running. So our suspect might sleep here, but he sure doesn't stay for long."

They moved to the sitting room. "Even I dust more than this," O'Leary remarked. "Maybe he only comes out to use the barn."

"Best way to find out . . ." Nigella said as they took the stairs.

"Bathroom," O'Leary declared.

There was no standing-water ring in the toilet. The cabinet over the sink held a brand of deodorant favored by athletes, a razor, and shaving cream.

"Definitely not things grandma would use." O'Leary held a toothbrush up to the light. "Still wet."

Nigella slipped off one glove and laid her palm on the bath mat. "Damp. He slept here alright. Let's find his bedroom."

"Holy shite," O'Leary said, stopping abruptly in the doorway of the second room down the hall. "For just a moment, I thought it was himself, sitting waiting for us!"

From the far side of the room the eyeholes of a black and silver feathered mask glared at them, lit by the daylight from a window behind. It was perched atop a dark hoodie draped over the back of a desk chair.

"Looks like we've found Nick's fancy dress from last night's Ethan Fox show." O'Leary pulled out his mobile and started snapping.

The room was clearly lived in: the bed was made haphazardly; a set of free weights lay beside the desk; and a pair of trainers sat against the door to a built-in wardrobe, dark sweatpants hanging from a hook above them.

"Eleven and a half," Nigella remarked as she moved the shoes aside and opened the wardrobe. "Not much here, but every damn bit of it is black. Oh Jesus." She picked up a knitted balaclava and held it out.

"I sure as hell hope we stop him before some poor soul is confronted by Nick wearing that." O'Leary straightened from his examination of the desk. "Plenty of fine-tipped permanent markers, just the sort you'd use if you wanted to leave a ranting note on the back of a tie."

Or a taunting note underneath an angel. The stupid note that has O'Leary calling me "Parker."

"Hello there," O'Leary said, shifting his focus to the bedside table. "*From the Shadows: The Architecture of Nicholas Hawksmoor; Nicholas Hawksmoor's London Churches; Hawksmoor: Maligned and Misrepresented;* and at least three books on British architecture that I'm betting mention Hawksmoor."

He began picking up the books one at a time, flipping through them gently. When he got to the third, photos fluttered to the floor. "Are these Polaroids?" he exclaimed, scooping them up. "Didn't know they existed anymore."

"O'Leary, you're so not on trend. They don't just exist; they're hot again."

"Looks like a church." O'Leary laid the photos on the bed.

Nigella moved forward to stare down at them. They were taken from artistic angles—the photographer clearly interested in beauty and composition as opposed to capturing a church the way a tourist would. Reaching out, she touched an exterior shot—a great arched doorway, set in a block of banded stone, topped by a lunette window and photographed at a dizzying angle to capture a series of free-standing, lighter-stone Corinthian columns and twin square turrets balanced above. "This is St. Mary Woolnoth. It's not ten minutes from the nick. I've been there."

"Lunchtime prayers, Parker?"

"No. Morning coffee. They have an independent coffee place with little tables right outside this door. Nice quiet place to sit." *It won't seem that way now, will it? I wonder, was I blissfully sipping away at my morning latte when he took this?*

She turned her attention to the remaining pictures. In the first, an up-angled camera captured elaborately carved wooden posts, treated with gold and supporting a gold-trimmed abat-voix. In the second, the camera took the viewer inside a cluster of three white fluted columns. And in the last, a brass chandelier hung straight down at the viewer from an expansive white ceiling delicately trimmed and framed on all sides by half-round lunette windows.

"Everything's from the same time period as the churches where Nick's already staged crimes. I've never been inside St. Mary Woolnoth, but given Nick tucked these away with a picture of its entrance, I am guessing this is what it looks like."

"I'll bet either Wren or Hawksmoor designed it then."

"Do we put St. Mary under observation? Might be the site of Nick's next abomination," Nigella wondered aloud.

"St. Mary Woolnoth and half of London thanks to the Great Fire. This case isn't going to make me an expert on architecture but it *has* taught me that that Wren rebuilt half the city after the fire. And Professor Rowan said Hawksmoor did half a dozen London churches as well. We surveil all those buildings, and there won't be constables enough left to handle London's everyday crimes."

Nigella gave a sigh, letting her eyes drop to the floor. The corner of a picture stuck out from under the bed near O'Leary's left foot. "What's that?"

"Must've missed one." He bent, then gave a low whistle as he straightened. "Wherever Nick's planning his next art installation, bet we see one of these."

The Polaroid in his outstretched hand showed a semicircle of carved figures in gloaming half-darkness. A bare-bulb work light had been set amid them, catching some more than others. Nigella recognized the Christ Church angel, although in the picture she didn't have wings.

There were three additional figures in the picture . . . three.

"Jesus," Nigella said grimly. "Forget churches—we need to find this place."

"Looks like a garage." O'Leary said. "Is that a tire iron leaning against that metal cabinet?"

"Looks like one," Nigella replied. "Let's have the boys at Wood Street enlarge this image until they can't enlarge it any-more."

"We'll get better resolution if we take the print for scan-ning, Ni." She never thought she would be so chuffed to hear the informal moniker return. "Let's take it. Finding this fucker's lair, that's more important than anything—even covering the fact we've been here. We find this garage, stake it out, and catch Nick bang to rights next time he drops by."

Nigella nodded. "Put the others back, but we take the sculp-ture gallery and pray he doesn't pull his pics out to admire before beddy-bye. Let's also hope, if we find this garage and stake it out, Nick doesn't have another body in tow when he arrives."

As they headed down the drive, O'Leary phoned DCI Grosvenor and asked him to put someone on the house but to make sure they were subtle.

Back on the main road, Nigella asked, "Quick lunch at our usual pub?"

"Sure," he said.

O'Leary joked with the waitress but was otherwise quiet until the food came. He took a bite of his battered cod, put down his fork, and looked at her. It was the most direct look he'd given her since she'd left him on the steps of Christ Church.

"If I'd lied to you, do you think we'd still be together?"

Nigella mentally staggered. That damn directness—so use-ful in their line of work, such a pain in the ass when it came to interpersonal relationships.

"You didn't have to *lie*. You just needed to leave things as they were." She looked at her salad, suddenly taking an intense interest in the distribution of the goat cheese.

"I don't know if this is just a Catholic thing, Ni, but we have what are called sins of commission and omission. Sometimes failing to act is just as wrong as an affirmative bad act. I think of lies that way. It got to a point where *not* saying I loved you felt like a big lie—a damning one."

Nigella felt a burst of white-hot anger—at herself for the cowardly way she had resorted to avoiding his gaze, and at him for . . . she wasn't sure. She raised her eyes to his face. "So you felt morally compelled to blurt it out over my shoulder while I was making coffee one Sunday morning?" He hadn't blurted it; he'd actually slipped an arm around her waist and murmured it into her ear as she stood at the counter, watching the pot brew.

"Apparently."

Damn you for that. We both lost best friends over it.

"And the next thing I knew," he continued, "you'd put the one lousy sweater and toothbrush I kept at your place in a bag, and stopped answering my calls."

"Be fair, O'Leary. I didn't ignore your calls without officially ending things."

"By text." There was a bitter edge to his voice. "Did it never occur to you I might have something to say? That, after half a year together, I deserved to be heard?"

How, Nigella thought, *did I ever let a man into my life for six whole months?*

But her anger had ceded ground, at least partially, to shame. O'Leary had a point, now that she heard it starkly spoken: he had deserved a hearing. Not that he could have talked her round, but because speaking his piece might have helped him let go. *And I'd love it if you would just let it go.*

"You're right. I should have picked up the phone." *At least a couple of times.* Nigella had avoided his calls for about three months, and then, after running into him at a funeral for an officer they'd both known, they had starting talking again—strictly about work, or at least as strictly as a man like O'Leary, with a penchant for mentioning her cat and other awkward things, could manage. "I'm sorry."

"Apology accepted. I guess it was for the best anyway." He gave a half shrug and picked up a chip. "Because sooner or later you would have met James, or someone like him, at one of those art things where I always felt foolish standing around, and I couldn't have competed."

You'd have done just fine. The thought was as disconcerting as it was unbidden.

"And you'd have realized," Nigella said, trying to deflect, "I was never going to stop treading on toddlers and start liking them. Let alone thinking of tucking my badge away in a sock drawer to start having them."

"Ni, I've never suggested any woman put anything in a drawer to be a mum. And," he said, leaning across the table, green eyes intense, "I never wanted you to be different. Hell, if lining up tins in your cupboard in perfect rows is your thing, have at it. I just thought we had more important things in common—like this job and how we do it."

"We still have that, O'Leary. Haven't we just come from casing the cottage of a killer? As an investigatory team, I don't think there are two DIs who can beat us—at least not where one of them is from the Met."

He gave a snorted half laugh.

I'm sorry if I hurt you. Say it, she willed herself. But the words wouldn't come out. Nigella *was* sorry. O'Leary was not just a very good cop; he was a very good man—simply not the man for her because he was the marrying type. The type who wanted to grow old with someone; who demanded not only to share a bed or a meal, but to be given entry into another person's soul. That sounded exhausting.

"Eat your fish before it gets cold, then lure the waitress over here with our check. We have a picture to dissect." She smiled, then made herself pick up her fork and take a bite. Normalcy was a thing she valued almost as much as order, and she would force it if she had to.

♦

The computer boys had the photo uploaded at lightning speed, and Nigella and O'Leary stood behind them as they went to work brightening the image. Even this step, without magnification, made a difference.

"Bugger me senseless if that isn't the nose of the Corsa at the front edge of the frame," Nigella said. "How'd we miss that?"

"Well, we know where the Corsa is, so that's no help," O'Leary replied. "But that might be." He pointed to a wall calendar next to the metal storage cabinet. "Zoom in on the writing," he instructed. "Emmerson Holdings Limited, Rental Properties."

Nigella leaned in until her hair brushed the shoulder of the officer at the keyboard. "Can you get even closer so we can read what's beneath it?"

It was a Hackney address.

"Keep at the photo," O'Leary said. "I'll call Emmerson Holdings. If we're lucky, their properties are all in North-East London, just like their office."

"No, if we're lucky," Nigella replied, "they don't have a couple hundred rental garages, because it would take far more than two Tweedles to check out that number." She didn't realize she'd used O'Leary's nickname until the tech officer looked up, puzzled. O'Leary, already halfway out the door, turned back and smiled.

"Can you print me a close up of the calendar?" she asked. There was a church at the top. It didn't look very Wren, but given the number of churches in the case, she'd rather ID it than not.

Pulling out her mobile, she said, "Siri, text O'Leary," then instructed him to ask the folks at Emmerson about the church.

Turning back to the photo, Nigella's eyes scanned slowly right to left, coming to rest on a workbench. "Enlarge those." She pointed to a line of metal containers. *Linseed-fucking-oil! Of course.* Next to them was a paper takeaway bag with writing on it. Her phone started ringing. "Figure out what that says. Hell, find every damn name or address in the photo—" She held up a hand, paused, and took the call.

"Phone trace is a bust." O'Leary's voice bristled with anger.

"What?"

"You heard me."

"That's not possible. Bloody technology—the trade-off for all this convenience is supposed to be a lack of privacy, but somehow Nick the prick gets to keep his?"

"He is a lucky bastard. According to our team, that phone is gone—just gone. And they got the paperwork needed to get the trace moving damn quickly. I mean they were trying to locate this thing within an hour of our ask."

That was fast by red-tape and paperwork standards, but apparently not fast enough. But maybe it wouldn't have mattered had they been on it in minutes . . .

"You know what I think?" she said.

"Burner," he replied grimly. "Destroyed the moment after he responded to Taylor's text. Paranoid bugger."

"And smart."

"I'd try to cheer you up by saying the smart ones are more fun to catch, but under the circumstances, I know we both wish this bloke was a hell of a lot dumber." He was gone before she could reply.

"Right." She turned back to the tech guys. "Make me that list of addresses and names. Make it for me yesterday. Send it to me so quickly I'm dazzled."

CHAPTER 15

Whitehall Palace

Sunday, November 4, 1666

A bead of sweat scuttled down the back of Margaret's neck like a beetle, and she chided herself for being nervous. After all, it was she who had sought this confrontation, deaf to Etienne's renewed pleas to leave Wren to God; obstinate in the face of his fears of what might happen when she confronted the monster who had killed Thomas and destroyed London's greatest church to satisfy personal vanity.

"Faith teaches we must do what is right, even in the face of danger," she'd reminded Etienne the night before. "The book of James says, 'Therefore to him that knoweth to do good, and doeth it not, to him it is sin.' Would you have me be a sinner?"

"Margaret, there are as many ways to do good as there are stars in the heavens," he had replied, pointing to the sky above them as they stood on the leads in the spot where they had first met, "and I wish you to live a long life so that you may do much of it. Is that so strange? Why must you press this?"

"I thought you liked my fierceness, the hawk in me."

"I do Margaret, God help us both. Yet the Bible also says, 'Blessed are the meek: for they shall inherit the earth.' Just this one time, perhaps, a bit of meekness."

Margaret smiled at the memory. Trust Etienne, even in his absence—for he was safely in the Volary Garden, doubtless by the doves' cage—to calm her nerves. He had argued passionately that, at very least, he ought to be with her at this moment. She had only succeeded in stilling his tongue by reminding him that he'd already agreed to her terms, agreed to let her see Wren alone, because she'd offered him the one thing he could not resist: herself.

Margaret had summoned Wren with two stark lines, choosing the Lord's Day because she was about the Lord's business—a thought that had fortified her to this point. Yet now her pulse thrummed. *Why can I not wait with equanimity for my moment to embody Justice?* Perhaps "Justice" was the wrong word; she was not *Justitia* and could not extract temporal justice. Margaret intended instead to be the conscience Wren did not appear to have; to set guilt and fear like twin worms inside him—as she'd told Etienne in Anglesey's library before he had persuaded her to temporarily abandon that mission—hoping that the combination would eat Wren alive.

The clock on the mantle sounded, yet there was no knock. That she should be kept waiting was inexcusable. Though she was but a woman, her social status and connections far surpassed Wren's. *Perhaps he is blinded and emboldened by his new fame.* In the weeks since she and Etienne had realized the truth about Wren, in Anglesey's library, the King had become firmly in the architect's thrall. Yes, Wren was very much in fashion now.

Is he confident enough to ignore me?

As the thought hung in the air like one of Etienne's rockets, a knock at last sounded. "Come," Margaret commanded, drawing herself up, preparing for battle.

Simona ushered Wren in. "I will be just outside," she said distinctly. As she reached the door, she turned, giving Margaret an "are you sure?" look.

Never more so. The fact that she experienced no desire to retreat at this, the last feasible moment, buoyed Margaret's confidence. She gave Simona a nod and then, as the door clicked shut, turned her attention to Wren. He looked decidedly wary.

He's not forgotten our last interview. And for as long as he lives, he will never forget this one.

Wren bowed. "Mistress Dove, you wrote that you had important information pertinent to St. Paul's I ought to hear before Their Majesties did."

The bait for the trap has been obvious. Margaret knew St. Paul's was his beating heart, knew the royal commission for its reconstruction was his greatest desire. *Desire is a strange thing. It inspires the best in us but also makes us change in ways no sane person standing apart from it could ever anticipate.*

Wren doubtless expected the construction of his new St. Paul's to be the greatest pleasure of his life. Margaret fervently hoped to make certain that pleasure was not unadulterated.

"Doctor Wren, did you go to the hanging of Robert Hubert?"

He started, as she meant him to. "No, Lady, I heard it was a gruesome thing, and I take no pleasure in the gruesome or ugly."

"Nor do I. Yet I went. And gruesome does not begin to describe it." Margaret swallowed the bile that rose in her throat at the memories—the sound of the crowd; the smell as, while twisting in the noose, the poor dying man's bladder emptied; the odor of blood as his body was torn to shreds; but most of all, the confusion and fear in his eyes. "To see a poor addled fool punished for a crime he did not commit—a crime that did not in fact exist—changed me forever."

Margaret's heart began to race unevenly in a manner she knew all too well. To fall unconscious before she'd had a chance to make her accusation . . . the idea was unbearable. *Do not betray me now,* she thought, realizing even as she lectured it that her body had never yet been amenable to her pleas. She stamped her foot angrily, and Wren jumped.

"Mistress, are you quite all right?"

"No. But that is to be expected, because while Hubert was innocent, you are not."

She stared directly into his eyes, expecting to see fear. Instead, he stared back with an openness that chilled her. She drew a deep breath. She'd rehearsed the words, determined to sound as a judge would in court, not like some hysterical woman whom Wren would easily dismiss. "Doctor Christopher Wren, I accuse you of arson and murder. I charge that on Tuesday, September fourth, in this year of our Lord 1666, while London burned, you broke open the doors of the western crypt at St. Paul's with a pries bar for the express purpose of setting fire to the books and papers there, and in commission of that terrible act, you murdered the bookseller Thomas Bradish by striking him with that same bar of iron."

Margaret expected a burst of anger similar to the rage he had exhibited the first time she accosted him. But Wren stood silent. No color rose in his neck. No denials sprang from his lips.

After a few moments during which his eyes gazed curiously into hers, he said: "How did you know?"

"Like you, sir, I am a scientist. I examined, I experimented, I concluded . . . oh, and I have your pries bar." She said the last sardonically, filled with a heady feeling of having power over her situation, of being in control.

"I needed St. Paul's to burn," Wren said matter-of-factly. "But it seemed determined to stand. The thought of all London in ruins but that hulking wreck of a church surviving . . . going on for another century while my plans for an extraordinary new cathedral turned to dust . . . You have seen my plans; you must understand then that I could not allow that! So I suggested to Bradish that the Stationers take their inventories to the crypt."

"You say this as if you feel no shame!" Anger collapsed the edges of Margaret's vision in on itself as her heart pounded ferociously.

"I am *not* ashamed. Why should I be? I did not go to the Cathedral to *kill*, merely to topple stone, to wipe clean a slate so that I could give the city a cathedral so beautiful that people all across England, and indeed on the continent, will declare it a wonder and a beautiful tribute to the Lord our God. I did not mean to kill Thomas."

This last was said softly. Margaret sensed a genuine regret that muted her anger.

Wren took a deep breath. "And I am not really to blame for his death—fate is. Or perhaps he himself was, with his obsessive fastidiousness, his need to check and double-check things, whether figures in his ledger or the seal on the crypt door."

Margaret's fury roared back, bringing a dreadful pounding at her temples beyond any she had ever known. She took a few steps to the right so she could rest her hand on the table to steady herself— the same table where she and Etienne had spent so many happy hours planning their telescope. "You dare to blame Thomas!"

"All right, fate then," Wren replied as if they were bargaining.

"Did fate wield the pry bar? How can you call striking a man over the head and then striking him again once he fell"—Wren's eyes widened, and he blanched slightly at this detail—"how can you call such savagery an accident?!"

"Because it was not part of my plan." There was a touch of pleading in his voice. Margaret could not be certain whether he was trying to convince her or himself that this fact made him less culpable.

"When I went down to the door of St. Faith's, no one was there. Brandish, like the other Stationers, had been gone for hours. I scraped away the clay along every seam because without air, fire soon chokes. Then I raised my bar and struck the door a vicious blow, but it left only the smallest mark. I struggled to crack the wood, striking again and again. And all the time I could hear cries from the church above that the roof was melting, could hear people fleeing. My hands were nearly raw when I finally breached the oak. I put the stubs of a dozen candles from my lodgings in through the hole, took my flint from my pocket and struck it. I'd lit all but one of the candles when I heard him—Bradish—asking me what I did.

"I turned and he was gaping at me. Then he rushed forward, snatching off his hat, seeking to press it over the flames I'd kindled."

Margaret was convinced that Wren no longer saw her—but somewhere over her right shoulder, he saw Thomas in that fateful moment.

"I had to stop him." His voice no longer explained, but asserted. "I shouted for him to stop, and he ran."

Little wonder.

Margaret had seen Wren's face when he was angry, remembered her terror as he'd drawn close to her—fists balled. Now, the near madness in Wren's eyes scared her once more. She was corseted by fear—squeezing the life and will from her, tightening her stomach into a knot, and compressing her lungs until she could draw no air.

Time enough . . . she'd promised Etienne. *"There is no fear in love; but perfect love casteth out fear."* The line from the Gospel of John came to her, bringing with it a great calm, and the power to breathe and speak. "You caught up with him in the nave, near the tomb of Thomas Kempe, Bishop of London."

"Yes."

"And you killed him. Tell me, how does murder fit with your planned tribute to God?" Fury rebounding, Margaret shook, and her vision narrowed until she saw Wren as though he were down a darkening hall.

"I could not let Thomas go because if he told anyone what I'd done, the commission for a new St. Paul's would be Pratt's or perhaps Evelyn's. And while the latter is a friend, he has not my vision. *My* new cathedral is what London needs and God deserves."

"Can you really believe God wants an offering stained by innocent blood? Our friend's was not the only body found. Although you may not have used your pries bar upon them, other souls perished when the crypt exploded: an old woman; a man with a red beard who the more gullible insist is a preserved saint popped out of his tomb. Perhaps others lie beneath the rubble. Even should your vision for a new St. Paul's come to stand in stone and glass, impressing all mortal men who see it, God will hear the blood of those who died cry out from the earth beneath as once he heard Abel's blood."

"God will forgive when he sees my dome." His eyes shone with a certainty she found sickening.

"You delude yourself. God forgives only those who repent truly and fully. You show no genuine remorse, sir, and sound anything but repentant. Whatever you believe as you stand here today, God's knowledge of your dreadful mortal sin will sit more heavily upon you with each passing day, spoiling the taste of food in your mouth and ruining your enjoyment of your new St. Paul's, should it ever rise."

His eyes grew wild, haunted. *Good, that is what I wanted. If he endures even a hundredth of the suffering he has caused Agnes, there will be some measure of justice in that.*

Margaret tried to take a deep breath, but her lungs were tight, and only the smallest portion of air seemed to enter them. *I must finish. I cannot falter or fail now.* "And Dr. Wren, while I am confident God will not forgive you, I am entirely certain I will not."

Finally the cunning emerged, crept into his eyes, pushing aside all else. And at his side, Margaret watched Wren's hands curl into fists as they had that September evening.

She felt a terrible presentiment that he would strike her. *Please, God, I cannot die at this moment of all moments—when I am so close to my object.*

"What do you intend to do?" His top lip curled back as he spoke.

"If I can thwart your plans, I . . . I . . ." Margaret stumbled over the words. "Their Majesties—" Her right hand rose to her chest, clutching. Then she fell.

Divine intervention, how else to explain it, I think, watching Mistress Dove collapse. She seems to go unnaturally slowly, clutching at the runner on the table as she sinks to the floor with a soft rustling of silk. She lands on her side, one hand pressed to her breast, utterly still. *Is she dead? "O my God: thou hast smitten all mine enemies upon the cheek bone."* As the son of a clergyman, who was a Chaplain in Ordinary , I know my Psalms.

A great clattering interrupts my thought as the last of the runner clutched in Mistress Dove's pale hand comes down from the table, bringing with it a pair of silver candlesticks. The door bursts open, and the young woman who ushered me to this meeting dashes in.

"Dear God, dear God!" she cries. Running past me, she falls to her knees, placing a hand before the fallen girl's mouth and nose. I hold my breath. She reels back in horror.

"Her heart has failed her at last." She says it softly, but the wail that follows is anything but.

"How can I help?" I ask, feigning concern where I feel only relief.

"Run and summon help!" She pulls Mistress Dove's head and shoulders into her lap and begins wailing again.

I do run, nearly as fast as I did fleeing the churchyard of St. Paul's and the streets beyond during the fire. But I do not summon help. That would be foolish. Mistress Dove looked dead, but the longer she remains without the ministrations of a physician, the surer I can be of her death.

And I need her to be dead. A dead woman cannot tell tales to Their Majesties, tales that might deprive me of St. Paul's and St. Paul's of me.

🔥

Westminster Abbey, London

Wednesday, November 7, 1666

I stand tucked in a corner at the choir's open end, watching them slide a stone into place, sealing Margaret Dove under the floor of The chapel of St. John the Baptist. I doubt, she would merit interment at Westminster were not most churches in London nothing but heaps, their churchyards blackened. But perhaps I am unfair. The Lady clearly had many friends, even if I was not one. As the Abbey Dean intones a final solemn prayer, he is ringed by courtiers. At the front of the knot, a collection of the Queen's ladies cling to each other, crying. They include the young woman I saw last cradling the dead woman. *That is a gaze I must avoid.*

I have seen enough in any event. Unless she haunts me as a ghost, Mistress Dove will bother me no more. I can forget her.

Can you?

The thought rises, but I push it down again, swiftly. I can. I *must.* And surely that is what God intended when he took her from my path.

Turning to go, I notice some other outliers along the north aisle. *My God, one of them is Thomas Bradish's wife, babe in arms.* I duck behind a column, panicked. Then I remember she has no reason to think ill of me—she cannot know what Mistress Dove discovered. Cannot know what I did. I could, if I like, offer her my condolences.

I peep round the column. Beside her, a tall man clutches a little girl's hand. Mistress Bradish it seems is a practical woman and does not wait to give her children a new father. I am of a practical bent as well, so I will be the last to censure her. I look at the man more closely. His face is familiar. I could swear I saw him at Bradish and Son . . . but I thought that about Mistress Dove too.

Perhaps it is best not to intrude upon the widow. What could I gain by it anyway?

Reversing direction, I slip down the south aisle and out into the crisp autumn air. Reaching King Street, I turn back for a look at the church. King Henry III had an architect's eye. But my eye is better, and the Gothic style is antiquated. Soon I will raise a church in a new style, like a phoenix from the ashes of our Great Fire, to the wonderment of Englishmen and God alike. My St. Paul's will put Westminster Abbey to shame.

"If I can thwart your plans . . ." I hear Mistress Dove as clearly as if she stood before me rather than lying in her grave. I half expect her to appear to me here in King's Lane, as Thomas appears in my dreams. Can the dead interfere in the work of the living? As a man of science, I cannot credit that thesis. And yet . . .

CHAPTER 16

Present-day London

Saturday

The boat was wooden, the figures wire.

"It's authentic," James said. "Not that all good art isn't authentic, but in this case I mean the boat made a trip in the Aegean. It held refugees."

Nigella circled the sculpture. It was interesting from every angle, stirring . . . and yet . . . Although she believed in public art, the whole installation made Nigella feel decidedly melancholy. The boat, once a vessel of hope for the displaced, would never arrive anywhere—just sit for all time in Brushfield Street near Spital Square, in the shadow of a modern office tower with a pub and a takeaway food place for a backdrop. Most disconcertingly, Nigella could see Hawksmoor's Christ Church at the end of the road, bringing poor, dead, wire-wrapped Ethan Fox to mind.

"Too early for drinks?" she asked, coming to a stop at James's side. "How about brunch?"

She needed a drink to push Ethan Fox out of her mind. But she also owed James. She'd evened the score in terms of ignoring texts. When James had texted late Thursday, asking her how her night was, she'd quite reasonably let it go because "involved a flaming man in a ball" seemed an answer likely to engender nightmares. But when he'd texted half a dozen times on Friday, she'd had no excuse for not replying. Unless a shitty bad mood was excuse enough.

She'd certainly been in one of those. Not only had she and O'Leary suffered a dead end on the phone trace, but Ethan Fox's agent had IDed him, which meant driving round to tell his next of kin. They'd returned to the incident room, demoralized, to find both phones ringing. Nigella had spoken with Andrew Smyth's brother, who, despite their advice, had gone to see his brother's body, while O'Leary handled Ethan Fox's weeping girlfriend. When the receivers went back in their cradles, they'd looked at each other and agreed they were done. The list of garages from the property company; names and addresses ferreted out from the garage photo; the new sketch of the suspect, reimagined with a tie and a shave—could all wait until Monday. As Nigella had poured herself the first of several glasses of wine Friday night, James had texted again, wanting to come over. She'd declined. Not even his chiseled naked form would have cheered her, and one of the best things about having a sex partner, not a life partner, was that she wasn't required to fake it. But now, unless she was ready to be done with him entirely, it was time to pay James back for ignoring him.

"It is never too early for drinks." James smiled. "We can have mimosas with brunch."

Nigella had to give him this—he didn't hold a grudge.

Ensconced in a sunny restaurant, menus in hand, Nigella pushed her recent glimpse of Christ Church from her mind and began, at last, to relax into the weekend.

"Let's get someone on those mimosas." James raised his hand to flag the server. "Hey, isn't that your partner in crime—or rather crime solving?"

Bloody hell! What was O'Leary doing in Spitalfields? Because there he was, standing at the hostess podium, with a petite blonde in a colorful sweater who she assumed was Amy.

James raised an eyebrow. "I didn't know we were double-dating."

"We are not." *Not dating, and not inviting them to join us.*

"So it's just an incredibly small world?" His tone smacked of jealousy.

"Apparently."

O'Leary hadn't spotted them yet. Nigella experienced an urge to scramble to the ladies', but she'd only have to come out again. And really, what was she hiding from? She remembered the last discussion they'd had of James—the raised voices, how the topic of their partners had become incendiary. She was trying to dodge a repeat of that. *Coward.* She put up her hand and waved.

O'Leary didn't look any more thrilled than she felt, but as the hostess took a pair of menus to a table in the other direction, he and Amy walked toward Nigella.

She rose. James looked confused, then did the same.

"Amy, I'd like you to meet DI Parker from City."

Nigella stuck out her hand. "I'm sure you're sick of hearing about me."

O'Leary's eyes did a weird thing, and he shifted from foot to foot.

"Not at all." The woman's smile was genuine. "Colm tries to leave work at work."

Since when? Nigella felt like she'd been slapped.

"Glad to hear it. This is James, and, as he can tell you, I never leave work anywhere for more than an hour."

"True." James grabbed her hand where it hung at her side, and there was no way to take it back without making a scene. "But I think all the criminal stuff is part of what makes dating a DI exciting."

O'Leary's eyes were the size of salad plates, presumably from the double whammy of James's use of the word "dating" and his assertion that hearing details from an investigation involving men crisped beyond recognition was exciting.

Nigella smiled so hard that her teeth showed. "Well, don't let us keep you from a lovely nonwork afternoon. Monday's coming soon enough, and with it all the excitement of mapping rental garages."

She was damn glad when the mimosas came moments after the couple wandered off. And gladder still that she couldn't see them from where she sat.

◊

O'Leary had the driver's side door open the moment Nigella's car rolled to a stop alongside St. Magnus the Martyr. Funny how seeing him at brunch had been awkward, but seeing him at a crime scene gone midnight wasn't.

"I know he's doing these after dark out of necessity," he said, "but part of me thinks he's determined to keep us from getting a decent night's sleep, to dull our wits and keep us from catching him."

She swung out of the car. "No excuses, O'Leary. If we're not catching him, that's on us."

"You're right—and that feels like shite." He hesitated. "Ni, I think the victim might be Neil."

"Oh God. Killing our witnesses would be a bigger fuck-you than that raised finger at St. James's. Why do you think it's him?"

"The victim is a rough sleeper and—"

"And Neil is the only homeless guy you know?"

—"if you'd let me finish. We have another note. Come take a look."

The line of screens abutted the wall of the church's tower. Overhead a large, black clock, touched in gold, crowned by a golden cherub's face, loomed. The minute they rounded the barriers, even before her eyes swept the full tableau, she saw the writing in huge block letters in chalk on the pavement:

YOUR POLICE ARTIST IS ANYTHING BUT. TIME IS RUNNING OUT, DETECTIVES. FASTER THAN YOU THINK.

Oh Christ, maybe it is Neil.

The figure on the ground wasn't a ball or a replica of Christ. He just lay like a man sleeping, but twisted by nightmares. And behind him stood a scorched figure, pointing accusatorily, not at the corpse, but at the detectives where they stood. This figure, too, was different from the ones before. He was half man and half still-unadulterated wood. He had a front, a left side, and half a back, but no right shoulder. And while his right leg was complete, his left was subsumed below the knee in an uncarved block. Most disturbingly, he lacked a face. Where it should have been, there was only a rough, rasped patch of angry burned wood. Wilkinson was beside him—torch focused on an ordinary petrol can, scorched. Looking up, he nodded at Nigella. "Petrol everywhere. My guess, this can was full, killer splashed it about and then lit the whole mess."

"What about the victim?"

Wilkinson picked his way gingerly around chalk letters and past the prone figure to join them. "Male. Further consumed by fire than his predecessors. I'd bet the massive dose of petrol helped achieve that, but then again we don't know how long he burned before this was phoned in." He paused. "Without an autopsy I can't be sure, but I've got a bad feeling about this one—I think he was alive when the killer lit him."

"Aw, no." O'Leary made a fist and punched his own hand for lack of a better target. "Poor Neil."

"Who?"

"O'Leary thinks, given the reference to the police artist, our victim may be the witness who provided the description for our sketch: a homeless man named Neil."

Wilkinson gave a low whistle. "We found a bag like a homeless person might carry against the side of the church. Used grocery sack full of an odd assortment of someone's treasures—half-eaten sandwich, dog-eared picture, couple of items of clothing. Haven't emptied it out and catalogued everything yet, but you get the gist."

"We'll take it," Nigella said. She turned to O'Leary. "The evidence boys have this. Let's wake the vicar."

She had to open the car door for O'Leary because he just stood there with the grocery bag, staring down at it. She cleared her throat twice before he took the hint and got in. "I was supposed to keep him safe," he mumbled. This time the fist he made slammed into her dash.

"How? By putting a police guard on him? Neil didn't like cops, and besides how in the living hell could you or I have expected the suspect to know about the sketch, let alone figure out who IDed him?" Nigella paused. Something about what she'd just said was needling her—what? She shook her head but the amorphous something got no clearer. "Stop beating yourself up, get on your phone, order up a round-the-clock uniform for Taylor's house, and tell them we want a man at Spiffy, starting tomorrow."

She started the car as he dialed.

"Ni," O'Leary said quietly as they turned a corner, "how *did* Nick know about the sketch?"

That was it, the thread she'd been trying to grasp. "Right. We haven't put it on the telly or in the papers. We haven't even shown it to Fox's agent or Smyth's brother yet—that's on Monday's list after they've had a bit of recovery time. Other than Nelson Taylor's kitchen, we've shown it in only one other place: GG&S."

"So either that cock-sucking son of a bitch was there when the Tweedle took it round and saw it—in which case he's right, and it isn't worth the paper it was printed on—or he has a contact who saw it and ratted on us rather than ratting him out."

"We're taking that new sketch to GG&S first thing Monday." Nigella flipped on the flashers and ran the next light.

"That's anger talking."

"You're the one punching dashboards."

"Yeah, I'm pissed beyond pissed. And I'm not suggesting you shouldn't be. When we catch this killer, you may have to write me up for slugging him, and I've never punched a suspect in my life. But we've used more resources on GG&S than anything else to this point, and what do we have to show for it? A goose egg. We could spend another couple of hours sniffing around there with what is starting to look like the worst police sketch ever, and be no closer to finding Nick. So that's not the top of Monday's list."

"What is?" Nigella slid the car into a spot along the curb by St. James's.

"You said it yourself Friday: we find the garage. Because there were three wooden figures in that shot, and there are still two left."

She nodded. "Alright, the glamorous task of mapping and driving round to rental garages is priority number one Monday, but for now let's get poor Sarah Ellis out of bed."

It took several rings to roust the vicar. "Please don't tell me there is a body outside my church."

"Outside St. Magnus the Martyr. And Ms. Ellis"—Nigella could see O'Leary's Adam's apple move as he swallowed—"we're afraid it may be Neil."

"No." Her voice was firm, full of denial, but there was raw terror in her eyes. Grabbing a jacket off a peg by the door, she pushed past them.

It wasn't dark inside the church. Random figures lay stretched out in the rear pews, and several of them shifted positions and muttered at the sound of her footfall, but Sarah Ellis kept moving. *Heading for Neil's pew—of course.* When she got there, the vicar put her hand over her mouth and let out a little sob. She spun round as O'Leary arrived, clearly prepared to comfort, and said, "He's there, he's right there!"

A sleeping but recognizable Neil lay at the far end of the pew. Nigella wasn't sure who looked more relieved—the vicar or O'Leary.

"Cup of tea?" The vicar asked, voice shaky. "You two look like you could use it."

"Yes, please." O'Leary's voice wasn't normal either.

He waited until everyone had their cup, then cleared his throat. "I am sorry, Vicar, but we're going to need you to take a look at a few things. Happy as are we all are that it is not Neil, somebody is still dead, and we have personal effects suggesting the man was homeless." He began spreading the contents of the bag on the kitchen table.

The vicar immediately reached for the snapshot—two kids and a dog, faded and with a corner missing. She drew a sharp breath "These are Joe's kids. He hasn't seen them in decades. But he treasures this picture."

The name sounded familiar.

"Is he a regular?" O'Leary asked.

"Yeah, one of the first the parish took on when we opened the doors and focused on this mission. He's at the heart of this place, along with Neil."

That's where she'd heard the name, Nigella thought. Neil had mentioned him when talking about the suspicious new bloke. "Can we go back over to the church and see if he is there?"

"He won't be. He's here for meals, he helps with orientation for the new fellows, and he takes a particular interest in the addicts, but in all the time I've been vicar, he's never slept here."

"Where does he sleep?" O'Leary asked.

"He's old style. Moves around. Sleeps rough."

"You have any contacts?"

"I'm afraid not. If he doesn't show up tomorrow, I'll call. But I can't believe he'd be the target of a killer. Why?"

That wasn't a question O'Leary was going to answer. "I know your boys aren't keen on coppers," he said, "but we're going to send some round. They'll be here twenty-four-seven until this mess is over. But we'll make them plainclothes and have them see you first so you can decide how to introduce them to the flock."

He began to gather up the things from the table and put them back in the bag. "Oh Jesus," he said under his breath, "I think we have another note." He held up a square of folded paper—bright white compared to the faded picture, with dots of sharpie bleeding through it. Nigella felt her stomach knot as she watched him unfold it—ready for another lengthy screed and hoping it didn't get personal like the last one.

Without reading out a single word, O'Leary refolded it and tucked it in his pocket.

For an irrational moment, Nigella thought he was keeping whatever was in it from her. Then she remembered: the vicar sat not three feet away.

Back in the car, she didn't even bother to start the engine. "Read it."

FRUSTRATION, ANGER, INJUSTICE: YOU KNOW THEM INTIMATELY, DON'T YOU, DETECTIVES?

O'Leary punctuated the end of the first line with an affirming nod. Then he continued:

SO DO I, AND SO DID NICHOLAS HAWKSMOOR. DO THEY COLOR YOUR DAYS AND DISRUPT YOUR SLEEP AS THEY DO MINE? GOOD, THAT IS MY INTENTION. PERHAPS THEN YOU'LL UNDERSTAND ME BETTER—UNDERSTAND WHY I RAIL AGAINST BEING KEPT IN THE SHADOW OF LESSER TALENT, JUST AS HAWKSMOOR WAS CONSIGNED TO OBSCURITY BY THE WORSHIPERS OF WREN. ASK YOURSELF, THOUGH: WHICH IS THE MORE BEAUTIFUL CHURCH—THE STUNNING WHITE ALTAR, SOARING SKYWARD, ON WHICH I PLACED ETHAN FOX, OR THE SQUAT, POORLY PROPORTIONED MONSTROSITY WHERE I LEFT THIS GENTLEMAN FOR YOU?

"Sounds like Wren is Nick's celebrity mistaken for a great talent; the false god from the tie," Nigella said. "The collector of big commissions he didn't deserve—at least in the mind of our suspect."

"So when Nick gave the finger to St. James's, he was giving it to Wren. Nick's hatred of Wren might please Margaret and Etienne," O'Leary said, "but it's not particularly useful to us in catching our killer.

🔥

Present-day London

Monday

O'Leary set a list in front of Nigella. "Emmerson Holdings only rents in Hackney. But they have more than thirty garages and storage lockers, even though the borough is only a little more than seven square miles."

She sighed. "Let's get them mapped."

"Right, I'll do that while you go to the morgue."

"Is that your idea of a deal?"

"No, that's me not wanting to go to the morgue so soon after lunch."

The morning had been paperwork, courtesy of the latest homicide. That was a little reality they never showed in TV dramas. More death meant more desk time: more reports, more lists, more calls. The vicar had rung to say Joe was indeed missing, but with only a first name and part of an old picture, he would not be easy to identify.

Evans stuck his head in. "Time's running out. Faster than you think," he recited grimly.

"Quoting the suspect, sir, or personally threatening us?"

"Neither and both, Parker. I'm just back from an unpleasant meeting with the DC Superintendent. Press and public are baying for blood."

She and O'Leary had seen the papers.

"We have three dead bodies in two weeks. People don't feel safe in their homes." Evans pulled a pastille box from his pocket, flipped it open to reveal the same antacid chewables that filled the candy bowl on his desk, and stuffed three in his mouth.

"To be fair," O'Leary offered, "Nick hasn't dragged anyone out of their home."

"Well, in case you missed this particular lesson at the Met, the public and the press aren't fair." He opened the little box again.

If he takes any more antacids, its duck-and-cover time, Nigella thought.

Evans snapped the box shut. "City officials are on the edge of piling on with the critics. And we know what happens once they do that, if we don't wrap this up and tie it with a bow."

"A cop gets sacrificed," O'Leary replied. "I didn't miss that lesson."

"I'm making the right noises," Evans said. "Tough case, top people—"

"All true." Nigella met his eyes. "But I know truth isn't enough either. Time *is* running out, so how 'bout you let us get back to it, sir?"

As Evans stalked off, O'Leary said, "What do you think he means by that anyway?"

"Evans?"

"No, the suspect. I mean he is, as your DCI pointed out, already killing people at a good clip. So what exactly is this new threat? Time is running out on what?" He began walking in circles around the conference table. "Time is running out before what?"

"O'Leary, stand still—you're making me dizzy!"

"Sorry. Nick's not just burning things willy-nilly. He's building art installations; he's trying to make a bleeding visual point. As far as we know, he has two figures left, and your friend James says these wooden men take significant time to carve. So realistically, how much faster or bigger can he work?"

"He can devote himself fully to the medium of flesh when he runs out of wood," she replied. "That'd be faster. Maybe *we* can move faster too—or we could if you'd leave off the vulture circles and map storage garages."

"Vulture," O'Leary mumbled under his breath as he pulled out his chair. "That's our killer. Probably circling his next victim. With our luck, it will be someone else tangentially linked to this case, so there'll be more guilt and, if anyone else figures that out, a chorus of recriminations about how could we not have known."

"Right." There was no use mincing words. When a suspect started killing witnesses, it was disastrous. "So after I'm done at the morgue, I'll pop in at GG&S—see if Mrs. Kay recognizes the updated sketch, and put her on alert. With Nick getting vindictive, this would be a good time to give Andrew Smyth's secretary, that nice architecture-student receptionist, and the useless guard who saw Smyth stagger out with the suspect but didn't recognize him, a bit of unscheduled leave."

🔥

Wilkinson had been right—damn him. Joe died by fire. Nigella stood on the pavement outside the morgue, gulping air.

"He'd been drugged, so we have to hope that dulled things, but all signs are that he was alive when he was set alight." Gwen Phillips's voice had made it clear that even after decades in her job, the victims on her slabs were people to her, not just evidence.

Worst way to die, worst way. Maybe not in everybody's mind, but in Nigella's—always.

Two little girls, it had started with two little girls down at the end of the terrace. Sirens at night; her mother, father, and herself, spilling out onto their front steps in Pimlico as the trucks roared past. The townhouse on the corner, with flames shooting out the side windows. Someone on the pavement in front of the house, screaming. Nigella was whisked back inside. Her mother sat on the edge of her bed, said the firemen were there now and everything would be alright. But it hadn't been. Because her friends Peggy and Milly—frightened and confused—hid in a closet together. Their parents couldn't find them. The firemen couldn't find them. Their names were called again and again, but they never came. They were recovered the next day, what was left of them. Ten-year-old Nigella had played hours of hide-and-seek in that house. She didn't have to imagine the inside of the bedroom closet; she could see it. She began having nightmares. She was "it," and she had to find her friends. But the house was on fire. After all these years, she could distinctly remember the panic of awaking from one of those dreams, always before she found them: the feelings of gut-wrenching guilt and failure.

So catch this bastard, she said to herself angrily as she worked to normalize her breathing. *Catch him before he can inflict that on anybody else.*

On the ride up the escalator through GG&S's stunning lobby, Nigella glanced down at her gray blazer and realized it was not just wrinkled, but rumpled—O'Leary-level rumpled. She hoped to hell he was mapping garages like crazy, not faffing around. *That's unfair; he's nearly as relentless as you.*

Waiting for the elevator, Nigella tucked the slender folder containing the updated sketch and a few autopsy notes under her arm, then pulled out her mobile. The ride up might give her time to glance over the morning obbo briefing from St. James's Piccadilly. The elevator stopped a single floor after she got on; some indistinguishable lawyer-like shoes and trouser legs moved through her peripheral vision as she typed instructions to Tweedledee to follow up on a car that had cruised past St. James enough times to be noticeable. She was finishing up her message as the doors opened again: her floor.

Heading toward HR, Nigella pulled the folder from beneath her arm, juggling it in her phone hand as she extracted the sketch.

What a huge difference. There is a resemblance to James, damn O'Leary for being right. A distinct resemblance. Nigella came to a halt, just staring. She felt someone behind her—close enough that her police senses tingled. Raising her eyes from the page, she was about to turn when James emerged from an office further along the hall, his arms full of folders.

"Detective Parker."

Why did he have to say it in that odd, ironic way—like they were in a farcical play rather than the middle of a gruesome murder investigation?

"What's that you've got?" James pointed toward the sketch in her hand, redirecting her attention.

Wham! Before she could answer him, someone slammed into Nigella from behind so forcefully that she staggered. Letting go of everything, she reached forward, expecting to go down arse over tit. Instead, after a couple of stumbling steps Nigella righted herself and whipped round as an explosion of folders and papers scattered around her.

A man was already on his knees a short distance away. "Oh God, I am sorry," he mumbled, hands frantically snatching up some of the mess.

I guess I ought to help. But for feck sake, why couldn't he look where he was going? As she began to stoop James came forward.

"I got this." He put up a hand to stop Nigella, then crouched down himself. "Rough day?" he asked the bloke who'd caused the crash.

"Aren't they all?" The fellow shrugged as they both picked up the scattered folders and sheets of paper. A moment later, he scrambled to his feet.

What the . . .?

James looked equally confused. "Hey," he called after the retreating figure, "the rest of this is yours as well!"

But the bulldozer didn't stop, or even break his stride. Just sprinted onward, calling, "Sorry to cause chaos and dash, but if I'm late to this meeting, I'll be looking for work," as he disappeared round a corner.

"What'd I tell you?" James looked up from where he still knelt, and shook his head. "This is a miserable, anxious place for the small fish."

"Do you see my sketch down there?" Nigella asked.

"Naw, just a mess of charts and case notes. Was it the killer?"

She nodded.

"Damn! And now I don't get to see him. Keep wondering if he's anybody I know."

He winked, and rather than just being annoyed, Nigella found her skin crawling.

Maybe the killer doesn't just look like James. Maybe it is him. And he is toying with me.

All the little "coincidences" flooded into her mind like dots connecting—the bird tattoo, the workout-boy physique, family in Surrey, how quickly he'd gone from finding out he knew a burned-up dead guy to wanting to get her in bed . . .

"You go on with your official police business," James continued, interrupting the growing and disturbing list assembling itself in Nigella's head. "I'll deal with this mess. See you later?" His tone was hopeful.

"Sure." Nigella was placating. *Someone will be seeing you later—following you actually, starting as soon as you get off work— but it won't be me.* It was time to stop shrugging off the creepy number of similarities between James and Nick. She'd radio from the car, put Tweedledee on surveillance duty immediately.

Maybe save a life by doing so.

🔥

O'Leary looked up from the large map he was standing over as Nigella entered. "All the garages are on here, but you forgot to give me that list of place names and addresses the photo boys compiled, so the only other location I've marked is that church from the calendar—St. James the Great, in Lower Clapton Road." He put a finger on a large cross on the map.

Wordlessly, she went to the stack of papers by her laptop, pulled out the list, and tossed it across to him. "Joe was alive when Nick lit him."

O'Leary dropped into his chair, list forgotten. "That's the shittiest thing ever."

"Yeah, and to top it off I lost the new sketch before I had a chance to show it to Mrs. Kay."

"What do you mean you 'lost' it? You don't lose things."

"I got plowed by some legal type who wasn't looking where he was going. Papers went all over the place. Guy must have picked up the sketch with his papers. He'll find it later and think, 'What the heck.'"

And I put my current sex partner under surveillance because, hell, he might just be our damn killer.

There was no fucking way she was saying that out loud, but it felt the cherry on top of her utterly shit-filled day.

Nigella started to take off her blazer, then gave up. "Let's knock off. Hit a pub. Have a drink or ten. Start over in the morning."

She half expected O'Leary to say no, but he stood, took his coat from the hook, and said, "I'll buy the first round."

Five rounds later, and cabbing it home because drink driving was not on her list of things to do, Nigella reached for her mobile. Not in its customary pocket. She flopped about in the back of the taxi like a fish on a riverbank, drawing odd looks in the mirror from the driver as she checked every pocket. No phone. Not in her bag either. *Sod it all!*

Inside her flat, Nigella dumped her bag just to be sure. Nope. Gone. She considered heading back to Wood Street and searching the incident room. Had she used her mobile there? She couldn't remember.

Nigella couldn't think straight, couldn't see straight. Majorly sleep deprived and pissed as a newt was not a good combination. Missing phone or no missing phone, it was time for bed. She'd just have to set the old-fashioned alarm on the bedside clock extra early, head into work, and get another mobile issued. Thankfully, she never stored anything confidential on it, and in any case, without her fingerprint or password, wherever her phone was right now, nobody was accessing it.

It wasn't the alarm that woke her. It was pounding on the door. The bedroom was pitch black, the clock read half midnight. Who the hell could be out there? And who had buzzed them through the main door?

Nigella grabbed the clothing she'd uncharacteristically dropped by the side of her bed and started pulling it on.

"Detective Parker, are you in there?" The voice was muffled.

Nigella was halfway down the hall when she heard the door give way. Instinctively she crouched, ready to defend herself.

The man caught her hand mid-swing.

"Parker?" It was Evans, and he sounded more relieved than angry. "Thank God."

"Guv'nor, you're going to have to fill me in." Nigella stared past him as her sitting room lights flicked on, revealing at least three uniforms. "Is there some particular reason you broke down my door in the middle of the night?"

"You didn't answer your mobile. You scared the shit of out DI O'Leary, and then you didn't answer your mobile."

"O'Leary?" She was becoming more confused by the moment. "The last time I saw O'Leary he was grabbing the taxi behind mine outside the Bell and Nettle."

"Yeah, that's what he told me too: a couple of rounds and he put you safely in a taxi. But about twenty minutes ago he got a text from your number—and I immediately got a call—because the person texting said their name was Nicholas Hawksmoor and that they had you."

That cleared the last fuzziness from Nigella's head better than four shots of espresso. "Where is O'Leary? Where?" The only reason Nigella didn't grab Evans and shake him was because he was her senior.

"He told us to get here fast, confirm you were missing. Said he'd meet us at the nick."

"Call him."

Evans pulled out his mobile. "I guess he's going to be relieved."

God she hoped so, but a sinister thought had crept into Nigella's brain, and it couldn't be banished except by the sound of O'Leary's voice.

"Rolled to voicemail." Evans held out the phone as if she'd want to leave a message.

Nigella grabbed it but instead of saying anything, hung up, opened his message app, and messaged her own number—"Nick is that you?"

The ping was almost instantaneous: "Yes, Parker. Smart. I'll give you that. Sorry, I don't have time to chat. Have a friend of yours at my place. We are going to create some art." And then he sent a wink. The fucking, murderous bastard sent a wink.

Nigella pushed past Evans and ran for the door. "The killer has O'Leary."

♦

The incident room was packed. Word had gotten round one of their own was in danger, and detective sergeants and detective inspectors turned up in droves. The cops from the Met stood intermingled with the cops from the City.

On the ride over, Nigella had made certain Evans contacted DCI Grosvenor in Surrey. The killer had said "my place," and grandma's property was certainly his place. The observation team in Betchworth said everything was quiet and dark, but they were on high alert.

"Have a friend of yours at my place. We are going to create some art." Other than the farm, that could mean only one spot: the garage. Or at least Nigella hoped it could only mean one spot, because the garage was the only other lead on their suspect's personal space.

"Listen up," she said. "We do this in teams and we do it quickly, or Detective Inspector O'Leary becomes this suspect's next victim." Her tongue was dry as dust and her throat tight, but she forced herself to say it because it was her job.

Looking down at O'Leary's map, Nigella swallowed hard at the sight of his handwriting, then grabbed a pencil and started sectioning.

"Have we got the warrants?" someone at the back asked as she handed out addresses.

"We will by the time you get where you're going," Evan's said. "We've got a magistrate rousted from bed. But let me be clear: when you arrive you cut locks, you break down doors— don't worry about warrants. This is an emergency. If we can't use evidence later, I'll live with that. Having an officer from the Met dead on my watch—that is something I can't live with."

Hearing Evans say "dead" was even worse than intimating it herself.

Nigella kept the remaining Tweedle for herself. She hadn't taken a section of the map. But that didn't mean she wasn't going out to hunt. Nigella knew the clock was ticking. *"Time is running out, detectives. Faster than you think."* Even running lights with sirens blaring, many of the Hackney locations were upward of twenty minutes out. And random legwork wasn't much better than guesswork. She'd be damned if she'd resort to guessing with O'Leary's life on the line.

Solve it, Ni. Use that brain of yours and solve it. The admonition came in O'Leary's voice, not her own.

"Make sure we have the gear for getting into places with padlocks and metal doors, then pull the car up and keep it running," Nigella ordered. She watched Tweedledum go, then radioed Tweedledee, praying he'd followed James to a storage garage with a definite address, one that she could race to, lights flashing.

If I only get one break in this case, make it this one.

Her slender hope dissolved, and her stomach contracted as Tweedledee told her he was standing outside a Spitalfields pub, watching through a window as James had a pint. Choking down her disappointment, Nigella took two deep breaths then thought: *What do I have?*

No mobile phone tower triangulation. As expected, the suspect had destroyed Nigella's phone after responding to her text. *Like he was waiting to taunt me and willing to take a risk to do so. And how the hell did he use my mobile without my passcode? Without my fingerprint?*

Nigella's glance fell on the list from the photo boys containing every place name and address they'd found in the Polaroid of the garage. The one O'Leary should have been arriving in a few hours to deal with. *Map them and pray for a pattern.* She grabbed a red marker.

The first item was an address off a Chinese takeaway menu: Nigella scrambled to find it. The next was a Tesco Express sack. Nigella googled. *How the bleeding hell could there be nine Tesco Expresses in Hackney?* She marked each, cursing at how long it took. It was when she marked the third item—the address of a hardware store from a receipt for linseed oil—that Nigella thought she saw a cluster emerging. Her heart raced as she googled a name stamped on a coffee takeaway cup. It was a one-off, on Lower Clapton road. There was definitely a grouping of dots now—a tidy knot surrounding St. James the Great. A line of six Emmerson units sat tucked behind some residences a short distance away.

She didn't wait for the elevator, just pounded down the fire stairs and out into the night. Her Tweedle was in the driver's seat, but she needed to hold the wheel, needed to know the car was being driven as aggressively as possible. So she displaced him and they shot into the night, siren screaming. "Radio Evans," she barked. "Tell him where we're headed. Tell him to reroute officers for backup, and if I am wrong about this, he can have my badge."

If you're wrong, quitting won't help.

They were the first on scene. Maneuvering down the narrow drive between two row houses, the squad car's headlights revealed a long dirt courtyard. At its far end sat six brick garages with corrugated roll-up doors. She shouted his name the minute she got out of the car. Listened . . . nothing. "Right! Get them open."

If I had both my sergeants, two sets of hands with bolt cutters. . . It hit her like a brick as they sprinted toward the nearest unit that her decision to have James tailed might prove deadly.

By the time the second door rolled up to reveal nothing but storage boxes, bile and panic were rising together in Nigella's throat. The dots had been convincing, but maybe her conclusion had been wrong. And if she was wrong, and O'Leary was still alive, out there to be saved and she failed . . . It was the first time she'd acknowledged that he might already be dead. After all, Andrew Smyth had been dead long before any fire was started.

At the third unit, Nigella caught a whiff of smoke. As the padlock dropped away, she hoisted the door herself. A vintage car fell under the beam of her torch. She raced to the next door.

The odor was stronger and underpinned with the abrasive scent of petrol. While her sergeant closed the cutters on the lock, Nigella banged on the door. "O'Leary, I'm here!"

In the moment of silence before the door began to roll up, she listened desperately for a reply. Two torch beams pierced the interior, revealing a pair of glistening wooden figures. One crouched furtively, head turned to show an entirely featureless face; and the other stood—head thrown back as if in ecstasy—beside a giant, wooden crate. At each figure's feet, cardboard boxes belched smoke. The resulting tableau resembled a ghoulish altar.

Victory. Nigella took the first full, deep breath since she'd sprung from the squad car. She'd been right, this *was* the place. But where the hell was O'Leary? Why wasn't he answering as she shouted his name? Her feelings of triumph and confidence fled as quickly as they had come. And then the cardboard box next to the crouching figure exploded into flames.

"Jelly, Jelly, ready or not here it comes!"

The voices of the dead girls in Nigella's head were silenced by another sound. As it was licked by flames, an erratic, feeble thumping came from the crate. Nigella raced across the petrol-dampened floor, aware that the whole garage could be an inferno in minutes. Skidding to a stop in front of the burning box, she reached for it. The heat was too much. The sound from the crate was louder. She had to stop it from catching fire.

Backing away, Nigella ran at the flaming box from the side, kicking it as hard as she could to get it away from the crate. A strip of the floor caught fire as it skidded away, and so did the bottom of her trouser leg. Staring at the flames that she saw but couldn't yet feel, her breath coming in ragged gasps, Nigella fought the instinct to drop and roll. Rolling in petrol was the surest way to be Nick's victim. Stooping, she began to frantically beat out the flames with her hands, hardly feeling the pain. She was extinguishing the last of them when a spark flew up, landing in her hair. Nigella saw it catch, just like in one of her fire nightmares.

This can't be how it ends—any way but this.

Desperation gave way to determination. In a single, swift motion, she yanked the blazer she'd thrown on up over her head, wrapping it tight to smother the flames. In the dark cocoon of gray wool and terror, nostrils full of the scent of her burnt hair, Nigella realized that there was something worse than being engulfed by fire. Failing. Panicking and failing to save those she'd taken an oath to serve, failing to save a fellow cop. She hadn't failed to save Peggy and Milly. She'd been only ten, and running into their burning house wouldn't have helped. But things were different now, *she* was different. And she wasn't going to fail to save O'Leary. She couldn't live with that.

Emerging from her blazer, Nigella dropped it over the box she'd kicked, now encircled by a pool of flaming petrol, counting on the wool to help smother the fire. Then she picked up the second smoking box, ran through the open garage front, and dumped its jumble of smoldering rags onto the open ground, nearly colliding with her sergeant carrying a crowbar. Still smoke rose around the crate and Nigella spotted two more boxes at its rear corners. "Forget the crowbar! Blast those!" she ordered, reaching out her hand for the tool so he could race back to the squad car for a fire extinguisher Somewhere in the distance she heard sirens.

Nigella thrust the end of the crowbar into one of the crate's corner seams, throwing her full weight behind it. She heard rather than saw the blasts from the fire extinguisher, choking and coughing as the powder from it mingled with the smoke surrounding her. She had to get the box open before O'Leary smothered. But she was not the right person for the job.

The right person is standing outside a pub in Spitalfields watching your lover have a pint.

Her sergeant appeared at her side. Dropping the extinguisher with a clank, he took the pry bar out of her hands, grunting and wrenching until, with a tremendous crack, the front of the crate came away. A figure, bound hand and foot with packing straps, fell into Nigella's outstretched arms, its weight driving her to her knees on the petrol-covered floor—it was O'Leary. A moment of scrambling, then her sergeant's flashlight lit, its beam hitting O'Leary's face. His eyes were unfocused, but the pupils contracted in the light, and he was breathing.

"Get an ambulance!"

Left in darkness as the sergeant ran for the squad car radio, Nigella bent low over O'Leary. "Colm, I have you. Everything is going to be all right."

Would it? How much smoke had he inhaled? How high had his core temperature gone? All her years of fire experience meant she knew exactly what to worry about. Thank God, the killer had put the incendiary boxes outside the crate, not in it, or even without flames O'Leary would have suffered scalding and burns.

The returning sergeant handed Nigella a small canister of oxygen, and she pressed the plastic mask to O'Leary's face as the packing straps binding him were cut away. As soon as he had a hand free, he tried to push the mask aside, lips moving soundlessly, but she pressed it back.

Sirens, not one but many, closer and closer, until the court-yard beyond the garage came alive with lights. O'Leary raised a hand again, pushed the mask away firmly this time. "Come on Ni—help me get up." His voice was hoarse. "If I let them roll me out of here on a stretcher, it's all anyone'll talk about."

"Don't be an idiot." But she beckoned to the Tweedle, and he hauled O'Leary to his feet. Nigella slid beneath O'Leary's other arm. The sergeant was congratulating her, but she hardly noticed. More gratifying by far was O'Leary's weight leaning into her and the sound of his feet shuffling unevenly over the concrete. As they crossed the garage threshold, leav-ing behind the smell of petrol and the darkness of pure evil for a moonlit sky and flashing cruiser lights, dozens of officers cheered.

Evans arrived as they lowered O'Leary to a sitting position at the rear end of the ambulance. "Parker, we've got the scene. You manage this fellow." He slapped O'Leary on the shoulder. "The trouble you Met boys get up to when we let you out of our sight for an instant." His gruff voice was openly tinged with relief.

The paramedics moved in—another oxygen mask, a blood pressure cuff, a finger monitor to measure blood oxygen. And all the time they were connecting him up, Nigella couldn't take her eyes off O'Leary, not even to get a look at the full scene, now illuminated by spotlights.

"Put these under your armpits," one of the paramedics said, explaining the need to bring down his temperature as she pushed a pair of ice packs up under O'Leary's shirt. "And these are for your groin." As she reached for his fly, O'Leary lifted off his mask.

"If you don't mind," he rasped, "I'll do those. And I'd like a bit of privacy. I have to work with you people."

Turning her back, Nigella saw Wilkinson emerge from a van, followed by a swarm of forensic types. "Press at the end of the alley," he told her as he brushed past.

"Right back," she said to the re-masked O'Leary, reaching out to unnecessarily brush back a bit of hair from his forehead.

Evans was bent over the pile of rags she'd cast out of the garage, shifting them with a screwdriver. "Press is here," Nigella said. "My gut says we send a uniform out, low-key it, don't make a connection to our homicides. Just an accidental fire—some homeowner refinishing furniture and carelessly leaving the rags about."

"Your case, your mate nearly incinerated, your call." He moved the screwdriver a bit more. "Is that an iPhone?" Nigella looked down: there was her mobile, smashed to hell.

The EMTs seemed relieved to see her as she returned to the ambulance.

"Detective Inspector O'Leary is refusing to let us run him to hospital."

Nigella sat down next to him in the open ambulance back. "Don't be a prat. You've been boxed up and smoked like a ham."

"I don't want to go to hospital."

"Give us a minute," Nigella said, and the paramedics retreated. "Is this a pride thing?"

"Naw, Ni, if it was that, would I be sitting here with ice in my nether regions?" He tried a smile. She gave him a look. He lowered his voice. "I—I don't want to feel like a victim."

She went to talk to the ambulance team. "Can you cut us any slack on the hospital thing?"

"Look," the senior EMT said, "he's on the border. His blood oxygen levels are okay; his temp is coming down; we've got him slugging electrolyte-charged water because he resisted an IV. But he could be dizzy, nauseated, confused."

"He is not confused now. So you're talking about running him in for observation?"

"Yeah."

"How about if I promise we'll keep him observed? We're going to anyway. Even if you take him to hospital, we will have a man on him. And there is no bleeping way any cop is going home alone after being kidnapped by a murderer."

The paramedics looked at each other. They were pretty obviously relieved—O'Leary must have been giving them a hell of a time. Their chief nodded.

O'Leary was slumped against the side of the ambulance but straightened as soon as he saw her. He was fighting to seem normal. She'd have done the same. Act normal and you'll feel normal, everything will be back to normal. Too bad that wasn't how life worked. She wanted to cry and didn't know why—she hadn't cried in years. And she'd won here, dammit—even if they didn't have the killer yet; she had Colm. Nick hadn't got Colm.

Nigella tapped a uniform on the shoulder. "I need a car, something unmarked," she said gruffly. "Come on, O'Leary— grab another bottle of that rehydration stuff, and let's get out of here."

She held the door, then leaned over and buckled him in. It was a sign of just how traumatized he was that there was no snide quip—no "You're not my nan." As they were waved out of the alley onto the main road, she said, "You know you can't go to your place, right?"

He didn't turn his head. Just looked straight ahead down the lighted street. "No argument on that. I don't want to be alone. That is the first time I've ever really thought I'd bought it." A tremor went through his body, as if he'd seen a ghost.

Probably his own.

The hair on Nigella's arms stood on end. "How the hell did he get you?" She tried not to sound accusatory, but along with relief Nigella was starting to feel angry. "Evans said you were headed to Wood Street."

"I was. Then I got another text. Nick changed the game. Told me he was at Saint James the Great. And he was. Clever wanker showed me only what he wanted me to see. There were what looked like two figures in the front pew. As I made my way forward, he must have come up behind me and whacked me on the head."

Nigella doubted he'd told the paramedics that, or they'd never have agreed to release him. "Why in the hell did you go to the church alone? Without phoning it in?" she snapped.

"Because I thought he had you." He exhaled. "When I came to, I knew where I was. I recognized it from the Polaroid."

"Your fucking chivalry is going to get you killed someday."

"It wasn't chivalry, it was loyalty. And *your* loyalty is what saved me Ni. We've all had moments when we know here"—he touched his temple—"we're in danger. But that's not what this was." He paused, took a slug of the special water and a couple of deep breaths. "This time I *felt* it here." He put a hand to his chest. "When he grinned at me through a black balaclava like the one we found in his room in Surrey. When he made me watch him pour petrol over those figures, when he put me in that box in the dark, when I started to smell smoke . . . I *felt* it was the end."

"But you were wrong. You're not dead," she insisted, as much for herself as for him.

He swayed on the elevator ride up to her flat, and Nigella put his arm back over her shoulder. The smells of smoke, petrol, and linseed oil clinging to him were overwhelming, reminding her of how close he'd come to being consumed by a madman's ambitions and flames.

They were barely inside before Nigella pulled the coat off him, threw it in the hallway, and slammed the door. She didn't realize she was crying until O'Leary wrapped his arms around her and said, "I'm okay, Ni. I'm okay." Then he put his mouth beside her ear and muttered the admission, "But God, I was terrified."

"You weren't the only one." The panic she'd experienced racing through Hackney, worried her deductions were wrong; the stark fear at that first whiff of smoke; the complete terror when the door to the garage had opened and she'd seen the box burst into flames—all washed over her afresh. "Damn it, O'Leary I don't care what Nick told you; you should have followed protocol."

"You don't always follow protocol—not when you think a life's on the line. That's what we cops do, Ni—weigh risks, make split-second decisions, fight like hell to save people."

And we don't always succeed.

Nigella knew failure was part of the job: crimes went unsolved, deaths weren't prevented. If you couldn't accept that, then you couldn't be a detective. And if you were good at your job, you solved and saved more than you lost. But O'Leary dead was *not* acceptable—not remotely, not under any equation.

She put her hands behind his head, pulled it down, and kissed him. He even tasted like smoke. And that made her frantic. Nigella started to unbutton his shirt, pulled so hard that she heard fabric rip. Then she made herself stop. *A minute ago the man couldn't even stand on his own feet.* "I am sorry, maybe you don't want—"

"Oh, I do." He tipped her chin up so he could see her eyes. "But are *you* sure?"

"As sure as I've ever been of anything."

And then there were four hands instead of two removing petrol-scented clothing. They stumbled from the tiny foyer into the sitting room and sank to the rug, a tangle of arms and legs, a frantic merging of bodies. For Nigella, it wasn't really about desire—except for an overwhelming desire for proof of life, for a way of convincing herself that O'Leary was flesh, blood, and safe. Seeing him hadn't been enough. Even touching him hadn't. But holding him, devouring him—the terror of his near loss was finally wiped away by the celebration of his continued existence.

When it was over, Nigella rose, held out a hand to help him up, and led him through to the bedroom. Wordlessly, they lay down face-to-face and fell asleep within seconds.

Nigella woke with the sun. O'Leary still smelled like smoke, but the odor was no longer disturbing. Nudging him, she said, "We'd better get moving. We have a killer to catch and now it's personal."

"It sure as hell is," he replied, blinking and yawning.

She threw off the covers. There was nothing awkward about standing undressed in front of Colm before shrugging on a T-shirt from atop the dresser; nothing odd about him sitting on the edge of her bed, naked, hair mussed, and stretching. Until his phone pinged.

"It's Amy." His voice dripped with guilt. "I forgot to text her last night."

"I think you'll be forgiven," Nigella worked hard to keep her tone ironic. "After all, you almost died."

"She doesn't know that."

Better for her.

"I'll let you handle that then, shall I." Nigella retreated to the kitchen, where she made much more noise than was necessary getting coffee on. Only when she had a full cup for him and his briefs off the sitting room floor did she return, hesitantly, to the bedroom.

O'Leary was sitting in exactly the same spot. "Well, that's finished."

Nigella set the cup down on the highboy and gaped at him. "Because of this? She never has to know." Nigella tossed him the briefs. "On my honor, O'Leary, I won't tell. If you've got something good, do you think I want to ruin that for you?"

He shook his head with a bemused smile. "Remember that discussion we had, Ni, about lies of commission and omission? I'm decent at a lot of things, but lying isn't one of them. I told Amy we were through not because I spent last night in your bed, but because I don't love her. I love *you*. However offensive that is to your sense of life's order."

He went into the bathroom, leaving the door open. Nigella watched his reflection in the mirror while he pulled a spare toothbrush from her medicine cabinet and did his teeth. By the time he'd straightened up from spitting, she'd made up her mind.

Joining him, she reached round and deliberately made the brush he'd set down parallel to the edge of the basin. "If you're going to start keeping a toothbrush here again, Colm, you're going to have to learn to do it properly."

She didn't say she loved him. She wasn't sure if she'd say it later, or ever. But Nigella remembered the utter soul-freezing panic of the moment his bound body had fallen out of that crate, and embraced the realization that he wasn't replaceable. That he meant more than a good fuck, and that he'd been right when they'd stood on the steps of Christ's Church and he'd suggested that the way they *were* together was more than just professional partners.

O'Leary turned and pulled her into his arms. Their kiss was all consuming, and the next thing Nigella knew, she was sitting on the edge of the counter with her legs wrapped around him, watching in the mirror as they made love.

When they'd unwound, O'Leary gave her his most disarming smile and said, "Not bad for a gaffer."

"Great," she said. "But if this relationship is going to become a distraction from the case . . ." She let the sentence trail off because there was no way she was going to reconsider, and because she realized she'd used the word "relationship."

She held her breath, waiting for O'Leary to poke fun. Instead, he said, "I have to shower. Linseed oil and petrol is not my cologne of choice. Go slug your coffee and let's get to work."

◊

The Met had a car out front at O'Leary's place. As O'Leary got out, Nigella said, "Throw every bit of what you're wearing in the bin. And while you're in there, if you have a few things you want to keep at my place . . ."

"I don't know." He flashed a grin. "I have some PTSD from that sweater-in-a-bag incident." Then he shut the door and headed up the walk.

Nigella fished for her mobile to ring James while she had a minute alone—to officially call a halt to their arrangement— then remembered she didn't have a phone . . . a little detail that had led to near catastrophe. *Only two people were with you at GG&S when the phone likely went missing—James and the man with the folders. You know lover boy isn't the killer because Tweedledee was on him every minute after he left GG&S. So the hit-and-run folder guy was likely the killer himself.*

"Colm," she said as he threw a kit bag in the rear seat and climbed in, "I think I met Nick yesterday—had to have, or how'd he get my mobile? I think he was the guy who knocked into me at GG&S. I'm ninety-nine percent certain. But we're one hundred percent certain you met Nick, and that means—"

"I have to talk about last night."

"Sorry."

"S'alright. I had the same thought as I was throwing my things together. So here's where we find out if I'm a good witness or the kind that makes you want to tear your hair out."

"Let's start with the damn phone," Nigella said. "Did you see him with it—see him text me back?"

"I heard him. He had me sitting on a stool, trussed up. He'd shown me the boxes—explained how he was counting on an exothermic reaction to finish his sculpture, was dying to see how that would work out." O'Leary took an audible breath and held it for a moment. "He laughed and told me that actually *I* would be dying, and that was the one thing he knew for certain about how it would work out."

"Cocky son of a bitch. Low opinion of the competency of the police."

"It's damn lucky for me that he underestimated the cops. Otherwise, he'd have lit me up directly like he did Joe."

She cringed. "Don't say that."

"Well it's true, and that was what I was most afraid of: the pain."

Nigella drove a couple of blocks before she felt confident enough of her voice to go on. "You said you heard him text. What do you mean? Because I still can't figure out how Nick the prick used my password-protected mobile."

"Siri. All that bastard did was say, 'Hey Siri, text Evans.'"

"The hack was that easy? Holy hell, we need to have the tech boys check that out and send out a department-wide memo."

"True, but maybe that's not our first priority."

"While Nick was running his mouth off, what else did he say?"

"He explained to me the dynamic tension he hoped to create between his wooden figures and my remains, but I wasn't particularly interested in the artistic aspect of his creation. Of course, I didn't tell him that; the longer he talked, the better. Then, when it was time to go in the box, he apologized."

"Jesus."

"He looked at me though those eyeholes—and by the way, I know Neil said brown, but I will never, ever forget those eyes, and they are hazel—and said I was clearly a 'true devotee and a disciple of my work.' What a Nick phrase, eh? Said that devotion to craft was something he and I shared." O'Leary flexed his fingers unconsciously. "That was disturbing. I really don't like to think Nick and I have anything in common. Then he patted my shoulder and said he was sorry to cut short my career but that a price had to be paid for our suppression of his work." They were pulled up at an intersection, and O'Leary turned his head and looked out the window.

"What else?"

"Nothing."

"Okay, then look me in the eye and say that."

O'Leary kept his glance out the window. "He said at least I had the consolation of knowing that I was dying for some . . . something."

A horn honked behind them, and Nigella realized she'd missed the light change. "Was that the last thing he said?"

"Directly to me, yes. He put me in the crate and drove the nails in—one of the worst sounds I've ever heard—then I heard his footsteps, heard them stop. I was waiting for the sound of the door. But instead, he started talking to the artist he takes his name from. He said, *Father Hawksmoor, patron saint of underappreciated artists, man overlooked and ridiculed, bless this work. When this door opens next, it will reveal my magnum opus. I only hope it will be worthy of you.*'"

"He thinks he's Hawksmoor—a victim." Nigella whipped her car into a spot in the Wood Street garage. "But he's really Wren."

Nigella thought of Margaret and Etienne's centuries-old case notes—of the pair's doggedness, their level of detail, how they'd found no justice and hadn't even been blessed with the time that she'd now have with Colm. Because she'd done a bit of digging one evening, drawn to the couple's story, wondering if the love they'd found had made amends for the unsatisfactory way their case had concluded. And she'd discovered there had been no time for that—Margaret had been interred at Westminster only days after the date on her letter. Nigella had never told O'Leary of that discovery, because it'd felt like she'd cheated by investigating the notes on her own, and because the idea of Margaret dead so soon and Etienne left grieving had been unbearable to Nigella in a way that made her uncomfortable. *And now, so close to his own escape from death, I certainly can't tell Colm that Margaret was not so lucky.*

"Margaret and Etienne made a compelling case that Wren believed his art was more important than other people's lives," she continued. "Wonder how Nick'd feel realizing he's connected to a man he abhors by that man's most loathsome quality."

"Ni, you're brilliant!" O'Leary's face lit up. "Nick'd *hate* that. He sees himself as aligned with the angels; a statement comparing him to Wren would make him furious. So that's what we're going to do."

"Colm, how does a furious killer help us? We don't need more bodies; we need fewer."

"Make someone angry enough Ni—blindly angry—you can trap 'em."

"So how do we trap Nick?"

"Haven't worked that out yet. But two of the best cops in London are on it—so we'll come up with a plan. Or maybe we won't need to. He works at GG&S—has to or how would he have been in the hallway to knock you over."

"I didn't fall over."

"Whatever. My point is Mrs. Kay could take one look at our new sketch and say his name. His real name." He gave her a genuine, wide O'Leary smile. And Nigella was so happy to see it, she bit her tongue rather than calling him an overconfident fool.

Inside the nick, cops of all ranks jumped to their feet and saluted as the pair passed. "Had I known getting nearly burned up was all it took to get the City crew to respect a Met officer, I might have tried it earlier," O'Leary wisecracked, but he was clearly moved.

When they reached their incident room, Nigella called up the new sketch, changed the suspect's eye color, and ordered it to print.

Evans came to the door. "I've got half the floor working on last night's incident. Oh and Wilkinson took core temps on one stray box of rags we found intact. You might want to put your hands over your ears and hum for this next part, O'Leary." When O'Leary just looked at him, Evans shrugged. "Suit yourself. Wilkinson thinks we had another fifteen to thirty minutes before all that petrol ignited. He says it takes considerable time for oil-soaked rags to go from heating to smoldering, to flaring. Which means your suspect set the stage, down to starting the exothermic reactions, *before* he even texted O'Leary. And about that—"

"I'll explain. Parker, you pick up a shiny new mobile phone." O'Leary apparently felt he was currently popular enough to interrupt the DCI.

The first thing Nigella did on her new mobile was disable "Listen for 'Hey Siri.'" That was one convenience she was never using again. There were a couple of texts from James. But he was no longer relevant—not as a suspect and not as a physical distraction. So she left him unanswered.

O'Leary intercepted her near the elevators, holding the newly printed sketch. "This is it, Ni, our last trip to GG&S."

"That's optimistic."

"I'm in an optimistic mood. Call it a new lease on life. We get a name on our boy, we get an address."

"And just trot round to his cubicle or run round to his flat and pick him up? That's not optimism, that's fantasyland."

Mrs. Kay took them into her office and shut the door. Nigella recounted the hallway crash. "We'd like two things," she concluded. "We have a new picture that we want to show very selectively—because we cannot afford to put our killer on the run if he isn't already—and we'd like a list of all non-solicitor staff out today on any sort of unscheduled leave." She pulled out the sketch and slid it across the desk.

"That's Josh Wright." Mrs. Kay's response was immediate, her voice calm. "I cannot believe I didn't see the resemblance before." Mrs. Kay opened a screen on her computer, clicked around a bit, then looked back up at them. "Wright is not in—so he is either late or not coming."

"We'd like to see his workspace."

As they passed through the outer office, Mrs. Kay stopped by a desk. "Mary, can you get me Josh Wright's address and emergency contact information."

The youngish woman seated behind the computer gave Nigella and O'Leary a wide-eyed look. "Oh no, Josh hasn't been hurt by the killer who got Mr. Smyth, has he?"

"No," Mrs. Kay responded with an unforced, even tone that impressed Nigella. "But the officers are worried about him. I'd appreciate it if you didn't mention that or anything about police interest in Josh to anyone. The last thing we want is another death." The girl nodded vigorously.

When they reached Josh's desk, Mrs. Kay whisked the young woman in the adjoining cubical away, leaving Nigella and O'Leary the chance to go over things unobserved. Wright's small corner of GG&S was entirely impersonal.

"No pictures. No 'I love my cat' mug. Nothing that isn't GG&S related." O'Leary slid the last drawer shut quietly. "Josh is Nick."

"Let's get the evidence crew over here." Nigella pulled out her new mobile.

"How about after hours—and plain-clothed?" O'Leary lowered his voice. "We don't want Nick to know that we know he's Josh, right?"

Nigella paused. There were only two forks in this road. They could go full reveal: name, details, and picture on every TV channel and in all the papers, launching a UK-wide manhunt. Nick would go to ground, but given the size of the net they'd be casting, somebody would get him. Might take days, weeks, but someone would. *But not necessarily us, and this is so personal for the City and the Met—for Colm and me.*

Or they could go stealth. Know more than Nick knew they did, and count on that advantage and their own policing to find him—to trap him.

It was knowing more that let me save Colm last night. And Colm thinks we have an angle to trap Nick.

"So you're for keeping his ID under wraps. That's not just about us getting to make the collar?" She asked because she wasn't sure of her own motives.

"No. I mean it's partly about that, sure. We've had all the ugly—the visits with next of kin, standing over charred remains."

Thinking you were going to be burned alive. Typical cop behavior not to mention that among the ugly.

"But it's more than that. Nick has to know by now something's gone wrong. I mean my death wasn't in the papers this morning. That means he's in a highly agitated state. I'm against anything that makes him panic—until we are ready to use that panic to our advantage."

She nodded.

O'Leary held the elevator door for her in that annoying way of his, but she let it go. "Of course, somebody could die on our ground while we continue investigating," she said, hitting a button. "We've been at it for just shy of three weeks. What if it takes us three more?"

"It won't. If we can lure him into a trap, the deaths stop. And I told you Ni, you've identified his pressure point: Wren. We're going to use his hatred of Wren as our bait."

"How precisely?"

"The idea's out there hovering—it just needs to come into focus."

She rolled her eyes.

Mrs. Kay looked up as they reentered her office. "This might interest you," she held out a list of dates. "Mr. Wright has been out several times lately—going back to the day your sergeant came first over with a sketch. He went home sick midday that day."

"Very interesting indeed." Nigella took the sheet. "How about an address?"

"I have it, but Mary tells me it is recent. Changed in the last couple of days."

"Burner, like the phone," O'Leary muttered.

"Emergency contact?" Nigella asked.

"Linda Shotton in Surrey."

Dead gran. Nigella wondered if that too had been updated. Didn't matter, it was a dead-end.

Nigella paused in front of the massive windows with the million-pound view just outside of HR. The sky was mottled gray, making the edges of nearby buildings look sharp as knives. The perfect sky for the frustration she felt. "Time to get inspired, O'Leary. What's our plan for trapping Nick?"

O'Leary gazed out thoughtfully. "This isn't just your ground, Ni; it's his. He comes here every day to work—or he did. We can see two of his six crime scenes from here." Nigella glanced at monument outside, then turned her eyes in the direction O'Leary was pointing and found the spire of St. Magnus the Martyr. "Let's lay our trap here, where he feels at home."

"I like that," she replied. "He feels comfortable so he'll be more confident—even over-confident."

O'Leary pulled out his mobile as they headed to the lift. "You want a Wren spot or a Hawksmoor one?"

"We just want close. I mean, seriously, do you think we're going to have a whole menu of choices?"

"As a matter of fact, we do. And one of them wins the pools—it's that church you have coffee out in the front of, the one from the pictures in Nick's bedroom. I can't believe I didn't think of it."

"St. Mary Woolnoth."

He held out his phone, and there was the front entrance of the church from a much more traditional angle than in Nick's Polaroid.

"Perfect. There'll be a certain irony in taking Nick down at a location he was likely casing for his work. But—and I hate to be a killjoy here—we have bait and a location, but still no blueprint for a trap." Nigella tossed him her keys. "You drive."

"Guess I am still benefitting from the almost-died-but-didn't effect."

"Nope, I need to think. So maybe try not to distract me by running anyone over."

Three blocks later it came to her. "O'Leary, the time has come for you to give your favorite tabloid a big exclusive. And after you do, we're going to stage a little art event with the help of our friend Professor Rowan—an exhibit and lecture for an audience of one."

◊

Present-day London

Friday

"Let's go over it again, make sure we're ready for this party." O'Leary threw the last of the takeaway containers in the bin as Nigella hung up her dishtowel.

They'd spent all week on the details of their plan for St. Mary Woolnoth. The whiteboard in the incident room was covered with them. Their team could probably recite the details backward. If anything, they'd had too much time to contemplate their plan.

Waiting until the one-week anniversary of O'Leary's kidnapping to spring their trap had been a nerve-stretching choice. But they'd balanced the need to make sure Nick had ample time to hear about Professor Rowan's lecture and exhibit against the risk he'd act out in the meantime, and decided the delay was necessary.

Of course there wouldn't really be a lecture or exhibit. But Nick could be forgiven for thinking there would be—all of London could be forgiven. The events had been announced at the end of an incendiary story in London's favorite tabloid—the story of Christopher Wren, arsonist and murderer, as set forth in Lady Margaret's notes. When he gave the tabloid this juicy, centuries-old gossip, O'Leary had offered some carefully drawn parallels to the current killer running loose in London. "Best to connect the dots for them. They are not exactly geniuses," he'd said with an eye roll.

His tune changed when he saw the headline emblazoned across the front page: "Sir Christopher Wren, Murdering Arsonist? Inspiration for Today's Monument Killer?"

"They may be bollocks most of the time," he'd conceded, grinning as he tacked the front page to the wall of the incident room, "but this, this is a masterpiece of journalism."

A smiling Nigella had raised her coffee in a salute. "I'd give my eyeteeth to see Nick read that piece. The part where they speculate he began his killing spree where he did in order to honor Wren . . . he must be howling like a dog. Read my favorite paragraph again."

"With pleasure:

Does this madman terrorizing London know the truth about his idol? Is the Monument Killer inspired by the gruesome actions that must make this nation reconsider Wren's legacy? Perhaps not, but one thing is certain: Like Wren, this killer thinks what he creates is more important than people's lives. We hope the police catch him soon because nobody should die for art, let alone for some second-rate carving of a man giving a church the finger.

The piece closed with the question of whether St. Mary Woolnoth ought to go ahead with a scheduled lecture by Professor Katherine Rowan, given Wren's newly revealed murderous history. Her talk, the tabloid made clear, was intended to honor the architect: insisting that St. Mary Woolnoth wouldn't exist as it did without Wren, and arguing that the church's actual architect, Hawksmoor, had been no more than a good-quality lump of clay whom Wren took on as a clerk and molded into a second-rate purveyor of English Baroque. The time and place for the lecture had been carefully listed.

Nigella and O'Leary had plainclothes officers hang posters and deposit flyers in the foyer of St. Mary Woolnoth promoting the lecture and emphasizing that, in conjunction with the Tuesday evening talk, there would be a small exhibit illustrating Wren's influence on St. Mary Woolnoth. Beside each mention of the exhibit, a handwritten note had been pinned: "To facilitate the construction of Tuesday's exciting exhibit, next Monday's choir practice is cancelled."

Nigella and O'Leary reasoned Nick would want Rowan stopped before she "defamed" Hawksmoor. They were counting on him to turn up to keep the professor from setting up her exhibit.

Monday night was go time. In the interim, they were taking no chances.

Katherine Rowan, had been shadowed 24/7 since she'd agreed, eagerly, to their proposal. Nigella had gone in person to ask—not because she'd been in any doubt of Rowan's reply, but to give Rowan a gift. "You are the scholar for this," Nigella said, handing over Margaret's case notes. "I know it will take time and research, but there is the making of a groundbreaking book here." As Nigella walked back to the car, where O'Leary sat, engine running, whistling, she'd smiled. It pleased her to give a fellow professional woman a leg up. And beyond that, it felt like a tribute to Margaret, a chance for the case she'd built so carefully against Wren to bring some modicum of posthumous justice. That would be a memorial more fitting to her than a stone in the floor of Westminster.

Leaving O'Leary in a parked car outside the Slade was about as far away as Nigella had allowed him to get since his near immolation. They were each unwilling to be out of the other's sight, even if they never directly talked about it. And every morning when Nigella woke up and rolled over to look at his sleeping profile, she thought, *Time enough.*

Now, as she opened the wine cooler and pulled out a bottle of Valpolicella Superiore, Nigella said, "Colm, this plan is so tight you could bounce a pound coin off it. So let's *not* go over it again. Let's turn on the stereo and have some wine on the sofa. I'll even let you pick the music."

"Right, but I'll pour, and you put on what you like. And we should probably turn in early in case Nick decides to haul us out of bed. After all it's the two-week anniversary of poor Andrew Smyth's installation at the temple."

"Let's not think about that either." Nigella took her glass from him. "Let's celebrate the one-week anniversary of those Polaroids slipping from Nick's book and ultimately saving your life."

"I'll drink to that." He raised his glass before setting it on the side table and settling in on the sofa, back against an arm, legs stretched out so Nigella could sit between them. She relaxed against his chest. They'd just clinked glasses when her mobile rang.

"Is that . . . James?" he asked.

"Oh Christ on a crutch, it is."

"Nigella Parker! You haven't been entirely honest with that young man, have you?" His imitation of her mum wasn't half bad—especially considering he'd never met her.

"It's been a busy week, Colm." She slid off the sofa because she couldn't very well dump James while curled up with Colm.

"Hey, Nigella." James sounded his usual brash, confident self. "I decided to go old school and ring because our text exchange has really fizzled. I'm starting to feel jealous—"

How the hell could he know?

"—of that creepy murderer. He is getting way more of your attention than I am these days."

"James—"

"I know, I know, catching killers is what you do. Anyway, I'm downstairs with a bottle of bubbly. Let's make a night of it."

She put her hand over the phone, but before she could even mouth the news to O'Leary the buzzer sounded. "Well, this is going to be awkward," he said. "I'd offer to go through to the bedroom, but wouldn't that just make things worse?"

"You can be the very devil, Colm. You know that, right?"

"It is part of my charm."

The buzzer shrilled again.

Sex-starved puppy. The words came into Nigella's head as she swung the door open to reveal James in jeans and a tight turtle-neck. He leaned in for a kiss, but she stepped back, gesturing for him to go through. He took two steps into her main living space, then stopped and stood staring.

"James, you've met DI Colm O'Leary."

"This is balls up!" He turned to face her. "I *knew* it! Don't even try to tell me this is just a work evening, Nigella."

"Wasn't going to."

"So how long has this mixing of business and pleasure been going on?"

"If you mean was I sleeping with O'Leary while I was doing you—no. I'm guilty of delay in telling you, but not deceit."

"Well, thanks very much for that." His voice dripped with sarcasm. "And here I thought we had something."

"We did, James—we had a hell of a good time. And please don't tell me you were looking for a happily ever after, or try to make me feel guilty. Because we were hooking up, plain and simple, and we both knew that from that first night when we left an art exhibit for drinks and a tumble less than an hour after we met."

"You're welcome to her, mate," James said, turning toward the sofa. "But I don't know why you're grinning, because if I can't handle her, I don't know what makes you think you can."

"I'd never try to 'handle' Nigella," O'Leary replied mildly. "She's a person, not a situation."

James laughed derisively. "You've got an enormous amount of confidence for an old man. Here," he said, placing the bottle he was carrying on the coffee table. "I'll leave this for you— because you obviously care, so when it's your turn on the short end of the stick, you'll need it to get legless. I, on the other hand, am heading out to find myself a good fuck at the nearest pub." Brushing past Nigella, he left, slamming the door behind him.

"Did you hear that? That knob called me an old man." O'Leary grinned. "Let's drink his champagne and get naked."

🔥

Present-day London

Monday

Hawksmoor certainly wasn't a hack. Nigella adjusted her earpiece and looked around slowly. *Nick the prick is right about that.* There was something appealing about the foreshortened squareness of St. Mary Woolnoth, about the way four trios of columns framed the heart of the sanctuary. Doubtless, if the sun hadn't already set, light would have poured through the lunettes above, but instead, the church's brass chandeliers—each identical to the one captured in Nick's artistic up-angled Polaroid—gave off a warm glow.

The stage had been set that afternoon: a trifold screen with scattered architectural drawings attached stood just to the right of the suspended pulpit; a pile of additional photos, each with bits of double-sided tape on the back, lay nearby, ready for her to get to work once the signal came; a canvas bag containing the parts of a metal easel lay unzipped. Everything arranged to paint the picture that Professor Rowan was in the middle of assembling her exhibit. A trap ready to be sprung.

Nigella added the finishing touch: turning on her classical playlist before depositing her mobile phone on the back of a pew—noticeably out of arm's reach. It was essential Nick feel confident to approach her—and in a space so full of stone floors and painted wood, the cover of music would make him less wary of the echo of his own footfall. *Not that I'd mind hearing him. After all he's a clever bastard, and if he gets the jump on me . . .*

Nigella's wig itched—they always itched—but she resisted the urge to scratch. As she'd put it on at home, she'd jokingly asked Colm if he fancied her in Katherine Rowan's characteristic blonde bob. "I'd fancy you with purple hair or no hair at all," he'd responded, "so be careful tonight."

She looked at her watch. Past eight. Where the fuck was Nick? If they'd gone to all this trouble and he didn't show . . .

"Suspect approaching down King William," the voice in her earpiece was soft but electrifying. Nigella picked up a photo, peeled off the backing and got to work. As she was positioning a block of text, the next signal came: "He's in."

Now she was flying blind. There was no balcony where an officer could crouch and give her a bird's-eye view of Nick's movements. But they'd placed microphones under a number of pews, and those were now funneling into her earpiece. As the Purcell on her phone reached a softer passage, she strained for any sound of him. Nothing. She drew the metal pieces of the easel out of their bag and began to assemble it, noisily.

"Box outside. Petrol, lighter, note."

Damn, looks like he plans to burn Katherine Rowan right here, and I am Katherine Rowan for the moment.

Then she heard it—a distinct thud. *Catch your foot on a pew, Nick?* The cop in charge of audio surveillance gave her a location: A2. Nick was close, but not yet close enough for her to turn round. As Nigella began to count down from twenty, the air around her seemed alive—as if wherever Nick was, she could feel his breath.

"Excuse me, what's that you're building?"

Nigella's body twitched involuntarily as if pulsed by an electrical current, and her muscles tightened, ready to go.

"Sorry, didn't mean to scare you—just curious."

"You don't scare me." Nigella turned and locked her eyes on the eyes of the devil who'd been burning Londoners.

She expected him to run. Most of them did. Not that he would have gotten far—the whole place had been ringed with police ever since the words "He's in" sounded. But Nick wasn't like most of them. He was smarter. He likely knew he had no exit, so instead, he took a step closer.

"It's almost better this way," he said.

"Yes," Nigella agreed. "I have been looking forward to saying this. Josh Wright, you are under arrest on suspicion of murder—"

That was as far as Nigella got before he lunged. The hands she'd been watching from the corner of her eye came out from inside his pockets. She dodged left, letting the large black flashlight slam into the screen behind her. The display toppled to the marble floor with a clatter as Nigella struck a blow to Nick's arm, forcing him to release the makeshift weapon. He gave a sharp cry of surprise, then his left hand rose.

Pepper spray—great. A whole night's worth of eyewashes.

Nigella took a breath, prepared to hold it, waiting for the blast. Then O'Leary came catapulting out of the pulpit where he'd been hiding. Nick swiveled at the sound of O'Leary's landing, arm rising as he turned, ready to strike. The arm froze mid-arc, then dropped.

"Why aren't you dead?" Nick's voice sounded both mystified and haunted. "I saw the little piece in the paper a day late— unidentified man dies in accidental garage fire. I was pissed they'd belittled you in death the same way they belittle me in life."

"Yeah, mate. Well, I was pissed that you nailed me in a coffin alive and walked away to let me burn to death." It was pretty damn impressive that O'Leary managed his characteristic wise-ass tone under the circumstances.

"What happened to the others?" Nick asked.

Nigella had no idea what he meant, but O'Leary seemed to. "They never caught fire, because DI Parker is a better cop than you are an artist. They're in the evidence lockup."

"Not destroyed!" There was exultation in Nick's voice, and he drew himself up, squaring his shoulders.

With all the people he's killed, the wanker's worried about the figures he carved. Nigella was about to promise Nick someone would take a chainsaw to the pair of wooden figures until all that was left were pieces the size of garden mulch. But this was Colm's moment, not hers. He was the one who'd been left to die in the company of the carvings.

"No, not destroyed." Her fellow DI's voice was quiet. "Too bad the same can't be said of Andrew Smyth, Ethan Fox, Joe, and the lives of everyone who cared for them."

"Art means sacrifice." Nick said it fervently, as if he were preaching a gospel. He stared intently into O'Leary's eyes, looking for something. *Could it be understanding?*

"Maybe." O'Leary pulled out his handcuffs, "But doing something *really* well requires *self*-sacrifice, not the sacrifice of others." For a moment time seemed to freeze. No one moved—Nigella wasn't sure she even breathed. Then Nick gave a slight nod, let the pepper spray drop, and held out his arms.

"That's why, in the end, you didn't make art, Josh. You made chaos," O'Leary said as his cuffs clicked around the killer's wrists.

EPILOGUE

Marylebone

December 1, 1666

The dining table was set and a merry fire crackled in the grate, pushing back the December cold. The elder Mistress Belland kept herself studiously between the fireplace and little Raphe, who had at last begun to toddle, while the younger Mistress Belland circled the table, pushing each Staffordshire plate further back from its edge, well out of the little fellow's eager reach. *I will have to speak to Mary about this . . . again.*

Glancing momentarily from Raphe to the clock on the mantle, the senior Mistress Belland clicked her tongue censoriously. "If they do not come from the workshop soon, I will march over to get them. Etienne is still not too old for me to grab by the ear. What can they be doing?"

Her daughter-in-law laughed, "You know very well, Mother—the same thing they have been doing all week: obsessing over the color of that new purple rocket they are determined to surprise the King with at Christmas."

"Well, if they chose fireworks over a warm supper, we shall dine without them. The mutton grows cold, and we both know how difficult cook will become if her egg pudding gets stodgy."

While his wife was shaking her head, old Monsieur Belland came through the dining parlor door. Etienne slipped in behind, dipping his head apologetically. "Sorry to be late." He picked up Raphe and sat down with the boy on his lap.

"Lucky you came when you did," his wife replied, setting Ellinor on a chair and ringing the bell for Mary before taking her own seat. "Your mother had very nearly decided to send you to bed without supper."

A smile split Etienne's face. "But we are not going to bed are we, my dove? We have an eclipse of the moon to observe with our telescope."

It was Margaret's turn to smile. "Do you think it will be very orange?"

"I cannot believe the two of you," Agnes Bradish said, claiming a seat and beginning to cut Ellinor's mutton. "All the women at the market and half the men in the pews at church say this eclipse is another ill omen."

"Nonsense," Etienne replied. "It is merely one of God's marvelous and varied natural creations to be studied and understood. Besides"—he reached out and took Margaret's hand where it lay beside her wine glass—"all the omens in my life are auspicious ones since Margaret rose from the dead to be my wife."

"It is a very different life than I ever imagined, and a much happier one." The sincerity in Margaret's voice brought a flush to her husband's cheeks and smiles to her in-laws' faces.

"Never thought I would have a baron's child at my table, let alone for a daughter." The senior Monsieur Belland puffed a bit.

"Shh, Father," his wife chided. "You know there is no more Mistress Dove, only our Margaret now and that is how it must stay—for all our sakes and safety."

Madame Belland was right. It was not only Margaret who would bear the consequences if the trick of her death was discovered. But after more than a month, Margaret had stopped fearing detection. She kept well away from Whitehall and those haunts of her years as a nobleman's daughter. And those few at court who had helped her stage her death would never tell. Simona, because she was a true friend who wished Margaret to be happy; the royal physician because he had been well paid and would lose his place should his complicity be discovered; and

Her Majesty the Queen because she saw Margaret's conversion to Catholicism and marriage in the Church of Rome to be the work of God and a positive good.

And as for the Phoenix, to him I am a fearful ghost. He would not believe his eyes if he saw me, and I will certainly never have reason to be inside St. Paul's again in my lifetime. My lifetime . . . Margaret looked into her husband's earnest face. *I cannot say how long it will be, but I know with certainty it will be a happy one.*

AUTHOR'S NOTE

First the thanks. Simon Turney, Hannah Thompson, and Anne Easter Smith, your British eyes were *essential* to keeping this Yank on track so that *And by Fire* avoids caricature in favor of authenticity. Thanks! I owe each of you a pint (or ten). Thank you to Dr. Casandra Kuba for consulting on the gory details. You punch far above my weight, so I appreciate that you made time for me and for my manuscript. Gratitude to my critique partners, each an uber-talented author in her own right, Eliza Knight and Kate Quinn, for helping me hone this novel far beyond where it started. And last, but never, ever, least—heaps of love and appreciation to my many-hat-wearing family members: Laura, Michael, Barbara, Katherine, Erin, and Colin.

Next a bit of history and a confession of sorts (no I did not set fire to London). While all the characters and events in the modern plot line of *And by Fire* are fictional, there are definitely actual historical events in the seventeenth-century plot line. The biggest, of course, is the Great Fire of London, which I've worked to portray in all its horrible, transfixing, and transforming reality. There are also individuals in my cast of characters who lived and breathed. Etienne Belland, for example, was indeed the son of the royal fireworks maker.

I am a careful and thorough historical researcher, but I am also a novelist. And novels are the very definition of fiction. Thus—as in all novels involving the real and the past—some facts in this book were created out of whole cloth because they were unknowable, and others were deliberately altered or fictionalized to serve the needs of my plot. Because without a plot, without a twist, what sort of crime novel would I have? So, I have asserted Sir Christopher Wren made certain old St. Paul's Cathedral was entirely destroyed while London burned. Do I have concrete evidence of this? No—but he had every motivation. As a historian whom I heard on NPR years ago said quite casually, Although the Great Fire of London has been many times confirmed to be accidental in origin, nobody benefited from the destruction of London more than Wren, who designed so much of what rose from those ashes, including his masterpiece, the new St. Paul's Cathedral. That thought—that Wren's dream of a new, gloriously domed St. Paul's likely became a reality only because the old cathedral burned during the Great Fire—was the spark for this novel. I hope you enjoyed the conflagration that resulted.